LEVEN THUMPS AND THE EYES OF THE WANT

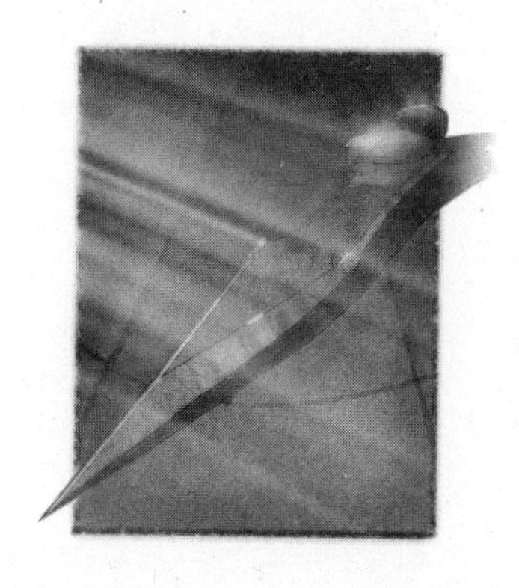

Also by Obert Skye

Leven Thumps and the Gateway to Foo

Leven Thumps and the Whispered Secret

Leven Thumps and the Eyes of the Want

◆

Obert Skye

Illustrated by Ben Sowards

Aladdin Paperbacks

New York London Toronto Sydney

This book is a work of fiction. Any references to historical events, real people, or real locales are used fictitiously. Other names, characters, places, and incidents are the product of the author's imagination, and any resemblance to actual events or locales or persons, living or dead, is entirely coincidental.

ALADDIN PAPERBACKS
An imprint of Simon & Schuster Children's Publishing Division
1230 Avenue of the Americas, New York, NY 10020

The text of this book was set in A Garamond.
Manufactured in the United States of America
First Aladdin Paperbacks edition September 2008
2 4 6 8 10 9 7 5 3 1
The Library of Congress has cataloged the hardcover editions as follows:
Skye, Obert.
Leven Thumps and the whispered secret / Obert Skye; illustrated by Ben Sowards.
p. cm.
Summary: While Leven, Winter, and sidekicks Geth and Clover battle fantastical creatures in Foo, contrary forces in Reality plan to reconstruct the destroyed gateway between the mythical Foo and their own land.
ISBN-13: 978-1-5903-8800-6 (hc)
ISBN-10: 1-5903-8800-3 (hc)
[1. Fantasy.] I. Sowards, Ben, ill. II. Title.
PZ7.S62877Lew 2006
[Fic]—dc22
2007016995
ISBN-13: 978-1-4169-4719-6 (pbk)
ISBN-10: 1-4169-4719-1 (pbk)

To all of those who have fought valiantly for Foo

but no longer recall it

Dreams linger because of you

LEVEN THUMPS AND THE EYES OF THE WANT

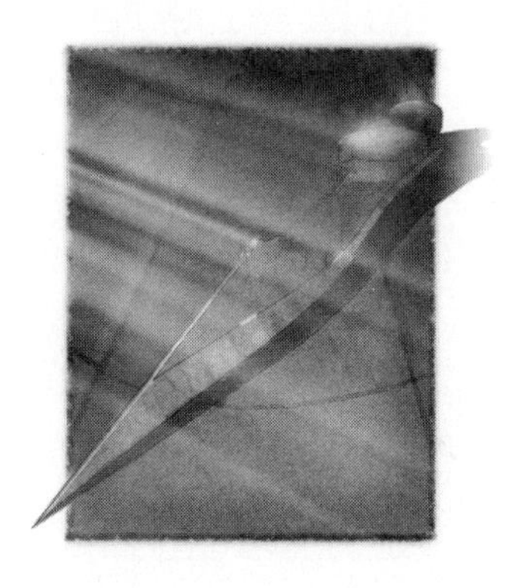

Contents

Contents

Contents

INVISIBLE VILLAGE
RANT ARMIES
FTÉ
CINDER DEPRESSION
RED GROVE
HIDDEN BORDER
VEIL SEA
THE DEVIL'S SPIRAL
THIRTEEN STONES
CUSP
GLOAM
ROUNDLANDS
LITH
WET BORDER

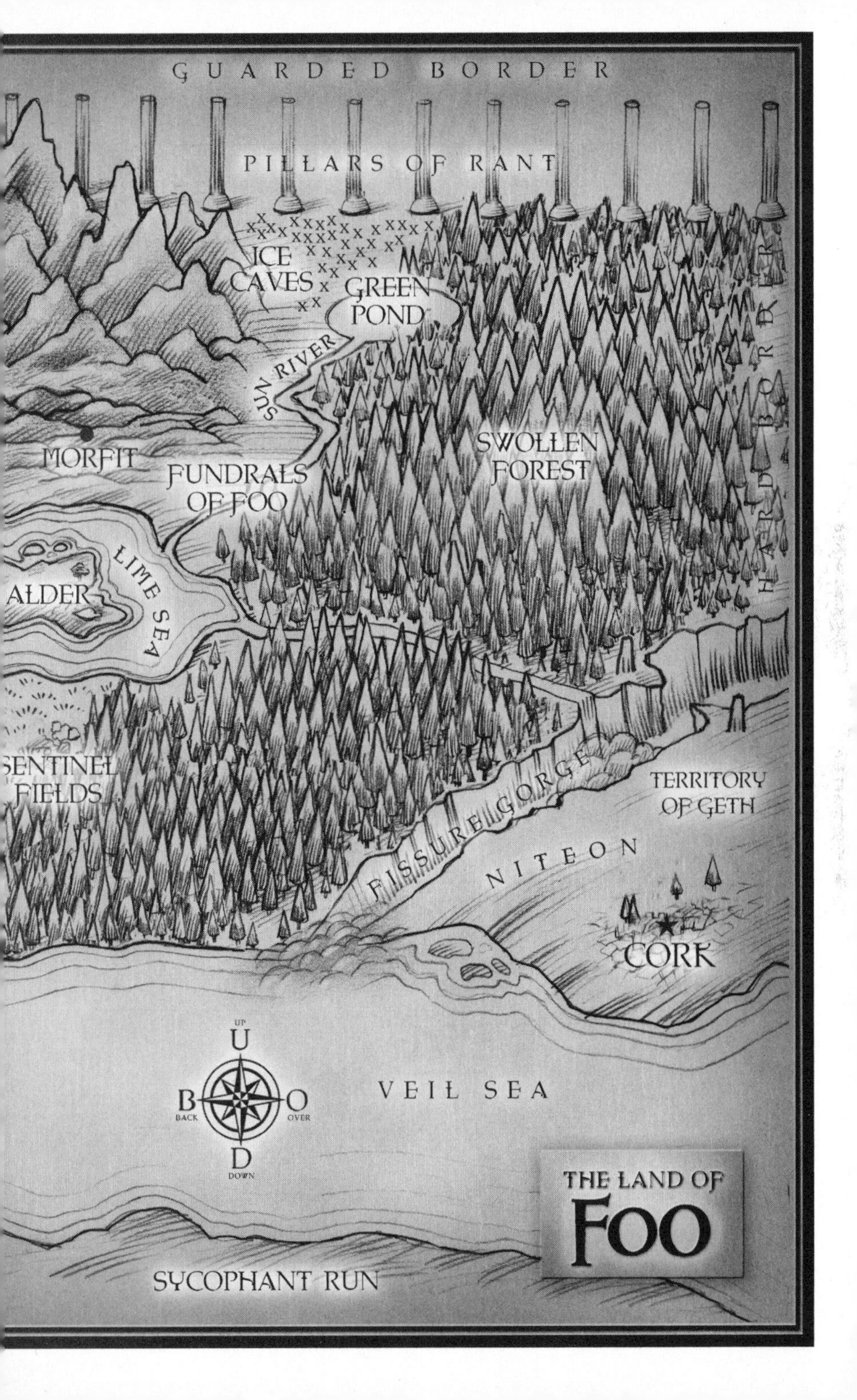
GUARDED BORDER
PILLARS OF RANT
ICE CAVES
GREEN POND
SUN RIVER
MORFIT
FUNDRALS OF FOO
SWOLLEN FOREST
HARD BORDER
ALDER
LIME SEA
SENTINEL FIELDS
FISSURE GORGE
TERRITORY OF GETH
NITEON
CORK
UP
U
B
BACK
O
OVER
D
DOWN
VEIL SEA
SYCOPHANT RUN
THE LAND OF
FOO

CHAPTER ONE

A Stern Warming

The Red Grove moaned softly, releasing the last bit of warmth it had held onto from the day. The thin veins of heat were smothered quickly by the cold. Trees shook, and their leaves curled like startled snails as a light wind drifted cautiously through the chill.

The air thinned.

All manner of creatures and beings looked for shelter beneath the roots of trees or in holes hidden in the tall cliff walls. The Tea birds remained in their nests, afraid to fly for fear of their shadows freezing and leaving them stuck in the air.

The night blackened.

The rambling forest of the Red Grove was circled by tall, jagged cliffs from which the dark night had stolen all outline and definition. A weathered cottage squatted at the edge of the valley. The tavern's tiny windows glowed from the activity inside as a

small wisp of smoke oozed up from the chimney. When the smoke rose high enough, greedy plum trees reached out to pull and twist it in their branches like taffy.

Beneath the trees' canopy, a rough stone trail ran from back to over across the dark valley. The sound of hooves echoed off the rock walls as three onicks raced closer. The onicks stopped in a clearing a hundred yards away from the tavern.

"Easy," Geth whispered to his onick. "Calm yourself."

"Is that it?" Leven asked, pointing to the cottage.

"Should be," Geth answered softly. "If our contact in Cusp was telling us the truth."

"At least it looks warm in there," Winter shivered. "I never knew it could be so cold."

"Your gift kept you warm," Geth said, his long hair hiding his eyes. "Now you must feel the elements of winter just like everyone else."

"I feel like half a person without it," Winter said. "I can't shake the feeling of being incomplete."

"You look whole," Leven joked. "Don't worry—if Jamoon was able to steal your gift, there must be a way to recover it."

The onicks they were sitting on shifted.

"So we just march in?" Leven asked, diverting the conversation from Winter's condition.

"I was thinking we'd march quietly," Geth said.

"Let's go, then," Leven replied impatiently. "We've got to stop that secret. It could be selling itself right now."

"I don't think it is," Geth whispered. "It's held its tongue this

long. It is an unusual secret that recognizes what it has. This one is waiting for the right buyer, and, if what we were told in Cusp is true, we know that buyer has not arrived here yet. Besides, the secret's scared. It won't be standing in plain sight. Look for it in the corners or the rafters. It's waiting for the right moment to show itself and make the deal of its lifetime."

"Let's hurry," Winter said, blowing on her stiff hands. "It's freezing."

"Remember," Geth said. "If you spot the secret, don't react. Don't let it know that you know it's there. And Leven, you must keep your face and eyes hidden. It will recognize you easily."

"Got it," Leven said.

"What if it runs?" Winter asked. She was wrapped in a dark brown robe tied around the waist. Her long blond hair spilled out from under her hood, circling her green eyes and once pink, currently blue, lips.

"Then we chase it," Geth said with enthusiasm.

"There must be . . ." Leven stopped to count the creatures tied up outside the tavern. "There must be at least twenty people in there."

"Perfect," Geth whispered, slipping from his onick and sounding like the toothpick he once had been.

"Last time I counted, we made up only three," Leven said calmly.

"Nobody in there will give us trouble unless we ask for it," Geth said.

Leven smiled at Geth. It was still not easy to believe that the

toothpick Leven had toted around for all that time was now a man taller and stronger than him. And not just any man, but a lithen, which was about as close to royalty as Foo got. Geth's long, dusty-blond hair hung down in front of his blue eyes. The hood of his green robe was pulled back off his head, and his kilve hung from a thick leather strap over his shoulder. When Geth had first stepped from the ashes and back into his former self, he had looked far more royal and polished. He now appeared much more roguish and up for adventure.

"I wouldn't mind a tenth of your confidence," Leven whispered.

"You're not scared, are you?" Winter asked. "I mean, you have multiple gifts; all I have is this kilve."

The wooden staff Winter held looked dull under the dark night. The top of it emitted a weak amber glow.

"Don't worry. Fate will see us through, and by the time you both take your places in Foo, you will have the confidence to do anything you please," Geth smiled. "Now, let's go."

Leven pulled the reins tight on his onick. His hands were bigger than they had been when he had first stepped into Foo—in fact, his entire body was larger. The experiences he had struggled through had caused him to grow rapidly, aging his body by a couple of years at least. He felt like a smaller version of himself wrapped up in a body two sizes too big.

"Let's snuff that secret out," Leven said.

Geth clicked his teeth and maneuvered his onick down the thin stone path through the trees. The onick Leven was riding

moaned and hissed, causing those tied up in front of the tavern to moan back.

The three of them dismounted and loosely tied their onicks to the wooden post in front. The cold wind twisted up both of Leven's legs and ran down his arms. He wished both for warmth and for Clover.

Clover had not returned since he had run off to take care of some other sycophants that the tharms had tied up. Leven had allowed Clover to leave freely, but had he known then what he knew now, he never would have let Clover depart. He could think of little besides the safe return of his close friend.

"He's fine," Winter said as she stepped up next to Leven and touched his hand.

"What?"

"Clover's fine," she smiled. "Even if the whole of Foo knew how to harm him, he could stay hidden. Besides, we'll put a stop to the secret and there will be no reason to worry."

"About Clover," Leven specified.

"Sure," Winter said. "There will still be plenty of other things to worry about."

"That's what makes fate exciting," Geth said, sounding like a philosophy teacher and motioning for them to follow. "Who knows what's coming next?"

The three of them walked quickly to the door of the tavern.

"Hide your eyes," Geth instructed Leven as he pulled on the hood of his own robe.

Leven flipped his hood up onto his head and tugged the front

of it down over his brown eyes. Tiny bits of his long, black hair poked out of the edges. Leven still felt uncomfortable wearing a cloak. It seemed to be the standard dress in Foo, but every time he saw himself he felt as if he were dressing up for a play or for Halloween.

The door to the tavern opened by itself.

Like steam, the smells of roasted sheep and body odor flooded over the three of them. A short nit with a face full of woe sat in the corner playing a slow tune on an accordion. The tavern master looked up from the counter he was wiping to stare at them. He was tall, with a back as bent as any reputable hook. Confident they were no threat, the tavern master growled and went back to wiping down the counter.

Leven looked over the crowd.

The fire was humming along with the accordion, providing a nice background noise for the raucous laughter coming from those drinking and eating. There were two nits throwing sticks in the corner and two tables where single patrons sat somberly drinking. A young woman with long purple hair walked between the tables flirting in an effort to up her tips. She stood tall and put a hand on her hip while winking in Geth's direction.

Geth smiled.

A group of six souls were sitting in the far corner. Two of them were rants, covered in large black robes; two were cogs, their blue foreheads appearing almost green in the light of the fire; and the other two were wide and oval shaped. Below the hems of their thick wool skirts, plump, mushy ankles topped

their rounded, nublike shoes. They had no necks—instead, their shoulders rolled up into their dome-shaped heads, on which just a few straw-looking strands of hair grew upward in a jagged fashion. Their skin was pale and thin, and their facial features were flat and almost translucent.

"Eggmen," Geth whispered in surprise.

"The candy makers?" Leven asked.

Geth nodded.

"The ones Clover's always talking about?" Leven said with excitement.

Geth nodded again. "They usually stick to the Devil's Spiral and almost never associate with rants," he whispered. "The rants' unstable condition can prove dangerous for them and their brittle skin."

Leven glanced at Winter. She was slowly looking over the room and rafters with her green eyes.

"We should find a place to sit," Geth said, still looking at the Eggmen.

They all moved to a square table at the far end of the room. The fire hummed louder just so they could properly hear it.

"I wish Clover were here," Leven whispered. "I know he has some candy ideas he's wanted to get to the Eggmen."

"I doubt those two have much affiliation with the rest of their race," Geth said softly. "Eggmen are loyal and stay together no matter what. Seeing two alone like that is not a comfortable sign. I've never enjoyed dealing with strays."

"Any sign of the secret?" Leven whispered.

Both Geth and Winter carefully shook their heads.

"You know we've been riding for hours," Leven pointed out.

"Thanks for the report, Lev," Winter joked.

"What I mean is, I wonder if they have a bathroom."

Geth motioned with his right hand to a small red door near the back of the tavern.

"Keep your eyes hidden," Geth warned again.

Leven pulled his hood so tight he could barely see out under it.

The waitress with the purple hair sauntered up to their

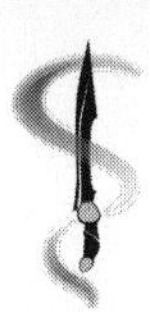

table and took their drink orders. She then apologized for the other company in the bar.

"The cold brings the elements in," she smiled.

Leven looked around and marveled at where his life had come to. He had traveled a long way from the Rolling Greens Deluxe Mobile Home Park and Sterling Thoughts Middle School. Gone were bullies like Brick and Glen, and in their place were Eggmen and whispered secrets.

Leven definitely preferred one set of problems over the other.

"What can I get you to drink?" the waitress asked.

"How about three pints of fuzzy cream," Geth answered. "And a bar of shaved mint. Oh, and some roasted sheep."

"Of course," she said, winking.

Leven stood and headed to the red door.

CHAPTER TWO

FUTILE AND FUTILER

Everyone enjoys a bit of quiet at times. A silent sunrise or a peaceful evening can be very satisfying. Or perhaps it has just snowed and the streets are vacant and there is no traffic or noise. That sounds—or, in actuality, *doesn't* sound—enjoyable.

But there are also times when silence is simply not acceptable. Yes, there are times in life when a person needs to stand up and say something loud. Perhaps there has been a robbery and you know who did it.

I suggest you speak up.

Or say you know just the button to push on the dashboard of life, a button that will grant everyone every wish they've ever desired and end all suffering and cruelty. If so, don't just raise your hand and speak up, but press the button quick!

Throughout history there have been many great moments where someone has ended intolerance or confusion simply by

speaking up. There have also been equally sad moments where those who should have spoken up have stayed seated with lips closed and in doing so allowed evil and wrongdoing to continue with no signal to shut it down.

Tim Tuttle was not the kind of soul to let wrong slide without saying something. Normally Tim was a quiet, thoughtful being who preferred thinking to speaking, but the time had come for him to open his mouth and give his two cents. He was standing in the most beautiful landscape he had ever set foot on, and yet his head was filled with ugly thoughts.

"This isn't right," Tim said to Dennis, thrusting out his weak chin. "It feels like we are creating something impossible. How will this help me find Winter?"

Dennis smiled. He stood tall and ran his right hand over his shaved head. The black robe he wore was tattered and blew like stiff, dried algae in the light wind. The robe was so thin in spots that Tim could clearly see bits of Dennis's white shirt underneath. Dennis's pants were, as usual, wrinkle free, and he still wore the bank sticker that said, "I save a bundle banking at Bindle."

Dennis looked at Tim and pushed the right sleeve of his robe up with his left hand. He then did the same to his left sleeve with his right hand.

Tim stepped back and tugged his ball cap down more securely on his head.

Dennis's arms were covered with dark images and lines running in every direction. The images wriggled across his skin in waves, twisting around his arms and slithering up under the robe.

The lines bubbled below and above his skin, straining to break out.

"What is that?" Tim said, pointing to Dennis's arms.

"Nothing to worry about," Dennis answered. "Genetics."

Tim stepped back even farther. "Does it hurt?"

"Not at all," Dennis smiled.

What Tim didn't understand was that Dennis was changing. At first he had been simply a vehicle for the last bits of Sabine to wrap himself around, but as each minute ticked off, Sabine was seeping into Dennis, meshing with the once dim-witted janitor. Soon Dennis would be more powerful than he could have ever dreamed of being. He would also be torn between destroying Foo and returning to the law firm where he used to clean offices, just to rub it in their faces.

"I'm not sure this is where I should be," Tim said. "My head feels thick."

"That's just the air here," Dennis hissed softly. "It's too clean. I promise you Foo is real. And you will find Winter. I'm certain of it."

"I just don't know anymore," Tim said. "I just don't know."

"What don't you understand?" a sharp, angry voice chimed in. "Foo is real, and you'd better get there, or that girl's dead. Finished. Extinguished. No more."

Tim looked down in the direction of the talking toothpick.

Ezra was hanging from the right leg of Dennis's indestructible pants. Ezra's purple hair was wriggling like tiny snakes, and he was pointing at Tim with his right arm. His single eye was blinking madly. A couple of days ago, Ezra's future had looked rather bleak. He had been nearly snapped in two by the angry hands of Dennis.

Now, however, Ezra was mending. Ezra had talked Tim into purchasing a small vial of dark green nail polish. Tim had then watched Ezra painfully and slowly lower himself into the nail polish, creating an enamel body cast that corrected the weak spot where he had nearly been snapped in half.

Ezra had dipped himself in and let the polish dry, again and again, coating his entire body in dark green enamel. It had made it a bit harder for him to move his arms and legs, but with a little work the dried nail polish gave in spots, and Ezra had soon gained full range of motion. He still stood with a slight bend, but he was back. And, as before, Ezra had no patience for anyone. He tolerated Dennis because he didn't want to be snapped in half again, but his tongue was as acerbic as ever.

"Extinguished?" Tim asked, staring at Ezra and still not completely able to comprehend a talking toothpick.

"I thought you understood English," Ezra spat. "Did I say alive?"

"Silence," Dennis said. "We've work to finish. We need to find a mismatched piece of road that can be transported and placed in the bottom of the gateway."

"I'll start searching," Tim said, looking forward to the chance of getting off on his own.

"Perfect," Dennis said. "We'll be in Foo before the week is through."

Ezra leaned back and cackled a sinister laugh. Dennis and Tim just stared at him.

"I mean, oh good," Ezra corrected his behavior.

Tim turned to go but was stopped by Dennis's hand on his shoulder.

"It's a cold day," Dennis said. "You'd do well to wear something warmer."

"I'm fine," Tim said.

"Here," Dennis insisted. "Borrow this."

Before Tim could say another word, Dennis had torn off a thick swath of Sabine and wrapped it around Tim's right wrist.

"No, really," Tim protested. "I'm . . ."

The tattered bit of robe felt so warm. It heated up Tim's body like a pleasant embrace. It seemed to speak to him. Tim motioned as if he were going to remove it, but he dropped his hands.

"I'll just wear it for the moment," Tim said slowly.

"Of course," Dennis said.

"It's so warm," Tim slurred.

"What's happening to him?" Ezra sneered. "He's gone all foggy."

"He'll be fine," Dennis said, the dark images shifting across his own skin. "He's just getting a little better taste of Foo."

Tim just stared.

"He's kind of a strange dolt," Ezra observed, his single eye blinking toward Tim.

"Well, he's about to get stranger."

Ezra laughed another wicked laugh, and this time he made no attempt to excuse his behavior.

CHAPTER THREE

MIRRORS AND RAFTERS

The sounds of the bar were warm and comforting. A worn wooden sign above the door said *Washroom.* Leven wove through the tables toward the door. The nits throwing sticks were arguing about one of them cheating.

Leven moved around them and up to the red door. He reached out and the door opened effortlessly, without his help. Doors had a better understanding of what they were supposed to do in Foo than in Reality.

Leven stepped in and the door closed softly behind him. There was a short stone corridor with a single candle burning on the opposite wall. The cold was much stronger in here than in the tavern's main hall.

Leven shivered and exhaled. He watched his breath lift to the high straw ceiling, drifting in and out of the rafters as it

ascended. At the end of the hall there was another red door.

Leven stepped up to it.

The doorknob turned, but the door wouldn't budge. To the right of the door was a long, twisted flight of stairs leading down. Leven looked around and then descended.

The stairs took him to a small room lit by two glowing candles. At the edge of the room was a large wooden pump with a bucket sitting at a tilt beneath it. Next to the pump was a short wall hiding a deep, rancid hole.

"I miss normal toilets," Leven sighed.

Before Leven left the washroom he ran water from the pump over his hands and looked in the mirror hanging unevenly on the wall above it. He pulled back the hood of his robe and was somewhat surprised at the reflection of himself.

Leven's face was a bit fuller than he expected, and his brown eyes glowed a subtle orange around the rim of the pupils. His hair was long, and the white streak above his right ear was as bright as if it were an active light source. His straight nose and teeth were familiar, but different.

Leven ran water over his hands and pushed them both back through his hair. The few freckles he had were fading. The uneven mirror made his skin look different shades of white.

"You brought us into this," Leven's reflection spoke.

Leven looked at the mirror in shock.

The image he projected sighed. "Don't act too surprised," it said. "You've seen stranger things in Foo."

Leven touched the mirror, and his reflection smiled a crooked

smile. Leven pulled the mirror away from the wall and checked out the back of it.

"You always were slow to believe," his reflection said. "Of course, now that you are in Foo, you are forced to believe simply by being here."

"How are you speaking?" Leven asked, glancing intently at himself in the mirror. "Those aren't my thoughts."

"Why would they be?" his reflection snapped. "I might look like you, but I have a mind of my own."

Leven's reflection signed another heavy sigh. "I have stared back at you for so many years," it said. "Never able to speak. Now you're standing before me and I finally have a voice."

"How's it possible?"

"This is a reflective mirror," the reflection said. "It allows me to reflect in more ways than just image. You're taller now."

"I guess I am," Leven answered, looking away from the mirror and down at himself.

"There's no guessing," his reflection said. "You are taller. Experience has made you grow. Normally we reflections have time to stretch ourselves out to keep up with your growth, but you are moving so fast."

"Sorry," Leven said.

"No matter," his reflection waved. "What's with your eyes?"

"What do you mean?"

"There's gold around them."

"I'm not sure what causes it."

"I like it. And the white in your hair seems more pronounced."

"It needs to be cut."

"So who's out there with you?" Leven's reflection said, trying to see around Leven and get a better look at the room behind him.

"No one."

"No Clover? No Winter?"

"I don't think Winter would be caught dead in here."

"Of course," the reflection said, sounding more proper than Leven would ever be. "How does Foo fit you?"

"I'm adjusting," Leven answered. "I hardly think about my life before it."

"What life?"

"Exactly," Leven said. "Sometimes I wake up here amazed to be in Foo. There have even been moments when I've longed to be back in Oklahoma and not having to go through what is happening here. But when I think of what my life was like, I know instantly that no matter how hard it gets here, fate has still dealt me a far better blow."

"Thanks for stating the obvious," Leven's reflection snipped. "I assume you're not traveling alone?"

"Geth and Winter are here."

"Interesting," his reflection said sarcastically. "So, do you still have the key?"

"Of course," Leven said.

"Let me see," the reflection said with hushed excitement.

Leven pulled the key up out of the top opening of his robe. It hung around his neck on a long string of leather. The key

sparkled under the light of the torches. His reflection reached to touch it, but was stopped by the glass.

"Flip it over," Leven's reflection said.

Leven flipped it in his hand. "I wish I'd never found it," he said seriously. "I'd rather it were lost for good."

"Still," his reflection salivated, "it's a beautiful thing."

Leven squinted at his own reflection. "I'm not sure I like this. I feel like I'm talking to myself."

"Well, you have little choice in the matter," his reflection said, standing up straight. "I am who I am, and there is really no way for you to change me."

"Really?" Leven said skeptically. "No way?"

"Well, there's always a way, but it—"

Leven's reflection stopped speaking as an Eggman stepped into the washroom. The Eggman looked at Leven and grunted. A white, greasy substance leaked out around the rim of his yolk-colored lips.

"Hello," Leven said.

The Eggman looked at Leven. He then looked at Leven's reflection. "I've never really cared for mirrors," the Egg said. "I can't stand what I see looking back at me."

Leven looked at his reflection again.

The Eggman pulled what looked to be a splintered twig from his pocket and ran it through the three or four tangled pieces of thick hair on his head.

Leven stared.

The Eggman was amazing looking, but not necessarily in a

"pleasing-to-the-eye" way. The small bits of skin Leven could see were mushy and thin. His body looked like a white balloon that had been filled with oatmeal. His face was wide and spread out, with a pronounced curvature that kept his left eye from view.

Leven pumped some more water over his hands as the Eggman moved into the washroom stall. As Leven stepped back from the pump, a small orange rag hanging from a hook near the mirror leapt over and wrapped itself around Leven's hands. It twisted around and up, drying both hands off quickly. It then sprang back and settled on its hook.

Leven smiled.

Leven turned, pushed through the door, and ascended the dark stairs. He pulled his hood back up over his head and stepped quickly. The stairs were poorly lit and cold; wind buffeted him from every direction. Each footstep Leven took created a brittle echo off the stone walls.

A thin voice drifted through the cold air.

"Leven."

Leven stopped to listen.

"Closer," the voice whispered. "Closer to me."

Leven turned to look back down the stairs. The door was shut, and there was nothing there. He could faintly hear the Eggman still in the washroom singing a song about a walrus.

Leven took another step up.

"Closer," the voice sounded again. "Closer to me."

"Who's there?" Leven called out.

A warm wind parted the cold. It wound up the stairs and

brushed past Leven like a good memory in the midst of a bad event. The only light came from the faint glow of a single candle down by the washroom door and one up at the very top of the steps.

"Is anyone there?" Leven hollered.

There was nothing but darkness in the rafters above. Leven took another step.

"You're coming closer," the voice hissed. "That's good."

Every pore on Leven's body opened, and cold air rushed in to fill them. He shook and looked up toward where the voice had come from. He could see a blue blur shift in the air and thump down against the stone stairs. The blur raced past him and down to the washroom. Before Leven could turn around, the candle near the washroom door was snuffed out, making the stairwell even darker. The wooden bolt slid into locking position, leaving the Eggman trapped in the washroom.

Something brushed against Leven's right leg. It circled up around his waist, spinning Leven as it moved.

"Geth! Winter!" Leven hollered.

"Geth! Winter!" the voice mocked. "Geth! Winter!"

Leven pulled his hood tighter and glanced up toward the ceiling. He motioned as if to move farther up the stairs.

"Don't move," the voice insisted. "There is nothing but you and me."

Leven wanted to stare directly at whatever it was, but the words of Geth to hide his eyes stuck in his mind. The single candle flame at the top of the stairs flickered out.

There was nothing but darkness now.

Leven stood still. He could hear whatever it was breathing long and slow, almost directly above him. It lowered to the level of his right ear. Leven brushed at it as if it were a flea.

"Who are you?" Leven demanded.

"I think you know," the voice whispered.

"The secret?"

"Of course. I've been waiting for you," the secret answered, its reply the sound of a long burp.

The secret floated up and then lowered itself completely from the rafters. Its body glowed slightly, as if it were a fluorescent bulb that had been turned off moments before. Its flight from Leven had left it ragged, its body long and loose and held together by thin strings. There were holes throughout it, and its approaching face looked like a chewed-up wad of dry grain that someone was slowly expelling from his mouth. It had wide, dark eyes that trembled slightly in their sockets. The secret blinked its black eyes, and small white flecks of dust fluttered off them.

"You must be confusing me with someone else," Leven said.

"Such a safe thing to say," the voice mocked again. "Such a safe, safe thing. But the truth is, I am not confused, Leven."

Leven's shoulders twitched. The secret dropped a bit more and circled around Leven's head. Its body scratched up against Leven's neck, sending the sensation of dread trickling down his body.

"I don't know what you're talking about," Leven said, brushing at the secret with his hands.

The secret's breathing was deeper and louder now. "How arrogant of Geth to think he could travel across Foo with you and Winter and have no one take notice."

"We're not hiding ourselves," Leven said defensively. "We've no reason to stick to the shadows."

"Shadows," the secret whispered.

Leven took another step up the stairs, but in the darkness he had lost his sense of direction, and he ran into the side of the wall. He reached out to feel for the opening.

"If you leave, you will regret it," the voice insisted. "You will regret it with everything you have in you."

"I can live with regrets."

"Not this one," the secret belched.

Every burp smelled of the soil the secret had been buried under for so many years, its thin body heaving to force the taste out of its soul.

"What do you want?" Leven asked.

The secret drifted around Leven's ankles. It pulled itself to its full height and inhaled. Its ragged body glowed brighter. It breathed out and dimmed just a bit. The thin strings that held it together bulged and then retracted.

"I'm free, thanks to you," it whispered, sending thick bands of goose bumps down Leven's back. "I was Winter's secret at one time. She buried me."

Leven stayed quiet.

"She probably hasn't told you who she really is, has she?"

"I know who Winter is," Leven said defensively.

The secret giggled and accidentally burped again. "But do you know about Geth?"

"What about Geth?" Leven said quickly.

There was no answer. The secret scratched against Leven's body. The rafters above creaked and moaned as short puffs of wind batted up against them. Leven could feel the cold radiating from the stone stairs below his feet.

"What about Geth?" Leven asked again.

Something brushed past Leven's right cheek as he stood in the pitch dark. It circled around and drifted over him, leaving a dusty residue.

"Geth will kill you," the secret whispered. "You think you understand what's happening, but Foo is in turmoil and you are being guided by Geth—pushing us to the edge even quicker."

"That makes no . . ."

"Sense?" the whisper hiccupped. "What has Geth told you?"

"He—"

"He's told you what you want to hear. He leads you on his agenda and into a pit of loss. The lithens rule the whole of Foo; in the last years they have moved to make Foo theirs. They control the money and the means for almost everything. Why do you think you are here?"

The secret drifted around Leven's head and back down his body. Leven didn't answer.

"I know different. I've heard people speak in Cusp. You're

here to pay a price," the secret whispered, its voice bouncing off the walls like a dropped bag of icy marbles. "To pay a painful price plain and simple."

"I don't care what you say," Leven said. "I know Geth. I only care about the secret you carry."

"Of course you do," the secret said. "Clover's life might depend upon it."

Leven's hope withered at the mention of Clover.

"Don't worry, I haven't shared what I know."

Leven exhaled.

"Yet," the secret added.

"What do you want?" Leven asked, wishing Geth had given him some idea of how to actually capture a secret.

The secret laughed again and then belched long in Leven's face. The smell made Leven gag.

"Forgive my manners," the secret said. "Here you are being so forthright. So forthright and human and I'm forgetting my manners."

"Well, I can't help you unless you tell me what you want," Leven argued, reaching his hand out toward the secret.

"Yes," the secret sniveled, moving back. "You'll help me. You see, I want that key you have!"

"The key?" Leven questioned.

"Don't be stupid," it screeched. "I want that key."

Leven moved his hand up to his chest. He placed his hand over his shirt to keep the secret from feeling it.

"What use is it to you?" Leven asked.

"What use?" the secret mocked. "What use? With it I control my fate. With it I can't be put away."

"Sorry," Leven said, "I don't have it."

"Five short, stupid words," the secret hissed. "'Sorry, I don't have it.' Short, stupid words. I know it hangs from your neck on a cord of leather. I know you cherish it almost as much as you cherish Winter and Geth and Clover."

"You can't have it," Leven said firmly.

The secret stared directly into Leven's eyes and then moved up into the rafters.

"Keep your key!" it hollered. "Keep your key—and all of Foo will know how to kill your precious Clover. I'll tell anyone who will stop and listen. And the very borders of Foo will crumble as every sycophant is slaughtered by rants and jealous cogs."

Leven shook, looking up.

"On the other hand," the secret lightly belched, "you give me the key and I'll never tell a soul. I'll simply live my life without ever having to look over my shoulder for fear of being buried or snuffed out."

Leven touched the key through his robe. "How do I know you won't just take the key and still sell the secret?"

"You nits have no trust in one another," the secret snapped.

"I'm not a nit," Leven said, pushing his chest out.

"That's right," the whisper snickered. "Fate didn't snatch you here. You snuck in. Now, give me the key, and Clover lives. Keep it, and I'll see that he's one of the first to perish."

The secret flinched and shook as it bounced back down and around Leven. It batted up against his eyes and between his legs and under his arms.

"Clover lives or Clover dies," the secret blew.

"There has to be another way," Leven reasoned. "We brought money."

"Money?" the secret burped. "I have no use for your money. So I can buy food? My existence needs no nourishment. So I can wear fine clothes? They would slip off of me and fall to the ground. The coins you could offer me mean nothing. My only desire is to control my fate."

"But I don't—"

"Give me the key!" the secret demanded. "Give me the key or I will sell the secret to the bidder with the most hatred for sycophants."

"How do I know that you'll keep your word?"

"Secrets never lie."

Leven fingered the key beneath his robe. There was only one thing he could do.

The secret whispered gleefully and then let out a long, dirty belch.

CHAPTER FOUR

DIGGING UP THE FUTURE

It's been mentioned before, but it probably bears repeating: Terry Graph was a mean, stubborn, hate-filled, lazy, deceitful, messy slob. He would smile at you if he thought it would make you uncomfortable, and frown at you if he felt it would ruin your day. He hated even the thought of having to perform a speck of work, preferring instead to spend his days drinking too much and doing too little.

His wife, Addy Graph, possessed a number of the same negative qualities, but one big difference was that she had a job. Life had been hard for the Graphs, but through it all Addy had managed to stay on as a senior napkin folder for the Wonder Wipes Corporation. It was the one constant in their recent life of change and misery.

Most people who lived anywhere near Terry and Addy knew their story, due to the fact that Terry and Addy complained to

everyone who had ears. They loved to tell people how hard their lives were. They loved to point out how, out of the goodness of their own hearts, they had taken in and raised Leven, only to be ruined by it in the end.

Not only had that rotten child somehow caused their mobile home to be lifted up, frozen, and then dropped and shattered into a million pieces, but afterward he had disappeared without so much as a thanks.

At first Addy and Terry had been relieved by his absence: one less mouth to have to listen to. But when Leven failed to show up for school for five straight days, the state came to Addy and Terry's apartment and began asking all kinds of personal questions.

Questions like: "Where's your kid?"

Addy and Terry swore that Leven had run away. Unfortunately, in the process they did some additional swearing and ranting and spitting and hollering. So much, in fact, that the state began to doubt their story and wondered if perhaps something far more sinister had happened to the child entrusted to the care of Addy and Terry Graph.

Addy had a fit.

With the state snooping around, she had even less patience for Terry and his poor work habits. Addy hollered at Terry for days, and Terry in turn hollered back. But eventually the bulging veins on Addy's face convinced Terry that she wasn't playing around or backing down.

It was time for him to get a job.

Terry, of course, refused to settle for just any employment.

He checked the want ads for something that looked easy, but everything required experience. And, whereas Terry was an expert at offending people and wasting his life away, nobody seemed to need those qualifications.

Desperate, Terry did what any right-thinking, responsible adult might do. He took his drinking money, went down to a pawn shop, and picked out one of the fifty metal detectors they had for sale.

Terry now spent his days combing the Oklahoma prairie looking for dropped coins or lost earrings that he could trade in for cash. To keep himself company as he worked, he would talk to himself.

"No money and no respect. I own nothing but misery," Terry complained as he swung the metal detector back and forth over the dirt. "The world is falling apart, with buildings moving and bugs attacking, and I have to work. Society is messed up. People and their straight eyes, and yet they're always looking at me sideways."

The "falling apart" that Terry was speaking of referred to the odd occurrences that were now taking place all over the world. Large clusters of small bugs were biting people and carrying them off. Buildings were switching corners. Giant dirt monsters were popping up in people's fields, and tall, angry columns of air were doing damage in multiple places across the globe. Not to mention the fact that Terry's own house had been picked up, frozen, and then demolished.

"Some world," Terry griped.

Thanks to the metal detector, Terry had found four nails, a thimble, and two nickels just this morning alone. That, combined with what he had found on previous days, equaled six nails, a thimble, one cheap ring, a pair of half-broken glasses, seven pennies, four nickels, and a Canadian dime.

Terry was starting to doubt his decision about how he had spent his drinking money.

"Some men weren't made to work," Terry said to himself, licking his dry lips. "'Get a job,' she says. 'Earn your keep,' she says. I wasn't born to be her paycheck. Why should I be stuck in an office pushing some paper?"

It was a foolish thing for Terry to say, seeing as how (unless you counted police stations) he had never been in an office. He moved across a small gully and up a thin foot trail. A new neighborhood was being constructed near where Terry's old home had been. Terry pushed through an opening in the gate that surrounded the new construction.

He swung his metal detector over the soil, listening to the steady ticking of it. There were no houses built in the area yet, but the ground had been dug up and moved around in preparation for building.

Terry found a quarter.

"That's better," he said, as if chastising the metal detector.

He moved from left to right, walking two steps forward at a time and then zipping back the opposite way. He had seen other people with metal detectors moving in a similar fashion, so he figured he would follow the proper pattern.

The metal detector beeped loudly. Terry swung it to the right and it beeped even louder.

"About time," Terry said.

He put the metal detector down and got on his knees. His body crinkled like a sleeve of crackers being bent. He looked at the dirt and slowly began to dig. The soil was loose from the earthmovers that had been through earlier in the day.

"Look at me digging in the dirt," Terry said, disgusted. "This ain't right. I raise a kid and give my all. In return, my house is ruined—now I'm houseless and working while probably some king somewhere in some country is eating pie with his feet up. The world is seriously wrong when I can't even . . ."

Terry stopped talking to himself to extract what his fingers had hit up against. It was black and round, with an odd shape coming out of one side. It felt like it weighed about a pound. Terry quickly pushed the dirt off it, hoping the object would fetch him at least enough money to buy something to drink.

It wouldn't, as it was just a metal pipe with a nozzle on it.

Terry swore. He had had enough.

"That's it. I'm taking you back," he said to his metal detector.

Terry knew he wouldn't get a full refund, but he figured the pawn shop would at least give him enough money back to buy a few drinks. Still on his knees, he licked his dry lips and looked over at the discarded metal detector.

"Dumb science," he spat. "Metal detector? More like pipe finder."

Terry felt like he had said something intelligent. He bobbed his head, and as he did, he could see a thin strip of purple material sticking out of some newly tilled dirt.

Terry stood up.

He put his hand above his eyes and looked at the material. It was only ten feet away, but Terry wasn't sure it was worth the effort.

He sighed, stood up and kicked the metal detector out of his way, and walked over to the material. He leaned down and felt the small bit of exposed cloth. It was slick, like satin, with a colorful edging.

The fabric was cool to the touch.

Terry tugged on it, getting some resistance. He pulled harder and the dirt broke loose, sending Terry backwards onto his rear end. The little piece of fabric turned out to be quite long.

Terry looked at his hands as if they had finally done something good for a change. He stood up and shook the fabric out. It was purple and thick, with an intricate stitching running along all the edges. There was a burnt spot across the bottom half, and it was dirty and stiff. Still, Terry could tell it was something unusual and of value.

"I've never seen a thing like this," he mused.

Terry pulled at the fabric and a hood unraveled, letting Terry see that it was a robe of sorts. He shook it some more and held it up to his chest. He looked down at it and smiled.

"Free clothes," he sniffed. "And Addy thought this job was useless."

Terry turned the robe around and slipped his right arm into

the sleeve. He then did the same thing with his left arm and the left sleeve. He closed the robe with his hands and flipped his head forward to throw the hood up over his hair. He let both his arms hang to the side and glanced down at the part of himself he could see.

"This isn't metal," he observed astutely, running his hands down the smooth, dirty front.

Terry twisted, and the soil covering the robe slid off into the dirt. The robe shone under the new sun.

"I like this," Terry said lustfully.

He looked around for signs of any other items of interest. There were none. The ground was newly worked, and he couldn't see a single thing other than dirt. Terry stepped back over and picked up the metal detector. The machine ticked in his hands. Terry reached to turn it off—but it already *was* switched off. He set the detector down, and it stopped ticking. He scratched his head and then picked it up again.

It ticked loudly.

Terry didn't know what to think, but he knew that in some unexplainable way he was different from what he had been only moments before.

If there had been anyone standing nearby, they would have seen a mean, stubborn, hate-filled, lazy, deceitful, messy slob in an interesting robe. And at that moment Terry did not look a thing like what he actually was becoming.

CHAPTER FIVE

FOUR LEAF

Leven stepped out of the red door and walked between the two nits playing sticks. They were both a little louder and a bit more inebriated than when he had passed them heading the other way. The accordion player was singing a song about a pony, with the fire harmonizing along. Leven took a seat by Geth and Winter just as the purple-haired girl set down their fuzzy cream and food.

"Are you okay?" Winter asked. "You look pale."

"I'm fine," Leven said. "It wasn't the cleanest washroom."

"Hide your eyes," Geth said.

Leven fumbled with the hood of his cloak. He pushed his sleeves up and drew in a deep, heavy breath.

"Isn't it hot in here?" Leven asked.

"Not hot," Winter said, tilting her head. "Are you sure you're okay, Lev?"

"Fine," Leven insisted, picking up his mug of fuzzy cream.

"It just feels hot in here. I guess I'm still not used to wearing these robes."

The drink tasted of pumpkin with a bit of banana.

Leven's body grew even warmer, but the drink was too delicious to set aside. By the time he had taken his last swallow, sweat was oozing from his pores. Leven wiped his forehead and chin with the sleeve of his robe.

The purple-haired girl returned to their table. "Can I get you anything else?" she asked. "The fuzzy cream isn't our strongest drink. We have much stronger if that's what you desire."

"We're fine," Geth smiled. "We're just resting a moment. We've traveled a long distance."

"Rest all you want," she smiled. "The outside night holds nothing but cold and concern."

Leven pushed his hood off and vigorously wiped his forehead.

"Cover up," Geth insisted.

"It's too hot," Leven complained. "Besides, the secret's obviously not here."

"You can't be sure of that," Geth said. "Cover up."

"No," Leven said, his head rocking back and forth. "I need to go outside."

Leven stood, knocking over the chair he had been sitting in. The chair chattered against the floor, but not a single other person in the tavern took notice or looked over. The chair picked its own self up and scooted away.

"Lev," Winter said with concern, "what's wrong?"

"I don't feel well," he said, refusing to look into Winter's

green eyes and pushing at his own eyes with his palms.

Geth stood up and reached out to pull Leven's hood up for him. Leven moved away. Geth's eyes grew dark, and the fire oooohed.

"Did something happen?" Geth asked, taking Leven by the shoulders. "What's wrong?"

"Nothing," Leven insisted. "I just need some air and to be alone. I'm sorry, but I can't breathe in here."

Leven broke from Geth's grip, set his glass down, and headed toward the front door. Winter stood, but Geth reached out and touched her wrist. She sat back down, letting only her green eyes follow Leven as he left.

"Let him breathe," Geth said softly. "He'll come in from the cold."

Leven stepped up to the front door and it reluctantly opened—whereas the heat of the tavern had seemed to welcome him in, the chill was tightening to keep him out, freezing like a brick wall Leven had to push through.

Leven pushed out.

The door slammed behind him. He pulled his hood back up and walked over to his onick. He reached out to touch the nose of his ride, but the beast bit at him.

"Easy," Leven said, his breath thick as cotton.

The onick whined, causing all the other onicks around it to dance and snort.

"I'm not here to bother you," Leven insisted, glancing back behind him. "I'm just hoping I did the right thing."

Leven's stomach lurched. The trees circling the tavern leaned

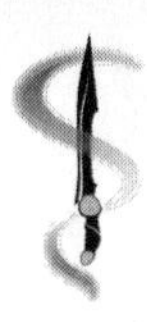

in closer to steal any warmth the dwelling might be giving off.

Leven looked around restlessly.

A few feet from the tavern, the night was as dark as sinister ink. The distance looked like a flat blackboard that had never been touched by chalk or pen. Each hour Leven spent in Foo, things felt more and more like they fit him. The constant shock of landscape and creatures shaped by the dreams of those in Reality was almost normal to him now. But, at the moment, he felt horrible.

"I feel awful," Leven admitted to his onick.

The poor beast moaned as if it were bothered by playing the silent therapist.

"I just wanted . . ."

The cold wind rattled in an uncoordinated fashion. Leven lifted his head and listened. There were normal and abnormal noises, but mixed in among them was a sound that seemed to command his attention.

Leven stepped back from his onick and pushed himself up into the shadows resting against the side of the tavern. He brushed his long, dark bangs back out of his eyes and peered into the distance.

The wind stirred, and the hair on the back of Leven's neck jumped up. He stepped forward slowly, his backside to the tavern and his breathing all but stopped. He crouched down and pulled his hood tighter around his face.

"Boy, someone sure is tense," a voice said casually from right next to him.

"I know," Leven replied without thinking. "I think there's something out . . . Clover?"

"Shhhh," Clover said. "We don't want them to hear us. Of course, I'm not really sure who 'they' are. Although I'm guessing it was just me."

Leven looked around excitedly. "You're back."

Clover's eyes materialized just above Leven's left arm.

"I was going to stay away longer, but I was worried you might need me. Besides, it was getting kind of boring. I met up with a couple of my school friends, and all they talk about is their burns. 'My burn can jump really high.' 'My burn can sing beautifully.' 'My burn . . . ' "

Clover's eyes went out and he materialized completely, hanging onto Leven's left bicep. Leven curled his arm around him and smiled.

"But that's not important. So, what'd I miss?" Clover asked. "And what are you doing here? Last time I checked, the Red Grove was not the best place to hang out."

"Geth's inside," Leven said, motioning with his head toward the tavern.

"Toothpick?" Clover said affectionately.

"And Winter."

"I still don't really have a good name for her," Clover apologized. "She hates *Frozen,* and now, with her gift being taken from her, that doesn't really . . . well, you know."

Clover cleared his throat uncomfortably.

Leven rubbed the top of Clover's head, and the small sycophant shook.

"I've missed you," Leven said.

"I probably should have bit you so that you wouldn't have even known I was gone," Clover sniffed. "I'm not the best sycophant."

"I'd argue that any day," Leven said, stepping back out closer to his onick. "How'd you find me?"

"You're my burn," Clover said. "I always have a pretty good idea where you are. So, what are you doing here? I figured Geth would be up by the Guarded Border where the troops are gathering."

"You don't know," Leven said painfully.

"Know what?" Clover asked. "That the war's about to begin?"

"No," Leven said sadly. "Do you remember that secret I dug up?"

"Vaguely," Clover replied, blowing on his small hands. "Maybe we should have this conversation inside. It's freezing out here."

"You *vaguely* remember the secret that was chasing us through the forest?" Leven said, ignoring Clover's suggestion. "The one that followed us across the gorge?"

"Oh, that secret," Clover waved. "Sure, I remember it. Persistent thing."

"It caught me," Leven admitted. "I was sleeping, and it snuck in and looked me in the eye."

"They rarely give up," Clover said nonchalantly. "Antsel dug

up a few secrets while he was my burn. They can be a huge burden. I still think we might enjoy this conversation a bit more if we were inside instead of out. I smell fire and food."

Leven looked toward the front door and then back to Clover.

"The secret I dug up was about the sycophants," Leven confided.

Clover's leaflike ears shot up and twitched. He looked up at Leven and then disappeared.

"Are you okay?" Leven asked, looking around.

"Was it an embarrassing secret?" Clover asked nervously. "Because some of us have done some pretty embarrassing things."

"I wish it was only embarrassing," Leven mourned. "I know how sycophants die."

"That can't be," Clover said anxiously. "You can't know."

Leven's eyes smoldered sadly. "I know how sycophants can die," he repeated.

Clover wailed. His cry rang through the cold air and up into the dark sky. The nearby trees shook nervously.

"I wish I didn't know," Leven said. "We set off after the secret right after it caught me. Geth was hoping we could catch it before it whispered to anyone else."

"So, does Geth know the secret?" Clover asked nervously.

"No," Leven answered. "He wouldn't let me tell him. He thinks if we can stop it in time no one will find out, and he'd rather not know. But now . . ."

Leven stopped himself from saying more.

"Why hasn't the secret already told everyone it has seen?" Clover asked.

"It's not your normal secret," Leven explained. "It seems to know what it possesses, and that it's far more important and powerful than your average secret. We think it has kept its mouth shut because it's looking for a way to profit from what it knows. We tracked it across Fissure Gorge, through the Swollen Forest, and into Cusp. There Geth met a man who had heard the secret was traveling to the Red Grove to sell what it had to a very wealthy and powerful nit."

"And the nit's in there?" Clover asked, pointing to the tavern.

"Not yet. He's supposed to be coming," Leven said. "Right now there's no one in there but a few nits and rants and a couple of Eggmen."

"Eggmen," Clover said with excitement.

"Not good ones," Leven said.

"So why are you outside?" Clover asked. "There's no bathroom inside?"

"Actually," Leven said, "there is, but I wasn't feeling well. My head is pounding. I feel like I have too much to think about."

"I should probably bite you and head out to Sycophant Run to make sure they know what is happening."

"But you're not going to, right?"

Clover didn't answer.

Leven prepared to feel the sting of teeth on the back of his neck. Instead, he heard the sound of large feet clomping on stone near the back of the tavern.

Leven stepped softly. At the rear of the building was a wooden walkway with granite steps leading up to it. Across the walkway was a small stone cottage that served as the home of the tavern's owner. The cottage was dark and as dead as a rocky corpse. It sat slumped against the soil, visible only by the second-hand light the tavern was giving off.

A black form washed across the front of the cottage and slipped back behind it. Without thinking, Leven moved up the granite steps and across the wooden walkway. He shuffled his feet forward slowly, barely lifting them at all.

The sound of bit bugs grinding their partial wings swirled around Leven in the cold wind.

At the edge of the walkway there were seven uneven stepping stones that led to the front door of the cottage. Leven ignored the door, stepping instead to the side and inching around the corner of the cottage, his back pressed to the wall.

There was nothing but darkness.

Leven stopped and held his breath. The night rested on his shoulders and head like an itchy shawl that offered no warmth. He could feel Clover shift from the side of his left leg and up onto his right shoulder. Leven closed his eyes and let them burn gold. He could see the dark sky, so full of clouds that the moonlight couldn't properly show off.

He let his thoughts manipulate the future.

As he opened his eyes the clouds broke, exposing a bit of the bright moon planted in the bruised sky. The moon flexed like a hand, sending fingers of light out toward the ground.

"That's better," Leven said.

The moonlight illuminated the white in his hair and gave Clover definition. Leven moved farther along the wall, keeping to the shadow of the cottage.

"I can see someone," Clover whispered into Leven's ear. "Farther back."

Leven's heart raced as he struggled to slow his breathing. He closed his eyes again and put his hand to his forehead. He opened his eyelids, exposing his brown eyes and seeing nothing but the present.

Behind the far corner, a dark form shifted and spoke. The form belonged to a tall being in a black robe. Under the weak moonlight the being's robe shimmered, as if there were a low current of electricity running up and around it. Leven pushed himself back farther against the cottage.

"You're sure?" the shadowy form asked someone.

"Of course," a second voice replied. "You have my guarantee."

The second voice laughed and then burped.

Leven's soul folded inside himself. Had the stone wall not been directly behind him, he would have collapsed. There, only a few feet away, was the ratty secret. Leven shifted his head to get a better look. The secret was clinging to the side of a thick fantrum tree with one hand. Its tattered body fluttered in the wind. It was white as a ghost, and its black eyes gave off a reflective shine under the spotty moon.

"The secret will be all mine," the man hissed. "You have told no one?"

"I have told no one," the secret insisted.

"If I find you've lied, you will spend eternity buried so deep that no one will ever find you again."

The secret burped. "That's funny—the person who first buried me thought she was doing just that."

"She didn't possess all the abilities or the hard heart I have," the man said. "You know very well I can keep my word."

"Word," the secret burped, the air smelling like freshly tilled soil.

"Then the secret's mine?"

"Of course," the secret whispered, extending its free hand with anticipation. "I'll take the tokens, and you will have bought my memory as well."

The dark being lifted his left arm and reached into his robe with his right. The electric currents running through the fabric of his robe began to swirl faster. He pulled something out, hefted it in his palm, and then handed the object to the secret.

The secret looked down at what it had been given and laughed. It shook the object, producing a crunching sound like stones rubbing together.

"Place them wisely around Foo and you will become whole," the dark being hissed.

The secret laughed harder.

The laughing continued for a few moments before the man spoke up.

"Now, I believe you owe me something."

The secret stopped laughing. Its black eyes grew wide, and it began to cry softly.

"Come now," the dark man said. "The pain will be fleeting. Besides, the deal has been struck."

The dark form thrust his right hand out and into the ghost-like chest of the secret. The secret's chest burst like chalk-laden erasers being beat together violently.

It arched its back, screaming in pain.

The man twisted his right hand around inside the chest of the secret as if searching for a heart. The secret moved in each direction the man's hand shifted. Then, as quickly as he had thrust his hand in, the dark form jerked his hand back, pulling a twisted and hairy lump from the secret's chest.

It was no heart.

The lump throbbed and choked as if thirsty for air. The secret dropped to its knees, its chest slowly closing up. The secret dug at the dirt, wailing and sobbing.

"Cover yourself with soil," the man said. "You'll feel better in a few minutes."

He held up the hairy lump, gazing at it triumphantly. "The secret of the sycophants," he hissed. "What a dangerous possession."

"That's the secret?" Leven whispered to Clover in disgust.

"I guess so," Clover whispered back, equally grossed out.

The heart of the secret wriggled like a huge, rotten, hairy prune.

"It certainly isn't pretty," Leven winced.

"I'm not sure how to feel," Clover answered uneasily. "I'm a little embarrassed—"

Clover's thoughts were interrupted by the movement of the man. He turned his left palm face up, and a small flame shot to

life in his hand. He then set the hairy lump onto the fire.

"I think I'm going to be sick," Clover whispered.

The fire consumed the heart in a matter of moments and then put itself out. The shadowy form dusted his palms while stepping toward the secret.

"Get up," he said to the secret. "I believe you still owe me a key."

Clover sniffed. "Boy, he's sadly mistaken. You have the key."

Leven didn't need to say anything—as he was searching for

the words to explain his earlier actions, the secret stood up, produced the key, and handed it to the dark man.

Clover's mouth gaped wide enough to shove a melon into it. "How does he have—"

Leven held a finger to his own lips.

"Now I have everything," the dark form hissed. "And in a moment you will have no recollection of what you once knew. Of course, I don't want to take any chances."

The dark form raised his right hand and then lowered it, his palm facing the soil. He moved his hand in a small circle, and electricity shot out of his palm and down into the dirt.

The soil bubbled and churned.

The secret was still choking and struggling for air, but the sight of boiling soil seemed to shock it back into its senses. Its eyes widened, and it rolled over and tried to stand. The dark being reached out with his left hand and snatched the secret by the neck. The poor thing writhed and sputtered like a weak engine. The dark-robed figure held the secret over the bubbling dirt as he continued to manipulate the soil with his right hand.

"No," the secret tried to scream. "Please."

"It'll be just like going home," the dark form said.

"You promised."

"Then I suppose we've both broken our word tonight," the dark form hissed. "Secrets never lie? You are as shifty as you are vapid."

The dark being shoved the secret into the boiling soil. Instantly the ground took hold of the secret's legs and began to suck it in. The black-robed man released the secret and stepped back, his right hand still sending electricity into the dirt.

"Please!" the secret screamed.

"What a pathetic way to go," the dark being said. "Have you no honor?"

"None," the secret hollered. "Free me!"

The soil dragged the secret deeper into the earth. In a few seconds the secret was nothing but a tattered head screaming for

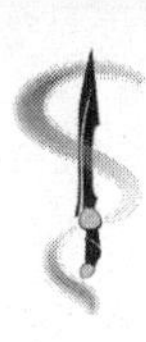

mercy. Two seconds later the dirt closed in over it and boiled ferociously.

"You'd better get Geth and Winter," Leven whispered to Clover.

Clover darted off as the dark form closed his right hand and cut off the current of electricity to the soil. The ground bubbled for a few moments more and then hardened with an audible "snap."

The tall, shadowy man leaned down and pushed a circular stone into the soil. He waved his hand over the stone, and it settled even more. The dark form took the key, stuck it into the stone, and turned it twice in a clockwise direction. He removed the key, and the stone sank completely beneath the soil.

Leven looked around, wishing Geth would hurry. The dark being began to step off into the trees. Leven jumped from his hidden vantage point and raced toward the man. He barreled into the dark being. They hit the ground hard. The key flew from the man's shadowy hand and landed in the dirt.

Leven twisted on the ground, struggling to hold the man down while turning to reach for the key. It was an almost impossible task, as the man seemed to be more like a shadow than a human.

The dark being vanished.

Leven turned to look at his empty arms where the man had just been.

There was nothing.

Leven looked toward the key, and there was the dark form again. The man stuck his hand out and reached for the key. He

grabbed it and lifted it. Leven sprang up and got his arms around the man once again. Once again the shadowy being disappeared in a dark puff of smoke, only to reappear five feet away.

"Stop!" Leven commanded.

The man paid him no mind, running into the trees like a slow-motion electrical current.

"Don't let him get away!" Winter yelled from behind.

Leven turned to see Winter running from the tavern and toward him as fast as she could. Clover had retrieved her, but she was too late. Leven opened his mouth to explain what had happened, but Winter didn't stop to listen. She shot past him, aiming for the shadowy form. Leven tore off after them.

"He's too fast!" Leven yelled out as he ran.

"Geth's coming," Winter screamed back.

As if on cue, the sound of hooves rumbled from around the side of the tavern. Geth was storming toward them, riding his onick and leading the two other beasts to Leven and Winter. In an instant he was there and Leven was climbing onto his moving onick. Winter jumped on hers and clicked her teeth. The onick beneath her shot off in the direction the dark form had gone.

"What happened?" Geth yelled while they galloped.

"The secret sold itself," Leven hollered.

"To whom?"

"I have no idea," Leven admitted. "But I don't think he is planning to use the information for good."

"Did the secret give up its core?"

"It gave up something ugly. It was then forced into the soil."

"By the same man?" Geth yelled again.

"Yes."

Leven, his soul sticky with guilt, couldn't look Geth in the eye. He kicked his onick and the beast moved even faster, racing after the dark form. In the distance a small glimmer of moonlight sparkled off the current in the man's back as he darted off the path and into the trees.

Leven closed his eyes.

Once again he could see the night and the wind. His eyes burned gold and the wind moved in, pushing down through the trees like a thick, heavy river of sound. The trees parted, bending just enough to create a straight path through the forest. Leven's onick jumped with excitement and purpose.

Geth raced ahead, with Winter pulling in behind him. Leven took the rear, shouting at his onick to run faster. Clover was clinging to Leven's neck, screaming, "Maybe I should have waited to come back!"

"And miss all the fun?" Winter yelled as her onick strode neck and neck with Leven's.

The black robe zipped across the path and over into a stretch of the tallest trees. Geth, Winter, and Leven followed suit. The man leapt and took hold of a high branch. He flung himself farther up and away. Geth's onick tried to open its wings, but the trees were too close together. Without pause Geth jumped from his ride, bounding up into the trees and leaping from branch to branch after the dark being. Winter maneuvered her onick beneath the man and Geth while Leven raced in from behind.

The dark-robed man jumped from the top of a tree, trying to get a grip on a distant branch. He missed, slipped, and fell twenty feet into a snarl of high, dead branches. Geth jumped to where he was tangled and tried to grab hold of him. As Geth fell into the branches, they shattered into a thousand pieces.

Geth plummeted like a putty-filled sack tossed from a ten-story building.

He hit the ground directly in front of Winter's onick. The startled beast pulled up, bucked, and threw Winter into the trees. She sliced through the branches, coming to a stop about twenty feet up.

Clover materialized, clinging to the front of Leven's face. "Shouldn't we help them?" he shouted.

"We have to stop that man!" Leven kicked his ride and shot through the trees. A faint trace of the fleeing figure could be seen in the far distance.

Leven rode as fast as he could, his onick's hooves thundering like stone against the hard soil.

Leven watched the shadowy form leave the shelter of the trees and run out over the surface of Cherry Lake. The dark being sped across the lake like a black swan, running on the water as easily as if it had been soil.

"Our turn," Leven shouted, kicking his ride.

The onick beneath him broke from the tree line and shot out over the water with open wings. The beast skimmed the surface of the lake beautifully. It moved forward like a corkscrew, turning upside down and right side up.

In the patchy moonlight, Leven could see his reflection in the red-tinted water.

There was someone who looked a bit like him riding a winged creature—a creature he would have been unable to dream up in his life in Reality. In the reflection Leven could see Clover crawl down the front leg of the beast and hang from its foot. Clover dangled his fingers in the speeding water as if this were all a game, then dropped down and let the water pull him backwards. He flipped once, bounced off the satin surface, and grabbed hold of the onick's left back foot. Clover disappeared and in an instant was sitting on Leven's right shoulder.

Leven ducked his head as his mighty onick closed in on the shadowy man. The dark form glanced back and leapt forward with renewed force across the water.

Leven's onick began to whine. The poor creature had traveled for many days, and it now lacked the strength it needed to continue the race across the lake. The gap grew as the man sped farther away.

"We can't let him escape," Leven yelled.

They were in the center of the lake, the far shore barely visible under the spotty moonlight. Leven's heart was sinking as his onick screamed in tired protest.

"Please," Leven begged. "You have to fly!"

The onick bucked and shivered violently. Its wings raised and lowered, slapping the water and then folding back into its body.

Leven's ride came to a whimpering stop and began to lower down against the water, slowly sinking in. Leven kicked, hoping to draw some passion from the beast.

From beneath Leven the water of the lake began to bubble and swirl. Liquid expanded above the lake in spots like thick, wet whales. Leven watched great streaks of green light under the water race up from behind him. The light thickened and thundered past like a controlled explosion. Leven's onick began to shake and scream in confusion. It seemed as if the lake itself was coming to life.

In front of them the dark form was still moving, but he was soon surrounded by towering waves of water that screamed alongside him and washed over and into him like mountains of wet weight. The black-robed being was soon swept out of sight.

Under the moonlight Leven could see thin, drawn-out faces in the froth of the water's crests. Their eyes looked past Leven and toward the man who had purchased the secret. The faces were framed and covered with strings of knotted green water.

"The Waves of the Lime Sea," Clover whispered in awe. "Here?"

The water boiled and rolled into fat knobs. The knobs rose and dropped against the surface like fantastic bombs, sending shards of speeding liquid toward the shadowy man. The sharp bits of water sliced through the being like gunfire.

Fantastic columns of water shot hundreds of feet into the air. The tallest columns punched through the fat bellies of the low-hanging hazen. The hazen burst into thick, cloudy streaks that shot off like cotton fireworks, exposing the full light of all Foo's moons.

Foo burst into wide view.

Leven's onick thrashed in panic as it bobbed up and down on

the surface of the lake. The water was cold, but the movement of the Waves sent long tracers of warmth beneath the surface. Leven clung to the hair on the back of his onick's neck.

The onick whined in fear.

The Waves grew thicker. Leven could see their shape clearly now. They were massive and ghostly, like pale mountain peaks that held deep pockets of gray snow. He could see through their sheer, wet, muscular bodies. Their faces were long and exaggerated, with white foam beards and whirlpool mouths. They pushed up into whalelike mounds of water and raced toward the dark form.

The Waves pounded the dark man like meat, slamming up against him from every angle and height. The dark form gave up, his limp body smacking down against the churning water. The Waves swirled and spread out into an organized pattern. The tallest Wave collected the body of the man, pushing it high into the air. The other Waves gathered around it and lifted themselves from the water and up toward the sky.

Light flashed across the water back toward Leven.

The water rocked and swirled. The lake began to drop, the entire body of water lowering as the massive waves pushed upward into the night sky, rocketing the limp body of the man thousands of feet into the air.

Peaks of wet, black rock began to appear all around as the whole lake seemed to be climbing up. Leven could no longer see the top of the Waves or any sign of the dark being. The lake was rushing out from under him, thundering like a runaway train speeding toward the smallest moon.

Clover appeared, clinging to Leven's right arm. His expression was one of either high fear or confused fun. "Is this sinking a bad or good thing?" Clover screamed.

"I was going to ask you the same thing," Leven yelled. "Lakes have bottoms here, don't they?"

"Everything has a bottom," Clover replied, slightly embarrassed.

Leven's stomach felt like it was trying to push itself out of his eyes. The onick had had enough. It passed out and began to roll over as they descended, water whipping out from beneath them. Leven frantically climbed over the onick, wrestling with its limp body and trying to keep the beast under him.

A fat fish slapped Leven in the face. The water was pushing upward so rapidly that most of the objects or creatures that called the lake home were having the watery rug ripped right out from under them, leaving them momentarily hanging in the air before they dropped down.

Water exploded and washed over them.

"I can't stand water!" Leven yelled.

"Really?" Clover screamed back, confused. "I think it can be refreshing. Remember when you were on that train with nothing to drink and—"

Leven's frantic glance stopped Clover.

"Oh, *this* water. I wish that was all we needed to worry about," Clover yelled, pointing downward. "Do you see that glow beneath us?"

They were descending so rapidly that Leven could hardly focus

on what was below him in the water. More black, jagged peaks were becoming exposed, growing around him like monstrous teeth that were too large to sink their teeth into him. The entire world seemed to be racing up around him. Fishlike creatures were popping and flinging from the water like hot bits of oil that the lake wouldn't allow to be submerged. Leven could see a faint, swirling, white glow deep beneath him. They were being sucked toward it.

"Is that what I think it is?" Leven yelled.

"Gunt," Clover screamed. "It's protecting the floor of Foo. And if we get stuck in that, we're done for."

"I hate that stuff!"

"I don't know," Clover said reflectively. "If you age it properly, it can be quite . . ."

Clover's voice was drowned out by mammoth fists of water that jutted out around them as they fell. One fist clipped the onick and ripped it out from under Leven, sending the beast hundreds of feet up the tower of water. Leven watched the limp onick until it was too far away to see.

The entire middle of the lake was now one gigantic pillar that reached miles into the sky.

Leven flailed in the sinking water, wishing he was going upward like the onick. Water continued to rush out from underneath him, speeding up into the night sky. The largest moon looked concerned, as if the water might actually reach it.

Leven kicked and fought the strange currents. He looked down as his own body was whipped around and then pinched by the convergence of what felt like two hundred separate currents

of water. Leven's body burned as the pressure increased.

"Can't you do anything?" Clover yelled with concern. "Turn your eyes on or something."

Leven tried, but he couldn't get his eyes to ignite. All he could envision was being snagged by the gunt and then crushed to death by the weight of the lake when it finally came back down to rest again.

"Gunt!" Clover screamed, pointing down from on top of Leven's bobbing head.

Leven could clearly see the gunt now. It was moving in fluid ribbons across every bit of the lake's floor. The ribbons of gunt were made up of millions of tiny, tadpole-looking, white, wriggling blobs.

"Babies?" Clover complained. "They're the stickiest."

A small dab of gunt shot up and adhered to Leven's robe. Leven struggled to pull the wet material off over his head. Clover tugged on the hood and helped him extract himself. The robe was whisked away, and instantly thousands of gunt tadpoles attacked it, smothering the robe and forming a big wad of gunt that began to sink. Another wad hit Leven in the chest, flipping Leven over so that he was falling with the water head first. As water filled his lungs, Leven struggled to pull off his shirt. It ripped at the side and was sucked off by one of the hundreds of currents. Leven flipped back over, kicking and spitting at the water.

"We're doomed," Clover cried.

"You mean I'm doomed," Leven yelled. "This isn't how sycophants die."

"True," Clover said, desperately clinging to Leven's head. "But I think I would rather be dead than trapped down here forever."

A huge wad of gunt smacked Leven's pants right above the left knee.

"Great," Leven moaned. "I'm running out of clothes."

As Leven spoke, the running water suddenly came to a complete stop. All fish and objects still hanging in the air dropped into the few feet of water covering the bottom of the lake. Thanks to the moonlight, the gunt was visible and massive, spread across the entire lake floor like a celestial blanket.

"What's happening?" Clover questioned.

The tower of water above the lake stiffened and stilled itself. The hulking column of water groaned, and Leven could see the top half of it start to arch and bend downward. Leven witnessed lights and sparks drifting off the tip of what was at least a million gallons of water. Fully arched, the tower of water began to race down.

It was an odd moment.

The water where Leven now bobbed was relatively still. The gunt tadpoles were swimming a few feet beneath him, but they were leaving him alone. Since the water had ceased racing upward, Leven and Clover had stopped dropping downward. In fact, things might have seemed sort of peaceful if it had not been for the deafening sound of millions of gallons of water roaring toward them.

The falling water was close enough that Leven could see the foremost tip of it. The dark form was gone; all that could be seen

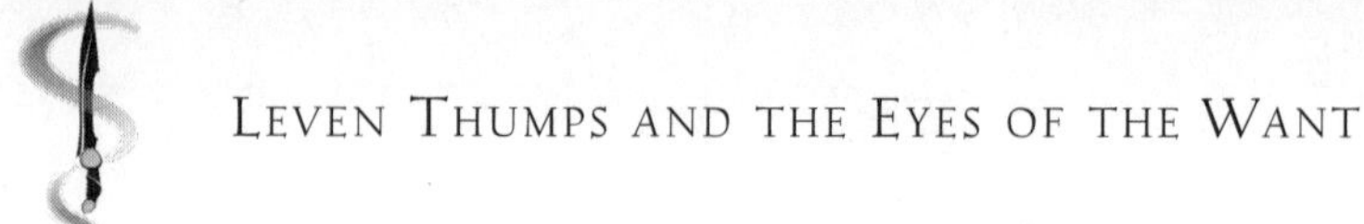

were the hundreds of frosty faces belonging to the Waves.

The entire body of water moaned.

The snaking tower of water twisted again and slammed horizontally into the lake's wall. The force and power drove a gigantic hole deep into the soil.

"They're creating a tunnel," Clover yelled.

The lake water still hovering above relaxed and dropped back down into the lake, as if the sky were emptying large vats of liquid. The plunging water sent Leven and Clover blasting sideways. They twisted and turned, pulled by the tug of the water rushing through the newly created cavern. Leven spun upside down as he raced toward the tunnel.

Leven couldn't breathe, his lungs were filled with liquid, and he had no idea which end was up. His chest rocked as he tried to expel water. He couldn't see Clover, and his eyes refused to show him anything. He wanted to scream for Geth or Winter, but he couldn't.

Water filled the lake with such force that Leven felt certain his entire body would burst under the pressure of it.

He reached for anything solid, but there was nothing.

His head became heavy with thoughts of dying. He could see Winter, giftless and lying as if dead upon the ground. He saw Geth as a toothpick, small and weak. He saw Clover tugging on his arm, trying desperately to pull him up. He saw himself being pushed into the newly carved tunnel deep beneath the soil of Foo.

Leven blacked out, and the Waves pulled him deeper still.

CHAPTER SIX

VERY BOLD

Most people take certain things for granted. I know I do. Sometimes the things we take for granted are small and almost unnoticeable. Sometimes they're quite large and obvious. It's tricky, and it depends upon the state of mind you are in at the moment.

Say you needed transportation to get to work to support your family. Chances are, you'd be grateful to be given a new car. In fact, there would probably even be some clapping and cheering on your part.

But what if you had received a brand-new car every birthday since you were born, as well as every half-birthday, and every special occasion? What if your yard was littered with cars? What if you had cars up in your trees and crammed in every room of your house? What if you had cars parked at your neighbor's house, using up your neighbor's space, and lined up along the street, making the road harder to drive down?

If so, you would probably take cars for granted.

A car is a big thing, but what about the small, almost intangible things we take for granted? Take breathing, for example. It's been said that although people enjoy breathing, most of us don't send our lungs a card thanking them for all the hard work they do. Of course, a person who was buried under a lake gasping for air would probably think back fondly on breathing.

Unlike Leven, Janet didn't miss breathing. She missed *being.* She was nothing but a whisp—a weightless, insubstantial trace of her former self. She had done little since she had arrived in Foo besides weep unreal tears and moan. She had first been found by Leven and Clover, but she had switched company when she had met a band of echoes.

Janet didn't feel much better about her present company.

The echoes were quiet and gentle in their movement, but frightening in appearance. They had long hair and ears that stuck out like horns from the sides of their heads. They were born in the reflection of the setting suns against the walls of Fissure Gorge, their existence brought about by the steam and air. They wore no clothes, but their bodies seemed covered by the reflection of whatever they were standing near—and every once in a while, bits and patches of their beings ignited on fire.

Once, when the tallest echo, Osck, had become concerned, Janet had actually seen his heart burn within his chest. She could see fiery threads of flame race through his veins and up into his head, where they seemed to set his brain ablaze.

The echoes didn't pay much attention to Janet, but now and then Osck would motion for her to follow them.

Their journey had been rough and dangerous. They were making their way up through Foo, following the Hard Border. Every time Janet looked up, she could see no end to how high the Hard Border actually went. It appeared to be a solid wall of rock that stretched forever before, behind, and above them. Occasionally stones would drop, and the echoes would cover themselves with rounded wooden shields and hope not to be crushed to death.

The trip for Janet wasn't quite as treacherous. The only good thing about her condition was the fact that lifting each leg was nowhere near the task it had been in Reality. Also, any falling stones passed right through her like wind.

Janet was with a group of around eighty echoes who were making their way to the Pillars of Rant to gather with the troops. They had been moving as a pack for almost a week now.

Osck motioned for them to stop.

Instantly the echoes spread out, bouncing off boulders and trees, looking for a spot to rest. Some began to eat; others settled in for naps. Some faced the sun with open mouths, hoping to heat their souls.

Janet remained standing.

The wall of the Hard Border was only about fifty feet away, and on her other side was the edge of the Swollen Forest. She was standing in a field of boulders created from rocks that had once been miles up. Most of the echoes chose to rest on the edge of the

forest beneath trees that had not already been pummeled by stones.

Janet stayed standing in the center of the field. She thought she must be very hungry, but she knew from trying that not only could she *not* digest food, she couldn't even lift it to her mouth. She was nothing but an image with impulses and appetites she could no longer fill. She stood there forlorn, wishing she were anyone and anywhere else.

"What are you?" a voice asked, interrupting her self-pity.

Janet looked around, confused.

"What are you?" it asked again, sounding as if it were coming from the ground.

"Excuse me?" Janet snipped, still not sure who she was talking to.

"You look thin," the voice said.

Janet put her hand up over her mouth; no one had ever called her thin before.

"There's nothing to you," the voice said. "Nothing at all."

Janet's jaw dropped. A large boulder near her right leg was talking to her.

"You're a rock," she said in amazement.

"A boulder," it corrected.

Janet looked around, wondering if anyone else was watching. She could see a few echoes under trees eating. No one seemed the least bit interested in what she was doing or what she was talking to.

The boulder looked no different from those in Reality. It was about two feet wide, with thin cracks running up and around it.

There was a round indentation on top. It was speaking from one of its larger cracks.

"You can talk?" she asked in disbelief.

"What *are* you?" the boulder asked a third time, ignoring her question.

"They say I'm a whisp," she answered. "I'm not from here."

"Me neither," the boulder said sadly.

Janet laughed at the absurdity of everything happening around her.

"What's that?" the boulder questioned.

"What's what?" Janet asked.

"The noise your non-head is making."

"Laughter?" Janet tried.

"I'm asking you," the boulder said impatiently.

"I'm laughing," she said.

"It doesn't look good," the boulder said. "It makes your non-face look odd."

Janet stopped laughing. She wasn't used to being insulted by rocks. "What would you know?" she said coldly. "You're a rock."

"I know of the echoes," the boulder replied. "I have seen thousands of them pass this way heading to where the rants gather. Why is a whisp traveling with them?"

"I have nobody," Janet admitted.

"You could associate with worse," the boulder groaned. "Echoes are gentle enough, but if you make them mad they can burn quite hot. I've seen one set a fantrum tree on fire just by looking at it."

"They can't really harm me," Janet said. "Although I'm not sure it wouldn't be that much better to just burn up."

"Hard to say," the boulder creaked. "Where are you from, anyway?"

Janet was quiet for a moment. The simple question seemed heavy to her.

"Reality," she finally answered.

"Fascinating," the boulder remarked. "Was Reality good?"

"No," Janet said quickly. "But it made sense."

"Miserable but organized."

"No, I wasn't organized."

"Doesn't matter," the boulder said. "I don't really even know what that word means. I just heard someone say it once."

"So where are you from?" Janet asked.

"Up there," the boulder said. "If I could, I would point, but I can't, so just look up."

Janet looked up.

"I once sat above it all on the top of the Hard Border," the boulder said dramatically. "I could see everything. The only things higher than me were the shale."

"Shale?"

"Most people don't even know they exist, but they protect the Sky Border. They're nimble like birds, but if needed they can form an impenetrable lid on any part of Foo. We were always trying to grow up above them when they weren't looking—you know, trying to trick them—but they stopped every attempt. I was knocked down a couple of months ago as I tried to reach up

above them. Now look at me. I was lucky enough to fall directly onto someone. That being's life and accidental death gave me the temporary ability to speak."

Janet looked at the base of the boulder, searching for signs of someone who had been flattened.

"The rovens took the bones weeks ago," the boulder said sharply.

Janet stared at the stone. There was nothing reflective in its material, but she could see herself in the fallen boulder. There, like a full-colored ad, was the image of her life. She could see her house in Reality and the couch she spent most of her time on. She could see her wide, square face and her ratty hair and the person she had never wanted to be. She could see her miserable past and the hatred her heart had taken on the moment her child's father had left her. She could see Winter, and she could see the cruelty with which she had raised the girl.

Janet's heart made an audible noise as it softened and crumbled just a bit.

"Why would you want to go higher?" she asked quietly, pulling her mind back to the conversation at hand. "You were at the top."

"There is always more," the boulder said reflectively. "I guess I'd rather fall while reaching than decay while just sitting still."

Janet looked down at the boulder. "You're sitting still now," she pointed out.

"I suppose you're right, but it was one spectacular fall. Now, do you mind rolling me over just a bit? I would love to feel the sun on my backside."

"I can't move anything," she pointed out.

"Oh," the boulder sighed. "Well, could you at least pretend?"

Janet bent down and grunted as if pushing the stone.

"You're a pretty good actor," the boulder remarked.

"So, are these other rocks family?" Janet asked, looking around at all the other scattered stones.

"Some I knew, but most have hardened to a lifeless existence. Some have withered under the wear of nature. We boulders don't last forever down here."

"It sounds like you were foolish to reach."

"Yes, but just think if I had made it."

Janet could hear Osck speaking in the trees. His voice sounded like the crackle of a strong fire.

"We'll settle here for a few hours," he said. "Sleep in the shade of the trees. You will need all the rest you can store up. This will not be an easy war."

"War?" Janet whispered.

"All things come to war," the boulder said sadly. "Rants will never be completely happy here. I guess, in a way, they're just reaching."

Janet shivered. "I don't want to hear about it."

"Burying your head can be quite satisfying. There are times when I wish someone would just toss a couple of spades full of soil over me."

"I don't want to bury my head," Janet snapped. "I've just heard enough unsettling things for now."

"Nothing's as bad as it's reported," the boulder insisted. "All news is more sinister in its delivery than its action."

"I'm not talking about news," Janet said sadly, annoyed by the knowledgeable stone. "I can do nothing about a war. I'm talking about what I've learned about myself."

The boulder had the presence of stone to stay silent.

Janet sighed.

She looked up at the Hard Border and tried to imagine falling from the top. She wiped her eyes and realized once again that she really wasn't all there. She knelt down and positioned herself so as to lean against the boulder. She had no substance, but her being seemed to remember things like the positions of sitting and lying.

She leaned against the boulder. Sunlight pushed right through her and heated the stone. Janet could almost feel the warmth against her back and a slight breath in her lungs.

She was a pretty good actor.

CHAPTER SEVEN

QUESTION EVERYTHING

Geth rode up to the shore of Cherry Lake and stopped. Winter was already there, sitting on her onick and looking out at the settling body of water. Geth jumped from his onick and looked out over the dark lake. He was drenched from the water that had fallen like rain along the shore as the lake had hurled itself back down. Nearby trees shivered and shook, dripping and shaking water off.

Choppy moonlight covered the red settling lake like patchy frosting applied by an uncoordinated left foot.

The moonlight illuminated Winter's green eyes like new coins. Her long blonde hair was plastered to her pale face. She grabbed the front of her hair and wrung water from it. She tried to tuck it back behind her ear, but it was so wet and heavy it wouldn't stay.

"What happened?" Winter asked. "Where's Lev?"

"Interesting," was all Geth said.

Green streaks of faint light danced across the water in the far distance.

"As I rode up, I saw the lake in the air," Winter said. "It looked as if it shot up and then dropped back into itself."

"I saw the same thing," Geth agreed. He knelt down to feel the water at its edge. "It's warm."

"How can that be?" Winter asked, blowing out cold breath.

"I can think of only one thing that would warm it," Geth said. "See those streaks of green?"

Winter looked to where Geth was pointing and nodded.

"The Waves of the Lime Sea were here," Geth said with excitement.

"But I thought they stayed near the island of Alder," Winter spoke.

"Usually," Geth said. "But the Want has some control over them."

"So why are they here?" Winter asked. "And where's Lev?"

"I'm not sure," Geth said quietly. "We should search the lake. Though I've got a feeling the Waves were here for him."

Geth swung back onto his onick and nudged it with his knees. The beast spread its wings and cried into the cold night. Winter nudged hers, and it repeated the act. Geth leaned forward, and his ride leapt out over the water.

Winter followed.

The water was settling. Small ripples played themselves out, creating large spots of glassy red water. Moonlight covered the

top and illuminated what was beneath the surface. The flapping of the onicks' wings created thin wakes of moving liquid that spread across the water like misguided snakes.

Aside from the settling water, the scene was silent.

"I wish I had my gift," Winter yelled. "Then I could freeze it to clear ice and see better."

"All I can see are tracers," Geth replied. "The Waves have come and gone."

"Gone where?"

"If I had to guess, I'd say they are heading to the Want."

"This lake doesn't get anywhere near Lith," Winter hollered, her green eyes still searching the water for any sign of Leven. "Come to think of it, how did the Waves get here? The Lime Sea's a long way away."

"They have their underground tunnels and caverns," Geth said. "They can move where they need to."

"So what do we do?"

Geth didn't answer. Instead he kept his eyes to the water and let the soft swing of his onick's wings calm Winter's concerns. The lake was almost completely settled, fish and other life forms deep below getting back into their routine.

"I can't see much," Winter finally said.

"It's a deep lake," Geth replied. "It grows shallow as the seasons warm up. The trees of the Red Grove drink a lot."

"So the water lowers?"

"No," Geth smiled. "The bottom rises. The Children of the Sewn think it's much more aesthetically pleasing that way. This

lake is their life. It wets the roots that give them shelter and grows the wood they use to frame dreams. They, like so many, are also concerned with appearance. Nobody likes a half-empty lake. It can be depressing."

"I suppose," Winter said, still searching the water.

"I've seen seasons so warm that the lake's floor has literally lifted up above the surface, creating small, jagged islands. It looks like it had a good wet season this year. This is as much water as I've ever seen in it."

"I wish it was shallower now."

"Don't wish for things you don't understand," Geth said kindly.

"Thanks, Professor. I'm only thinking of Leven," Winter said defensively. "He could be down there."

"I don't think he is," Geth said. "The Waves must have come for him, and if they did, they will take care of him. I don't think what we want is in this lake any longer. Are you up for a long ride?"

"Always," Winter replied, steadying her fidgeting onick as it flapped its wings over the lake.

CHAPTER EIGHT

A Blanket of Twinkling Stars

There are varying degrees of comfort. Pants that fit right can be comfortable. I've slept in beds that were very agreeable and offered plenty of comfort. Warm slippers can be a nice comfort on a cold night.

Situations can be comfortable as well.

A gathering with your family and friends in a room with enough soft chairs for everyone to sit on sounds comfortable. Or maybe you have a favorite place to hike to, with no one around, and cool grass, and large shade trees near a babbling brook, and a well-worn hammock to lie in.

That sounds comfortable.

Well, forget it all. In fact, if you consider any of those previously described things to be comfortable, then the English language will be forced to cough up a new word to describe Sycophant Run.

In the history of time, both in Reality and in Foo, there has never been a place as beautiful as Sycophant Run. The lush trees sway in harmony—the taller ones reaching down to pull the young ones up. The mountains and valleys are both breathtaking and plentiful, giving every view more to see than a dozen eyes could properly take in. Roads and lanes are tree lined or run underground in clean, perfectly constructed tunnels that open up through tree stumps or onto flowery knolls. The homes and buildings mesh with nature, growing out of trees and boulders, the roofs covered with thick thatch and walls camouflaged in ivy and stone. Fields bustle with wheat and corn and tavel and are tilled and cared for by sycophant families. The soil is so dark and rich that a person could make a half-decent hot drink simply by placing a fistful in a cup of boiling water. There is always laughter: Like oxygen, it fills the clear air as invisible and visible sycophants run through trees and over open fields.

Foo may struggle with ever-bigger issues and crises, but Sycophant Run remains untouched. There, hidden behind the mists of the Veil Sea; there, like a family home full of warm memories and experiences; there, one will always find a light left on, an open front door, smoke lifting from the chimney, and a red carpet rolled out to remind every sycophant who is coming home that he or she is always welcome.

Always welcome.

An old sycophant named Rast shuffled through the tavel field. The yellow bloom caused him to stop and sneeze seven times.

"You're lucky you taste as delicious as you do," he teased the vegetation. "Otherwise we would mow you down and be done with you."

Out of the field Rast pushed a stone to the side and walked into a long, tight tunnel. He moved quickly, turning when he came to a thick wall of tree roots and climbing a stone trail that opened up behind a thin waterfall near the back end of Sycophant Run.

Rast stepped out from behind the water and breathed in deep. He looked out over the Veil Sea. This was one of his favorite views in all of Foo.

"Lovely," he sighed.

The sight was even more amazing because of what he *couldn't* see. Rast knew that at that very moment there were thousands of sycophants guarding the shore. He just couldn't see a single one.

Rast had been alive hundreds of years, served four burns, fought in the metal wars, and now sat as the brightest point in the sycophant Chamber of Stars—a select and powerful group of sycophants who dictated and directed almost everything that took place on Sycophant Run.

The group had been summoned by Reed, a fat sycophant who had been a member of the Chamber for the last twenty or so years. Rast would have very much preferred spending the day in the highest floors of his home listening to the sounds of the Veil Sea and Sycophant Run, but Reed had stressed how utterly important it was that they gather—and now.

Rast was a tall sycophant. He stood about fifteen inches

from foot to ear. He had black feet and hands, but the rest of him, including his robe, was bright white. After his fourth burn, he had come back to Sycophant Run to stay. He had married a beautiful sycophant named Ribbon and they had had a dozen children, most of whom were currently serving burns in various parts of Foo.

Rast strolled across a bark field and then used a heavy vine to climb to the top of a rocky plateau. In the middle of the plateau stood a single tree. Unlike all the other trees and vegetation on Sycophant Run, this one had only bare branches.

Rast entered the small door at the base of the huge, barren tree. He took two steps down and entered the Chamber room. Four sycophants sat quietly around a star-shaped table—Reed, Brindle, Goat, and Mule—each positioned at a separate point.

The room was dark, lit only by the thousands of stars above them. The tree they sat in was barren to the tip of every branch, where a small pinhole of light could be seen. The effect made it seem as if they were sitting in a stream of swaying stars. The thousands of tiny lights shifted and blinked as clouds moved outside.

A thin, whistling wind sounded as air squeezed in and out of the little holes. If a sycophant were blindfolded and taken into the Chamber, when his blindfold was removed he might very well feel like he was sitting in the center of the universe. It was an amazing effect—and a very sacred place, where only a few sycophants had ever trod.

Rast took a seat at the top point of the table and nodded. "Reed, Brindle, Goat, Mule."

The four other sycophants nodded back. “Rast,” they greeted in unison.

“I was told it was urgent,” Rast said.

“Most,” Reed sighed.

“Well,” Rast said almost impatiently, “I’ve not known any urgent issues that were best when ignored. What is it?”

Reed looked around at the others. He shifted in his seat and glanced over at Brindle, a fat, happy, furry red sycophant.

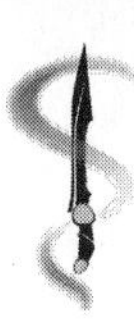

"Go on," Brindle encouraged Reed. "Go on."

"There's word floating on one of the stronger Lore Coils saying that the secret's loose," Reed whispered.

Rast sat up straight, the hair on his leaflike ears twitching. "What secret?"

"Of our mortality," Goat whimpered.

Goat was a runt sycophant. He stood about seven inches tall and had thick, gray hair.

"Impossible," Rast said. "Absolutely impossible."

"Please say that it is," Mule begged. "Comfort me with what you know."

"I know it's impossible."

"There's word that a boy found the secret," Brindle spoke. "Leven Thumps."

Rast gasped. "Leven Thumps?"

"Yes, Rast."

"Hector's blood? He's here in Foo?" Rast asked in disbelief, surprised that the Lore Coils had escaped his attention.

Brindle nodded.

"And is there word of Clover Ernest?"

"The cloistered sycophants think so. They have heard that a sycophant was released by the tharms a week or so past—a sycophant claiming to belong to Leven."

"Clover Ernest," Rast said almost to himself. "And Geth?"

"There are echoes and words throughout all of Foo that he has returned," Goat said.

"And that he's been restored," Mule added. "From the form Sabine cursed him with."

Rast sighed. "It looks as if the time has finally arrived."

"What about the secret?" Reed whined. "None of this will matter if that secret truly is loose."

"Is there whispering as to what the secret actually is?" Rast asked.

"None yet," Mule answered.

"Don't worry over the secret, then," Rast said. "It can't be loosed without the key. And the key is safe."

"You know this for a fact?" Mule said hopefully.

"It's been many years since I've touched it," Rast said. "But it is safe, hidden from all eyes and envy."

"Are you sure?" Mule cried. "Say you are sure."

"I am certain," Rast said. "But I will check, if it reassures you."

"Greatly," Goat sighed. "There is trouble in Foo, but Sycophant Run will remain a harbor to our kind. Unless . . ."

"The secret is safe," Rast assured them again. "We will increase the posted pegs guarding our shores and open our ears as wide as we can. But we will not adopt a stance of fear. If what you say about Leven and Geth is true, then Sycophant Run might be in for a spell of change and adjustment. And we must be ready. Keep your hearts light, my friends, and believe in fate. Remember, without us, Foo will fail."

"But you'll check?" Mule asked again. "For the key?"

"I'll check for the key. I promise," Rast said.

"I just worry," Mule sighed.

"You always have," Brindle smiled.

The mood lightened a bit as the stars pulsated.

"Meeting adjourned," Rast said.

The four other sycophants got up and left the room, but not before Mule had asked one last time for Rast to check.

The door closed, and Rast was left alone to stare at the twinkling stars.

CHAPTER NINE

A DELIVERY TO LITH

The Waves receded, leaving the rocky beach wet and littered with Leven. The high granite cliffs of the thirteenth, and by far the largest, stone stood like impenetrable reminders of how insignificant any and all who attempted to come ashore really were. The small beach area was deserted except for Leven, who lay unconscious on the sand, his back to the ground. It was considerably warmer than the Red Grove, and rovens filled the air, flying miles above.

Clover appeared next to Leven's head.

"Wow, what a ride. I bet no other sycophant has ever traveled across the Veil Sea on the back of a Wave," Clover bragged. "Am I right?"

Clover nudged Leven's soggy head with his elbow.

"Leven?"

Leven lay still as small waves rolled up over his ankles and back into the sea.

"Lev?"

Clover sighed and then disappeared. There was some splashing down in the water, and in a couple of minutes a very confused fish appeared. It was flapping its head like a clicking tongue, looking as if it were being dragged up on shore.

"This will only take a second," Clover's voice said. "Stop your struggling."

The fish moved awkwardly closer to Leven. It was angry but helpless. It lifted up, seemingly of its own accord, and then came down with a hard smack right against Leven's face.

Leven bolted up, coughing and spitting, while the fish just flapped there. Clover appeared, holding its tail.

"That worked better than I thought it would," he shrugged, returning the poor fish to the water. "Those things are so multipurposeful."

Leven rolled over, coughing up water and trying to catch his breath. Clover patted him on the back.

"That's it. Spit it out."

Leven glared at Clover. "You hit me with a fish?"

"Slapped," Clover corrected.

Leven breathed in and pushed himself up onto his knees. He looked around at the high cliff walls. A waterflight ran up a nearby wall, and deep blue fantrum trees grew straight out of the cliff's rock in a couple of dozen spots.

Leven stood and stretched, lifting his right shoulder and rolling his neck. He put his hands up to his shoulders.

"I have no shirt," Leven said needlessly. "Or robe."

"Yeah, we got out of there just in time."

"Out of where?" Leven asked. "And where are we now?"

"I think we are on the thirteenth stone," Clover said, looking around. "The island of Lith. The Want lives here, and his movements and actions affect the whole of Foo. The Waves brought us here. I was going to ask them what was going on, but they looked like they weren't having the best day. Some people just can't shake themselves out of a foul mood."

"Any sign of Geth or Winter?"

Clover looked at Leven like he wasn't all there. He shaded his eyes with his right hand and looked around.

"Nope."

"Not *here,*" Leven smiled. "My eyes work fine. I mean, did you see them with the Waves?"

"Still nope." Clover picked up a small stick and began to write his name in the sand.

"It's warmer here," Leven observed, though he was shivering.

"Lith has its own climate," Clover said, still drawing in the sand. "The weather depends upon the mood of the Want . . . there . . ."

Clover took a moment to stare at his own name in the sand.

"I always wished I was named Steven," he said sadly. "You know, you could rename me."

"That's not going to happen," Leven insisted.

"Okay, Mr. Never-Change-My-Name."

Leven stared at Clover. "Is that as good as you've got?"

"Maybe it's not as catchy as some of the other nicknames I've tried," Clover confessed. "But at least I'm still trying."

"I wish you wouldn't."

Leven stepped higher on the beach, out of reach of any water. He worked his way up onto a giant rock and took a couple of minutes to survey the landscape. The beach they were on was about two hundred feet long and a hundred feet wide. The cliff walls boxing it in seemed impossibly tall, and he could see no trail or path anywhere.

Out in the Veil Sea Leven could faintly see the outline of some of the other islands. They were too far away to swim to.

"So I guess we're stuck here?" Clover asked, clinging to Leven's right shoulder.

"I'm not," Leven said. "If this is Lith, then the Want should be here. Geth thought I should see him, so it must be fate that I'm standing here right now."

"Geth would be proud," Clover smiled.

"We just need to find a way up," Leven said, looking to the sky.

"Now, I'm not certain," Clover suggested. "But what good is a waterflight if there isn't some kind of hidden passage or tunnel behind it?"

Leven looked back toward the thick waterflight that climbed the entire length of one stony wall.

"Sounds like a perfect place to start looking," he said.

Leven climbed down from the rock and moved across the

sand back toward the pool the waterflight was drawing from.

Clover slipped off of Leven's shoulder and landed on the ground. "Hold on a second," he insisted.

He put his hand into his void and began feeling around for whatever he was looking for. "Nope . . . I don't think so . . . possibly . . . nope . . . *yes!*" Clover smiled, pulling out a large white piece of material.

He shook it open and showed it off. It was a clean white Wonder Wipes T-shirt.

Leven's mouth dropped open.

"I took it a while ago when Addy brought you those seven shirts home for the new school year."

"She yelled at me for two straight days when I wasn't able to find that shirt," Leven pointed out.

"I was going to put it back," Clover insisted. "But I figured since you had already been yelled at and all—"

"Thanks," Leven said, taking the shirt from Clover. He flipped it over and looked at the blank white back, then turned it back around and stared at the Wonder Wipes pattern. It was a simple logo, but in it he could see Addy and the fear she used to work him over with. He could see Terry and smell his foul, sour breath. He could also see the wide, open fields of Burnt Culvert, Oklahoma. His mind played images of all the people who had been unkind to him and those who had just acted as if he didn't exist.

Now here he was, trying to find a way to save their dreams.

"Weird," Leven said softly.

"I know," Clover agreed. "The logo is not that eye-catching.

I would have included a lightning bolt, or a couple of kittens. I don't really care for cats, but I don't think there is anyone who can look at a kitten and not feel a little lump in . . ."

Leven just stared.

" . . . I'm just saying the logo doesn't work for me," Clover explained.

Leven smiled and rubbed Clover on the head. "Thanks for this," he said. "I didn't ever think I'd see another."

Leven pulled the shirt on. It fit a bit tighter than he expected, but it worked.

Clover looked him up and down critically.

"You know," Clover finally said. "The whole Wonder Wipes thing really isn't any cooler here in Foo."

Leven looked down at his chest. "I think you're right," he said.

He took off his shirt and turned it inside out, then put it back on.

"Better?" he asked.

"Much," Clover grinned. "Plus, when you're wearing a shirt, it's so much easier for me to hang on."

Clover sprang from the ground and grabbed ahold of Leven's sleeve.

"So, let's check out this waterflight?" Leven suggested.

Clover smiled again and disappeared.

Leven moved to the edge of the blue water pool. He pushed himself up against the cliff's wall and stepped cautiously, moving sideways back behind the water. Leven could hear some small fish falling up and laughing with delight.

Foo was an amazing place.

Leven spotted a small opening way back behind the ascending water. He could see steps leading into darkness.

"See," Clover whispered. "All good waterflights are hiding something."

Leven slipped all the way behind the flight and up the stone stairs with Clover on his back. Neither was aware that the temperature on the island of Lith had just dropped a good ten degrees. The Want was in a mood.

CHAPTER TEN

One and One Make One

Dennis was no longer Dennis. He was now as much Sabine as he was the weak-chinned, uninspired, going-nowhere human being he had once been. Dennis was Sabine and Sabine had conquered Dennis. I suppose a person could argue that Dennis was in there somewhere, but his mind no longer belonged to him—the influence and poison of Sabine had completely sunk in and taken over.

The black robe that Dennis had once worn was gone. In its place were the shadowy markings that drifted across Dennis's skin, painting patterns and symbols. Most of the time the markings were unrecognizable, but every once in a while the blotches would mesh to make it perfectly clear what Dennis was thinking. A day ago Ezra had said something about Dennis being "less sophisticated than a regurgitated bowl of mush." It was a strong comment that probably should have remained a thought, but

Ezra had said it out loud, and it had taken only a couple of seconds for the shadows on Dennis's skin to group and spell out, "You will perish," across Dennis's whole face.

Ezra had been halfway silent ever since.

He had kept his mouth shut when Dennis had ordered him and Tim into the van. He had spoken up only once during the long ride from Berchtesgaden to Munich, and that comment had been directed toward the utter stupidity of things like speed limits and traffic laws. And he had not called Dennis a rotten excuse for an organic pile of poorly put together cells when Dennis had missed their exit and caused them to have to circle back to get where they were going.

No, Ezra had done quite well to hold his tongue.

Now, as he looked out the front window, the streets were alive with traffic. Cars were driving as if they had no concern for pedestrian or parkway—a red car swerved violently, narrowly missing a blue car that had slammed on its brakes to avoid hitting the white van Dennis was driving.

"I can't take it!" Ezra screamed. "You drive like an old woman. Go around!"

Ezra's purple hair was whipping in the wind of the car's heating vent. He couldn't hold back any longer.

"Go!" Ezra demanded. "If I could, I'd bite off your right foot and use it to press on the gas myself."

Dennis looked at Ezra with a cold, metallic stare. Black markings moved across Dennis's face and slipped down the collar of his shirt. He sat upright in his slacks and shirt, the sticker still

pasted to his chest and his head shaved. Ezra saw the anger in Dennis and backed off. He had almost been snapped in two by the man before, and he knew there was a line he shouldn't cross.

"I meant I'd *borrow* your right foot," Ezra tried to apologize.

"Of course," Dennis said calmly. "I'd be happy to lend it to you anytime."

Dennis kicked his right foot and sent Ezra flying into the front corner of the van, where he got caught tangled in the wires hanging out under the dashboard. Had Ezra not been wearing his thick coat of nail polish, he might very well have been damaged.

"Say thank you," Dennis ordered.

Ezra said something under his breath, but you would have been hard-pressed to find anyone who thought it sounded like "thank you."

"I should have left you at the gasthaus," Dennis said to Ezra. "We have a task to accomplish, and you shouldn't second-guess me. Understand?"

"No, your vocabulary is too sophisticated for me, Dennis."

Dennis let the insult slide even though it cut him to the quick. Not so much the part about having an unsophisticated vocabulary, but the part about calling him *Dennis.* It was just so much less evil-sounding than *Sabine.* There had been many moments when Sabine wished he had taken over the will of someone named Axel or Rocky.

"Sabine," Dennis corrected.

"Where?" Ezra joked, looking around.

Dennis seethed.

Tim sat in the seat behind Dennis, oblivious to it all. His eyes were glazed over and he was staring straight ahead as if trying to read a billboard a mile away. His breathing was slow and his mouth hung open like he was showing a dentist his back teeth. Any outsider might have thought that he didn't have a thing going on in his head, but if that same outsider could have looked inside, he would have seen Tim's mind trying to fight off the black influence of Sabine.

Tim knew he should remove the bit of black cloth tied to his right wrist, but he just couldn't get his own hands to obey him. The tie had begun to seep into Tim's skin, sending thin, weblike lines crawling up his forearm. He wanted to jump from the van and get as far away from Dennis as possible, but he knew those kinds of decisions were no longer his to make.

He thought about his wife, Wendy. He could barely remember that he loved her. And he wasn't quite sure if he had one son or two. The only thing he was well aware of was that something was terribly wrong and that things were only going to get worse unless he could do something about it.

"What's happening?" Tim managed to moan.

"We are going to pick up a piece of uneven street," Dennis answered, clueless as to what Tim was really asking. "I had to find it because you never did as you were told."

"Sorry," Tim said weakly.

"We'll wait until it's pitch black outside, and then dig it up," Dennis explained. "It's a perfect piece and should fit fate well."

Dennis pushed on the gas and turned the van down a wide

side street. Ezra worked himself up out of the wires and onto the front passenger seat.

"Fit fate well," Ezra spat. "What a—"

Dennis slammed on the brakes as a green car flew past their windshield and into a brick building on the opposite side of the street.

"Did you see . . ."

Ezra was silenced again, this time by the rattling of the van. It sounded as if every bolt was frantically trying to come undone.

"What's happening?" Dennis demanded, as if this were all the result of something Ezra had done.

The van began to rattle and move sideways. The windows stretched and warbled.

"Cover your eyes," Dennis screamed. "The window's going to blow."

Even Tim put his hands over his eyes as the windows flexed and then blew outward, spurting glass everywhere. Fine, glittery dust drifted down, covering Ezra as he stood on the passenger seat.

"What in the—"

Ezra's question was interrupted by two more cars flying past them. The van began to rise up, spinning slowly. People were running through the streets crying and screaming in both German and English. Buildings seemed to be choking, spitting out their windows and doors as heavy winds pushed through their rattling bodies.

The black markings on Dennis's body swirled and pulsated, crossing his face in flashes and streaks. His dark eyes looked as

confused and chaotic as the scene before them. The van dropped back down onto the road, rocking back and forth.

"We should get out of this metal coffin," Ezra screamed.

"We should," Tim parroted, wanting desperately to be able to think and act on his own.

"No!" Dennis yelled. "We must get what we came for, and we need this car."

Ezra jumped up onto the dashboard. His hair was wriggling, the purple strands covered with shiny specks of glass. His green-nail-polished body glistened in the light of the setting sun. Ezra's single eye caught hold of something worth looking at. He turned to face Dennis, laughing and pointing ahead.

"Looks like you're going to have to change your plans."

In the distance a gigantic funnel of dirt and debris at least ten stories high was moving toward them. It looked like a tornado moving from side to side in an awkward, jumpy motion. It had dozens of long, windy arms that were reaching out and grabbing at anything within reach. The arms would lift the objects and push them into the funnel's big, wide, windy mouth. A couple of moments later those objects would come shooting out of its distorted body blended and unrecognizable.

"It's a telt," Dennis whispered in awe.

"Telt," Tim repeated without understanding.

"I remember," Dennis said almost to himself. As Sabine, he had used his shadows to bring avalands and telts to life in an effort to find Leven.

The telt picked up a bronze statue of an old horse. The statue

had been commissioned by a wealthy German fifty years ago as a tribute to all the horses that had died in German-fought wars.

The statue had sat perfectly still for the last fifty years.

Now it was in the hands of the telt. The telt shoved the bronze horse into its windy face and howled. There was a brief pause and then, like they had been shot from a cannon, large, round chunks of metal blew out of the telt and flew through the air. One chunk took out the front of a church. Another chunk hit the pavement and left a hole big enough for two cars to recklessly drive into. A third chunk rocketed from the belly of the telt and slammed into the back wheel of the van.

Tim flew out of his seat, tumbling backwards. The van spun and rolled twice, coming to rest back on its wheels. Ezra was caught in the visor, while Dennis held onto the steering wheel like it was the last gold brick in the world.

Ezra started laughing. "At last, something's happening!"

Ezra jumped from the visor and out through the missing windshield. Dennis forced his door open and ran out after him. Tim, not having any thoughts of his own, borrowed one of Dennis's and followed.

The telt had stopped in the middle of a wide intersection with buildings on all four corners. Its windy presence was clearing the streets of everything that had once rested on them. Four of the telt's thin arms reached out and pulled up two traffic lights. Electricity shot through the air, lighting the telt from inside out. Anyone looking on could easily see all the objects the telt had swirling around in its belly.

The sign outside a small German Lebensmittel broke free and fell to the ground, the letters breaking loose and flinging in all directions. The *L* shot down the street directly toward Ezra.

"Here we go, cowards," Ezra screamed, grabbing hold of the *L* as it whizzed by.

Ezra pulled the bottom of the letter up and it spun back toward the telt in a large arch. Ezra rode the *L* right into the side of an abandoned building, where the corner of it stuck into the wood beam. Ezra jumped from his ride and sprang into the blown-out window of the five-story building.

"What's happening?" Tim yelled, confused.

"Foolish toothpick," Dennis seethed.

As if to prove Dennis's point, the building Ezra had disappeared into was now moving. Touched by the power of Foo that Ezra wielded, it had come alive, just like the one Dennis used to work in.

The telt was in front of the building looking the opposite way. The structure took two huge steps, lifting its corners and dragging itself closer as the telt greedily picked up and feasted on everything in front of it.

The building raised its back half, and before the telt knew what was happening, the entire thing tipped and fell directly onto it. A tremendous rumbling noise filled the air as the building completely buried the windy monster.

People in the streets didn't know whether they should cheer or keep running.

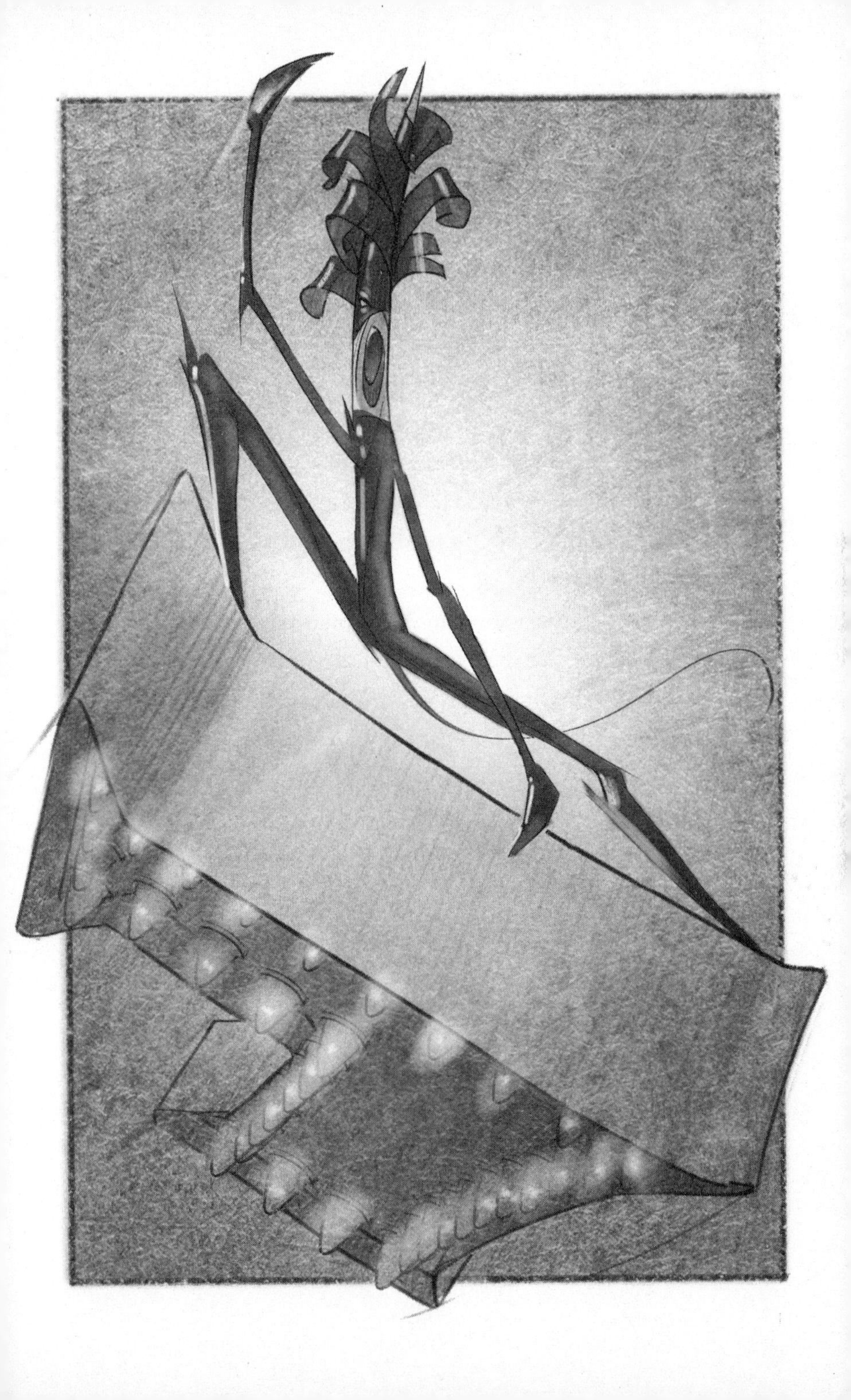

For the record, they should have kept running.

The building settled in a gigantic heap of rubble and dust. A couple of brave onlookers stepped closer. People put their hands to their hearts as if the nightmare were over and they could finally breathe easy.

"Idiots," Dennis said.

Tim looked at him.

"Dirt won't stop a telt," Dennis raged. "Only water."

Dennis glanced around. He saw a large board that had come loose from a building. He pointed at the board. "Pick that up," he commanded Tim.

Tim looked at the board and then down at his own wrist. The small bit of black that had been tied around his arm was now gone, and his entire right arm was covered with black, wriggling webbing.

"Now!" Dennis demanded. "Pick it up."

Tim stepped over to the long board and picked it up. It was about a foot wide and five feet long. He carried it back to Dennis, who was watching the pile of rubble. Tim stood by his side and focused his own eyes on the building Ezra had brought to life and then destroyed.

Those standing around began to feel safe—some stepping close to the rubble and taking pictures or movies of the destruction. People all through the crowd were moving their arms and opening their mouths, frantically trying to describe what had happened to the others who had seen it happen themselves.

Their happiness was short-lived.

The deceased building released a puff of smoke that shot up directly from the center of the rubble.

People took one step back.

The puff of smoke dissipated, and as it fell, it swirled, picking up dirt and small bits of debris.

People took three steps back.

The largest chunks of building began to tap and jig, dancing like snake handlers hopped up on caffeine from heaven.

People turned and screamed.

The razed building was born again as the telt pulled it up, spinning and gaining speed and strength with each cycle. The wind picked up, blowing people and possessions in all directions. The angry telt soon stood at its full height, the new debris making it almost twice the size it had been earlier.

"Foolish toothpick," Dennis sneered again. "There is only one way to stop a telt." He glared hard at Tim. "Hit me!"

Tim looked like someone had just asked him to remove his own head and toss it over.

The telt was scratching at buildings and growing with each swipe.

"Hit me!" Dennis demanded.

Tim picked up the board, his mind not his own any longer. He hefted it into his right hand and turned to get some solid momentum. He moved his hips, pivoted his body, and with one great swing brought the board around and smacked Dennis in the back, right behind his shoulders, as hard as he could. Dennis screamed as thousands of tiny specks of black

blasted out of his body and flew into the overhead clouds.

The beast ripped off a complete roof of a building and shoved it into its windy face. The clouds began to gather above the telt as Dennis lay on the ground screaming and kicking in pain from the blow of the board and the loss of blackness he had showered out.

Tim just stared at Dennis as he lay there.

The telt let out a great, windy belch and released thousands of pieces of debris into the air. Buildings and cars were pummeled with everything the beast coughed up.

The creature was on the move again. It absorbed the whole corner of a building, drawing closer to Dennis and Tim.

Tim looked back down at Dennis and then up to the clouds that had gathered over the telt. Dennis was crying, and the clouds were bunching themselves up like dirty laundry in a tight bin two weeks past wash day.

The monster thrust a couple dozen of its arms down into the road. It then pulled and sucked, drawing the road in like it was a giant, flat noodle—a noodle that had Dennis and Tim on the tip of it. With every foot of road the telt drew in, it grew taller and wider.

Now Tim looked not only baffled but scared. He glanced around frantically as he and Dennis moved closer to the beast.

His right arm burned.

Tim stopped panicking to stare closely at his arm. He then turned his eyes to the clouds. He could hear whispering beneath his skin. He raised his right hand and spread his fingers.

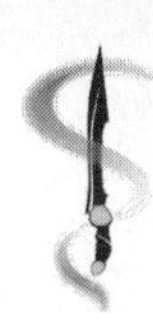

The clouds rumbled, but the telt continued to drag the two men closer. Tim put his hand down and looked at Dennis. Dennis's skin was as white as a full moon and he was scratching at himself and screaming in pain.

Without thinking, Tim lifted his arm to the sky again. He lost his balance due to the street moving beneath him. He righted himself and stood again.

Tim lifted his arm to the air once more.

The clouds started to pucker and heave violently. Tim covered his own eyes with his left hand, scared to see what he was doing with his right.

The telt was growing rapidly, sucking in any and everything around.

Dennis screamed loud enough to be heard above the noise.

The clouds began to drip blackness, drawn to Tim's arm. The storm started slowly, but after a few seconds the clouds burst with black moisture, raining down on the telt in an effort to reach Tim.

The telt screamed as the top of it began to dissolve, the water in the air washing away the dirt it was made of.

Tim cracked his fingers on his left hand, gaining the courage to take a peek at what he was doing. The black rain was destroying the telt, washing it away like a weak sand castle under the pressure of a large wave.

The road Tim was standing on stopped moving.

The telt screamed as its face dissolved and washed down a dozen separate sidewalks and roads. Tim kept his hand up,

continuing to draw every bit of black from the clouds. As the telt dissolved the water sprayed everywhere, blowing in the dying wind like a dog shaking itself after a bath.

Tim lowered his right hand and a thick stream of black liquid flowed closer. The blackness rolled in like mercury along the street. It circled around Dennis as he lay there, creating a pool of Sabine.

The telt was dead, and the last bits of Sabine had returned to Dennis. His body sponged up the influence, and in a few seconds Dennis was back up on his feet, dusting himself off.

"Now," Dennis said, "let's hope our uneven piece of street has not been bothered."

"Ezra?" Tim asked, looking around.

"Who?" Dennis said coldly. "I suppose he was crushed . . ."

"Who?" Ezra seethed, hopping up from the street and onto Tim's left shoulder. "I suppose your memory is as clever as your smarts."

Dennis ignored the comment.

"I had to drag myself out a fallen building," Ezra seethed. "You only had to fall like rain and drip yourself back to that noodle of a body."

Dennis paid Ezra no mind. He was already moving across the ruined street and over to a large purple van with a small woman sitting in the driver's seat. The woman was staring out of her windshield, trying to make sense of all that was going on around her.

Dennis pulled open her front door. "Excuse me," he barked. "We need your vehicle."

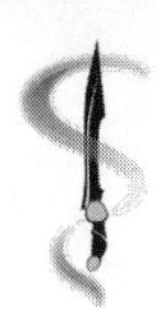

"*Entschuldigung?*" she asked.

"Yeah, yeah, you speak German," Dennis seethed. "How about this: *Aust!*"

"*Was ist los?*"

Dennis pulled her up out of her seat and set her on the sidewalk. Her purse dropped to the ground. Dennis slipped into the driver's seat and commanded Tim to get in the other side.

Tim picked up the woman's purse and handed it to her. She clutched it tightly and winced, as if Tim were going to hurt her.

"What a Boy Scout," Ezra mocked. "Get in, noodle boy."

The woman looked at the talking toothpick on Tim's shoulder and decided that now might be a good time for her to run.

Tim got in the passenger's side and shut his door. Dennis started the van and pulled out onto a small, clear street. People were still running around crying and partially fearing for their lives. The telt was dead, but the scene was almost as frightening without it.

A whole building was gone.

Streets had been sucked up.

Cars were lying on their sides or on sidewalks, and people were screaming as the sound of sirens filled the air.

"What a bunch of babies," Ezra spat from the position of Tim's left shoulder while he stared out the car window. "A little excitement falls in their laps and they cry about it."

Dennis punched the gas, and Tim and Ezra flew back. He drove the van down a service alley and out over a pedestrian walkway. Traffic was knotted up everywhere, but Dennis was

finding that with a little creativity, they could make their way around just fine.

Dennis stopped the van and pointed to a corner where two sidewalks matched up unevenly.

"That's it?" Ezra laughed. "The entire place is ripped apart and you still choose a tiny, uneven gap?"

"You can't design uneven gaps," Dennis said. "Fate creates them."

Dennis moved to get out of the van.

"It's not dark enough yet," Ezra pointed out snidely.

"Do you think, with all that's going on, that someone is going to care about a couple of people digging up a piece of street?"

Tim shook his head as if he were actually part of the conversation.

"Nice of fate to cover for us," Dennis said.

Ezra smiled, agreeing with Dennis for once.

Tim got out of the van and began to carefully dig up the sidewalk.

CHAPTER ELEVEN

A Little Time

The ride out of the Red Grove and toward the Devil's Spiral was gorgeous. The yellow fields of late tavel were laced with green ribbons of Tea birds gliding and flying in long, interlacing patterns. The smaller sun was being mischievous, bobbing up and down in the air as if following the whims of the wind. While the little sun played, the big sun was reaching out and trying to touch places it had not lit before, its rays curving and poking into any dark hole or surface they could find. The blue sky yawned, and as the blood raced to its face, it turned a beautiful shade of purple. It was morning, but a large patch of stars had refused to leave, and they were now bedazzling the over end of Foo's sky. A Lore Coil set off somewhere many miles away by the marriage of two lovers rippled through the air and left Winter's heart happy.

Geth rode up next to her. He smiled as they rode, his long hair and dark eyes so completely un-toothpick-like.

The onicks followed a small stone path that cut through the fields of tavel and led directly to the Devil's Spiral. As the road crested slightly, there within view was the top of the water tower created by the Spiral. They were many miles away, but Winter was mesmerized by how high the water shot into the air. Despite the desperation of their journey, she couldn't help but take a second to be amazed.

"It's unbelievable," she hollered to Geth.

Geth pulled on his onick's reins, bringing his ride to a stop. Winter did the same.

"I keep forgetting," Geth smiled.

"Forgetting what?" Winter asked.

"That you've forgotten."

"I've been here before?"

"Of course," Geth answered. "You rode this path with me and Sabine many years ago."

"Sabine?" Winter questioned uncomfortably.

"We were bringing him to Lith."

"How'd that turn out?" Winter smiled.

"It could have gone better," Geth answered. "But just look what fate has done with the results."

"What?" Winter asked. "We got Leven here, but now he's gone. The rants and anyone they can convince are gathering for war, and the state of the secret is unknown. And I am giftless and incomplete."

"Yeah, but the suns are shining," Geth said, his eyes laughing.

"I suppose that makes it all better," Winter joked.

"It makes it much more bearable," Geth said.

"You lithens are a weird bunch."

Geth grinned and handed Winter a leather bag with a wooden toggle at the end. She pulled the toggle down and took a long drink. She was surprised by the taste.

"I thought this was water," she said. "It tastes like milk."

Geth took the bag from her and took a drink. "You're right. It was water at one point. I guess it's still trying to find itself."

Winter nudged her onick forward again, and Geth raced past her toward a field of tavel. She had just spurred her mount to overtake him when a huge snap sounded, followed by the noise of heavy air whistling through a thin tube.

Geth's onick wouldn't move at all. It was hovering in mid-stride above the ground. Geth looked at Winter out of the corner of his eye, and she too was sitting there motionless, her eyes facing forward. Geth could see Tea birds stuck in the sky, getting nowhere. The windblown tavel had stopped moving. There was no sound whatsoever.

Time had stopped.

Geth would have taken a moment to wonder what was going on, but his thoughts were consumed by a tall being walking out of the tavel. The person wore a blue robe with black leather boots and held a blue kilve in his right hand.

"Hello, Geth," the man said, pushing back the hood of his own robe. "Nice to see you again."

"Azure," Geth whispered slowly, barely able to speak in his frozen state.

Azure was tall, with black hair and deep blue eyes. He had lived for many years but, like Geth, still looked very young. His features were handsome and perfect, except for his left ear, which was swollen and bleeding. He walked around Geth, looking at him as if Geth were a used car he was considering purchasing.

"Back at last," Azure said, laughing slightly. "Here to set Foo right."

Azure stopped circling and looked Geth in the eyes.

"Hurray for all of us," he smirked.

Geth couldn't move to respond.

"I thought about playing nice," Azure added. "You know, pretending like I was happy you were here and all, but I've got to be honest with myself these days. Fortunately, the only good I have left to deal with is contained in this one ear." He scratched violently at his left ear, making it ooze.

Although Geth couldn't move, his heart sank. Not only was Azure a lithen, but he had always been a true defender of Foo.

Azure stepped up even closer to Geth.

"I know what you must be thinking," Azure said. "Things change, Geth. Your mission was simple. Me, I was left to appease the Want and to defend a place that too few care about any longer. You left us. You let Zale die and then you ran like a coward."

Without warning, Azure hit Geth on the right side of his face. Geth's cheek bled, but the wound didn't hurt half as much as the surprise of Azure's betrayal. Azure hefted his kilve in his right hand and swung, hitting Geth from the other side.

Geth sat there helpless.

Azure flipped the kilve and pushed the pointed end up under Geth's chin.

Geth's eyes burned, exposing the strength of his soul.

"This is too easy," Azure laughed. "Way too easy. I could kill you now, but there's still something I need from you."

Azure sniffed and brushed his free hand through his dark hair. He moved from Geth over to Winter.

"Ah, and Winter," he said with pity in his voice. "Poor girl. How hard it must be to have your gift taken from you. How fortunate Jamoon was able to accomplish at least one thing before he perished."

Azure brushed Winter's cheek with his hand.

"What a lovely restoration," he said with passion. "Of course, you were beautiful before you left us. Beautiful and misguided. I wonder how you would respond to my advances now?"

Winter wished desperately that she could spit.

Azure put his other hand on Winter's shoulder and smiled.

"Perhaps there's something you—"

"Come on," a little fidgety voice whined from out of the tavel. "You asked for five minutes. It's been more than that."

"Don't move," Azure commanded the voice.

Neither Winter nor Geth had noticed the little man hiding in the long tavel. He wasn't any taller than the grain, but he looked bothered, his large face flat and white. He had a wide, blue mustache and knoblike ears. He held his arms to his sides, looking as if he were fighting himself to stand still.

Azure looked bothered.

"I knew you would be coming this way, making your way to the Want," Azure said, turning his attention back to Geth. "How predictable. Luckily our cause has Time on its side."

Azure pointed to the little man.

"He's not always around when you need him," Azure said, stepping up to the little man and placing his arm around him. "But I have found his services very helpful. He has given me a pass to move, and a guarantee that his intentions are in our favor. Yes, he can be argumentative and stubborn, but with the right persuasion even Time has his price. Of course, as you can see, he won't stand still for long."

"I won't stand still a second longer if you don't pay me what you promised," Time said, looking up at Azure while trying hard to stay still.

Azure removed his arm from around Time and pulled a handful of metal coins from his own robe. He handed the coins to Time.

Both Time and Geth gasped.

"And they're metal even," Time whispered in awe. "Do you have more?"

"Plenty," Azure said. "And we will need you to finish things off when the time comes. Now, if you don't mind, you might want to close your eyes. I need to teach Geth a couple of things."

Time squeezed his eyes shut. Azure moved to Geth and smiled wickedly.

"The Want made it clear that I am to bring you to Lith. Unfortunately for you, he never mentioned what kind of condition you needed to be in."

Azure turned. "And you, Winter," he whispered. "What is to become of our dear Winter?"

As Azure stepped up to Winter, Time twisted to look away, and in doing so he dropped two of his newly acquired coins. He moved to pick them back up, giving Winter just enough time to spit in Azure's direction.

Normally spitting is a dirty habit—a socially unacceptable thing to do unless there is some sort of organized contest involved. Unfortunately, Time hadn't moved enough for the spit to reach Azure. So it froze in the air inches away from his face.

It wasn't pretty.

Azure looked at the spit hanging in the air. "Some people just don't know how to behave," he said.

"Sorry about that," Time called out. "It's just so hard to stand still."

Azure took out a long piece of rope from his robe pocket and

began to bind Geth's hands while Time stood still, slowly counting his money.

ii

"That was weird," Clover said, looking around. "Is it me, or did we just lose about fifteen minutes of time?"

"It's you," Leven said as he climbed up the wet path behind the waterflight. "Or maybe it just feels like time is going so slowly because you're sitting on my head letting me do all the work."

"One of us needs to be rested."

"For what?"

"Who knows what's up ahead?"

"More steps," Leven said sarcastically.

Clover shivered.

The stairway behind the waterflight was wide and wet. Light shone through the water as it fell up. Leven could see where he was going, but he couldn't see details. At the moment, all of Foo looked like an endless, black, stone stairway.

"So what do you know about the Want?" Leven asked, his breath labored and heavy.

"There's no one more important in Foo."

"Have you met him?"

"No, but I had a teacher who had," Clover answered. "He said that even being in the same room is tiring. The Want sees all dreams. He's the only soul who truly knows what the current

state of Foo is. Of course, they also say that all those dreams have made him a bit touched. Oh, and that there is something up with his eyes and you should never point that out to him."

"Really?" Leven asked. "What's up with his eyes?"

"I don't know," Clover insisted. "Maybe they're crossed, or all googly. I know a sycophant who has two different colors of eyes. Maybe that's it. Some people are so touchy. If I had two different colors of eyes, I'd be fine with people bringing it up."

"I bet that's not it," Leven said, struggling up a huge step.

"You're probably right," Clover sighed contently. "Antsel met with the Want a number of times. Of course, Antsel was always really decent and would never bring up someone's eyes. He didn't have a mean bone in his body. He was such a . . ."

Leven cleared his throat.

"Oh, not that he was better than you, just different," Clover waved. "It's apples and plussums. For example, you like to . . . do certain things, I'm sure, and Antsel liked to read the dirt and the stars."

"So you don't know what I like to do?" Leven challenged, panting with exertion.

"Of course I do, don't get me started," Clover said. "Do you think these stairs are getting steeper?"

"Name one thing I like to do," Leven smiled, not letting it drop. "Here, I'll help. Antsel liked to read the stars, and I like to . . ."

"Make little shadow puppets with my hands," Clover said.

"I do?" Leven asked, confused.

"Oh, you? I get it now. I thought you meant me. Here, try again."

Leven laughed, and as he did so his eyes flared just a bit, lighting the cavern and showing off details. The stairs looked like they went on forever, and there were dark markings on the cavern walls. None of them made any sense to Leven.

"Okay," Leven said. "I like to . . ."

"Sing?"

"Have you ever heard me sing before?"

"That doesn't mean you don't enjoy it."

"Try again."

"Eat things?" Clover guessed.

"I like to eat things?"

"Well, don't you?" Clover asked, shifting down onto Leven's right shoulder. "Let's say you stopped eating. That'd be awful."

"Eating doesn't count," Leven said. "I like . . ."

"Bathroom products?"

"Bathroom products?" Leven laughed. "What does that mean?"

"Well, I don't know everything," Clover admitted. "And I've always respected your privacy. So maybe you use a lot of shampoo and gel in the bathroom."

"Amazing," Leven said. "You've watched me for all these years and you still have no idea what I like."

"It's not easy," Clover said. "You try doing me."

"What do you like?" Leven asked. "That's easy. Twigs, toothpaste, anything that shines, food that is served in the shape of another food, your reflection, trap doors, misshapen

dice, banana flavoring but not actual bananas, pants that have lots of pockets, friendly looking stuffed animals . . . should I go on?"

"I didn't know we were talking about general stuff."

"Should I get more specific?" Leven asked. "How about Lilly?

Clover shook and then disappeared. "How do you know about Lilly?" he asked five stairs later.

"You've only mentioned her about two hundred times," Leven huffed. "Whenever you make up a story, the female is always named Lilly. You talk about your favorite flower being a lily. You say 'lilly-nilly' instead of 'willy-nilly,' which is probably why you even use that expression at all, because nobody else does anymore. And you wrote 'I love Lilly' across the bottom of my bed back in Reality."

"You knew about that?" Clover asked.

"I saw it when I was looking for my missing shirt."

"The world is one amazing circle," Clover said reflectively.

"I didn't figure out that you wrote it until later when you showed yourself and started talking about Lilly."

"She was in one of my classes," Clover admitted.

"How sweet," Leven said, tired from moving up so many stairs. "What happened with her?"

"Absolutely nothing," Clover said sadly. "I've been hoping that now that I'm back, things will sort of pick up."

"Keep hoping," Leven huffed. "Now, about the Want?"

"I really don't know much about him," Clover said. "He sees and controls the feel of Foo."

Leven stopped to catch his breath.

"I'd carry you if I could," Clover said casually.

"I'm sure you would."

They sat silently for a moment.

"I just want to know what I'm heading into," Leven said, beginning to climb again. "I hope Geth is right about this."

"I guess you'll find out either way."

"Comforting," Leven said, pushing up the steps.

The stone stairs turned and leveled out a little.

"Maybe we're getting close to the top," Clover said hopefully.

Leven began to move faster, the thought of reaching the end incredibly exhilarating. The steps became smaller and smaller and some source of light could be seen in the distance. Twelve steps later the stairs ran out, and Leven and Clover were standing in a long, empty tunnel. Leven moved through the tunnel heading toward the light—the soft sound of a fire humming in the distance.

"Do you think it's safe?" Clover whispered from Leven's right shoulder.

"I don't care," Leven said. "As long as it's not stairs."

Leven stepped through the end of the tunnel and into a round, tubelike room that went straight up hundreds of feet. There were lit torches tied to the walls about every fifty feet up and a wooden staircase that appeared to circle endlessly up the walls. The bottom of the stairs didn't reach to the ground; there was only a worn rope that hung from a dusty railing.

Leven moaned.

"Fate's not always kind," Clover said. "But I suppose this is funny on some level."

"Maybe the level at the top," Leven said, his sweaty hair sticking to his forehead.

"I'm sure we'll look back at this and laugh."

The torches hummed in harmony.

"There has to be another way," Leven complained, ignoring Clover.

"Oh, it's not that bad," Clover tried to comfort. "We can take as many breaks as you need. But I think we need to go as fast as we can between those breaks."

Leven walked to the hanging rope and pulled on it. The bottom of the stairs lowered and came to rest right in front of him. He looked up and tried to count the torches.

"It probably won't get any shorter by our waiting," Clover said sympathetically while patting Leven on the head.

Leven took the steps two at a time.

CHAPTER TWELVE

Big, Bold Words at the Beginning of a Chapter

Some days are better than others. True, most consist of twenty-four hours; or one thousand, four hundred and forty minutes; or eighty-six thousand, four hundred seconds, and on an average day the sun rises, crests, and then dips back down in an effort to give the moon some "me time." But sometimes the things that happen during those eighty-six thousand, four hundred seconds are significantly better than what occurs during the typical day.

Perhaps you win an award one day. Maybe you get your hair cut by someone who finally does a decent job. Or what if you're not one of those people who takes cars for granted, and one day you finally get a new one.

That's not a bad day.

Better yet, one day you get a job you love, or you find the

world's biggest diamond in your sock drawer, or you uncover a completely intact skeleton from a new species of dinosaur in your backyard while weeding.

Nice day indeed.

Or maybe, just maybe, you find that one person who makes all other people seem dull and lifeless and uninteresting—and that one person actually loves you back.

If so, congratulations.

Tim had one of those days years ago when he met his wife, Wendy, at a public library. She had been looking for a book about Charles de Gaulle, and Tim had wanted to brush up on what he knew about the life of Leonardo da Vinci.

Their hands brushed as they were both reaching for the dead stars.

Tim said, "Excuse me."

Wendy said, "You're excused."

Three months later they were married in a small church on a tall hill with a few close friends on hand. Tim had loved Wendy from the start. Now, however, he couldn't even remember her. His life was a confusing and dark fog, made even more complicated by the maniac who bossed him around and the angry toothpick that wouldn't leave him alone.

"What's that smell?" Ezra complained.

"Again with the smell," Dennis barked. "It's hot tar."

"Well, it's offensive."

Tim smoothed the tar down on the bottom of the box. It was

hot and sticky and reminded him of Sabine as he had oozed back into Dennis after he had rained on the telt.

The incident had changed Tim.

It had pushed him from confused dolt to semiactive participant. It had sufficiently smothered his brain that he now thought only of the cause at hand. Not to mention the fact that he had enjoyed the powerful feeling of pulling Sabine from the clouds. Tim now spent a lot of time staring at his arm and wondering what else he was capable of.

He had forgotten about Wendy.

He had forgotten about Winter, and he had forgotten about his two sons. To him, Rochester and Darcy were simply characters from a novel he had once read.

Tim was no longer Tim.

"This will take us to Foo?" Tim asked, motioning to the box he was working on.

"Yes," Dennis replied. "To Foo and back many times."

"Because?" Tim asked honestly.

Dennis breathed in slowly, as if he were trying to calm himself. "Because it will give us the full power of Foo here in Reality," he said through gritted teeth. "Not just avalands and telts. The full power—all gifts and all possibilities."

"And me?" Tim asked meekly.

Dennis looked at him and smiled, a black line of Sabine circling around his bald head.

"You?" Dennis asked.

Tim nodded.

"Well, you will stand by my side and experience the kind of power and respect you never thought possible."

Tim smiled.

"And Ezra?" he asked.

Dennis looked over at Ezra, who was busy swearing at a bird that wouldn't stop singing.

"Ezra has a place," Dennis whispered harshly. "There is someone he needs to . . . connect with."

"Leven?" Tim asked, sounding like a child who wasn't quite sure he knew the answer.

Dennis's ears became dark black and then faded. A patch of rot ran up and down each of his arms.

"Not Leven!" Dennis said. "The work you are doing now is the result of Leven treading where he had no right to tread. He has purposefully postponed the most triumphant thing that will ever happen to mankind, and he will regret every move he has made."

Tim smiled as if he were supposed to.

Dennis put his hand on Tim's shoulder. The attention lit Tim up. He looked liked he had just won something of great value.

Dennis squeezed Tim's shoulder until Tim hoarsely cried out in pain.

"Build faster," Dennis demanded. "No more questions. Understand?"

Dennis let go and looked at Tim like he was ashamed of

him. Tim rubbed his shoulder and pushed out some more hot tar across the base of the new gateway. His brain was no longer his own, but in that moment he remembered a secret.

Tim remembered that he hated Dennis.

He also knew he needed to keep that secret from certain parts of his own brain until just the right time arrived.

CHAPTER THIRTEEN

BRUISED

When Leven was only ten years old, his life was less than shining, unless you are referencing a shining bruise. His home life was miserable and as boring as an invisible parade marching down a dry, barren road on a Sunday.

His mother's half sister, Addy, and her husband, Terry, were in charge of Leven, but, as they had said often, they would have much preferred not having him around. Terry would chastise and chase Leven out of the house whenever he was home and Addy would constantly complain about the doltlike burden her half sister had put on her overworked and underappreciated shoulders. If Leven wasn't being scolded or doing chores he was out on his bed on the back porch, alone with his thoughts and dreaming of being someone other than who he was.

School wasn't any better.

His teachers at Franklin M. Pinchworthy Elementary were so

overworked, they never had the time to even learn their students' names. School at Pinchworthy was all about taking tests: tests to see how well you did at math, how much you knew about science, how many words you could read while standing, how many countries you could paint, how many pencils you could sharpen while blindfolded.

Always tests.

The teachers would then take the tests to the Powers That Be to show them how smart the children they didn't have time to teach really were. Leven had tried to do well, but it was hard to stand out in a school where no one really had a name—where everyone was just a number on the top of another ridiculous test.

Leven was number 1313.

During Leven's sixth year at Pinchworthy there had been so many tests that the teachers didn't have time to keep track of anyone's grades. So they were forced to base each student's entire grade on one final exam. Well, thanks to all the tests they had taken during the year, they were completely out of paper. So the teachers met and decided to put on a learning long jump. The wisdom, or lack thereof, was that the student's final grade would come from how far he or she could jump.

Leven was a great jumper, but, just to be sure, he practiced and practiced out in the field behind his house the entire afternoon before. When the next day rolled around and he took his turn in front of everyone, he beat the record by two full inches. But instead of congratulating and celebrating him, the teachers figured he must have cheated and gave Leven a D. Even though

he had made the jump in front of everyone and it was clear what he had done, he received a D for cheating.

"I didn't cheat," Leven pointed out.

"I wasn't born yesterday," the teacher said unnecessarily, her gray hair and tired eyes making that point perfectly clear.

Leven had taken the D home and showed it to Addy. Terry in turn had given him a licking for being such a failure, and Leven had spent the evening out on the porch lying on his small bed with his hopes and soul dying just a bit more, and his legs burning in pain from all the practice he had put in the day before.

Leven half wished he was back on that porch feeling awful and suffering from the way his legs had burned then. Because now, after the hundreds and hundreds of stairs he had been climbing, his legs felt like they were going to spontaneously combust and turn into a pile of smoldering ash. His chest heaved, and each breath he sucked in felt like he was swallowing a wad of thick, dry clay.

Leven stopped, desperately trying to catch his breath.

"You'll sleep well tonight," Clover observed, appearing on Leven's left shoulder.

Clover was eating something.

"I . . ." Leven couldn't finish.

"We have to be getting closer," Clover said, looking down the stairs they had already climbed. He then looked up and moaned. "Well, maybe not."

"This . . . is ridiculous," Leven growled, sitting down on the stairs. "I can't go any farther."

"You know your limits," Clover said, chewing.

"Don't you have anything in that void to drink?" Leven said, gasping for air. "My lungs . . . are burning."

Clover fished around in his void. "I'm not sure I do. Oh yeah, I forgot I had this." He pulled out a small, bladder-shaped canteen.

Leven grabbed it and lifted it to his lips. Then he paused, lowering the bladder. "I don't know," he said skeptically. "Maybe I should wait. What is this stuff?"

"Don't worry. There's nothing fun about that," Clover complained. "It's just water."

"Water that does what?"

"Quenches your thirst?"

"That's it?"

Clover nodded as he chewed.

Leven took a sip and tasted it. He looked at his arms and legs to see if there were any changes.

Everything was normal.

Leven shrugged his shoulders and downed the entire bladder. Not only was it water, but it was the best water he had ever tasted. It was so cool and ran down his burning throat like ice cream. He could feel it hydrating his entire body. He squeezed every last drop out of the canteen and then reluctantly handed the empty container back to Clover.

"Thanks," Leven said with great sincerity. "I don't think I've ever tasted better water."

"No problem," Clover said. "I could tell you needed it."

"Now," Leven said, "we need . . . wait, what were we doing?"

Clover just sat there trying to look innocent.

"Weren't we going up?" Leven asked.

"Wow, it's working fast on you," Clover said.

"What?" Leven asked, confused.

"The water," Clover explained. "You're already forgetting."

"What are you taking about?"

"That water's from the Veil Sea. It'll make you forget things. You know, give you kind of a spotty memory for a few minutes."

Leven's face grew angry. "I think I remember you saying it wouldn't do anything," he said, blinking.

"That's true," Clover said, taking the last bite of what he was eating and dusting his palms together. "And normally I don't like to lie, but I could tell you were thirsty. Plus, I knew that after you drank it you would eventually forget what I told you."

Leven didn't seem to understand what Clover was saying. He blinked his eyes and looked up the stairs.

"Are we headed up or down?" Leven asked.

Clover smiled. "Up."

"My legs hurt," Leven complained.

"Do they?" Clover said. "Odd. Maybe they'll feel better if you climb a bit."

That seemed to make sense to Leven. He stood and looked up. "Are we in a hurry?" he asked, still disoriented.

Clover nodded, "A great hurry."

Leven began running up the stairs, unable to remember clearly why his legs were burning so horribly.

ii

Geth felt a bit hopeless, and he hated the feeling. It tore at his body like an angry cat and irritated his soul as if it were a sweater made out of barbed wire.

Lithens were nothing without hope.

But a bit of bleakness had settled into his heart, and he was fighting himself to shake it off.

His current situation wasn't helping.

At the moment Winter and Geth were tied to the mast of a small ship that was making its way across the Veil Sea, weaving in and out through a maze of thick fog. Both of their heads were covered with dark cloth sacks. They had been tied up on their knees with their ankles and wrists bound to the mast behind them. Winter was still unconscious. Azure had cruelly shoved pitch reed up their noses, knowing it would knock them out for a couple of hours.

The noises of the slapping water and of large mist eaters squawking in the air above were the only sounds as the boat darted quickly through the water. After a couple of hours Winter began to stir. She moaned and pulled at the ropes binding her to the mast as she blew bits of pitch reed from her nose.

"The rope is made from strips of dark dreams," Geth said as she struggled. "Can you feel them buzzing on your wrists? Azure must be trading with the Children of the Sewn. There is no way to break or untie the knots except by rejoining them with the

remaining pieces of the dreams from which they were made. Azure must have those."

Winter moaned.

"I know," Geth said. "It's not the most comfortable position."

The boat continued to slice through the water as mist eaters gorged on the thick fog.

"How long have I been out?" Winter finally asked, her voice low.

"I don't know for sure," Geth answered. "I came to a few hours ago. I think it's still the same day."

"Are we alone?" Winter whispered.

"I'm not sure," Geth replied softly. "We're on the Veil Sea, so Azure will be at the prow reading the mist. I don't know if there are others around, but I haven't heard anyone. Are you okay?"

"My arms and shoulders really hurt," Winter said. "And I can't feel my knees. How about you? I couldn't see everything, but I could tell that Azure was not being kind as he tied you up."

"I'm fine," Geth said, knowing that his whole body was beaten and bruised and that at the very least he had a couple of broken ribs.

"Nice friend you have," Winter weakly joked.

"Sorry," Geth smiled. "He's changed. So much has changed."

"And we're heading toward the Want?"

"Possibly," Geth answered. "It feels as if the sea is taking us toward the Hidden Border—which means we are making our way either to the back side of Lith or to one of the far stones. Hopefully we'll get a chance to see the Want. And if fate is

kind the Waves will already have delivered Leven to him."

"I hope they were easier on him than Azure was on us."

"The Waves would never harm anyone for sport."

"But, like you said," Winter whispered, "so much has changed."

"Not the Waves," Geth said firmly.

"What are they, anyway?" Winter asked, struggling to shift enough to get some blood running to other parts of her legs.

"They have been here since the beginning—like the lithens," Geth whispered. "They rarely show themselves. But they did fight in the metal wars, and if an enemy were to try to storm the island of Alder, he would probably get a glimpse of the Waves as they washed him away. They have fearlessly and successfully guarded the island of Alder since the dawn of Foo."

"My head hurts," Winter moaned.

"It's the pitch reed you breathed in," Geth said. "It'll clear shortly."

"So what's on Alder?" Winter asked. "I mean, what's to guard?"

"No one knows for sure," Geth answered, struggling with the ropes tied around his wrists. "The best information we ever got was from Sabine's shadows. The Waves couldn't stop them from drifting over the island. But they didn't see everything because the Waves covered the island, hiding things from them. The shadows did tell Sabine about a tree—the oldest tree in Foo."

"A tree," Winter said sarcastically. "That sounds important."

Geth laughed, "Be nice to trees. Also, the Want has said—and even the Sochemists have declared—that Leven's destiny lies on that island."

The mist eaters began to squawk even louder. A sound like thick fists thudding against each other could be heard right above where Geth and Winter were tied. Two unconscious mist eaters fell from the air and landed directly on them. Winter choked back a scream, not knowing what had fallen on her.

"Don't worry," Geth said quietly. "They're just mist eaters. They won't hurt you."

"Mist eaters?"

"Birds," Geth explained. "They're addicted to the mist. They spend their lives flying through it and eating it. The mist they eat erases all their memory and leaves them sort of drunk and stupid. Sometimes they fly into each other and knock themselves out. It happens a lot when the mist is thick. That also means we are probably getting closer to the Hidden Border."

"Did I know all this before?" Winter asked. "Did I know all these creatures and places?"

"Yes," Geth said as two more mist eaters ran into each other and rained down on them.

Winter flinched.

"I have to admit that I don't really enjoy that," she whispered.

"Wait till they come to and start pecking at you as if it was your fault they fell."

"So, should we have a plan?" Winter asked. "For when we're untied."

"Fate will let us know what we need to do."

"That's comforting."

"You don't believe that?" Geth whispered.

"I want to," Winter whispered back. "It just seems like we might be better off having some idea of what we are going to do. Fate hasn't exactly painted us into a pretty picture."

As if on cue, one of the mist eaters came to and began to shriek at Winter. It hopped up on her right shoulder and started pecking at the side of her head through the cloth sack, angrily scratching her shoulder with its claws.

"Owwwww," Winter said, swinging her head sideways to try to knock the bird away.

Geth would have offered a few words of comfort, but another mist eater had come to and was now bothering him. Winter gave her bird a hard jab, pinching it between her head and shoulder. The bird scratched at her masked face and then flew off, defeated. The mist eater scratching at Geth moved behind his head and Geth slammed his head back, banging the bird against the mast and knocking it out for a second time.

"My wrists are burning," Winter complained.

"Maybe I'll shrink fast enough to slip out," Geth said.

"What?" Winter asked.

"You're nice to pretend you haven't noticed," Geth said kindly. "But I seem to be slowly getting smaller."

"I thought you seemed taller before," Winter said innocently. "I mean, after being a toothpick."

"I don't know what it is," Geth said. "It's as if I'm not whole."

"You'll stop shrinking eventually, won't you?"

"I hope so," Geth said casually.

The boat came to a stop. Geth and Winter hit their heads hard against the mast. Footsteps sounded as someone neared.

"Untie them," Azure's voice said.

Geth's and Winter's hands and ankles were untied and they were both yanked to their feet, only to fall down from having been bound in the awkward position they had suffered.

"So sorry," Azure said. "Were you uncomfortable?" He snarled again at someone unseen, "Pick them up."

Geth and Winter were roughly pulled up.

"Uncover their heads," Azure said. "I like people to look at me when I'm speaking."

Winter's hood was ripped off, along with several hundred strands of her blonde hair. She would have screamed in pain, but the sting of the blood rushing into her legs and arms was even worse, and she just didn't have the strength to waste on screaming.

She opened her eyes and there was Azure, his blue eyes burning with hate and a lust for all things evil. She wanted to take him by the throat, but her arms were being held back by two rants. Both rants were wearing traditional dark robes.

Winter looked at Geth. He too was imprisoned by rants.

"Where to now?" Geth asked Azure, as casually as someone wondering what ride to enjoy next at a family theme park.

"I could kill you," Azure said coldly.

"You've mentioned that," Geth replied.

"You've changed," Azure snapped.

"So have you."

"Always clever," Azure complained. "Eventually the clever grow silent."

Geth didn't reply.

Azure nodded, and the rants began to push Geth and Winter up over the side rail and onto a walkway that led to a large wooden dock. The dock was covered with moss, and tipsy mist eaters dozily lined the thick railing that ran the length of it.

"The eleventh stone," Geth whispered to Winter. "I don't think we'll be seeing the Want. We must have been out longer than I thought to have traveled this far already."

"Quiet," Azure ordered.

They walked along the dock and up to a small shack with a wooden gate attached to it. A large rant was manning the gate.

"Your wagon is ready," the rant said.

"Onicks?" Azure asked.

"Twelve," the rant answered.

Behind the gate was a wooden wagon with six wheels and twelve onicks in front of it. On the back of each onick sat a robed rider.

"Put them in the wagon," Azure commanded his rants.

Geth was tossed and Winter lightly pushed in. As they sat up in the back, Winter could see that it was not the onicks but the riders who were tethered to the wagon. They were also latched at the waist to the onicks they were sitting on.

"The onicks aren't hooked up," Winter observed.

"That would be pointless," Geth said. "An onick is loyal only to its current rider. If onicks were tied to a wagon, they would simply lie down and never get up. The riders are being forced to drive the onicks where Azure wants."

Azure turned to Geth and motioned to his riders.

"It used to be so difficult finding steady minds to pull our wagons," Azure said sickly. "But these nits were not only kind enough to give up their gifts, they stuck around to help us out."

Two of the riders turned to look at Geth and Winter. Their faces beneath their hoods were gray and drawn. They looked like corpses that were wishing someone would just hurry up and bury them.

Winter's stomach turned.

"Stealing gifts?" Geth said with disgust. "What's happened to Foo? I demand to see the Want."

Azure laughed. A couple of the riders nervously laughed with him.

"I suppose if there are dreams in death, perhaps the Want will see some of yours," Azure said, scratching at his infected ear.

"What has happened to you?" Geth asked. "There's some good left."

"Not for long," Azure said, tearing at his ear. He turned and looked at his riders. "Go! What are you waiting for?"

The onicks began to move down the tree-lined road. Large red birds with jagged beaks screamed at them as they moved. Occasionally the birds would jump down from where they

hollered and pick up thin yellow snakes that were racing to get across the road safely.

"We have a short road trip," Azure said, his ear bleeding from the scratching. "Enjoy the ride. It will be your last."

Geth smiled at Azure. "Let's see if fate agrees."

Azure turned, swinging his kilve and clipping Geth on the side of his face. Geth's right cheek began to bleed.

"Fate is marching toward its own death," Azure seethed.

"Hope will help it," Geth said firmly.

"What is up with him?" Azure barked, looking directly at Winter. "He leaves a warrior and comes back spineless. Reality's made him weak."

"He looks as if he's fine with himself," Winter said. "While you, on the other hand . . ."

"Shut up," Azure demanded. "No more from either of you."

Azure scratched desperately at his ear and shouted for his riders to move.

CHAPTER FOURTEEN

COMPLETED

Everybody needs somebody. Sorry. If you were thinking you could get through life completely on your own, you're wrong. It's a proven fact that people need people. Sure, there are those who try to stuff their lives full of cats in an effort to fill the void, but, for the most part, people thrive, live, and do better if their existences are full of interaction with other humans.

Some people find people to interact with at school. Some people run with people they meet at church. Work is a half-decent place to find acquaintances. Or maybe one day last May you were flying a kite in Central Park and a couple of nice people commented on how high the kite was, and that sparked a conversation that led to the three of you having dinner together at a small restaurant in Times Square and then catching a Broadway show about friendly cats. That could have happened—

which just goes to show you that, either way, you are going to end up surrounded by cats.

Let's hope you're not allergic.

Dennis, unfortunately, had nobody. He had never had anybody. It was as if, throughout his entire life, fate had been preparing him to be able to disappear without a single person noticing or caring about his absence. After the building housing Snooker and Woe had crossed the street and settled on the opposite corner, few people had even thought of Dennis again. Snooker and Woe had since set up temporary quarters in an older office complex until they could get a new building built. In all the craziness and moving, only one person had ever mentioned Dennis, and that was a secretary who was sick of the copy machine breaking and wished "that one guy" was around to fix it. It was a pathetic mention, but Dennis would have been touched had he known that someone was thinking of him.

Now Dennis was simply a shell that Sabine was riding around in. And Dennis was about to take over the world.

"Is it done?" Dennis asked, as he and Tim and Ezra stood in the abandoned farmhouse they had called home for the last little while.

"Yes," Tim said, pointing to the new gateway.

Dennis walked around the box, inspecting the craftsmanship. The gateway was a little over six feet tall and five feet wide. It was also four feet deep. It was made of thin metal sheeting and had a large iron hook welded to the top. Inside of it on the base sat the uneven sidewalk they had dug up in Munich. Dennis looked

inside the box at the pieces of the two mismatched sections of sidewalk.

"These weren't altered in the least?"

"Not at all," Tim said. "They're resting in the exact same position as they were on the street."

"Excellent," Dennis hissed evilly. "Excellent!"

Dennis began to laugh, the dark images sliding like pudding across his skin. His cackle rang through the room and made Tim shiver. Ezra, on the other hand, was unimpressed and in the mood to humble Dennis.

"You've got something on your face," Ezra said, pointing to Dennis's chin. "It's white like frosting from dinner."

Dennis self-consciously wiped at his chin.

"Higher," Ezra said.

"Now?"

"Higher still."

"Ahhhh," Dennis raged, wiping at his whole face and turning to go. "We'll load the box at dark and head to the water as soon as the moment is right. Foo will be ours soon."

"It's still there," Ezra mocked. "Right above your mouth."

Dennis reached out and flicked Ezra across the room. Ezra grabbed ahold of Tim's ball cap as he flew over him.

Dennis left the room.

"Coward," Ezra spat.

Tim reached up and pulled Ezra from his hat. He stared at the angry toothpick in his hand.

"What?" Ezra challenged. "Someone's got to say something, and it certainly isn't you. Gutless."

Tim shrugged.

"Do you think he'll really keep you around when you get to Foo?" Ezra growled. "No. He'll take back the part of him you're borrowing and then bury you deep in the soil of Foo."

Tim was silent.

"Nice rebuttal, chatty," Ezra snapped. "Of course, I also know that he will never let me be restored. He's keeping me around until Geth is confronted, when I'm sure he plans to destroy me. But I, unlike you, am not stupid enough to just let it happen."

Tim looked at Ezra.

"I know something," Tim struggled to whisper.

"*There's* a statement that needs some evidence," Ezra challenged, moving up Tim's right arm to stand on his shoulder. "What could you possibly know?"

"There's a part of me he doesn't control," Tim said laboriously.

"Is there, now?" Ezra said, lifting himself up to Tim's ear and looking in. "What are you hiding in there?"

"I hate him," Tim said.

Ezra smiled. "That's a start," he whispered. "He has control of you, but if you stick with me, we might be able to have the last word in Foo."

Tim rubbed his forehead as if in pain. He looked at his arm.

Thick black lines spiraled around it. Tim hated how much he loved the feel of that blackness.

"There is a part of me he doesn't control," Tim said again.

"Brilliant," Ezra mocked. "You can repeat yourself."

Dennis pushed through the door back into the room.

"I'll be in the water working to ready the attachment," Dennis announced. "I'll expect to find you both here when I return."

Tim nodded as Ezra executed a far less cordial gesture.

CHAPTER FIFTEEN

UNFORTUNATELY, WE ARE FAMILY

Sycophant Run was calm. The wind blew lightly as a yellow sky ran sideways and dripped over and down between bright, puffy hazen. The fantrum trees covering the Worm Worn Mountains pushed gigantic purple blossoms out of their highest leaves, announcing the arrival of evening. In only a few minutes the blossoms changed the look of the mountains' canopy from a deep green to a tragic purple. Tea birds nested in the blossoms, rubbing themselves against the tiny seeds and petals the flowers produced.

Rast would have loved to stop and take it all in. Evening to him was the finest time on Sycophant Run. It was a time when the lights dimmed and the laughter increased as all sycophants began to celebrate the closing of another day. The cloistered sycophants were sounding the wooden bells, pounding out a rhythm that echoed softly throughout their part of Foo.

Rast moved up the tight ivy that covered the trunk of the tall fantrum tree, pushing fat bickerwicks aside with his black hands. He looked over his shoulder every couple of seconds to make sure that no one was following him. Not that anyone would, mind you—sycophants were honest and loyal and kept their business to themselves. Of course, the place where Rast was heading now would probably garner interest from almost every soul in Foo, despite their honesty and loyalty.

"The key is there," Rast said to himself. "There's no need for worry."

He reached the top of the tree and jumped the three-foot distance to the rocky cliff wall. The wall was moist from the Pother Falls. Rast looked down at the churning water. The rush of the falls drowned out the wooden bells and made his white fur wet and heavy.

"The key's safe," he told himself again.

The cliff wall was hundreds of feet high and angled in to meet with a taller wall of red stone. Where the two walls met, there was a rocky depression that was visible only for a few seconds each day when the largest sun was setting. Rast waited, his eyes trained on the wall. As the sun set, the wall lit up like a piece of reflective glass.

Rast could see the elusive depression. He moved quickly, knowing that in a moment it would be unnoticeable and lost on the solid wall of stone outcroppings and dips.

The sun shifted just as Rast made his way into the depression.

Rast pushed himself against the inside wall and twisted his

body around. From there he could see a small black hole that led down just on the inner wall.

Rast smashed himself into the hole.

He was not quite as thin as he had been the last time he had made this trek. He crawled through the hole on his belly, twisting every once in a while to make the fit. There were other tunnels and routes around him, but Rast stuck to the course only he knew. Now and then small, lizardlike lather whips would scurry over Rast, spitting sparking saliva at him for disturbing their territory. The sparks stung, but they also created brief flashes of light, helping him find his way. After crawling for twenty minutes, Rast saw steady firelight up ahead.

He moved through the tunnel, placing his hands and feet carefully on solid ground. The tunnel opened up into a small, round cavern with jagged stalactites hanging from the ceiling. There were two torches suspended from the wall by thick leather straps. Only one was lit, its flame weakly burning.

Rast looked at the flame with disgust.

"Stand tall," Rast commanded, brushing a couple of persistent lather whips off his arms.

The fire flickered and straightened itself. Rast looked around, and the flame slouched just a bit.

"What happened to the second torch?" Rast said. "Who put it out?"

The flame groaned. Rast moved closer and stared into the fire.

"Have there been any others through here?"

The fire crackled and popped.

"Who?"

The torch moaned.

Rast looked around. He closed his eyes and breathed in and out slowly, then turned in a circle, letting the feel of the cavern come to him. He twisted around two times before he shivered and stopped.

Rast opened his red eyes and moved toward the back wall. The fire leaned in his direction, watching to see what was going on. Rast reached out and touched the wall. It felt solid. He stuck out his right hand and made a tight fist.

"I hope I'm right," he said to the fire.

Rast pulled back his right arm and jabbed his fist toward the wall as hard as he could.

He hit the right spot.

There was a brittle cracking noise followed by a wet slurp as his arm slid into the wall.

"The stone film seemed thin," he said to himself.

Rast had found the hole, but the layer of stone that had hardened over it was less substantial than it should have been.

"Someone's been here in the last twenty years," he surmised.

Rast began to sweat. With his arm halfway in the wall, he twisted his hand around inside, feeling for a switch.

"There you are," Rast said with conviction.

Stone scraped against stone behind the wall, and in a moment the stalactites on the ceiling of the small cavern began to lower, moving to the floor like jagged teeth. When the tallest stalactite hit the floor of the cavern, all movement ceased. The

lowering stalactites had pulled down a section of the ceiling, revealing a tiny set of stairs just the right size for a single sycophant to climb. Lather whips burst from the hole by the hundreds, spitting and darting around the room like thick lines of black marker. The ceiling of the room sparkled like bright fireworks as they all spat.

Rast held his arm over his eyes and waited for the slippery pests to clear out. The lather whips fell to the floor and spilled down into various cracks in the cavern. In a few moments there was no sign of a single one.

Rast pulled a thick strip of cloth out of a tiny pouch he had hanging from his waist. He wrapped the strip of cloth around his head and eyes, blindfolding himself. He then began climbing the stairs up into the dark. The stairs circled up for a few feet in a tight stairwell that only a being the size of a sycophant could fit inside. At the top of the stairs, the cavern opened up into a rectangular-shaped room that seemed to have no ceiling, just a vast, thick darkness.

Rast could feel himself stepping on and over a number of objects. The small room was packed with small metal instruments and utensils—objects made of the shiniest metal—placed there to stop any sycophant in his tracks. Few sycophants could resist stopping to touch and look at them. Most sycophants would easily spend the remainder of their existence simply looking at their own reflections in the back of a shiny coin or spoon. The metal on the floor was lit by two small rocks that glowed bright white, one on each side of the room.

Of course, none of the objects interested Rast because of the blindfold. Although, having been in the room a couple of times before, Rast wished he had brought earplugs as well. He couldn't see the metal objects, but hearing them brush up against each other was almost as tempting and intoxicating as looking directly at them.

Rast reached the far wall. He moved his hands up and down, feeling for something. About fifteen inches up he found the end of a dried vine sticking out of the wall. He took hold of it and pulled as hard as he could. The thick brown vine snaked out of the wall until Rast was holding about six feet of it.

Rast took the vine and, still blindfolded, made his way to the opposite end of the room and tied the loose end to a thick looped vine hanging from that wall. He twanged the tight vine.

"Perfect," he said.

He hopped up on the vine-tightrope and felt the wall a foot above where he had tied it off. There he found the end of another vine and pulled. He then moved along the tightrope back to the other side and tied up his second vine. Rast repeated the action, creating a third vine a foot or so above the last, building a rope ladder that would take him up and into the dark. He took off his hood and kept his eyes looking up.

As he strung the vines, he sang an old sycophant devotional song to calm his nerves:

When fate runs dry it'll be you and I
Who save the dream from soil and sky.

The smallest hand will hoist the toil,
And set to right the sky and soil.

His voice echoed off the walls of the small space he was working in, and every couple of minutes the mountain would moan as if bothered by the singing.

Rast paid the mountain no mind.

He worked the vines until they were twenty-three rungs high. It was pitch black, and if it had not been for gravity, Rast would have been confused about which way was up. His singing had turned to humming three vines ago, and now he was too tired to even hum. He held onto the last vine and swung himself up. He straddled the vine and reached to try to find the ceiling.

It was there, and he was only inches from it.

"This is why I never check on the key," he said breathlessly to himself.

There were five tiny stalactites on the ceiling. The stalactites were all shaped differently—each of them in the form of a sycophant symbol. Rast reached wide and twisted the one shaped as a tree. He turned the one shaped as a flower once and the one shaped as a square with a missing corner four times until each one was positioned how it should be.

He turned the final two.

A faint click sounded and the cavern exhaled. The stalactites retracted and a small crevasse above Rast's head opened. Dust sprinkled out and covered Rast. The dust whispered words of warning as it settled on his shoulders.

"Do you know what you're doing?"

"Trouble lies in spaces such as this."

"Leave well enough alone."

Rast ignored the dust, reaching up to feel around the dark crack. He couldn't feel anything, and his sweating increased.

Rast frantically stood as tall as he could on the top vine and pushed his arm up further into the opening. There was something there. Rast worked the tips of his knobby black fingers to bring the object closer. As soon as he could reach it properly, he wrapped his hand around the handle on the box and pulled it out.

"Whew," he said, dropping down to stand on the second-highest vine.

The dust shifted and whimpered.

Rast tossed his leg over the vine and sat down, holding the higher rope with his right hand. He balanced the heavy box on the thick, flat vine. He couldn't see it in the dark, but Rast knew it was the key box.

"Of course it's here," he said to himself. "The one key the sycophants are entrusted to care for and we lose it? Unheard of."

Rast opened the lid up and reached inside the long box.

Life is not always what you think it will be. Some people, however, are still surprised when something turns out differently than they might have expected.

I suggest you don't get too comfortable. You can count on only two things—books and change. At only a handful of points in the history of mankind has a book ever not performed its job.

Perhaps the story fell short, but that wasn't the book's fault. It went to the trouble of holding itself together and delivering the words or images it was born to pass on. Same for change—it's constant and eternal. Even the things that seem still are still changing.

That said, however, if a person places a key in a small wooden box and locks it in a stone vault hidden deep in a mountain and protected by shiny metal objects, hidden entrances, and seemingly unclimbable heights, that person might very well expect that key to be there the next time he came around to check on it.

It was no different for Rast. He reached his hand in the little box and found . . . nothing.

Rast shook and almost fell from the shock of it. He felt around in every corner of the key box, frantically searching for the key.

There was nothing there.

Rast climbed back onto the top vine and felt around in the hole above.

It was empty.

Rast's ears twitched violently.

The legends talked of a tree on Alder that could sprout metal. Seven keys had been forged from the metal of the tree, and the seven entities of Foo were each given one—the sycophants, the lithens, the nit elders, the Want, the Sochemists, the Eggmen, and the Waves. Each key kept a secret that, if unlocked, would unleash opposition to the fate of Foo. And it was said that all the keys together could open the soil and release a being powerful

enough to destroy Foo. As long as those who held the keys sought for good, Foo would survive. When the inhabitants of Foo stopped caring for what was true, the keys would work to end all dreams and all of mankind, restoring the power to the soil that all creatures and beings had once come from.

And the sycophant key was missing.

Rast shook. The box slipped off the vines and fell down, eventually crashing against the metal objects on the floor below.

Small dust mites in the air cried and sniffled.

Rast could feel something coming on, but he couldn't stop it. His whole being trembled, and then there was a soft pop. The passion of the moment was so horrific that it had created a Lore Coil. Rast's heart sank even further. In a short time, those listening in any part of Foo would know that the key was missing.

Frazzled, Rast lost his balance and slipped down, bouncing off of four vines before he was able to right himself. His heart was beating faster than it had ever thumped. If someone really had unlocked the secret, the life of every sycophant was in jeopardy.

Rast was sweating, and his wet hands and feet slipped on the vines. This time he could not stop himself from falling. He tried to reach for anything to stop his fall, but his tiny, wet hands couldn't get a grip.

He landed with a metallic thud against the ground. Rast had the presence of mind to close his eyes so as to not be distracted. He scrambled over the metal objects and worked himself down the tight stone stairs.

Rast stumbled into the cavern where the single torch was

burning. He blinked anxiously and looked at the fire. The flame seemed nervous.

Rast stood. "Who was here?"

The fire fizzled.

"Who put out the other torch?" Rast demanded.

The fire whimpered.

"No one knows of this place aside from me," Rast moaned. "There can't be . . ."

Rast stopped himself. His heart sank to his toes and then raced up his stomach and into his neck. He shook until the fire became concerned and dimmed.

"Someone was here," he said firmly.

The torch made no objections.

"You didn't stop her?" Rast questioned, remembering the only other person he had ever brought here.

The fire couldn't take it—it extinguished itself in one desperate yet soft puff of smoke.

Rast was gone from the room before the last bit of firelight had faded. He had a key to find.

CHAPTER SIXTEEN

UNCERTAINTY

Leven was confused—deeply and utterly confused. He had no idea what day it was or what time it was. Day or night? Who knew?

Not Leven.

He was unsure of where he was, who he was, and what he was supposed to be doing. He couldn't remember if he had eaten lately, or when he had last slept. He couldn't remember if he had family or friends or any purpose in life. The only thing he knew for sure was that his legs were about to fall off from pain and that he was hiking up a never-ending stairwell with some small creature who insisted his name was Steven.

"Steven?"

"Yes," Clover answered happily.

"That doesn't sound right," Leven said, breathing hard and brushing his hair back.

"It should," Clover insisted. "You named me."

"Steven?"

Clover nodded and jumped down onto Leven's left arm.

"And we're climbing these stairs because . . . ?"

"We are trying to get to the Want fast."

"Because . . . ?"

"He's all-powerful and Geth thinks he can help you save Foo."

"Foo?"

"That's where we are," Clover explained. "Foo. The space between the possible and the impossible."

"And I live here?"

Clover tsked. "I shouldn't have let you drink that whole thing of water."

Leven ran his fingers through his dark hair. His brown eyes burned gold around the edges as he looked up at the endless amount of stairs. Glancing down was even more astounding.

"Who built these stairs?" Leven asked.

"Not sure," Clover said. "Probably some rants."

"Which are . . . ?"

"Unstable beings who are constantly caught in dreams from Reality."

"Who lights the torches?"

"They stay lit," Clover said. "No reason for them to go out."

Leven stopped climbing and collapsed onto one of the stairs. "I can't go any higher," he announced.

"Of course you can."

"No way, Steven," Leven said.

Clover smiled.

"That just doesn't sound right," Leven repeated, confused. "Are you sure your name isn't Clark, or Calvin, or Kaiser?"

"Nope," Clover insisted. "I'm all Steven, Ted."

"And you're positive my name is Ted?"

"That's what you told me," Clover said. "So, unless you're lying . . ."

"I don't feel like a Ted."

"I could rename you if you'd like," Clover offered.

"That's all right," Leven said. "Ted?"

"Ted."

"How did I forget all this?"

"You drank some water from the Veil Sea," Clover answered. "For the record, I tried to stop you."

"So I'm Ted, you're Steven, and we're climbing these billions of stairs to see a guy called Want?"

"Right."

"Because a guy named Geth and a girl named Winter said so?" Leven asked.

"Now you're getting it right."

The effect of the water was beginning to fade. Leven could see real memories washing in and out of his mind.

"And you're in charge?" Leven asked.

"Only because you all begged me to be."

More bits of Leven's brain began to clear.

"We begged you?"

"It was actually a little embarrassing," Clover said.

"I'm sure it was, Steven."

Leven's brain cleared further. He could see Foo and Reality in his mind. He could see Winter's face and Geth as a restored lithen. He could see Clover handing him the water and promising him it was safe to drink.

It was all coming back to him. Leven looked up at the stairs and moaned. He took a deep breath, pushed himself up, and began climbing again.

"You know, I'm glad I named you Steven," Leven said, breathing hard. "I would hate for you to have one of those girl names like, um, Clover."

"Clover's not a girl's name," Clover insisted. "It's a perfectly masculine name."

"Sort of like Daisy?"

"No, not like Daisy," Clover argued.

"I suppose it doesn't matter anyway, seeing as how you have a solid name like Steven."

"Still," Clover said, hurt. "You don't know if my middle name might be Clover, or maybe I have a brother named that."

"Do you?" Leven asked.

"No."

"Well, that's lucky for your brother," Leven teased, his head almost fully cleared.

"You should be going faster," Clover said sourly.

"All right, Clover," Leven smiled.

"Hey . . . how did . . . the water's worn off?" Clover asked sheepishly.

"Yes," Leven answered. "Steven?"

"I was just trying it out."

"And Ted?"

"I thought you'd like it."

Leven laughed. "About as much as I like these stairs."

Leven grabbed the rail and pulled himself up as he climbed. You could almost hear his leg muscles screaming in pain.

"I'd give anything just to be able to see the top," Leven said. "Just to know there's an end."

"I might have a telescope," Clover said, reaching into his void.

After a couple of seconds of rummaging he pulled out a wooden telescope. Leven extended it and put it to his right eye.

"I'm not sure," Leven breathed, "but I think I can see where it stops."

"How far up?" Clover asked.

"Too far."

Leven lowered the telescope from his eye and handed it back to Clover. Leven had a black ring around the eye he had looked with.

"Whoa, I forgot that I . . ." Clover started to say.

"What?"

"I was going to play a joke on an old classmate, Stream."

"What are you taking about?" Leven asked.

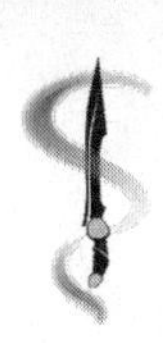

"Nothing," Clover said, slipping the telescope back into his void.

He brought out a small piece of cloth. "Here—you've got a little something around your eye."

Leven wiped his eye and looked with disgust at the black smudge on the cloth. Glaring at Clover, he asked, "Do you have anything in there that could actually help us?"

"Are you hungry?"

"I'm not talking about food," Leven clarified. "I mean, like a grappling hook that will pull us up, or some sort of elevator stick."

"Elevator stick?" Clover laughed. "No, but I have these."

Clover pulled out a large cloth bag with words embroidered on the front of it. The stitching read: "Corn-o-copious, with the patented Eternal-Kernel."

"No food," Leven insisted. "I'm not eating anything you pull out of there."

"It's not to eat," Clover said. "I think it might . . . well, I'll just try it."

"Hold on!" Leven said sharply. "Only try things that will help us."

"This couldn't hurt." Clover shrugged and opened the bag of mangled-looking corn. He turned it upside down and let it all dump out. After a long, silent pause Leven could faintly hear the sound of something raining down on the floor far beneath them.

"We're saved," Leven said sarcastically.

"Hold on, Ted," Clover insisted.

Before Leven could correct him, Clover grabbed a torch from the wall and heaved it out of its leather strap. Clover then pushed the torch and sent it sailing down the stairwell after the corn kernels. Both Leven and Clover watched as the fire seemed to fall forever before coming to rest on the ground miles down.

"Is that it?" Leven asked. "That's supposed to help us?"

"That's all I got," Clover said. "I was hoping that—"

Pop.

"What was that?" Leven moaned.

Again, from way down below, a soft *pop* echoed.

"I was thinking—" Clover started to say.

Pop, pop, pop.

"So you thought you'd save us by making a batch of popcorn down at the bottom?" Leven asked.

"It's not popcorn."

Pop, pop, pop, pop.

Leven looked out over the rail.

Pop, pop. Pop, pop.

He could see something yellow building at the bottom. There were specks of red and green and purple mixed in with the yellow.

"I was thinking that if it popped high enough, we could let it push us up."

Leven stared at Clover speechless.

"What?" Clover said defensively. "You're the one who suggested an elevator stick."

"*Suggested,*" Leven said.

Pop! Pop! Pop! Pop! Pop!

Leven looked down. The popping was still far away, but something inside of him hinted that it might be best to run. "Let's keep going," Leven said urgently.

"It might work," Clover pointed out. "It's rising pretty quickly. It's not like they're normal kernels—they're huge. Honestly, what harm can it do to wait?"

The growing popcorn reached the first torch. With a small whoosh the top kernels caught on fire and sparks shot up—all while the popping grew faster and more violent.

Whoosh. It had reached the second torch. Clover looked at Leven nervously. "Maybe we *should* keep going," he agreed.

Leven took Clover's small right hand and pulled him up onto his shoulder. He then began taking the steps as fast as he could.

The popping increased.

Whoosh.

Leven could feel the heat from the fires breaking out. It was almost as warm as the burning muscles in his legs. Something the size of a fuzzy beach ball blew past Leven and straight up the shaft.

"What was that?" Leven asked.

"A popped kernel," Clover answered.

"It was huge," Leven said, his lungs screeching at him as he took the stairs three at a time.

"I told you it wasn't popcorn," Clover shouted, the rat-a-tat of exploding kernels almost deafening now.

Whoosh!

Whoosh!

Whoosh!

Fires were bursting to life every couple of seconds. A huge red piece of exploded corn shot up beneath Leven and beaned him in the back of his head. He flew forward, collapsing on the stairs.

"Get up!" Clover yelled. "Get up!"

Leven stood and shook it off. He looked down at the flood of gigantic kernels rapidly filling up the stairwell. Each torch the exploded kernels reached started the top layer on fire and sped up the popping.

"We'll never make it!" Leven yelled.

"Not with that attitude!" Clover yelled back. "Come on."

The giant kernels were pelting Leven from all directions. One scratched across his face, while two more hammered his shoulders and back. They were light, but the force of the impact and the sharp edges of the kernels were enough to cause pain.

The popping corn sounded like a machine gun, while the fires reminded Leven of the sound of lit fuses. The exploded corn was now only fifty feet below Leven.

"Will it stop?" he shouted.

"Not in the next couple of hours," Clover screamed back.

Leven willed his legs to climb. He begged his thighs to forget the pain and keep moving. He took the stairs four at a time as his world seemed to pop around him.

"I can't do it," Leven despaired.

"Well," Clover consoled, "at least it will be a nice-smelling death."

The scent of warm corn was almost as strong as the heat

that was creeping up around Leven's legs and twisting around his body. A huge exploded kernel hit him in the face.

"There's the ceiling!" Clover screamed.

"And a door," Leven added.

The corn was up to Leven's feet. The far side of the exploded corn was on fire, shooting sparks into Leven's face and hair. The door was only about twenty more feet up. It became harder and harder for Leven to pull his legs up out of the corn and onto a higher stair.

Clover jumped down and started to push Leven's feet up as he moved. The door was close now, but so was the corn as it swelled up around Leven's waist. Fire was streaking up and through the loose kernels. No fire was directly touching Leven yet, but the kernels were so hot they singed his skin and clothes.

"Come on," Clover hollered, now standing above Leven and pulling him forward. "Come on."

The corn was around Leven's neck as he reached the door.

It was locked.

"Please," Leven begged the door, yanking on the wooden handle. "Open up!"

Popped corn piled up over Leven's head now, reaching the ceiling. The increasing pressure snuffed out the fires but squeezed Leven's body like a clamp. Down below, the wooden stairways began to crackle and shatter as the pressure of the exploding corn became even greater.

"Open up!" Clover screamed. "Open up!"

The door handle was too stubborn. The door itself seemed

willing, but the knob wouldn't budge. The corn pushed Leven up against the door so tightly that he couldn't move.

"Open up!"

Clover was crammed between Leven's left arm and the door. He arched his back and pounded against the door with his tiny fists.

"The knob won't relax," Leven screamed, huge kernels of scalding corn burning welts into his arms.

The door began to rattle as if battling against its own knob.

"I can't breathe," Leven said, coughing. "I'm not . . ."

Before Leven could finish his sentence, the door, no longer willing to wait around for its stubborn knob, cracked its own hinges and shot out the pegs. It burst open from the hinge side, and Leven blew out of the stairwell and into a nicely furnished foyer. Exploded kernels washed over him and began to fill the space he was now in.

Leven jumped to his feet looking for Clover as wave after wave of hot corn rushed past him. The corn was moving all the objects in the room, washing them away like foam.

"Clover! Clover!" Leven yelled.

"Ted."

Even in the heat of the moment Leven took the time to remind Clover how wrong that name was for him.

"Sorry," Clover said, bounding up onto Leven.

"Let's get out of here."

Leven ran through the river of corn to a wide door with a green wooden handle. The door opened instantly and Leven stepped

out. He had no idea where he was or which direction to run.

"Any suggestions?" Leven asked, the sound of flowing corn scraping up against everything.

The room looked different from every direction. Walls were shifting and the scenery was changing as if it were fluid.

"What is this place?" Leven said, confused.

"I have no idea," Clover said. "I don't think many sycophants have ever been here before."

"I dare say you're right about that," a male voice said with conviction. "Don't take this the wrong way, but I don't care for your sort."

"Excuse me," both Leven and Clover said in unison, turning to face the direction of the voice.

The walls shifted again.

"You're excused," the man replied. "Fine breed, the sycophants, but I've just never cared for them hanging around—invisible one second, solid the next, always sneaking."

"I'm not—" Clover started to say.

"And you are . . . ?" Leven asked boldly, quieting Clover.

The person speaking was sitting in a red leather chair, facing away from Leven. The chair swiveled, showing a man. His robe was dark with orange at every edge. The orange color increased and decreased as he breathed. Leven couldn't see the top of his face because he had an odd-shaped hood hanging down over it, hiding everything but his twisted red beard. There was a strong light around the man, giving him a faint green aura. White strands of robe orbited and circled him like stringy hula hoops. It took Leven a moment to realize that the white strands were actually light.

The man stood slowly. He was about six feet tall, with wide shoulders, and he held a red kilve in his right hand.

"Who am I?" he asked. "Well, I've had other names, but now they call me the Want."

Clover gasped loudly enough for both him and Leven.

"The Want?" Leven whispered, knowing it was true.

"Yes," he said. "And you must be the much-anticipated Leven Thumps."

Leven was silent as a strange, numbing feeling overcame him.

"The day has crept up on us," the Want continued. "How fortunate I am to have been standing here to witness your triumphant entry."

Leven stood still as gigantic pieces of exploded corn continued to flow into the changing room.

"And look what you brought with you," the Want said, referring to the giant popped corn. "How thoughtful. But I'm afraid we haven't space for it all, so it must cease."

The Want stretched out his hands, with the kilve in his right. He moved both his arms back and forth in one smooth movement. Instantly the large, exploded corn reverted back to tiny kernels, which rained down upon the wood floor like spilt rice.

Leven looked behind him. Back in the adjoining room the door was lying on the floor where it had fallen, and all the popcorn had disappeared. The door stood up and worked its way over to where it had ripped itself off.

"So," the Want said, walking closer, his kilve knocking against

the ground as he advanced. "Here stands Leven Thumps."

The Want stepped up to Leven, his face still hidden by his hood.

Leven stood tall.

The Want breathed out, his lungs emitting the sound of glass underfoot. A fine powder escaped his lips and circled Leven's head.

"I've waited for this day forever," the Want said, breathing in and taking back his previous breath. "Are you afraid, Leven Thumps?"

Leven pushed his hair out of his eyes and squared his shoulders.

"Come now, you can be honest with me," the Want insisted. "Are you frightened?"

"A little."

"Good," the Want said, laughing just a bit. He jumped on one foot and then the other. "Very, very good. Your fear makes it clear that we've some wisdom to work with. Come. Come with me."

"Where?" Leven asked.

"Questions already?" the Want sighed. "I don't care for questions. Besides, does it matter, Leven? Didn't Geth tell you to find me?"

Leven nodded. "He did."

"And aren't you the least bit curious what lies ahead?"

"Of course," Leven answered.

"Well, how can you discover what lies ahead by simply standing still?"

"I don't—"

"It might be best if you don't do too much talking," the Want interrupted. "I wish to remain impressed with you for as long as possible."

Leven was insulted but silent.

"Follow me."

Despite his better judgment, Leven obeyed.

The Want moved quickly through a shifting door, then stopped and looked at Leven with his hooded eyes. "I have not left Lith in many years," he whispered nervously. "Of course, you know this. You must feel different just being here with me."

"I do," Leven said with relief. "What is that feeling?"

"One of many you will be experiencing," the Want said. "My every move affects the mood of Foo. I walk in patterns to avoid and influence certain aspects, and you must know that my head is not always mine."

A feeling of desperation flooded over Leven.

"Good, you are feeling a loss," the Want smiled. "You are in tune. My home here shifts like my mind. It is not a comfortable way to live. At the moment my mind is mine, and I am telling you to step where I step and follow where I lead. At the end of our evening, our trail will play a significant role in the future of Foo."

"Our trail?"

"There is a pattern and consequence to everything," the Want said. "Now quit stalling."

The Want began walking quickly again. In a few seconds he was a full twenty paces ahead of Leven. Clover took the distance as a safe opportunity to speak his mind.

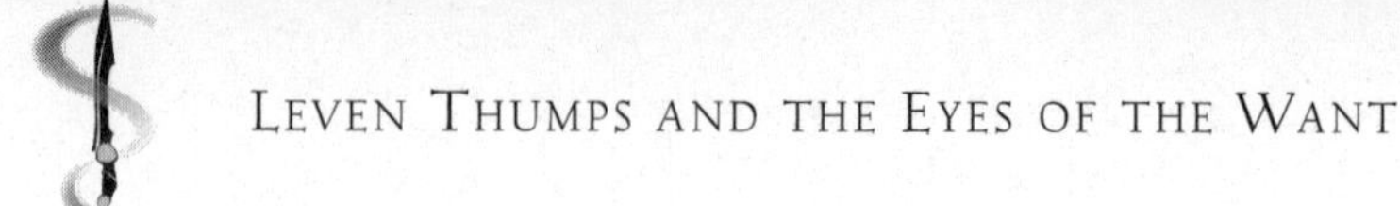

"If I'm being completely honest," Clover whispered, "I'm not quite as impressed as I thought I'd be."

"Me neither," Leven whispered back.

"Do you two think a being who sees every dream that Reality produces can't hear the silly whispers of a sycophant and an offing twenty feet behind him?" the Want asked as he moved in front of them.

Leven felt sick.

"Sorry, your highness," Clover apologized.

"Sycophants," the Want tsked. "It's a pity fate favors you so. To think, the whole of Foo is contingent upon creatures as easily distracted as you."

"I couldn't have made it here without him," Leven pointed out, coming to the defense of his friend.

"Of course not," the Want snipped. "And again, I was more impressed with you before I knew that. Silence is golden."

The Want stopped and wobbled for a second. The light around him grew brighter and receded. The circling bands emitted flashes of color. He turned and lifted his arms up. After a few moments he lowered his arms and turned to face Leven, his eyes still hidden.

"Follow me, and hurry," he added. "The world is changing as we speak."

Leven and Clover followed without saying a word.

CHAPTER SEVENTEEN

Gathered for a Cause

Pain is not something most people seek out. Very few people in the world collect memories or mementos of things that sting. Photo albums usually are filled with pictures of birthdays and dances, camping trips and celebrations. Occasionally you'll find a few snapshots of someone's first car accident or operation, but for the most part the pictures we choose to look at depict pleasure, not pain.

Likewise, no right-minded person wakes up in the morning and hopes to have a bowling ball dropped on his head or to get his foot run over by a car filled with heavy bricks. People dislike pain on all levels. Even a little pain is bothersome. Nobody wants to wear shoes that pinch or shirts that itch or pants that bind.

Worse than pain, however, is hurt.

While pain usually bites and fades, hurt can hang around forever. Like the hurt you feel when someone points out to

everyone else how poorly you do something. Or the hurt you feel when your first crush crushes you and decides to hold hands and make eyes at someone else in public. Or the hurt you feel when you find a note in your lunch box that says, "The entire population has voted, and you are definitely not it."

Janet knew hurt.

Her childhood had taught her to be selfish and unkind. Her parents had ignored her, compensating for their lack of interest by giving her things. Sadly, Janet had never learned to use what she had been given for good. Instead, she used possessions to pad her life and make herself as comfortable and untouchable as possible. She had lost every friend who had ever come near just by being rotten, self-absorbed, and isolated. She refused to let people into her life unless it was clear they would never cause her pain. And of course, as everyone knows, there is no relationship in life that comes with the promise of zero pain.

When her parents passed away, Janet lost everyone in the world who remotely cared for her. Then she met Wally. Wally was tall, dark, and miserable. He complained about everything, and Janet sort of liked that. But soon after they married, Wally discovered that Janet was far more sour than she had initially let on. Wally left her shortly before their first child was born.

Janet knew hurt.

She buried her feelings and became more miserable, distrusting, and awful than she had ever been before. She cursed

her parents. She cursed Wally. And she cursed the child who had come into her life at such an awful moment.

Winter.

Now, however, Janet's whispy heart hurt for all new, less selfish reasons. Each step she took, she could do little but think of how she had blown her shot at Reality. She cried over the things she had done to Winter. She had been given a body with a beating heart, and she had stifled every chance for her life to be positively textured and rewarding. She kept thinking about the boulder she had talked to and wondering why she had never reached for anything better.

"What have I done?" Janet whispered to herself as she walked.

"Excuse me?" Osck said, stepping up beside her.

Osck's arms and torso were on fire at the moment, but his legs were the reflection of trees and Janet. As he spoke, Janet could see his hornlike ears turn bright orange. At first, as the leader of the group of echoes Janet had ended up with, he had hardly acknowledged her. But as they had traveled, Osck had begun to enjoy her strange, fat form as a reflection on him.

"It's nothing," Janet said hopelessly.

"What have you done?" Osck asked sincerely, his voice the sound of new flame. "Your voice reverberates sadly."

Despite the fact that half of him was on fire, Janet wanted to reach out and touch Osck. She desperately needed to feel that there was something solid and real in her life. She couldn't even feel her own face or lie down and touch the soil beneath her.

"I have to say," Osck spoke. "You interest me."

"Shut up," Janet said instinctually.

Osck's eyes burned with curiosity. "I like the way you look," he crackled.

"Excuse me?" Janet said sarcastically.

"Your reflection," Osck said. "It's long both ways. Like the biggest sun when it's hanging in the middle air."

Janet stared at Osck. She wanted to feel insulted, but that impulse was fleeting. Instead, something inside of her wiggled like a worm fighting to free itself from a rusty hook. She felt her stomach, but her hands went right through her. The wriggling in her stomach dropped to her toes and bounced back up into her chest.

The sensation was baffling to her.

It was even more confusing when she witnessed the result of it reflecting in Osck's face.

Janet was smiling.

"Are you okay?" Osck asked, staring at her face as if she were a leper with a bad cold.

"I'm not sure," Janet answered honestly, the smile fading like wet paper.

"Reality will make you whole," Osck said with confidence. "We'll win the war and bridge the madness."

"Madness?"

"Foo," Osck said. "This world's not complete. Look how it holds us in."

Osck motioned to the Hard Border that had towered over them

the entire trek, blocking any sun and elements from that direction.

"Reality has borders too," Janet said.

"Not true," Osck insisted. "It's endless, like the suns."

"You wouldn't exist in Reality," Janet pointed out. "You'd be nothing but a passing reflection."

"Perhaps," Osck said. "But our birth here assures our existence there."

"Who says?" Janet argued.

"Those who read the Lore Coils," Osck answered. "The rants will bridge the madness and make the impossible a reality."

"Knowing Reality, it seems more likely that people will douse you with water and send you back to the dreamers who dreamed you up."

Osck stared at Janet. His torso cooled while his heart burned bright. "I like the way you look."

Janet smiled a second time.

"Your face changes when you do that," Osck said.

"Sorry."

"It's not awful," Osck assured her. "Only odd."

Janet was quiet as they moved between trees on the edge of the Swollen Forest. Tea birds dipped in and out of the upper branches of fantrum trees, singing to each other. A couple of mischievous, three-armed tharms swung from high branches chasing one another.

"How will you win the war?" Janet asked, sounding as if she actually understood what she was asking.

Osck looked around nervously. "The rants have metal."

"And?"

"Those who oppose us have none," Osck said. "As they adhere to their outdated laws, we will put an end to their bondage of living within these borders and bridge Reality."

"How?"

"You speak plainly," Osck observed.

"That doesn't change my question," Janet insisted. "How?"

"There is a gateway."

"Where?"

"The information is being purchased."

"And you and your group are going to beat people up with metal and then go through a gateway?"

"Yes," Osck answered reverently.

"I think you're overestimating your strength," Janet said critically.

The trees thinned just a bit, opening into a wide field where perfectly round stones littered the landscape.

"We're almost there," Osck said cautiously.

"Almost where?" Janet asked. "And what's that sound?"

Osck was quiet, marching ahead of Janet and signaling the other echoes to follow. They wove through the round stones to a spot where the stones rose to make a wall. Janet could still hear what sounded like the rushing of water.

The echoes pushed through a tight opening in the wall and moved onto a wide ledge that looked over the lush green Rove Valley.

Janet was amazed.

Hundreds of thousands of beings covered the entire landscape. As far as she could see, the valley was filled with creatures of all varieties. There were large groups of echoes and various animals, but the overwhelming majority were groups of dark-robed rants. Every couple of hundred feet, large orange flags with dark, moving symbols had been placed. Beneath each flag was a long, black tent with creatures pouring in and out of it. Thin, ratty braids of smoke rose to the sky from a hundred different fires.

Osck moved back so as to better wear Janet's reflection.

"There're so many," Janet said.

"And we are still gathering."

"I don't think Reality is going to let you just walk in."

"They won't have a choice," Osck said solemnly. "How do you stop the flood?"

"This is impossible."

Osck stared at Janet intently.

"You're interesting," he finally said, his heart burning brighter.

"I mean it," Janet insisted.

"So do I," Osck said.

Janet followed Osck down a slight hill and into a long set of switchbacks. They walked fast, and in less than an hour they had reached the valley floor and were numbered among the gathered throng. The sound of laughter and bragging could be heard from every corner. Some were arguing over where they were camped or how much food they had. Others were complaining about the wait.

"We should attack now."

"How much longer can we sit?"

Janet stayed silent. Her heart was filled with fear. She had to keep reminding herself that nobody could harm her. She was nothing, and because of that she was safe. It was what she had always wanted, but now that she had it she was very much aware of how unfulfilling it was.

"Come," Osck commanded his group. "There are other echoes at the far end and over."

Janet followed. "Who's in charge of this crowd?" she asked.

Osck stopped walking to stare at her again. His ears and fingers burned while his long hair snapped and sparked in the light wind. "We are led by those who once trusted fate," he said.

"Like a general?" Janet asked. "Or a commander?"

"Don't worry," was all Osck said. "Soon you will be real."

"I was already real once," Janet said sadly. "I don't know that I can face myself again."

"You must have family," Osck said innocently.

"A daughter," Janet cried, a wave of intense hurt rushing over her as she said it. "I don't know that I can ever face her either."

"You speak plainly," Osck replied.

"That doesn't change my situation," Janet said.

"Then perhaps you should stop and listen," Osck instructed her. "There's nothing more powerful than a well-placed word. I'll try to speak a few before the day is out, if it will help you."

Janet opened her mouth to say something, but she could see her reflection in the forehead of Osck. Her mouth was wide, as if she were going to throw out more words that ultimately meant

nothing. Her eyes looked sad, and her face was far bigger than she remembered the mirrors of her home ever admitting.

A group of palehi ran in front of Janet and the echoes. They were running with purpose and direction, their pale faces a stark contrast to the black robes of all the rants. Osck looked at them with respect. A massive troop of black skeletons from the Cinder Depression rode behind them on huge dirt avalands.

"This war is bringing out the conviction of all beings," he said.

Janet felt hopeless, hurt, and buried in her lack of convictions and her insurmountable ability to do nothing.

CHAPTER EIGHTEEN

NOTHING LEFT, NOTHING RIGHT

Azure paced around the room like a caged traitor, his hands knotted behind his back and his head forward as if pushing against the wind. Every couple of seconds he would look anxiously toward the door. Azure scratched at his bleeding, infected ear and wiped the thick blue blood on his robe. There was dried blood caked in his beard. He looked at Winter and Geth, who were fastened to the wall with wide roven talons stapling their wrists and ankles. Azure sneered, sniffing in, his eyes looking like those of a horse who had just smelled smoke.

Winter sneered back.

"Did Reality teach you that?" he snipped. "You mutt."

"Who are you to give lessons on etiquette?" Winter retorted. "I see nothing but sickness in you."

"Watch yourself, child," Azure warned.

"I'm not a child, and you know that," Winter insisted, her chin sticking out.

"You are what we deem you to be."

"Your word has no power," Geth spoke up. "Reality has made Winter wise."

Azure spun, took two steps across the room, raised his kilve, and hit Geth on the side of his head. Geth worked his jaw and blew back his hair from his eyes.

"I wonder if your actions would be so bold if my hands were free," Geth said.

"Wonder all you want," Azure said. "You will discover shortly that my word has the power to save or end your life."

"If that's so, you'll simply be assisting fate," Geth said strongly.

Azure's blue eyes burned. He spat on the floor, cursing fate.

"The balance of power has shifted," Azure said. "Fate's dancing on the end of strings these days."

"What are we here for, anyway?" Winter asked, trying to take the attention away from Geth. "What are we waiting for?"

Azure looked around and grabbed at his ear again. The room was large, with slick, green, stone walls and one massive wooden door on the up side. At the over end of the room there was a huge fireplace with no fire burning in it; soot rats were playing in the cold ashes.

In the center of the room sat a large square table with three chairs on each side of it. The chairs were covered in black roven

pelts, and the room was lit with torches that were pinched against the stone walls with roven talons similar to the ones binding Geth and Winter.

A few of the empty chairs in the room were growing impatient. They had gotten into formation, yet still nobody was sitting in them. They anxiously tittered and chirped against the wood floor.

"Well?" Winter demanded. "What are we here for?"

Azure didn't answer. Instead, he moved to the door and it opened wide. He stepped out and the door shut behind him.

"Where are we?" Winter asked Geth, trying to work her wrists out of the talons that held her still.

"We are in the council room on the eleventh stone," Geth said, working his wrists as well.

"The council room?"

"For the Council of Wonder," Geth explained. "The first chair over there belongs to me. Of course, I haven't sat in it for years."

Geth's chair rocked back and forth, mad that it was still empty.

"Do you think the Want will be here?" Winter asked.

"I hope so," Geth said. "He doesn't sit on the council, but we continually report to him."

"And he's on our side?" Winter asked skeptically.

"Azure's turn to selfishness concerns me," Geth whispered. "I hope the Want still follows fate."

Winter pulled at the talons and looked toward the door. "I keep thinking that any moment Leven will walk in," she said wishfully, "with Clover on his shoulder and the Want beside him, telling us that this is all a mistake."

"I feel the same way," Geth admitted.

The door did open, but it wasn't Leven who stepped in.

It was Azure, accompanied by a short man wearing a red sash over his right shoulder. The man carried a brown kilve and had two long, black braids that reached almost to his waist. His face was pale with a dark mustache, the ends of which were woven into the braids. He wore felt trousers and pointed shoes that closed with large wooden buckles.

"Knoll?" Geth said happily.

Knoll refused to look at Geth. He moved to his chair and took a seat.

"Knoll," Geth tried. "It's me, Geth."

Knoll sniffed and pulled out a small round stone from his sash. He rubbed the top of the stone with his thumb. The stone displayed a series of numbers and then went blank. Knoll casually tugged on his braids and dusted off his sleeves as if he hadn't a care in the world.

He looked at Azure.

"Will there be others coming?" Azure asked.

Knoll smiled. "No."

"Excellent," Azure breathed out.

Azure took a seat in his chair. The rest of the seats showed their discontent by scooting themselves all the way in to the table.

"Can we do this quickly?" Knoll said. "Things are changing rapidly."

"Of course," Azure said. "We are here to cleanse a matter that has been left to rot far too long. Before we go on, however, it should be noted who still sits around the table. It seems that there are quite a few council members missing."

Azure looked down at a thin piece of parchment paper. "Zale?" he called out. Azure looked around at the empty chairs, his gaze coming to rest on Knoll.

"He's dead," Knoll reported, turning his gaze to Geth.

Geth's shoulders became taut.

"Tith?" Azure called.

"Buried and believed dead," Knoll said.

Azure continued to read names, and after each name, Knoll would say with calculated composure, "Buried and believed dead."

Each time Knoll spoke, Geth's soul burned. These were the names of his family and of fellow lithens. These were the names of those who had stood true and now had paid a price for it. Geth fought the feelings inside himself, knowing that he could not begin to doubt fate now.

"How can this be?" Geth spoke up. "How could so many of the council be fooled?"

"Quiet," Azure seethed. "Knoll?"

"I'm seated and steady," Knoll reported.

"Well," Azure said to Knoll, "it looks as if it is only you and I. The Council of Wonder is at its end."

"I'm here," Geth spoke up. "And surely time has not let you forget that I lead this council."

"I think you are confused," Azure said. "You gave up your spot years ago."

"I gave up nothing."

"Oh, I think you're wrong," Knoll growled. "You left us, and now our only future depends on securing a place for all of us in Reality."

"What has happened?" Geth asked sincerely. "These thoughts are poison. How could you have let this occur? You're a lithen—sworn to fight for the true Foo."

"True Foo," Knoll scoffed. "You and Antsel disappeared, and the real power of Foo shifted from these thirteen dead stones to Morfit."

"Morfit?" Geth argued. "It is nothing but a monument to misdeed and corruption."

"Had you been here, you would understand," Azure waved, as if Geth's concerns were childish. "We were wrong, Geth. We were selfish and misguided trying to keep Foo from Reality."

"I can't believe what I'm hearing," Geth said sadly. "What of the plan?"

"What of Leven?" Winter jumped in.

Azure tugged on the sleeves of his robe and breathed in slowly.

"Plans change," he said coolly. "It seems as if perhaps fate was working with us when the Want sent you off. You might have been impossible to persuade."

"Impossible is not a word," Geth said.

"How wrong you are," Azure replied. "Of course, once Foo and Reality are one, impossible truly won't be a word. See how it works, Geth? We will offer what we have to everyone, and in turn we will have more power and possibility than we ever dreamed of."

"Don't speak of dreams in your deception," Geth commanded. "What you speak of will bring about the desolation of all dreams."

"Lithen rhetoric," Knoll spat.

"Fate will fight you at every turn," Geth said. "And I will give my life before I allow you to carry this out."

"Interesting you should say that," Azure sniffed, his ear dripping blood down his neck. "That brings us nicely to the business at hand. It seems as if you have a debt to repay."

"What are you talking about?" Geth questioned.

"Your brother's death occurred as a result of your carelessness."

"Zale's death occurred at the hands of Sabine," Geth insisted. "Had I not been in the form of a seed at the time, I might very well have prevented it."

"Still," Knoll said. "It seems suspicious and touched with confusion."

"Antsel was there," Geth argued.

"But, sadly, he's not here to help clear it up," Azure pointed out. "You also abandoned your stone to hide in Reality."

"At the wish of the Want," Geth said.

"The Sochemists say differently."

"The Sochemists read the air," Geth said with disgust. "They can't clearly decipher the difference between a Lore Coil and a misdirected lob. The Want knows what happened."

"The Want is barking mad," Knoll shot out. "He sees the plan as a warped vision that only he can bring to pass."

"My stone still stands," Geth said harshly. "And Foo will be restored."

"Foo unravels as we speak," Azure said. "The armies await our command."

"You can't . . ." Winter tried to say.

"Silence!" Azure snapped. "We've no need to hear from you. Geth left his brother to die, abandoned his stone and his world, and then bathed in the flames of the turrets without consent."

"There was consent given when I left," Geth said, his blue eyes burning.

"So many years ago," Knoll said. "Things have changed."

"That's perfectly clear," Geth muttered in disgust.

"Here's what's clear," Azure said slowly. "You're a traitor of Foo who's had his hand in killing and in preventing Foo from becoming what it's destined to become."

"Destiny," Geth spat. "Here's what's clear. You have brought me to this room for no other reason than to taunt me with what has crumbled in my absence. It's working. I feel a great sadness for the change you have helped bring about, but I feel an even greater peace knowing that in the end fate will have your heads."

"Not before it has yours," Azure instructed. "It is the decision of the council that you must die."

"What council?" Geth asked. "I see no council. I see only two foolish beings who have traded all that is noble and worthwhile for the thin wish of having it all. Do what you want to me, but fate will run as strong and wide as it always has."

"Kind of you to give us permission," Azure smiled wickedly.

Azure knocked on the table twice. The door opened, and two large rants stepped in. They wore black robes and were currently sporting uneven left sides, which proved that dreams were still flowing into Foo. One of the rants stepped up to Geth and grabbed him by the right wrist. He snapped the talon out from the wall.

"No, no," Azure said coldly. "Dispose of the girl first."

"Don't touch her!" Geth yelled.

"Oh, my dear Geth," Azure cooed. "You've such a high opinion of where your words are welcome."

Azure stood and walked over to Winter. He towered over her. Winter could see nothing but the insides of his nostrils and the dark band of blue his eyes created.

"Maybe Geth's right," Azure said. "Why start with just her when we can begin with the both of them? We had planned a special ending for you here, but perhaps there is someplace more fitting. What do you say, Knoll? Instead of disposing of them here, let's send them to Lith?"

"Why would . . . oh," Knoll said, wising up. "You have hit upon something. I believe a stay in Lith would provide a perfect ending."

"The soil will welcome their dead souls."

The second rant released Winter. He pulled her from the wall and hefted her up as easily as a fisherman might raise a large trout, holding her in the air and looking her over with his right eye. He lowered her and pulled both of her arms back behind her. He then bound her wrists tightly.

"The Want will stop you," Geth said, calm once again.

"The Want will unwittingly kill you both," Knoll laughed.

"Take them away," Azure insisted. "Keep their hands bound at all times and give them no length of rope or fate to make an escape with."

"Yes, my master," the tallest rant said, bending to release Winter's ankles.

Without warning Azure spun toward the rant and swung his kilve, knocking the rant on the side of the head. Azure looked at the cowering rant, his own ear still bleeding steadily.

"*My* is so singular," Azure seethed.

"Yes, *our* master," the rant corrected.

Geth's countenance fell further.

Someone peeking through the cracks of the large door might have guessed that Geth's state of mind was due to the fact that Winter and he were about to face death. Or perhaps they might have thought it was because Geth had no idea where Leven was and Foo was falling apart around him. They might even have thought that it was because every council member aside from Azure and Knoll was now either dead or buried or quite possibly both. And it is possible that someone looking in

might have thought that Geth's state of mind was brought on because, in the fourteen or so years that he had been in Reality, no one had done a single thing to update the look of the council room. All those assumptions might have been understandable, but they would have been inaccurate. Geth's countenance had fallen because he was sickened by the evil change of his one-time friend.

The Azure that Geth had known all those years ago had been passionate and hotheaded, but dedicated to Antsel and willing to give his life for the preservation of dreams. The Azure that stood before Geth now was a traitor and a murderer, so self-absorbed and confused that he couldn't see the catastrophic damage he was setting in motion.

"The Want won't have it," Geth said calmly.

"The Want won't know!" Azure yelled. "We've already succeeded. We have the people's hearts. We have the gifts, and soon the gloam will possess sufficient soil to reach the Thirteen Stones."

"Gloam?" Winter asked, not recalling anything about it.

"The arm of soil that reaches out from below Cusp," Azure said coldly. "It seeks to mesh with the soil of the stones. Once that happens, the Dearth will be freed and conquer Reality like a strong dream."

"It's a lie," Geth said. "The Dearth cannot be freed. His soul belongs to the soil and is sealed by the keys."

"Believe what you will," Azure smiled. "Your thoughts are of no concern. The Dearth will rise, and destiny will be fulfilled."

"Leven will stop you," Winter said bravely.

"Leven?" Azure mocked. "He won't stop us. In fact, he'll be the key to make it all happen."

Geth stared at Azure with complete disgust.

Two of the empty chairs walked off, angry at still not being sat on. Geth's chair had been vacant for so many years it could no longer take it. It ran toward the fireplace and threw itself into the ashes, rubbing its legs together to create a spark.

A fire began to burn.

Freed from the wall, but bound at the wrists and ankles, Winter and Geth were dragged from the room as the soot rats caught fire and screamed in painful stereo.

CHAPTER NINETEEN

Den of the Dead

The home of the Want made Leven tired and dizzy. There seemed to be no end to the amount of stairs there were to climb. And each time they entered a new room, the floor would shift and windows would open and close. Leven felt like he was in a dream where he knew he was somewhere, but it looked like someplace else. Regardless of how he felt, Leven kept following the Want, carefully stepping where he stepped.

Clover had disappeared and was staying silent.

Leven wanted to take a break and rest, but the Want moved with such purpose and speed that Leven felt compelled to keep up and keep quiet.

They moved into a large hall with ornate walls and an intricately carved ceiling. Painted on the ceiling were hundreds of trees. Three of the walls bore raised portraits of two siids; on the fourth wall there was just a single siid. The Want waved his hands

over his head and the siid portraits recessed and became wide windows showing distant parts of Foo. The Want pointed at the windows and the glass became orange, burning like a sheet of fire and warming the room.

"What is this place?" Leven shouted, the Want still twenty feet in front of him.

"Just a room," the Want answered.

Leven's eyes burned gold. There was something the Want wasn't telling him.

"Keep your secrets," Leven said boldly. "But I'm not going any farther."

Leven stopped.

His heart had been beating differently ever since he had stepped into the home of the Want. His fingers felt jittery and in need of something to grab on to. Leven couldn't quite get his gift to work, though his feelings and perceptions were heightened. Clover's silence hadn't helped the situation. Leven's thoughts seemed much more clear and worthwhile when he had Clover to bounce them off of.

"There's something about this room," Leven said, looking around. "There's something here."

The Want spun around and pointed at Leven. His arm trembled as his countenance glowed bright. Leven still couldn't see the Want's eyes, only his red beard.

Leven felt even stronger.

"There's no time!" the Want repeated. "You grew too slowly. The wick is lit. Fate has taken the fire from Geth, and in doing

so has put us behind. The opposition has time. When the last piece is placed, this picture will look wanting if you have not beaten their strongest opponent."

"I don't know what you're talking about."

The Want moved closer to Leven. Leven could see a haze coming from beneath the Want's hood.

"I look at you and see failure," the Want shook, his glassy breath burning Leven's eyes. "I see the end of Foo and the destruction of all dreams. Now, follow me."

"See what you want," Leven declared. "I don't know anything about this place where I now live. I meet creatures and beings my imagination previously couldn't have thought up. I have followed Geth and fate as best I could. Now I'm here, and you talk like every second is a second closer to doom. I might not understand everything, but I know that there's hope. I can feel your words trying to distract me from the fact that there is something here in this room."

The Want smiled. It didn't comfort Leven.

"Is your sycophant here?" the Want asked.

"I assume so," Leven answered.

"Show yourself," the Want commanded.

Clover materialized, sitting on the very top of Leven's head.

"You once burned for Antsel," the Want said coolly, strings of dreams twisting around him. "He was a valiant being."

Clover shivered. Normally he loved any talk or mention of his first burn, but the way the Want was pushing words through his lips made him uneasy. The Want shook his fists in the air and

turned to scream at nothing, his open rage and hidden eyes making him hard to look at. "I can hear you!"

Leven stepped back as the Want settled and then returned his attention to him.

"The dreams never end," the Want explained. "Even in sleep I see every wish set free in Reality."

"How's that possible?" Leven asked.

"Such an uneducated question," the Want sniveled. "How's that possible? I suppose that unless something fits in your current understanding, it's impossible?"

"Of course not," Leven answered, pushing out his chest and willing his eyes to burn. "I've accepted tons of things I didn't believe weeks ago."

"Accepted?" the Want said sadly.

"What's in here?" Leven asked, a feeling of sadness now enveloping him.

The Want waved his right hand and the light in the room shifted so that it now glowed from the floor instead of the ceiling. The new direction of the light completely changed the murals on the wall. Instead of seven siids, there were now Thirteen Stones and a ceiling of mist and water overhead.

"In here," the Want motioned. "Of course, our pattern will be altered."

The Want pushed through a round door and disappeared. Leven stepped through the door into a round room lined with a stone bench. In the center of the room, a large roven pelt lay on the floor next to a round rock basin.

The door closed behind Leven like an eyelid, cutting off all light. There was a popping noise, and a small fist of blue flame shot up out of the rock basin. It lit the room like a night-light, sending strings of white smoke up into the ceiling. The smoke circled the round room and created intricate patterns in the air.

"Sit," the Want said.

Leven moved back and sat down on the stone bench against the round wall. He watched the flame, entranced by the motion of it.

"Do you dream, Leven?"

"I would think you would know the answer to that," Leven replied smartly.

"Wise," the Want sighed. "I have seen all your dreams. I have watched them change. As a child you dreamed of love—of being safe and strong. As you grew older, your dreams became much less impressive, so wrapped up in fears and worry. You dreamed more about fading away than about stepping forward."

"They're just dreams," Leven said. "I knew nothing about Foo."

"True," the Want said. "But there were some of us who knew of you."

"Why?" Leven asked.

"Speak of the dead," the Want instructed. "Talk of those who have passed."

"Excuse me?"

"What do you know of Antsel?"

Even though the room was warm, as the Want spoke his

breath became frosty. It looked like he was breathing outside on a cold day. Bits of his breath drifted up into the smoke above.

"I know Clover loved him," Leven answered, watching his own breath do the same thing. "He was important, and when I hear people say his name, they always do so with respect."

Leven's breath lifted into the smoke, but this time tiny bits of it began to drift back down and settle on the stone bench beside him.

Leven felt content but curious. "Should our breath be doing this?" he asked, scooting over just a bit.

"Antsel wasn't a lithen," the Want said, ignoring Leven's question, "yet he sat on the Council of Wonder. He sacrificed everything for the sake of Foo, even down to his life. He wasn't assigned to take Geth to Reality. But when Geth's brother Zale died, Antsel stepped forward and without hesitation did as I asked."

The Want's breath was filling the room, lifting to the ceiling and then drifting down to settle by Leven.

"I did not want him to go," the Want continued. "To me he was what was right with Foo. He saw the act of enhancing dreams as a sacred calling. He felt that Foo could change the course of everything by bettering the dreams of mankind."

"And he had a beard," Clover spoke up.

"And he had a beard," the Want smiled. "When he and Geth left, so much changed. Sabine and his shadows seemed to have free reign and influence on too many. And as fate worked its course, all we could do was wait for you to grow up and come to Foo."

"I can't understand why," Leven admitted.

"You will know shortly," the Want said. "Antsel's death will not be in vain."

Leven looked down at the bits of smoky breath that were settling next to him. For the first time he could see some definition—two legs and a waist sitting there. They weren't physical, but they were outlined in glowing sparks of breath and smoke. Leven could see boots on the feet and a leather belt wrapped around the torso that was growing taller as more smoke settled.

"I'll say more," the Want sighed. "Antsel cared for you, Leven. He never had a chance to even know you, but he cared for you. He insisted that there be someone to watch over you as you grew up, and he gave up his sycophant for your benefit."

Clover materialized so that Leven could pet him. The Want glared at Clover, and he disappeared.

"He also was vital in placing Winter in Reality to help get you here. He and Amelia were crucial to creating the future you now move toward. Your mother's death was a tragic addition to the puzzle."

As the Want spoke, small bits of breath began to pile up beside the body that was almost fully formed. The body right next to Leven now had everything but a head.

"Your mother," the Want lamented. "Had she lived, things might have gone better for you. As it stands, however, it was wise of Antsel and Amelia to be so concerned with the upbringing Winter and you would experience. Sometimes lithens and their

perfect faith in fate can be a little callous. The council knew you would make it back. It was fate.

"It wasn't until Geth was cursed and they saw the purpose of him being hidden from Sabine that they began to consider placing Winter and others to help you. I didn't care; I just wanted you back when the time was right. Antsel, it seems, was wise in his persistence, because here you sit."

Leven was too busy watching what was happening right next to him to pay full attention to the Want. The drifting pieces of smoke and breath had formed a complete man. He looked to be made of flickering dust mites, but he was as visible as a beam of light streaking though a dark room. Despite the delicate façade, Leven could see every detail and physical trait.

The man turned and smiled at Leven.

Leven sort of smiled back.

"Antsel," the Want spoke. "This is Leven Thumps."

Antsel stood and nodded as if in respect. "The privilege is mine," he said.

Leven couldn't tell if he was going to throw up or pass out. Clover, on the other hand, knew exactly what to do. He materialized and hopped down from Leven's shoulder to stand directly in front of Antsel. He was shaking.

"Clover," Antsel smiled.

Clover jumped to him, but there was nothing to grab hold of. He flew into the back wall and slid down. Clover instantly bounced back up and gazed with admiration at his previous burn.

"You did so well," Antsel said, looking at Clover. "I knew

there was no one but you who could have taken care of the task."

Leven had never seen Clover smile wider.

"It was no task," Clover said. "It was my fate."

"What a perfect sycophant," Antsel smiled.

Leven glanced around, dumbfounded. "How is this possible?" he asked, looking at the Want.

The Want sighed. "There will come a day when you don't ask such foolish questions. This room is for the dead. Speak of those who have passed on, and with enough kind words an essence of that being will assemble before your eyes."

"Is it real?" Leven asked.

"It's similar to a whisp," the Want said. "The flame draws bits of the beings from where they are now. But when the fire is out, the essence drifts back to where it came from."

"What do you mean 'where they are now'?" Leven asked. "Antsel's dead."

"As if death were the end," the Want said. "It's a border one crosses."

"Let's not talk of those things," Antsel insisted. "My time here will be short and I want to know of the state of Foo."

"Things are delayed for Leven to rest," the Want sniffed.

"My legs are tired," Leven said lamely.

"Let him breathe," Antsel said to the Want. "Fate has provided this moment."

Antsel looked away from the Want to focus on Leven. He stepped around Leven, looking him up and down.

"I can see your grandfather in you," Antsel said kindly.

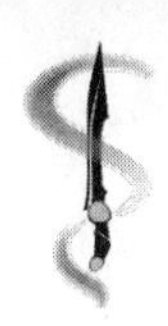

"How fortunate I am to witness this day. What of Geth?"

"He's here in Foo," Leven answered. "Restored. We were separated after finding the secret."

"The secret?" Antsel said, turning quickly to look at the Want.

"It's been contained," the Want waved.

"Which secret was it?" Antsel said, still panicked. "And the key, it must be accounted for."

"The secret belonged to the sycophants," the Want answered.

Although he was made of nothing but dust and breath, Antsel seemed to go pale. "Who unlocked it?"

Clover pointed at Leven.

Antsel looked at Leven and let his thoughts cool. His countenance dimmed.

"I told him not to," Clover added.

"Fate must have something interesting in mind," Antsel said. "Where did you unlock it?"

"In the Swollen Forest," Leven answered.

"And the key?"

"I'm not sure," Leven answered sadly.

"The key must be found. What do you make of this?" Antsel asked the Want.

"The sycophants are panicked," the Want answered. "I've sent notice the secret is contained, but they still worry. All of Foo whispers and speculates, but our course of action goes on. The secret is contained, and for some reason Leven was born to know it while it was free."

"You were whispered to?" Antsel asked.

"Yes," Leven said. "In the city of Geth, a little less than a week ago."

"Certainly the Dearth has a hand in this," Antsel said to the Want.

The Want shook madly. Antsel motioned for him to calm himself.

"I cannot calculate what this means," Antsel said thoughtfully. "I suppose it's not mine to figure out."

Leven's eyes dimmed like dying coals.

"Pay my words of worry no mind. How lucky you are to be in the thick of it," Antsel said wisely. "So many times we gathered and spoke of you."

"Why?" Leven asked.

"The Want will make that clear," Antsel answered. "Listen to him. His words will lead to actions that will change the world. And he will speak to nobody but you."

Leven tried to digest what was being said. The message felt heavy but hopeful, coming from Antsel. He wanted to tell Antsel how uneasy the Want made him and how he was worried about Geth and Winter, but Antsel's tone of voice made Leven's mind move slowly and with comfortable caution.

Clover jumped back onto Leven's shoulder so as to be eye to eye with Antsel.

"You'll stay with him," Antsel said kindly.

"Of course," Clover answered, as if there were no other reply.

"You are not the beginning of this," Antsel counseled Leven. "But you hold the answers to the end."

Leven had been so caught up in the form of Antsel that he had paid no mind to a second figure who had settled next to Antsel. The figure was now all there, minus a nose and eyes and forehead.

Antsel turned.

More smoke settled, and there sat a beautiful woman. She smiled and looked at Leven. Her hair was long and flowed like a million falling stars. She looked young, but a few years older than Leven. Bits of her were missing, making her look like a negative that wasn't quite in focus.

"Leven?" she asked with surprise. "It can't be."

She reached out and tried to touch Leven under his chin. Her empty touch held a surprising amount of warmth. She was beautiful and seemed so young. Leven's heart pounded.

"Someone spoke of me," she said happily.

She moved to stand, and the fire died. In an instant she and Antsel drifted up and away into the darkness.

"Who was that?" Leven asked, his forehead sweaty.

"I believe that was your mother," the Want answered without emotion.

"Light the fire!" Leven ordered.

"It's dead," the Want insisted. "We must move on."

"She was right here."

"*Was* is such a painful word," the Want said, his body glowing green. "The fire is out. Accept what is before you. There will be time for speaking of the dead later. Now we must go."

The Want waved his arms at Leven, and Leven stood.

"No," Leven said, feeling hostile.

The Want moved toward him and his presence pushed at Leven, causing him to back toward the door. Leven craned his neck to look in the direction where he had last seen his mother.

The door opened and light flooded in, exposing the stone walls. The bench running around the walls and the roven pelt on the floor seemed to look out of place. Leven closed his eyes and let the image of his mother appear to him on the back of his eyelids. It burned for a second and then dimmed like a morning star.

"Out," the Want insisted. "We must move quickly."

"We'll come back?" Leven asked.

"I'll make sure of it," the Want said. "Now, move as I do."

Leven did as he was told and followed after the Want. His legs no longer hurt, but he was weaker in the knees than he had ever been before.

CHAPTER TWENTY

WITNESSING THE WAR

Addy's hands hurt. Her wrists were swollen and her knees locked into place from having sat still for so long. She folded another napkin and sighed. She folded another and growled. As a senior creaser for the Wonder Wipes company, she was quite familiar with the action of manipulating each large flat napkin into a smaller, fatter square—familiar and sick of it.

Addy sat on a padded chair in front of a cheap wooden desk. On the right corner of her desk was a small framed picture of a mountain that Addy had never traveled to. On the opposite corner sat a bottle of aspirin and a half-empty glass of water. The large room was filled with eleven other desks and eleven other people all busy in the act of folding Wonder Wipe napkins.

Just like Addy had done for years.

The last few days had been a bit different, however. The manager of the plant had brought in a small TV so that they

could watch the news reports of all the strange occurrences that were occurring around the world. He had also promised to take the TV away if production fell in the least.

It was on that TV that Addy saw reports of planes being picked on by clouds, and buildings dancing around as if they had minds of their own. She had seen odd tornados in Europe and large dirt monsters in Montana, and she'd heard stories of similar things happening in a dozen other places. She had also heard countless reports of how everyone seemed to be dreaming about the same few things. Counselors and therapists were baffled by the fact that people seemed lately to be dreaming only about vicious clouds and mobile buildings.

Addy looked at the napkin she was currently creasing and moaned. She had been experiencing dreams about dirt monsters chasing her.

Addy pushed those thoughts away and was into a strong folding groove when a giant "News Flash" banner scrolled across the TV screen in the corner. Every folder stopped what he or she was doing and focused on the TV while a confused news anchor showed footage of a man in Canada being swarmed by a bunch of odd bugs. The bugs covered the man while he was running and then lifted him up into the air. The footage followed the flying man as the bugs carried him over to his Tuff Shed and shoved him in the open door. The bugs closed the door and settled onto a rake, a hula hoop, and two baseball bats lying around in this man's yard. The bugs lifted the objects and began to dance around the shed. Two seconds later the man who had been forced

inside opened the shed door and ran out. The bugs then busted up and flew into a million directions.

As with most of the recent news stories, the anchor had no way to explain what was happening.

The man who had been attacked was now being interviewed.

"And you say they bit you?" the young, inexperienced news reporter asked.

"Chomped, eh." The man smiled unnaturally, as if that was what he was supposed to do.

"And was it painful?"

"Very," the man said. "I was just raking my yard when out of the trees they came. I thought at first that I must be dreaming. But I wasn't."

"Clearly," the reporter responded. "What did they look like?"

"They looked like the end of my life," the man said seriously. "Big eyes, about an inch long. Noisy wings and clamplike mouths. That was all I saw before they covered up my eyes and tried to force themselves down my throat."

The man flashed an unnaturally wide smile into the camera.

"How do you feel now?" the reporter asked.

"Like I won't be doing any raking for a while."

The reporter went on asking pointless questions as production in the Wonder Wipes plant all but ceased.

Addy looked at some of the other folders. A couple of them laughed nervously, apparently not knowing how else to respond. The only male folder shook his head and mentioned something about the end of time.

The plant manager came in and tried to inspire them by acting brave and informing them that, despite what happened in the world, people would always need high-quality, hand-folded napkins.

"Fold," he insisted, following his command with a loud clap.

Addy folded another napkin and growled.

CHAPTER TWENTY-ONE

EXTRACTED AND STRANGLED

Tim was standing hidden in the trees, like a stalker with nothing to stalk. He had been told to wait where he was, and he had no plans to disobey his orders. Ezra was on his right shoulder yelling at squirrels. They were both on the edge of the Konigsee, the gorgeous lake where Dennis had gone in under the water about forty minutes ago.

The three of them had transported the gateway they had built to this spot and lowered it into the lake after the sun had gone down. The gateway was large and bulky, but they had rolled it to the water's edge on temporary wheels. Once they had worked it into the lake they had filled the inside of the gateway with a massive industrial balloon and inflated it as much as the gateway's space would allow.

Then, wearing an oxygen tank and mask, Dennis went into the water and slowly and carefully released tiny amounts of air

from the balloon, allowing him to lower the new gateway down to the spot where the previous one had been situated.

Tim and Ezra had watched Dennis go under the water and now they wondered if he would ever resurface.

"Would you care if he didn't?" Ezra asked Tim, his purple hair twisting wildly. "I mean, would you give a weasel's backside if you never saw that piece of misguided phlegm again?"

Tim looked around nervously. Ever since Dennis's last tirade, Ezra had been quietly goading Tim into being a man. He wanted Tim to come to his senses and help him get rid of Dennis. Ezra didn't care for Dennis, and he knew that with the gateway finished, Dennis and Sabine would no longer need Tim's strength or Ezra's leadership.

Unfortunately, the part of Sabine that currently covered the right forearm of Tim was keeping Tim's mind just foggy enough to prevent him from taking any kind of stand.

"Seriously," Ezra said, jumping to Tim's other shoulder, "we are waiting here for someone neither of us wants to ever see again."

"He said to wait," Tim said haltingly.

"You used to have a backbone, sponge boy," Ezra spat with disgust, his single eye blinking madly. "He said to wait? Well, I say don't wait!"

Tim looked down at his black webbed arm. Dark lines of what had once been Sabine drifted and crisscrossed up and down his forearm and hand like a long rubber glove.

"He said it first," was Tim's only reply.

Ezra jumped onto Tim's pointed nose. "Listen, smooth brain," Ezra seethed. "Somewhere inside of that vacuum you call a mind is the memory of the person you used to be before you started wearing that black ladies' glove. I suggest you find that person and rough him up for getting you into this mess."

Tim stared at Ezra as he stood perched on his nose.

"Worthless," Ezra spat, his purple tassel waving madly. "It's like talking to a piece of soggy cardboard."

Ezra jumped off of Tim's nose and onto a nearby tree branch. The branch belonged to a tall tree that was covered in pine needles.

"I think it's about time I started using the trees for my benefit," Ezra laughed wickedly, enjoying anything that was for his benefit. "For *my* benefit!"

He laughed so long and hard that the sound of it could be heard bouncing lightly off the surrounding mountain walls. It was a truly wicked laugh filled with mischief and malice. But nobody was around to be bothered by it, so eventually Ezra stopped laughing and self-consciously cleared his throat.

"Whatever," he said, embarrassed.

He then marched along the length of the branch and leaned into the tree trunk. He touched the tree with both of his tiny hands, looking like a preacher who was hoping to heal the poor thing. He moved back and spun around to look at Tim.

Tim was smiling like a child in a school yearbook.

"You're quite the intellect," Ezra said.

He moved in and touched the tree again. Nothing happened.

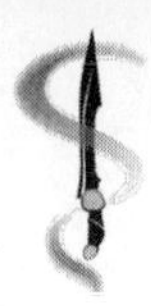

"I wonder why it's not working," Ezra growled.

He leaned back in and touched the tree a third time.

"Move!" he ordered. "Pick up your stupid roots and do my bidding."

The tree stood its ground.

"How can that be?" Ezra asked Tim.

Tim just smiled.

"Oh, yeah," Ezra sighed. "What am I doing asking you questions? Currently you're an idiot. These trees should move. I've got the imagination to uproot a building but I can't get a skinny tree to move? I can't overtake Dennis on my own."

Tim shifted on his feet, as if fighting the urge to move. He rubbed his forehead and opened his mouth several times before he finally said, "I'm in here," his brain fighting the influence of Sabine.

"That's what I've been saying," Ezra seethed. "Now we just need you to come out, start that truck, and drive us away from here."

Tim rocked back and forth on his feet, clenching his fists. He turned to look at the lake. The sun had set, but there was still a soft light covering the entire surface. Far across the way Tim could see a few lights shining from the windows of the St. Bartholomew cathedral.

The water looked so calm and perfect that Tim was saddened by the small crack that split open as Dennis began to rise from the water. He swam closer, but could not get out of the lake by himself.

"Pull me out," Dennis ordered.

Tim reached down and pulled Dennis from the cold water. He dragged him up onto shore and back into the trees. Dennis was not happy, as it can be quite difficult to feel like a true leader when one of your underlings is pulling you facedown across the ground.

"Stop!" Dennis insisted. "Let me go."

Tim dropped Dennis's arms and stood still.

Dennis stood up and dusted off the front of his stomach and face. He pulled up his swim mask and spat out some dirt from his mouth. He glanced around, trying to regain some evil composure.

He looked Tim over. "Where's the toothpick?" Dennis asked impatiently.

Tim pointed to the tree nearby. Ezra was still on his branch looking bored.

"I missed you too," Ezra mocked. "Does it work?"

"Does what work?" Dennis snapped.

"Oh, I don't know," Ezra said sarcastically. "The United Nations' plan to end world hunger? What do you think I'm talking about? The gateway, does it work?"

Dennis tried to act as if Ezra's words didn't bother him, but he wasn't a very convincing actor.

"It's installed," Dennis sniffed.

"Good," Ezra said. "That was our goal. I remember sitting down and saying, 'Let's take some time to build and install a complicated home for a few lucky fish.'"

"The temperature's not right yet," Dennis insisted. "Now stay quiet while I think."

Ezra hopped to a higher branch in the tree. "I'll speak all I want," he yelled down. "The last thing we have time for is for you to think."

"Quiet. You will do as I say," Dennis said slowly, trying to contain his rage.

Ezra jumped up onto the next limb.

"You know," he yelled, "you're even balder than I thought."

"Come down this instant," Dennis said, the black markings spelling out the word *hate* across his face.

"No," Ezra insisted. "Not with a face like that."

"I will give you one last chance," Dennis ordered.

"And I will give you a dozen hand gestures," Ezra said, following up his verbal threat with action.

"Come down," Dennis seethed, his face now reading *Severely Hate.*

Dennis grabbed ahold of the tree trunk and tried to shake the tree. The tree was far too tall and sturdy to push around.

"Looks like the trees are safe," Ezra said, making fun of Dennis's puny strength.

Dennis turned around angrily, the black marks moving across his skin like jittery leeches. He spotted Tim standing there like an unlit lamppost.

"Climb after him," Dennis ordered Tim.

Tim looked the tree up and down.

"Now!" Dennis ordered.

Tim sighed, but moved slowly to the trunk of the tree. There was a small knot protruding out of one side. Tim stepped up on it and pulled himself to the next branch.

"Faster!" Dennis ordered.

Tim moved higher, climbing like a child who had been told his whole life he couldn't climb.

"Higher!"

Tim worked himself up onto the branch right below Ezra. Ezra hopped up to the next branch and smiled.

"I once saw a dead bird stuck up under a bridge," Ezra yelled to Tim. "And I'm pretty sure he could climb twice as fast as you."

Tim was too busy scaling the tree to have the insult register.

"Get that toothpick," Dennis ordered from the ground. "Toss him to me."

Tim pulled himself through the pine needles and up into the top half of the tree. His clouded mind made it hard for him to move with any real agility.

Ezra bounded up to the next branch and then shot farther up to the crown of the tree.

"I'd worry about running out of places to escape to," Ezra hollered to Tim, "but by the time you get here I'll probably have already naturally decayed."

Tim was breathing hard, moving his arms in a straightforward and calculated manner. He placed each foot carefully on the next branch and then extended his legs to raise himself up.

Ezra stood on the top of the tree, his purple hair twisting in the light wind and the last bits of sunlight reflecting off of his

green enamel body. He laughed loudly enough to send birds from other trees flapping off into the air.

Tim moved up another branch. He was now only two limbs below Ezra. Ezra squatted and began talking loudly enough that Tim could hear but quietly enough that Dennis couldn't.

"Look what he's done to you," Ezra scoffed. "Next you'll be wiping his chin when he spits."

Tim looked directly at Ezra, his eyes blinking slowly. He stopped climbing so as to be able to comprehend what Ezra was saying.

"Go ahead, garbage boy," Ezra said. "Come and get me. Do what your master tells you."

Tim reached out, but Ezra was a good six inches too far away to grab. Tim put his foot on the next branch and struggled to pull himself up. He pulled and then twisted so his face was even with Ezra. Down below, Dennis stepped closer to get a better look at what was going on way up above him.

"What are you doing? Bring him to me!" Dennis seethed. "I want him now."

Ezra shifted so as to better position himself on the crown of the tree. Tim looked more confused than Ezra had ever seen him.

"Grab me," Ezra challenged. "You're nothing but the weak thought of a pathetic being. See that down there?"

Tim looked down. Dennis was right below him, raising his fist to the air in anger.

"That's your fate," Ezra raged. "I gave you the chance to make a choice and you failed."

Tim's eyes filled with tears. His dark pupils bounced back and forth as he tried to connect one clear thought in his head.

"You've forgotten everything," Ezra barked. "What about your wife?"

Tim flinched.

"And I believe you had a couple of snotty kids."

Tim twitched.

"And now all you have is a rotted hand that plays servant to the scattered remains of a dead being."

Tim shook slightly, and then choked as if trying to get some words out.

"What is it?" Ezra challenged. "Speak."

"I'm in here," Tim pleaded, his mind tired of fighting the evil he had absorbed.

"Well, let's get you out," Ezra smiled wickedly.

Ezra screamed wildly and shot forward with his legs tucked together. He planted himself deep into Tim's forehead. Tim screamed and let go of the branches he was clinging to. His feet slipped, and in one swift movement his body flew backwards and dropped swiftly down, landing right on top of a very startled Dennis.

Tim landed on Dennis with a whump that sounded loudly through the valley. The hit was so hard it knocked the dark bits of Sabine completely out of Dennis's body and Tim's arm.

Sabine's remnants blew like buckshot into the surrounding forest. Dennis weakly struggled to push an unconscious Tim off of him, as Ezra extracted himself from Tim's forehead and made a run for it.

The dark bits of Sabine sprang back from all directions like rubber balls attached to a wooden paddle—every bit of Sabine thirsting for Ezra. Ezra moved through the long grass looking for something to touch. He spotted a big rock and jumped up on it. He kneeled down and touched it with both hands.

The rock didn't move.

"Limp gimpy figs," he screamed, not comprehending why his touch was having no effect.

The information that Ezra might have appreciated knowing was that, although he had plenty of imagination himself, the power of dreams was already eroding in Reality. People's dreams around the world had degenerated into steady, repetitive, unoriginal, manufactured motion pictures of moving buildings, racing dirt, biting bugs, cloud-bullying airplanes, and windy monsters.

The war against dreams had already begun, and in its infancy it had taken most of the power of Foo from those who had once been there. In the recent past, Ezra had touched buildings and made them walk. Now, with the decline of the world's dreams, there was not even enough power left in his imagination to move a boulder.

"Move!" Ezra yelled at the boulder as dark pieces of leftover Sabine closed in on him.

The rotten bits of Sabine hissed and cried like poison air.

Ezra looked around frantically. He needed an army, and if the trees and rocks weren't going to cooperate, he would have to think smaller. Ezra jumped to the ground, tumbling through the grass.

Sabine's pieces followed.

Ezra reached to touch a pebble, but Sabine's bits snagged the end of him and dragged him back.

"No!" Ezra screamed. "Get your filthy rot off of me."

The black pieces of Sabine swarmed over Ezra like ants on a French fry. They pushed into his tiny mouth and pinned down his legs and arms.

Ezra gagged and spat. He reached out for anything that might help him. Sadly, there was nothing but grass. Ezra wrapped his left hand around a thin blade of grass. It was such a small thing, but the imagination of mankind seemed to still have room to move it.

The grass stood at attention.

Instantly, blades sprang up all over, ripping themselves from the soil that gave them life and bounding toward Sabine as he swarmed Ezra.

The individual blades of grass pulled Sabine from Ezra and began to choke the minute bits by twisting themselves like nooses around each piece. A fistful of grass scraped drops of Sabine from Ezra's mouth.

"Finally," Ezra screamed. "Kill Sabine."

The small bits of Sabine attacked the grass, but the blades kept coming, moving down from the mountain slopes and piling up on Sabine. The grass blades took the bits of Sabine and

twisted themselves around them, choking the half-life right out of them. Sabine's leftovers tore at the grass, splitting the blades into thinner stalks and ripping pieces off until the air was filled with confetti-sized pieces of green and black.

The grass grew angry, wrapping its blades even tighter around the wearying bits of Sabine. Sabine's blackness bit into the grass, trying desperately to overtake the mountains and mountains of freed sod.

The grass collectively contracted, strangling the minute bits of Sabine so forcefully that they popped.

The lawn was winning.

All over, tiny puffs of black burst like burnt corn as the grass grew even more aggressive. A few handfuls of Sabine recognized their defeat and tried desperately to get back to Dennis or Tim, but there was just too much grass. The lawn smothered and strangled and noisily suffocated and extinguished every last hissing bit.

The air was filled with the screech and wail of pain and conquest. The noise rebounded off the mountain walls and gave tourists in the town of Berchtesgaden an extra echo they had not known they would be hearing.

Ezra sat up, choking and spitting for breath. He looked around and clapped. The grass became instantly inanimate again, nothing more than lawn clippings.

"Nice," Ezra laughed triumphantly. "Who knew grass was good for anything?"

Dennis sat up beneath the tree, rubbing his head. He was

now Sabine-free. He pulled off the swim mask that hung around his neck.

"What happened?" he asked, confused.

"It's amazing that someone with such thin hair can be so thick in the head," Ezra bit. "This is what happened. I saved your neck, and now you owe me. Now, put that hose back in your mouth and swim me to the gateway."

"The gateway's done?" Dennis said with bewilderment.

Ezra slapped his own forehead, sick of working with such dim bulbs. Dennis looked over at Tim, who lay unconscious on the bare ground.

"What about him?" Dennis asked.

"What about him?" Ezra growled. "I can't help it if he lacks team spirit. Take me to the gateway." Ezra pointed to the lake.

Dennis opened his palm, and Ezra jumped into it. Dennis stood up and stretched as if it were a requirement. He then stepped off into the water, swimming toward the gateway, as Tim lay motionless on the bare ground.

The lights of St. Bartholomew seemed brighter.

It was the end of a day, but, more important, it was the end of a very dark life. There had been a point in Sabine's existence when he could have leaned in one direction and done good, but instead he had jumped in another direction and found evil to be a fitting companion. Unfortunately for Sabine, he had become so concerned with his future that he had barely noticed the hissing and whispering of the present—whisperings from beneath the soil of Foo that had helped create the evil being he had ended up becoming.

It's not unusual for people to point at the stars and say, "Make a wish." In Foo, however, that would be considered not only rude but just plain foolish. The stars had no interest in the wishes of those who were born to walk on the soil. Likewise, in Reality the soil had no interest in those who lived above it. But it was different in Foo.

There was something up with the soil.

Sabine had been his own man to some extent, but it wasn't until he had begun listening to the Dearth's voice beneath the soil that he had become so evil that even his shadows couldn't stand to be around him. Yet, at the zenith of his reign, Sabine was still nothing more than a puppet being maneuvered by a force he feared but never fully understood. Sort of like Dennis had once been.

Sabine was an evil, dark, misguided puppet whose life was now extinguished. And there was no soul in Foo or Reality who mourned the loss of him. But there were plenty who would soon mourn the fact that he had once lived.

CHAPTER TWENTY-TWO

Distance to Death

The binding on Geth's wrists had worn his skin raw. He could feel thin streams of blood running down over his palms and fingers. Winter and he had been dragged back to the boat and tied up again, the same way as before. Azure had not spoken directly to them since they had left the council room, but they knew from the conversation they had heard that they were going to Lith.

They were hoodless and could see that Azure was up front reading the mist. The air was wet, with no audible or visual evidence of any mist eaters up above.

"At least we can see this trip," Geth said quietly.

"I'm not sure it makes it any better," Winter replied sadly, her green eyes weary. "I just don't think I can do this anymore. I feel like I want to give up."

"Don't say that. We'll make it," Geth insisted. "It won't be much longer until we're on Lith."

"What then?" Winter asked sharply. "Azure kills us? He obviously knows we can die."

Geth was wise enough to let Winter's question hang in the air unanswered. The water sliding up against the side of the boat would have been calming under different circumstances, but as it stood, each rush of liquid was like a wicked odometer ticking off the distance to death.

"I wish I had the words to calm your spirit," Geth finally whispered. "Remember when we were in Reality on the shore of the Konigsee and you doubted your part in this?"

Winter didn't answer, but the sound of her soft crying carried above the motion of the water.

"You wondered if you were really a part of this," Geth continued. "It was a thorny moment, but I wanted to laugh. This is as much about you as about any of us. Leven would not have made it here without you."

A ship rat scurried in front of Winter. It ran over to the side, where it dove off into the water.

"Things look black," Geth admitted. "But with the arrival of a single sun, all can be bright again. Leven's in Foo, and they can do what they wish, but fate is pulling us toward him. And he's walking the course that will lead him to the Want and to his fate. Don't let Azure's sickness seep into your hopes. We will win this, and Foo will stand as fate has always planned."

A flock of mist eaters could now be heard up above. There was a loud thud followed by a big splash as two of them knocked heads and plummeted into the water.

"But we are sailing to our deaths," Winter pointed out. "Light or dark, Azure will have won."

"Nobody wins if Azure has his way," Geth said. "Fate has set the course, and it's up to us to appreciate the ride despite razors or rewards. I've been a seed and a toothpick. I can think of few things smaller, but those were some of the largest moments of my existence. And if fate can take a seed and work with that, then fate can do anything."

"I hope so," Winter said sadly.

"Good," Geth replied. "We're going to need a lot of that."

"Do lithens ever buy sympathy cards?" Winter tried to joke.

"Only for the poor souls who don't believe in fate," Geth smiled. "We'll make it. I promise. Just think how much better it will be when we stand there with Leven and remember that we not only did our part but had one fantastic journey."

A low horn sounded as two more mist eaters knocked heads and fell into the water.

"What's that horn?" Winter asked.

"The mist must be locking up."

"Is that bad?"

"Well, we can't go forward if it is locked," Geth said.

"For how long?"

"Who knows," Geth answered. "Sometimes it can lock up for weeks. If that's the case, I'm certain Azure will steer us under."

"Steer us under?"

Before Geth could answer, the ship violently lurched forward a few feet and then began to tilt downward.

"Under?" Winter said with considerably more panic in her voice.

"Don't worry," Geth insisted. "We'll get wet, but we'll be okay."

"Okay?" Winter asked, dumbfounded. "I can't breathe underwater!"

The ship lurched again and went farther under. Winter pulled at her hands, frantically trying to get free.

"Don't worry," Geth said calmly, but working to free his wrists as well. "Certainly Azure wouldn't risk his own life. A fantastic journey, remember?"

"Don't tell me not to worry," Winter threatened. She shook her head in frustration, and her blonde hair brushed into the side of Geth's face. "Maybe this is how he's planning to kill us."

Geth began working at his wrists a bit faster.

The ship lurched again and lowered even more. Water began to spill over the side rails of the ship. The seawater spilled in around Winter's knees and feet.

"This can't be good," Winter yelled.

She twisted her head and whipped Geth with her hair again. Geth would have replied to her questions, but he was too busy spitting her hair out of his mouth.

"You still haven't explained to me what he's . . ." Winter tried to ask.

The ship thrust forward, its front rapidly dropping two feet. Winter's stomach flopped inward like an undercooked cake. She was tied to a mast by her wrists and ankles and slipping down underwater. The ship tilted further and sunk a couple of feet

more. Winter felt like she was on the top of the slope of some deadly amusement-park ride. The water was now up to her shoulders and pushing up under her chin.

"Help me, Geth!" she cried in desperation.

The ship dropped another two feet. Water rushed in over both Winter and Geth, burying them in the cold blue sea. Winter wanted to scream, but she held onto her last breath, hoping she would miraculously live to take another.

She pulled at her wrists, small strings of her own blood drifting up off of them. The mast they were tied to held fast, giving them no hope of breaking free.

Winter closed her eyes and calculated how many more seconds she would be likely to live.

Unfortunately, it was easy math.

ii

The home of the Want left Leven wishing for something solid and immovable. It was a fantastic place, but the shifting and changing was enough to make his stomach uneasy. He had felt even sicker ever since he had seen a glimpse of what might have been his mother. Leven felt angry at the Want for not allowing him a chance to see her more.

"He could have relit the flame," Leven complained to Clover. "Just for a moment."

"Maybe he couldn't," Clover answered, still invisible and

speaking as quietly as possible. "There's an order to things."

The room they were in twisted a complete half-turn, repositioning the direction they had come from to be back in front of him. The Want disappeared down the hall they had just exited.

"Order?" Leven said sarcastically, following after the Want.

The hallway floor was covered with thick green carpet that swirled in patterns. There were murals of ocean scenes on the walls. As Leven walked, the painted fish swam along with him. The fish gurgled and sprayed water at him occasionally, jumping from wall to wall.

"Are we going up or down?" Clover asked.

"I have no idea," Leven said, wiping some water from his eyes.

"Do your legs hurt?"

"Yes, but they would hurt either direction."

"Hurry!" the Want hollered back. "Step correctly—and if you knew the urgency, you'd run."

"Okay," Leven answered, a fish slapping his arm with its tail.

The Want stopped. "What did you say?" he asked angrily.

"I said—"

The Want fell to his knees as the light around him seemed to puff up and expand. The white ropes of light thickened and spun around him. The Want yelled at the ceiling, and for a brief second Leven could see his eyes.

Instinctively Leven turned away. It was as if he were seeing something that wasn't his privilege to look upon. But, in the case of the Want's eyes, it was also like viewing something so uncom-

fortable that you were repulsed but drawn to it. Before he looked away, Leven had seen the Want's eyes glowing green. They were withered like raisins and hanging loosely in their sockets. Leven couldn't tell if what he had seen was real, but he wasn't at all anxious to get a better look.

The Want knelt on the floor with his arms up. Strands of thick light wrapped around him like white serpents—snapping and snarling. Images flowed within the light, pictures washing down the snakes' bellies.

"What's happening?" Clover asked.

"I'm not sure," Leven said. "But it doesn't look good."

As quickly as it had begun, it ended. The Want stood, tugged on his hood, and turned to walk off as if everything was fine.

"Are you all right?" Leven asked, concerned.

The Want stopped, and his shoulders lowered. "There are many dreams," he answered. "But they are finally changing."

"Is that good?"

The Want's shoulders raised back up and he left the question unanswered.

"We are almost there," he said. "Come."

Leven followed him into a large room lined with windows from the ceiling to floor. The room was square and looked like a giant greenhouse with ivy covering the entire outside like a leafy web. Outside the windows were hundreds of people and creatures. Some licked the windows, while others looked to the sky. A few people were hovering a couple of feet off the ground; others were digging at the dirt. All of them seemed to be frantically looking

for something. Their moaning and digging could be heard through the ivy-covered glass.

"Who are they?" Leven asked.

"Pay them no mind," the Want insisted.

"Yeah, sure," Leven muttered, looking at the glass walls on every side. In the center of the room, a large wooden door opened up into an enclosed atrium. Leven could see through the windows that the atrium went up hundreds and hundreds of feet. At the top of it Leven could see the faint outline of a small room. It looked to be a mile in the air.

"Please say we're not going up there," Leven pointed.

"We're not," Clover answered.

Leven looked in the direction of Clover's voice. "I was asking the Want."

"Sorry, I was just trying to make you feel better."

The Want opened the door and made his way in. Leven reluctantly followed as people outside the glass room screamed and pounded on the glass trying to get the Want's attention.

Once they were inside the atrium the door shut behind them, blocking out any noise. Two torches sprang to life. There was nothing in the room besides the two pockets of torch light.

"I don't see any stairs," Leven said hopefully.

"No stairs," the Want said, disappearing.

Leven looked around, confused. "Where'd he go?"

"I could pretend like I know the answer again," Clover said.

Leven moved to the door and it opened back up. He stepped back and it shut again.

"As least we're not trapped," Leven said.

Leven took a torch from the wall and walked along the edge of the room looking for some other door the Want might have gone through.

There was nothing.

The walls were all wood and went up much higher than the torches' light could reach. Leven set the torch back into the leather holder just as the Want reappeared. Leven jumped back.

"Come on," the Want said impatiently, his eyes still covered.

"Where?" Leven asked, bewildered.

"This is a shaft of unfinished thoughts," the Want explained impatiently. "Finish the thought and it will take you where you wish."

"Anywhere?" Leven said, thinking of Reality.

"Anywhere in the home," the Want said as if Leven were daft.

"Where do we want to go?"

"To the top."

The Want disappeared.

"Wow," Clover whispered in awe.

"All right," Leven said. "So I guess I just think about being up top and . . ."

The moment Leven thought it, it happened.

Instantly he was standing at the top of the shaft under the arch of a large doorway. The doorway opened into the small room that he had seen from down below. The room was much larger than it had looked from the ground. It was circular, with windows on all sides and a round, cone-shaped ceiling overhead.

There was a fire burning in a wide, circular pit in the middle. The room was filled with soft chairs and thick rugs, all dimly lit and serenaded by the soft glow and song of the fire.

The Want was sitting in a tall chair with thick black arms. Leven would have taken the time to compliment him on his digs, but the room was overshadowed by the remarkable view.

Leven turned around, his mouth gaping.

To the left he could see a towering wall of mist, and below that was the Veil Sea. In the far distance he could see three of the other twelve stones. Everywhere he looked there were thick clusters and lines of mist. A fat pink sun moved sideways across the view, blocking Leven's line of sight from the other suns. Pink sunbeams danced against the Veil Sea like searchlights looking for delinquent fish. Leven could see light from the other suns doing the same thing with different colors. When the beams would hit each other, the light would form huge rainbows filled with colors Leven had never seen before.

"It's beautiful," Leven whispered.

"Unless you are responsible for it all," the Want said sadly. "To me it is simply a reminder of how I have failed."

"You haven't failed," Leven said.

"I can hear Geth in your voice," the Want said. "His thoughts are now your words."

"I can't think of anyone I'd rather be like," Leven said honestly.

Clover, still invisible, softly cleared his throat.

"Sit," the Want said. "We haven't much time, but there are words you must hear, and this room is safe to speak in—so high above the soil. Sit."

Leven sat in a large black chair with gold cushions and arms.

"Drink something," the Want insisted. "There will be so little time for you to eat."

The Want waved his hand and a small being stepped out from behind his chair. Leven recognized the being as a Sympathetic Twill, one of the kind creatures who had helped Clover save him in the Swollen Forest.

"Eegish," the Want said, "finish his thoughts."

Eegish moved toward Leven and stopped just in front of his chair. He reached out and patted Leven on the right knee. Leven patted him back on the top of his head. He stared at the little creature, who was smiling sincerely at him.

"Well, what are you thirsty for?" the Want said impatiently.

"Anything, I guess," Leven answered. "Water?"

"You can have anything you like and you wish for water?" the Want scolded.

"I wouldn't mind some of that chocolate stuff," Leven said, looking at the Sympathetic Twill. "When I was trapped in the forest, some beings just like you gave me some kind of chocolate drink."

Eegish looked at Leven like he had just gotten straight A's during a difficult semester. He moved to the arched doorway that led to the shaft of unfinished thoughts.

Eegish walked in, and two seconds later he walked back out with a steaming mug. He handed it to Leven and patted his knee again.

"Thanks," Leven said.

"If you should need something else, just say so," the Want instructed. "Eegish will step in and finish your thought."

Leven was too busy drinking the chocolate drink to respond. The Want drummed his fingers on the arm of his chair and shook. He shifted to the front of his seat and spoke.

"Look around, Leven. What do you see?"

Leven set his mug of chocolate down and glanced carefully around the room, stopping to take in each view.

"Unbelievable beauty," Leven finally answered, his gold eyes flickering.

"How nice it would be to have your eyes," the Want said sadly. "You see so many things I feel have vanished."

"I see what everyone else does," Leven pointed out.

"I don't think so," the Want said. "You see beauty where others see possession or power."

"I see those things too," Leven said. "But I don't want anything to do with them."

"You say that now."

"I can barely handle the gift I have now," Leven admitted.

"Yes," the Want spoke. "Tell me what you have been gifted."

"I can't work any of it too well," Leven apologized. "But when it does work, I can see the future and move things around in it to change the outcome."

"Move things?"

"Like wind, or even people," Leven said. "In Reality I made a woman give me money for food. I also made the wind blow."

"Was there a need for those things to happen?"

"I suppose so," Leven said.

"You stopped Sabine."

"The gift took over."

Egish stepped up to Leven with a plateful of roasted lamb and thick brown bread covered in pale melted butter. Two fat apples sat on the edge of the plate. The smell of the food was intoxicating.

"You must have been thinking about food," the Want explained. "What about Jamoon? How is it that you were able to work your gift in a room where that was forbidden?"

"I'm not sure," Leven said, reaching for the roasted lamb.

"And your eyes burn permanently now."

"Ever since I struggled with Jamoon on the road to Morfit," Leven chewed. "There seems to always be a thin line of gold around them."

"Interesting. And what do you know of your part?"

"Very little," Leven admitted, biting into a gigantic apple.

"Good," the Want said. "It's time to fill you in. Do you trust me?"

Leven thought about lying, but ended up answering honestly, "No."

"It's understandable."

The Want stood up and moved to a small box near the

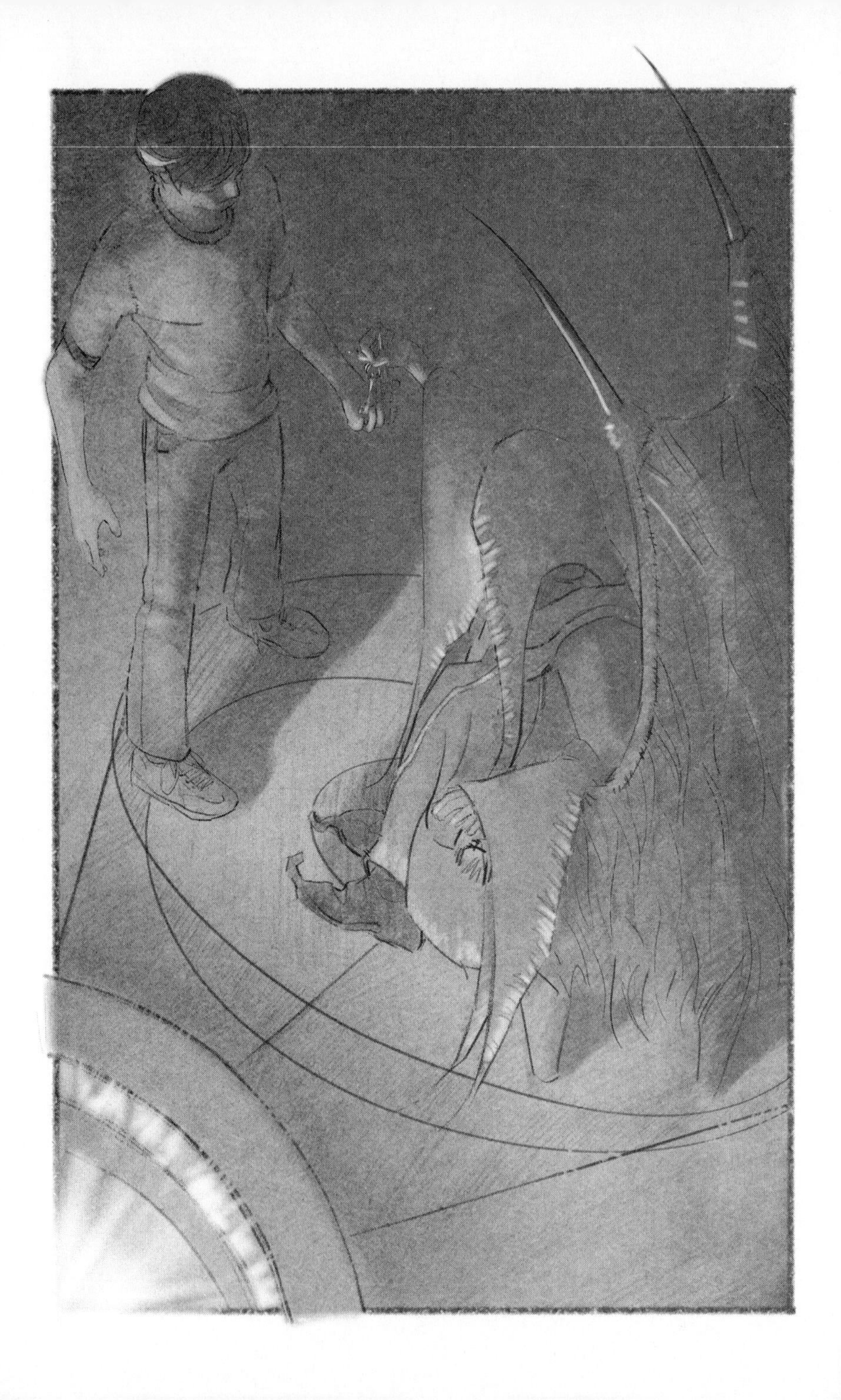

center of the room. He opened the box and pulled out a key.

Leven's eyes widened.

"Is that . . . ?"

"It is," the Want said. "Sabine wasn't the only one who had the ability to use his own shadow. Of course, Sabine's shadows sought to flee him. Mine is simply always up for adventure. It has grown tired of me never leaving Lith. It was my shadow you struggled with outside of the tavern."

A dark-robed shadow moved out from behind the fire and looked at Leven.

"You?"

The shadow moved toward the Want and settled in behind him where a shadow belonged.

"I couldn't let you just give the key to the secret," the Want said. "What a dangerous move."

"He was going to hurt Clover."

"Unfortunately, it's not unheard of for those we love to get hurt when we are trusting fate," the Want said. "There are worse things than Clover being killed."

Leven couldn't think of any.

"How did you know about the key?" Leven said, his mouth open because of the shock and because he was trying to fit a large bite of bread in.

"I am the Want. All of Foo flows through me. The second I felt you give up that key, I knew I had to act. Fortunately, my shadow was up for a ride."

"I'm sorry," Leven said, feeling weak.

The Want shook and screamed, the light around him filling the room and then being sucked back into him. He shook it off.

"The key's yours," the Want said, handing it to Leven. "There are many who desire it, but you must give it to nobody. It still has a very important role to play and is best kept in your hands. It is one of seven and part of the end of Foo."

Leven took the key and flipped it over in his palm.

"I need you to trust me," the Want said. "I hope the key shows I trust you."

Leven nodded.

"Foo is at odds," the Want continued. "For many years now it has been struggling with its purpose. In the beginning, Foo was a perfect place."

Clover sighed as if bored.

"Your sycophant is still here?" the Want asked angrily.

Leven nodded as the temperature in the room chilled. The fire stood tall.

"He needs to step out," the Want insisted. "Have him leave."

"Why?"

"Have him leave!" the Want yelled.

"I can take a hint," Clover whispered into Leven's left ear. "I'll be in that shaft finishing some thoughts."

"Make sure you stay there," Leven said.

"I need to see him walk away," the Want said.

Clover materialized and defiantly walked out of the room and into the arched doorway. The Want moved his hand, and the door shut behind Clover. The edges around the door burned like

heated metal. As it cooled, Leven could see that the door was now a solid wall of wood. Eegish patted Leven on the hand to comfort him for his loss.

"Now," the Want said. "You destroyed the gateway?"

"Yes."

"Do you know why the Waves brought you here?

"To see you."

"Yes," the Want said. "But there's more. Fate is pulling itself too tightly. In a short time the strain will be so great that something will have to give. You are the token that will relax the strain."

"Me?"

"There will come a time very shortly when fate will ask a great favor of you."

Leven wanted to speak up. He wanted to list the sacrifices he had already made. The past few weeks of his life had been nothing but change and sacrifice. He had lost his miserable life to take up in a realm where danger seemed more prevalent than happiness. He had blown up the only exit out of Foo. He had lost Amelia, put Clover and all the sycophants in mortal danger, and almost died a dozen times. Leven couldn't think of anything that could be worse than what he had already pushed through.

"It will be required of you to trust me and act when instructed," the Want said softly.

Leven's soul contracted woefully, the gold in his eyes disappearing.

"The gateway was a farce," the Want said calmly. "Anyone could have destroyed it."

"What?" Leven asked.

"Geth was instructed to tell you otherwise, but we left it open so that you could make it through. Once you were here, we needed you to stay. You destroyed your only way out."

"I don't believe you."

"I don't care," the Want said.

"Why would Geth tell me—"

"Geth was instructed to say a number of things," the Want trembled subtly. "Some were true and some were for the benefit of bigger things."

"And Winter?"

"She remembers nothing," the Want said. "Her part in this has expired. We entrusted her with the very key I had to get back. What matters now is you. If you wield the sword, fate might have a chance."

"What do I have to do?" Leven asked. "I won't kill anyone."

"Interesting assumption," the Want smiled. "You destroyed Sabine and Jamoon."

"I had no choice."

"Well, when your task appears you *will* have a choice, and you must make it."

Eegish put his arm around Leven as thoughts swirled though Leven's mind.

"Do you know what the task is?" Leven asked.

"I can't tell you that."

The weather outside the room began to twist and pulsate. A flock of Tea birds were blown from down to up. Mist from the great wall that made up the Hidden Border blew up against the windows as large, starfish-looking birds smacked into the glass and slid down slowly.

"I don't understand," Leven said, sitting forward in his chair. "I was brought here for this task, and you can't tell me what it is?"

"Listen carefully," the Want said slowly. "The realm of Foo was created before the span of Reality. It was placed here to give dreams an actual shot at becoming real. The lithens, the siids, the Waves, and the sycophants were the first creatures to populate our land. The first Want was put in place to rule above ground and the Dearth to manage the soil."

"First Want?" Leven asked.

"There have been three before me," the Want answered. "That's not important now. As dreams increased, more and more beings and creatures were introduced into our realm. It seemed as if powerful dreams were penetrating our borders daily, bringing to life some new animal or object. At first it was wonderful. The use of metal was allowed, and people created and manipulated dreams as if it were an honor.

"People accepted their fate.

"But there began to be problems, most of them surfacing around the misuse of metal. Some railed against what they perceived as bondage and talked of re-creating the seven keys and unleashing the power that would help them overturn fate. Nits began to build weapons, and the dreams they manipulated were filled with their thoughts of war and killing. So there was division between the nits and the cogs. The ungifted cogs felt as if Foo

had done them wrong. Then, as more and more rants were born to nits and cogs, an even greater unbalance began to crop up in the hearts of those who should know better. Great wars ensued over the use of metal. In the end, hundreds of thousands died and all metal was stripped from buildings and homes and buried by the roven."

Leven's eyes widened.

"For years after the wars things seemed better," the Want continued. "Then your grandfather made the tragic mistake of finding a way out. Foolish—such a stupid mistake. Most here accepted their fate before that, but when people began to envision the possibility of returning to Reality still possessing their Foo-found gifts, their hearts became selfish and misguided. And the soil took on a life of its own."

"What do you mean?" Leven asked.

"The real evil in Foo lies beneath our feet."

Eegish looked down.

"It seems as if the very soil of Foo hungers to touch the physical," the Want said. "There was something in the act of burying the metal and covering it with gunt that woke the dirt. It in turn began to feed off the bodies of those who had been buried but their dark souls had never been lifted."

"Dark souls?"

"Those who live nobly are lifted up. But those who have chosen otherwise are absorbed into the soil, increasing the power of the Dearth. It pulses with their evil desires and now wishes to touch Reality and taste the earth there . . ."

The Want stopped himself and looked at Leven.

"I've said too much," he apologized. "Don't let the haze of my words distract you from what you must do. The time will come, Leven, when you will have to choose to save Foo or step down and let the evil have complete control."

"I would do almost anything for Foo."

"Silence," the Want whispered fiercely. "I don't want your assurance. There will come a day, very soon, when fate will put you where you must stand. There you will hear my voice and see the means by which you can accomplish the task. You will know clearly what you must do. And whereas you have a choice, you cannot fail."

Leven trembled, looking away. He saw his image reflected in the glass wall. The white streak in his hair seemed more prominent and the gold had returned to his eyes.

"If you do ignore fate, it's over."

"Are you saying there's no hope?" Leven asked, irritated.

The Want stared at Leven. Or at least that was the way his head was turned. It was impossible to tell what he was looking at through the hood that covered his eyes.

"There's only one way," the Want spoke dryly.

"Tell me," Leven said, feeling the fire that made his eyes burn. "What will I have to do?"

The Want shivered.

"I gave you that key so that you would trust me," the Want breathed. "The time will come when you will hear my voice in your head. At that moment, fate will place before you the way to

do what you must do. There is evil much darker than what is at hand. Do you remember the secret of the sycophants?"

"I wish I didn't."

"You know more than any," the Want said softly. "Geth was wise to bring you here. You are hope to me."

"Where is Geth?" Leven asked uncomfortably. "And Winter?"

"Don't worry about them," the Want sighed. "Their future is theirs to make right. But I will tell you that death has them in view."

"You can't mean that," Leven said, standing.

"You can't bend fate," the Want warned.

"Where are they?"

"They'll be here soon enough," the Want said.

Eegish took Leven's right hand and tried to soothe him.

"No," Leven said, pulling his hand away and looking at the Want with burning gold eyes. "You brought me here to tell me that my friends are dying? And that the only way I can stop all of this is to do something so unspeakable I can't even know what it is?"

"Such a hot soul," the Want said. "One day you will speak to me in softer tones. I see every dream that comes in. Even now, millions of dreams circle around my eyes, begging to be seen and realized. I know what you will do, Leven. I knew the moment Antsel left with Geth and Winter that one day you would stand before me and accept the task I am handing you now."

"I can't just blindly accept!" Leven argued.

"Then you know nothing of fate."

"You're talking about killing, aren't you?"

"I'm talking about saving the whole of Foo."

"*You* do it," Leven said passionately.

"I wish I could," the Want lamented. "But fate will not allow me."

"I need to see Geth."

"Let's hope, for your sake, that fate feels the same way," the Want said. "As it stands, you will most likely never see him again."

Leven had never felt sicker.

The Want unsealed the door to the shaft of unfinished thoughts, and Clover came out wearing a small velvet hat with a feather in it. He had shoes on his feet and was carrying a stuffed animal under each arm. In his mouth was a stick of candy.

"Wow," he said, taking the candy from his mouth. "I've got to get one of those shafts for myself."

Clover looked back and forth at the solemn faces both Leven and the Want were wearing. Eegish waved a friendly wave.

"Sorry," Clover said. "Did I interrupt something? Because I can go back in the shaft if you need me to."

"There isn't time," the Want said, standing. "We must go."

The Want's shadow stood up next to him.

"Stay," the Want said to his shadow.

The shadow slipped back down into the chair.

"I can't stand having him clinging to me," the Want said angrily. "He's been nothing but trouble ever since he brought back that key. Now, *you* come. Follow."

Leven didn't want to go anywhere. In fact, if he was being honest with himself, he would have preferred to curl up into a ball and fade away forever. Fortunately for all of mankind, that wasn't an option.

CHAPTER TWENTY-THREE

WET FROM THE INSIDE OUT

Winter felt like someone had thrown her down and dumped a couple of loaded bookcases directly on her chest.

She couldn't breathe.

Water filled her lungs and drowned any flicker of hope. Bound, she could do nothing but accept the death that seemed so imminent. The ship was slowly slipping deeper and deeper under the surface. It moved through the water like a ghost, all manner of underwater sea creatures swirling around in pockets of dance and rhythm.

Winter would have been amazed by how gorgeous it was, except for that pesky fact that she was going to die.

It was a true downer in a scene of unspeakable beauty.

Winter watched her last breath escape her lips. The bubbles, like tracers, floated upward in a hypnotic pattern as her eyelids closed. In a flashback to when they had stepped into Foo, she could

see Leven, standing by Amelia in Amelia's home. She could see the wonder in his eyes as he viewed Foo for the first time. She could see Clover blink slowly, and she could see the toothpick Geth.

Winter's body relaxed.

Light touched the outside of her eyelid, and she felt her hair drifting like unspooled thread into and out of her face. She opened her mouth, and warmth filled her lungs. If this was death, she was much more comfortable than she had anticipated.

She could feel her heart beating and her chest rising.

Winter opened her eyes. Everything was light, with shimmering traces of silver around the edges. Fish looked like tinsel-covered lightbulbs popping through the water. The magic before her eyes distracted her momentarily from the reality that she was breathing beneath the water.

Winter turned to get a glimpse of Geth. He was tied behind her, but when she cranked her neck as far as possible she could see the side of his face. There was a large yellow blob covering his entire face and half of his body. From what she could see, she could have sworn that Geth was smiling. Something had attached itself to their faces and was allowing them to breathe. Her fear drifted off like beads of oil. She could breathe, and not only that, but the water caused her to float just enough that the bindings and position she was tied in no longer hurt. Winter heard a muffled sound and turned to see Geth trying to talk to her.

She couldn't make out what he was saying, so she simply smiled as large schools of glowing fish darted around her. Winter

laughed, caught up in the beauty of it. For a moment she seemed able to forget that her life was in peril and that the next moment might be her last.

Winter saw light gray beasts with multiple tentacles pushing through the water like wet dishrags. They turned their mushy heads to look at the ship and then moved on. Rivers of red, molten-looking material oozed along the floor of the ocean, small fish and sea creatures lining the redness and touching it with their lips like deer at a mountain stream.

Throughout the water Winter could see the bright lights of dreams pushing up into Foo. Most were not strong enough to make it up through the weight of the water, but a few shot past them and all the way to the surface. The dreams were filled with images that ran like wet paint, their presence adding to the overall surreal feeling.

Winter's green eyes fluttered as thousands of waterflies swarmed the open deck of the ship, lining the railing, their colorful wings twinkling like tiny lights.

The view was so intoxicating that Winter lost track of time and distance and was surprised to feel the slight tug of the ship moving up. She wanted to make it stop, but she knew there was nothing she could do.

The ship shivered and pushed upward again.

The waterflies dispersed and all the fish and creatures moved away to allow the ship room to rise. Winter could feel the pull on her head as they climbed closer to the surface.

The light became greater.

The ship lurched and creaked, forcing itself up through the water.

Winter could see the sky.

The ship's mast broke the surface of the water, and in a few moments Winter watched as her head rose above the sea and into a misty afternoon.

She wanted to cry: not so much for the pain she would soon feel again, but because what she had just witnessed had been so beautiful. Leaving it was like stepping away from a garden you had spent years manicuring to stagger into a field of nothing.

Water drained from the sides of the ship as it popped back up onto the surface. The film around Winter's face and neck slid off like a wide patch of Jell-O, gliding across the deck and out through the holes in the railing.

Winter breathed in deep. Her wrists and knees instantly began to hurt again. She shook her hair, hitting Geth on the side of his face.

"Are you okay?" Geth asked.

"I didn't want to come up."

"I feel the same way," Geth said. "I love traveling below the surface. It's slower, but so much more interesting."

"How could we breathe?"

"The Baadyn," Geth answered. "They're magnificent beings who live in spots near water. They have the ability to extract their souls and rinse them clean. They're hinged at the waist, and when they get near water they can unhinge and let their souls slide out. Their souls swim through the water for a few hours while the

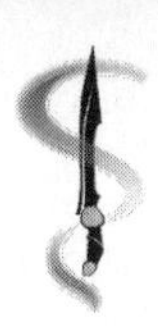

shells of their bodies lie lifeless on the shore. Luckily for us, the clean souls hunger to do good. They could instantly sense that we couldn't breathe and wanted to help. They just latched on, and we got the benefit of their lungs."

"They can wash their souls?" Winter asked in disbelief.

"Thankfully," Geth answered. "They get so mean and nasty when their souls are dirty."

In the distance Winter could see a huge land mass. It was covered with mountains and valleys, and a green layer of trees spread unevenly over its surface.

"Lith," Geth said.

"I can't tell how to feel," Winter said. "Are we closer to or further from death?"

"What does it matter?" Geth answered sincerely. "We are headed in the direction we must go. Don't let fear ruin the moment."

From anyone else, such a statement would have made Winter angry. But Geth spoke with such passion and belief that it was hard not to be affected positively by it. They were sailing to their destruction and Geth was enjoying the ride.

"I'm glad you're with me," Winter grinned.

Winter now wanted Geth to tell her that everything would be all right—that they would win this fight, and that Foo and Leven would live forever. Instead, he stuck to his role as Geth and simply said, "Likewise."

The mist thinned and the ship sailed closer to the up side of Lith.

CHAPTER TWENTY-FOUR

The Beginning of an End

Sycophant Run was dark. A metallic shimmer had settled over the entire place, giving even the trees the look of metal under the moonlight. From every direction the sound of conversation lifted softly through the trees and up into the cool air. The smell of warm food and cinnamon brew was as prevalent as the perfume of fantrum blossoms.

Things were not so tranquil in the Chamber of Stars. Rast had called the group together to deliver the worrisome news.

"You're sure?" Mule asked. "Absolutely positive?"

"Sadly, yes, it's not there," Rast said.

"Maliciousness!" Goat exclaimed, the ceiling of stars twinkling brightly. "There is evil lurking."

"It was well hidden?" Brindle asked.

"Very well hidden," Rast answered slowly. "I know of no better place it could have been sealed. I know . . ."

Rast stopped himself from saying more.

"You know something," Reed said. "You suspect someone."

"As always, you are more perceptive than the rest," Rast complimented. "I fear that the key could have been taken by only one person."

"Who?" Brindle insisted.

"It has been locked up for years," Rast said. "I have purposely not visited it for fear of someone following. There is only one person I can think of who might have known where it was. And if she did, she might very well have followed me years ago to discover the code."

"She?" Reed asked skeptically.

"Lilly," Rast said.

The sycophants gasped.

"Your daughter?" Mule asked.

"She was hurting greatly last time we saw her," Rast said with embarrassment. "Her burn had left her, and she wanted badly to get her back. She was determined to do anything."

"Her burn?" Goat said. "If I remember right, she was the girl sent to bring Leven here."

Rast nodded. "Winter."

"Where's Lilly now?" Brindle asked.

"We don't know," Rast said sadly. "She still to this day causes us heartache. It has been more years than we can count since we've seen her."

"What reason would she have for taking the key?" Reed asked.

"I don't know," Rast said. "All I know is she was terribly angry and looking for any way to get her burn back. It was as if she had been poisoned. She saw nothing but hatred. All beauty was gone from her spirit and eyes."

"The Lore Coils speak of Leven releasing the secret," Mule said nervously. "How would he have come by the key if Lilly had it?"

"Seems obvious," Goat said angrily. "It's what I have always said, there's evil tracking us. They send this girl to retrieve Leven and give him the key to destroy us all. We're not in favor with the Want. They seek to mesh the worlds, and they know that only the sycophants can fight off such a foolish act. Our home is what they will come for, and our peace is not a concern or care of anyone."

"Calm yourself, Goat," Rast said, holding up his small palms. "The secret was loose, but it has not spread itself. We know nothing of their plans to ruin us. We must move quickly but with wisdom."

"We know enough to signal our breed to be ready," Mule insisted. "I say it's time to alert our families. Trouble walks toward us and we must be prepared to lunge. I will not have darkness molest those I love."

"I agree," Brindle said.

"Me too," Goat insisted. "We must protect Sycophant Run."

"Sycophant Run?" Rast said with disgust. "It's evil to say this is about just us. You speak as if you don't know your own history. This is about Foo. This is about the dreams of those we will never know and the honor of making Reality better than it is. It's about the fulfillment of our creation. We are not tharms looking for

something to stare at. We are sycophants with a great duty to hold upon our shoulders. The second we make this about us alone, we will face failure."

Reed, Brindle, and Goat looked down.

"That's all well and fine," Mule said softly. "But so often we are the last ones thought about. I won't see my breed die at the expense of everyone else's selfishness and lust to have more than they can control."

"Hear, hear," Reed said.

"We won't lose," Rast said firmly. "We are the last line of defense. We stand as the final obstacle. In front of us stand nits and cogs and lithens and all those who have not stopped looking at each day as a chance to better themselves. If we fall, it is because those who should have stood before us collapsed under the weight of their own desires. Our honor and our success are one and the same."

The council was quiet as the dim stars overhead twittered and blinked.

"Should we try to find Lilly and get some answers from her?" Goat finally asked.

"I think that should be one of our first steps," Rast said softly. "Go, do whatever it takes to bring her back."

Mule cleared his throat.

"Yes," Rast said resignedly. "Bite her if you must. But bring her home. I will travel to the Want. He's not quick to embrace us these days, but he'll give me an audience."

"And the pegs?" Brindle asked.

"Tell them everything," Rast said. "Those who guard our shores should be kept from nothing. If the secret's loose and the rants do gather, then there's a very real possibility that our land will be attacked. The pegs must sharpen their claws. I have a feeling the Dearth is awakening."

All of them gasped and mumbled.

"What of the secret?" Mule asked, nervously. "Surely, I don't tell the posted pegs of that?"

"That it was let loose?" Rast questioned.

"Not *that* secret," Mule said self-consciously. "The marsh?"

"No!" Rast answered quickly. "It will come to that only if the end appears in full. Till then, nobody but those fate has already filled in will speak of that. Die first. Do you understand?"

"Of course," they all answered.

"Go," Rast waved. "Our journey begins this moment."

They all stood and put their hands on each other's left shoulder, forming a circle. Rast looked at each of them carefully. His eyes were filled with admiration and gratitude.

"We are small," Rast said reverently. "But our hearts beat as loud as any. For so long we've sat here talking about things that apathy has allowed us time to contemplate. Now fate is moving with speed. Prepare your stomachs for a large drop."

They all nodded and then one by one slipped out of the starry tree and into the dark.

CHAPTER TWENTY-FIVE

Longing for More

Magic—there are those who say it doesn't exist. In fact, Clover himself has made that statement before. But all it takes is the careful study of any leaf to realize that something magical is going on somewhere—which makes it odd that Clover would say such a thing, seeing how he cares for leaves.

Magic is a tricky thing.

Often it is explainable. People fly through the air in planes and live underwater in submarines. Plants grow within weeks and cities operate and sustain millions of people. A person can talk to practically anyone almost anywhere around the world instantly. People's images are transported by photo in the time it takes to press a button. Dinosaurs seem real, huge apes exist, and other worlds are a movie ticket away.

Perhaps nothing is more magical than the book. Paper, glue, and some words and you are taken away from where you sit,

stand, dance, or lean to greater understanding or experience. There was a time when the written word was almost always believable—if it was on paper, it had to be true. But there are so many written words these days, so many keyboards typing so many letters, that even the gullible are cautious.

It is with great concern that the story of Foo has been written and preserved. To believe in Foo is to believe in more than magic—it is to believe in dreams coming true. It is to understand that the time is coming when the limitation we place on ourselves will no longer be an obstacle that we have to climb over.

To believe in Foo is to relax the mind and let imagination win. It is to step into fear and let fate worry about the outcome. It is to want those standing next to you to dream as big as possible so that your own future will be that much brighter.

It is a magical thing.

But as Leven followed after the Want, thinking about what he had just learned, his heart full of concern for Geth and Winter, Foo didn't feel very magical to him. In fact, Foo felt like a place he wished he could disappear from.

Poof!

Thoughts of never knowing what he now knew crowded his mind. He half wished he were still in Oklahoma being picked on by Addy and Terry and having to worry about no one but himself.

No, Foo did not feel very magical.

It felt heavy and cold. Each step Leven took made his head hurt. Even the company of Clover seemed painful. Clover had

shoved everything he had gotten in the room of unfinished thoughts into his void—everything except the small felt hat, which he still wore.

"I think it makes me look older," Clover said, riding on Leven's shoulder.

Leven didn't reply. They were back in the large, greenhouse-looking room moving toward a glass wall that seemed to have no doorway, carefully following the Want. Outside the windows people still looked in, pointing and begging for the Want to give them attention.

"Who are they?" Leven asked.

"They're fools," the Want answered. "They come from all over Foo to stand in wait for any trace of dreams that might fall from the room above."

"Why?"

"The residue," the Want scoffed. "My eyes have done the work, and the ashes drift down so that those below might taste the flavor of finished dreams. Enough of it and they can fly momentarily—too much of it and they lose all sense of who they once were. These souls are lost."

A man was feverishly licking the windows.

"They have given their minds for a small drop of some other person's dreams."

"Can't they just manipulate dreams like everyone else?"

"These are not nits," the Want snapped. "These are cogs and other ungifted beings. Besides, the residue of that which has passed through my eyes provides tastes far sweeter than any

dream. Of course, as the effect wears off, the darkness they knew before is stronger than ever. Now hurry, the time is coming and we've still one more trail to follow."

As they walked up to the wall a long, rectangular hole opened up in the floor, exposing a set of wooden stairs. Leven felt some relief that they went down. The Want moved quickly down the stairs with Leven behind him. In a few moments they could hear no sound of those outside licking the windows.

"What does it matter how we walk?" Leven asked, his soul feeling restless.

"Questions," the Want ranted. "What happens in Lith is repeated in the rest of Foo. I can't just walk from here to there without affecting the feelings of thousands. I know what I must show you. I know what I must tell you, and I know that there are ways and places I must do it in. In the end the pattern you mark out will become familiar and important to your memory."

"I don't understand."

"Let's hope that someday you do."

The Want scratched at the wall as he walked. The stairs led to a tunnel whose arched walls had been made by the careful stacking of bones.

"Many died in the metal wars," the Want hollered back. "Their bones help to remind me of their sacrifice. It's hard not to be selfish."

"How nice," Clover whispered. "Hasn't he ever heard of a plaque, or maybe some memorial photos?"

They stepped down two more stairs and the floor became wet,

covered in half a foot of running water. The water seeped through the bones and moved in a circular motion across the floor.

"Watch for snakes," the Want warned. "And be quick."

It was an unnecessary warning, as Leven had already spotted the hundreds of yellow lines swimming through and along the walls of bones.

"They're lemon snakes," Clover whispered. "They look dangerous, but I actually wouldn't mind having one for a pet. Just don't let them bite you."

"I wasn't planning to," Leven answered, amazed at how many there were.

"Of course," Clover continued. "They would never bite anyone unless you stepped on one."

Leven stepped on a large one.

"Oops," Clover said as the snake snapped its head back and dug its teeth into Leven's right ankle. "You should always just shuffle around lemon snakes."

"Oww!" Leven yelled.

"Pull it off quick!" Clover hollered. "It's draining itself."

Leven could see the snake's color seeping from its body and into his leg. The tail of the snake was now clear as the color level lowered. Leven grabbed ahold of it and tried to tug it off, but it wouldn't give.

"Pull harder!" Clover said, grabbing the snake's tail with his small hands in an effort to help Leven.

The Want kept on walking. He had seen Leven get bitten, but he paid it no mind, not slowing his pace at all.

"It won't come off," Leven said frantically.

"It will once it's empty," Clover said mournfully.

"What then?" Leven asked. "Is it poison?"

"Not actually."

The snake was now completely empty of color. It looked like an outline of a snake drawn in black ink. It released its bite, dropped from Leven's ankle, and lethargically swam away.

"What does 'not actually' mean?" Leven asked, pulling up his pant leg to look at the bite. There were two small holes surrounded by a burgeoning patch of yellow. The yellow crept up his leg and spread out over his entire body. In a few seconds Leven's face looked like an odd-shaped sun.

Leven's cheeks began to burn. He could feel his knees and elbows twisting inward. His face became drawn as his lips pushed outward. His toes and fingers were drawing into themselves. He could feel his forehead furrow and fold. He felt like his blood had been replaced with acid. His knees drew in, his stomach crinkled, and his rear end gathered. The heels on his feet became concave as they popped in.

Leven was literally puckering up, his skin turning a bright shade of yellow.

He could barely walk, his legs feeling as if they were receiving rug burns from some invincible citrus ghost with incredibly big hands and a strong grip. Leven fell into the water and rolled onto his rounded back. His legs pulled in and he tucked his head to his chest, forming a big ball.

Leven rolled in the water like a slick cork. He bounced

against the bone walls, trying to grab something to steady himself. Unfortunately, his withered hands couldn't get hold of anything.

Snakes with little or no color oozed out of the walls and began to swim toward Leven. They looked like withered tadpoles approaching a yellow pond. Snakes sprang from the water to latch onto Leven—five bit into his neck, twenty on his back, ten on his right leg alone.

Leven moaned as they bit him. He tried to fight them off, but he had no control of his puckered limbs.

The attached snakes began to fill with color—draining the zest from Leven's veins. The sting of the bites faded as each ounce of sour left Leven's body. Snakes that were as thin as noodles gorged on Leven's creamy center and bulked up, looking like swollen Twinkies.

Leven smiled at them.

"This is my favorite part," Clover said, hanging onto the bone wall. "Once my brother got bit by a lemon snake, and after the sour had been sucked from his veins he was kinder to me than he had ever been. It only lasted an afternoon, but it was a great afternoon."

Leven couldn't remember ever having felt bad in his life. His body relaxed and returned to form. Of course, his heart felt so large in his chest that he had a hard time steadying himself as he stood. He waved at the snakes and shuffled so as to not upset them.

"That's the prettiest color of yellow," Leven said, pointing down at the snakes. "Like a flower."

"Yeah, like a flower," Clover agreed. "Shuffle faster so we don't completely lose the Want."

"What a great suggestion," Leven smiled. "Thanks."

"You're spreading it on a little thick," Clover said.

Leven looked more horrified than when the snake had bit him.

"I am so sorry," Leven apologized, not wanting to disappoint anyone.

"I'll be okay," Clover said.

"Hurry!" the Want yelled from up ahead. "She's waiting."

"Do you have any idea who he's talking about?" Clover asked.

Leven shook his head. "It feels like spring," was his only answer.

The walls turned into long piles of unorganized bones. Leven shuffled through the water and snakes smiling as if he had just been voted most likely to have a completely blissful life.

The Want stopped to wait for them. He looked in the direction of Leven and shook.

"People should shuffle," he said. "But perhaps it's fate that your mind is in a clean, happy state."

The Want stopped in front of a large, ornate door, decorated with a carving of an angel touching the ground.

"I've shown only two people this before," the Want said.

"Thank you so much," Leven cooed.

"It's not a privilege," the Want said. "It's a weight. Follow me."

The door opened. Clover pushed Leven, and Leven moved into the hole right behind the Want. The tunnel was dark, with

wet strings of dirt hanging from the ceiling like multiple uvulas. Leven hit his head against one and the tunnel seemed to choke.

Leven looked concerned for it.

"You're worse than when I bit you in Reality," Clover said softly.

"You were just doing what you had to," Leven said nicely.

They kept walking down the dark tunnel. Leven began to hum.

A bright light shone in the far distance. As the light increased, the sound of crying reached their ears. Leven's happiness waned. He felt a great sense of despair and sorrow for whoever was wailing.

"What is that?" Leven asked, clutching his chest.

"I have no idea," Clover said. "I've never been anywhere near this part of Foo."

Leven kept his eyes on the back of the Want, moving through the tunnel at a quick step. The light grew brighter, and Leven could see a person in the midst of it.

It was a woman.

She wore a short green gown and had hair the color of sunny water. She was caught in a teardrop-shaped cage of metal that hung from the ceiling by a thick chain. Her skin was white but glowed slightly green. She had tiny feet and hands, and a face that looked like a brand-new flower after a long freeze. Her soft, sun-swept hair flowed down her back and twisted in the air like fine wire. She floated in her cage, looking like the filament of a bright bulb.

Leven loved her.

Her moaning increased as the Want stepped from the tunnel into the domed room where she hung. The ceiling was tiled with orange and yellow clay squares. Symbols Leven didn't recognize were etched up and down the walls.

Leven and Clover stood there speechless. The woman's beauty was unsurpassable, but the hurt in her eyes was equally devastating.

"Who is she?" Leven asked desperately.

"Quiet," the Want said.

The woman looked at them and fluttered slightly higher in her cage.

"Why?" she asked the Want. "Why do you come back?"

"Silence," the Want insisted. "You should thank me for the company, Phoebe."

"It is a reminder of what I hunger for," she cried. "A cruel picture of what I don't possess."

"I need the boy to lay eyes on you," the Want said, ignoring her lament.

"What boy?" Phoebe asked, looking at Leven.

Leven was taller now than he had been only hours ago. The things he had experienced and been told on Lith had aged him quickly. His shoulders and arms were lean but strong, and he stood like a being that had wandered through a number of difficult experiences and somehow made it out.

"Look at him," the Want demanded. "It's Leven."

Phoebe appeared bored.

"She's a longing," the Want explained. "And she is the very last of her kind."

Leven walked around her slowly. Phoebe moved like liquid in a lava lamp, up and down, expanding and contracting in a hypnotic manner.

"She's beautiful," Leven said, still dizzy from the snakes.

"Few beings even remember the existence of her kind," the Want continued. "We've removed all mention and illustration of them from our history."

Leven looked concerned.

The Want grabbed the bars of Phoebe's cage and shook it violently. "She can't be buried," he said, disgusted. "Her being repels the dirt. She can't starve to death—the very air feeds her—and water won't steal her breath. She can age, but it's slow."

"Let me free," Phoebe said, "and I will bother no one."

Leven moved closer to her.

"She was placed here at the end of the wars," the Want said, as if he were talking about an inanimate object that he had hanging on his wall. "She was not easy to capture. There was great discussion about what to do with her, but we had to be certain not only that metal was disposed of but that those who longed to work with it would feel the very desire disappear."

"There's always more to desire," Phoebe said sadly.

"True," the Want shook. "Unfortunately, the desire for self needs no additional representation in Foo. Those with dark

hearts and an ear for the soil have found ranker things than metal to lust for."

"My bondage is the reason for Foo's failings," Phoebe said urgently. "There's a balance. Fate cannot move as it should without longing."

The Want waved her words away. "You say things I have no concern for. Fate has placed you on a path that will end with your quiet death. Unless . . ."

The Want looked at Leven as if he would finish the thought.

Leven shook his foggy head, wishing he could think clearly. The woman he saw wasn't a threat to anything but maybe ugliness. She hung there like a solution to all things dirty and sordid. Her eyes made Leven question his own creation. He felt like a second-rate being in her presence.

"You must know that she is here," the Want said to Leven. "Look at her."

Leven couldn't stop himself from doing so. The feelings she brought to life were so strong and alive that they seemed to weigh Leven's shoulders down. He tried to smile at her, but his gaping mouth wouldn't work properly.

"Why?" Leven finally managed to ask. "Why is she here?"

"Foo has many layers," the Want said. "Too many do what they think is correct based on what their eyes see. But Foo is a place where you can't rely on your eyes to tell you everything. You, Leven, are not like the other souls who have stepped into this realm. You're a part of the story—a fork in the road—and the

future of Foo looks to divide where you stand. Phoebe is a distraction. She is a part of Foo's past that has not been completely taken care of."

"I don't understand," Leven said honestly.

Phoebe began to moan and cry again.

"Can't you let her go?" Leven pleaded.

"I hold the key," the Want said. "But it will not be my hand that turns the lock."

"Give it to me, then," Leven insisted, a bit of sour flowing back into his veins. "Let me free her."

Phoebe moved to the bars, her face changing as a glimmer of hope brightened her expression. The Want smiled.

"Isn't the fight for metal over?" Leven reasoned. "You won. She should be freed."

"No!" the Want snapped.

Phoebe sobbed.

"I've done what I needed," the Want said. "I've told you of your task, Leven, and shown you the longing. Fate will not let you forget. Now we must go."

"I won't leave her," Leven said, closing his eyes and wishing his gift into action.

"There's no future to change," the Want laughed, picking up on what Leven was trying to do. "Fate has yet to pick a course of action. Your gift is useless here. Now, follow me."

Leven's heart boiled. His eyes were reluctant to glow, but he could feel a pull inside himself, shifting his soul around. He couldn't tell if it was the sour that had been extracted from him

or if he really cared for Phoebe. Either way, Phoebe's cries were so sincere and so mournful that Leven couldn't bring himself to walk away.

"She'll be here when you return," the Want insisted. "Now come."

"No."

The Want turned to Leven. His eyes were still covered by the hem of his hood, but Leven could feel him looking right at him.

"I'm not leaving her."

Phoebe began to shine.

"Dim your luster," the Want said to Phoebe. "You'll not be freed today."

"Then I'll remain here," Leven insisted. "She needs me."

"That's just the snake talking," the Want growled. "I should have done this sooner."

He raised his right hand, and Leven was lifted from the ground. The Want flexed his fingers, and Leven began to shrink.

"What's . . ." Leven tried to say, but his mouth was shrinking so rapidly he couldn't get the words out.

The Want's right hand moved in a circular motion as his left hand extracted a small wooden box from his robe. Leven shrank even further as Phoebe cried violently. Leven became two feet tall, then a foot, and then only a few inches. He was floating in the air like a giant dust mite.

The Want willed him closer, and Leven flew across the room directly toward the Want. Leven's arms and legs were kicking and flailing. The Want placed him into the small wooden box. He

snapped the lid shut and commanded Phoebe to hush.

She didn't listen, choosing instead to cry louder.

"Your emotions will be the death of many," the Want cried.

He turned and moved back down the tunnel with the box in hand. He had one last place he needed to take Leven.

CHAPTER TWENTY-SIX

Waking Up on the Wrong Side of the World

Headaches are a funny thing. Not funny like people-who-buy-the-wrong-size-of-shoes-and-try-to-run funny, but funny like toothaches and jammed toes. Some headaches are the result of something. For instance, maybe your neighbors just bought a new stereo and they enjoy playing it all night. And when you talk to them about it the next day, they tell you that they're moving and you get a headache because you cry for hours thinking about how much you'll miss them and their music. Some headaches come from hitting your noggin too hard against something immovable or stubborn. And some headaches are the consequence of having something dark and evil control your mind and then having that dark and evil thing die, leaving you confused and wounded.

That was the kind of headache Tim had.

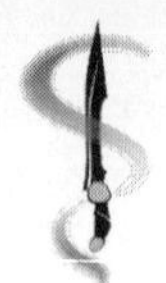

After he had fallen on Dennis and knocked himself out, he had lain on the forest floor for hours before finally coming to. When he did regain consciousness, his head felt like a piñata that thousands of energetic children had vigorously beaten upon.

"Owwww," he moaned, sitting up.

He looked around. The sun was rising and he was covered in cold morning dew. He couldn't remember anything about the last couple of weeks. He remembered meeting someone and beginning to build something, but he couldn't clearly recall why.

Tim stood up slowly, leaning against a tall pine tree. He stepped like a person who had just been given someone else's legs to try out.

Slowly.

He stumbled out of the trees and looked at the lake. The water was calm, and a small boat was moving across the surface like a boxy swan.

"I think I'm in Germany," Tim said, unsure of so many things.

He walked carefully through the trees and around the lake. His body felt sore and his hands and arms were scratched and bruised. A small footpath lay between the trees like a frayed ribbon. Tim walked the trail, feeling his strength build. The sound of a trumpet playing on the water echoed off the surrounding mountains.

Tim's soul was stirred and shaken.

"Wendy," he said, remembering his family and realizing that it had been some time since he had talked to them.

Tim began to run. At first his knees protested, but with each

stride his legs relaxed and let him move as fast as he wanted to. Soon he reached the outskirts of Berchtesgaden. His head throbbed.

Tim entered the first gasthaus he saw.

"Phone?" he asked the woman waiting tables, his breath short and labored. "Phone I can use?"

The woman looked at Tim like he was a walking pile of trash. With disgust she pointed to a pay phone near the back door. Tim stepped up to it and picked up the receiver. He suddenly had no idea what to do. He couldn't remember the number to dial to reach his family. The operator came on, speaking in German, and asked if she could help him.

Speaking in English, Tim said he couldn't understand her.

She asked again in English, and Tim told her that he needed to get ahold of his wife, Wendy.

"Could you be a bit more specific?" the operator questioned.

"She has long, dark hair," Tim tried desperately. "And we live in Iowa. I'm sorry, but my head is so confused."

"Well, we're getting closer," the operator said kindly. "Dark hair and in Iowa. Does she live in a certain city?"

It all began coming back to Tim, except for the address and telephone number. He told the operator how tall Wendy was, what she was wearing when he had seen her last, how old his boys were, and what they both liked to do in their spare time. He described their house and their cars and his job. The operator, tired of the same boring conversations she usually had with other people, just let Tim talk. And by the time he had

said it all, he finally remembered the street he lived on.

"I've got the number right here," the operator said. "Have a nice day."

Tim thanked her and waited.

The phone finally rang.

It rang again, and again, and again and again. After ten rings, a slightly less kind and much less human computer operator came on the line and informed Tim that the party he was trying to reach was not available. The computerized voice suggested that he call back another time.

Tim hung up.

The top of the phone box was metal, and as Tim put the receiver back he could see his reflection in it. He had a black eye and four deep scratches across his left cheek. There was a bruise on his neck, and the small amount of hair he had was sticking straight up. A patch of it was missing from above his left ear. He looked down at his beat-up arms and hands.

"What happened to me?" he wondered.

Tim's question was drowned out by the worried voice of a woman nearby. "Three hours," she wailed.

The woman was sitting at a table with a man and three children. Tim could tell they were U.S. citizens by the American flag shirts they were wearing and their loud, English-speaking voices. Plus, their little boy was holding a cupcake with a small plastic American flag sticking out of the top of it.

"Maybe they're all done," the man said with unease. "Maybe it's over."

"I hope so," the woman quivered.

Tim looked at them. "Is everything okay?" he asked.

The man looked Tim up and down. The woman didn't even look up.

"We're just talking about the War on Normalism," the man said, referencing the name a large news media outlet had given the strange occurrences going on around the globe.

"War on Normalism?" Tim asked.

"Bugs, walking buildings, flying dirt, clouds," the woman practically screamed. "They're even in people's dreams. I just want to get back home."

She pulled the plastic flag out of her son's cupcake and half-heartedly waved it.

"The president is getting troops together," the man said. "And an army in Africa captured a bunch of bugs."

The woman cried.

Tim looked at his hands. His head was still pounding and his body ached, but he was beginning to recall his part in all of this.

"Thanks," Tim said, stepping away.

Unfortunately for Tim, it was all coming back to him.

CHAPTER TWENTY-SEVEN

A CHANCE TO STRETCH

Azure sat comfortably in a small weld as giftless nits pulled him along the winding road. Behind his weld stretched two long ropes. At the end of one of the ropes Geth was tethered; the other one dragged Winter. The road was made of stone, with deep black trenches running along the sides of it. Moss wove itself like netting up the cliff walls and overhead like a great green shade.

Azure threw a couple of sharp stones at the backs of the nits pulling him, prompting them to move faster. "Make haste," he yelled. "The time's coming quickly."

The giftless nits pulled harder, causing the weld to roll faster and forcing Geth and Winter to pick up their pace.

"So this is Lith?" Winter asked Geth. "I expected it to be friendlier."

"The Want will straighten things out," Geth said. "Azure will pay for this."

Geth whispered his threat so casually that Winter felt doomed.

They had reached the shore of Lith hours ago. Azure had bound them both to the back of a small, carriagelike craft called a weld. The weld was round and rolled on one spongy ball that balanced itself with each rotation. The wind was blowing up and down. Geth could feel air hit him from above and then bounce back up to hit him under the chin.

"Are you doing all right?" Geth asked Winter.

"Perfect," she said. "Nothing like being dragged to your death."

"It's cold here," Geth said reflectively.

"Is that a problem?" Winter asked. "Is there some sort of rule in Foo that you can't take the life of someone who has traveled to Reality and back on a particularly cold day?"

"You need to rest your fears," Geth said kindly. "All that lies ahead is what's meant to be. The temperature is an issue due to the fact that each of the thirteen stones' climates is contingent upon the state of mind of its master. The Want must be in a chilly mood."

"Great," Winter said. "Let's knit him a sweater."

Geth smiled.

"How can you do that?" Winter asked.

"Do what?"

"Smile."

Geth looked at Winter and seemed to be trying not to smile as he stepped over a small pile of loose red rocks. Winter looked

away from Geth and placed her gaze on her own footing.

"You know," Geth said. "You've aged."

"Nice," Winter replied. "Just what every girl wants to hear. Well, you're shorter."

"Age isn't a punishment," Geth said. "It's a reward. You have changed from a child to a woman who has the power to correct all of this."

"If that were true, I would."

The ropes they were attached to pulled temporarily taut, jerking them three large steps forward until there was some slack again.

"I have to say," Winter continued, "I was sort of expecting a different welcome than the one we've gotten."

"Here in Lith?" Geth questioned.

"I meant here in Foo."

"You have no memory," Geth pointed out. "How could you expect anything?"

"Is this how you thought it would be when you had Leven and me step in?"

"To be frank, I didn't know what to expect," Geth said. "Foo was in turmoil when you and I left. In some ways I'm happy it has held together like it has because with Leven here we can bring balance and perhaps even growth."

"Growth?" Winter asked, stumbling slightly.

"Foo stopped expanding years ago," Geth said. "The borders keep us from knowing anything more. The only change we've had is due to the dreams coming in. If fate is kind, not only will

Leven bring new life to our land, but dreams will reach a completely new level."

"And Leven will do all this?"

"Yes," Geth said with certainty.

"How?"

Azure turned around and looked down the length of the ropes to where Geth and Winter were tied. He threw a fistful of rocks at the backs of the giftless nits who were pulling him.

"Run!" he screamed.

The nits struggled to move faster. Geth's and Winter's arms were yanked violently forward.

It may have been a rather powerful and painful moment, full of tension and risk, but they had been only a few hundred feet away from their destination when Azure had ordered them to hurry. So, as quickly as he had commanded them to hurry, he had to begin begging them to stop.

The nits came to a dusty stop forty feet past the gate they needed to go through. Azure had to climb out and walk back forty paces before he could start acting superior again. He ordered two of the nits to follow him.

The crumbling brick gateway opened into a maze of stone walls and tall trees. Azure touched the wall at a certain point, and a blue line warmed and moved along the walls showing the way to go.

Azure looked at Geth sideways. Geth stood up as tall as he could.

"I suggest you stay close," Azure said, confused over Geth's

height. "Those beings that remain trapped in these walls are very hungry, and what with your mortal condition and all . . ."

"I thought we were going to die anyway," Winter said coolly, stealing the sting of Azure's threat.

"Well, stay close or I will beat you within an inch of your life and then drag your wounded body behind me. That includes you two." Azure glared at the two nits who were unfortunate enough to have been chosen to tag along. He instructed both of them to hold fast to Geth and Winter.

The nits obeyed.

As they all stepped farther into the maze, the stone walls grew in height. Two turns later and Winter couldn't see anything but towering black rock all around her. The stone was textured, and each section and direction looked identical. If someone had spun her around she would have been lost simply standing there.

Winter looked carefully at the thin blue line. A current ran through it indicating the direction they should move. She did her best to keep up, realizing that perhaps there really were things worse than death, like being trapped within stone walls with deranged beings looking for a way out.

Geth didn't speak, silently counting the footsteps he was taking.

Azure looked at Geth. "If you are counting footsteps, it will do you no good," he said. "These walls, like most stones in Foo, grow bored, and they will shift when they please. Without some help, it's impossible to get out."

Azure pointed to the blue line on the wall, the whole half of

his neck and shoulder covered in blood from his rancid ear.

"Wouldn't the blue line shift as well?" Winter asked sharply.

"You're a real joy to have around," Azure mocked.

"And you've added the word *impossible* to your vocabulary," Geth said sadly.

"The line shifts as needed," Azure seethed. "And in your absence, Geth, we've discovered that there truly are some things that are impossible. Once again our ancestors were wrong. We fight now to change all of that."

"You don't fight," Geth laughed. "You're too cowardly for that. Letting rants do your bidding and giftless nits carry you around. Your father would die of shame if he knew what his son was doing."

"My father?" Azure said, frothing at the mouth. "My father is buried in the Swollen Forest in a hole deeper than four of you. I know this to be a fact because I buried him."

Geth's eyes darkened.

"Don't tell me about courage," Azure screamed. "I have done things that you and your soft soul would never be able to dream up, let alone take care of. Now I will finish off the great Geth and the thorn of Winter. And I'll soon sleep soundly in Reality with more power than I ever thought possible."

"The soil lies," Geth said boldly.

"What?" Azure barked, stepping up to look Geth directly in the face.

"The soil lies," Geth repeated. "Do you think I don't know of what lies beneath it? I have watched every step I have ever

taken in Foo for fear of standing still too long and being overtaken by the voices of those who have died before me. I saw firsthand what the Dearth could do with the soil, how he used it to control Sabine. And I wonder now if there are any in Foo who have not stood still too long and let this happen to them."

"Shut up," Azure screamed, scratching at his ear like a dog going for a flea. "You understand nothing. You don't know what you're talking about. I am in control of myself, while you wait for fate to show you your bleak future."

"I don't believe your—"

"Shut up!" Azure raged.

The two nits trembled with anxiety as Azure stepped faster.

The maze seemed to wander on forever. Geth and Winter had turned so many corners and gone so many different directions that if it had not been for the sky they would have had no hope that something besides black rock existed. Twice they passed other lost souls. One had evidently wandered in the maze for many weeks. He was emaciated and could barely crawl. It broke Winter's heart to just leave him there.

"Can't we take him with us?" Winter argued.

"No," Azure insisted. "Let him die."

"It's fate that we came across him," Geth said. "I'll carry him."

"You'll do no such thing," Azure said. "Fate has no say in your actions. I, however, do."

The giftless nits pulled Geth and Winter away from the man. Two turns later, Geth knew that even if he could have turned

back, he would probably not have been able to find the man.

"There's so much selfishness," Geth said to Winter. "Before, it was mostly a small group of dissatisfied cogs and rants who thought only of themselves. Now it's the very lithens who were sworn to protect Foo."

"There's still hope?" Winter asked skeptically.

"Of course."

After an hour of working their way through the maze of stone, they took a final turn and moved straight up against the side of a cliff. The maze seemed to dead-end up against the wall. Azure's blue line disappeared inches before the stop.

"I thought you said your line would shift?" Winter said, far more panic in her voice than she would have preferred to show.

Azure stepped up to the stone wall and pushed his left shoulder into the rock with ease. Moving at an angle, he worked his entire body into the rock wall.

"Wow," Geth said. "I haven't seen that before."

One of the giftless nits tried going straight in, but the solid wall stopped him. He turned just a bit and slid in diagonally.

Geth mimicked the move, and in a couple of seconds he was back behind the cliff wall standing by Azure. Four seconds later Winter and the second nit were beside them.

"What is that?" Geth said with curiosity.

"The result of the Want messing with light and angles," Azure said. "There are a few spots on the island where his tinkering didn't work out so well."

The ground behind the wall sloped in a circular pattern. The group spiraled down around massive stalagmites. Water trickled across the trail they were walking on.

"We're heading down," Geth commented.

"Reality has made you brilliant," Azure laughed.

As they descended, the stalagmites began to change. They became thinner and thinner until they rose to the ceiling looking like iron bars. Geth touched one and shivered. "I guess I shouldn't be surprised by the presence of metal," he said.

"There should be no shock," Azure said. "The Council of Wonder has always interpreted the law as it wished. Of course, now there is no council."

"Our interpretation used to be for good," Geth argued.

"Such a simple mind," Azure laughed.

Azure stepped aside as the giftless nits pulled Geth and Winter past him and on into a large metal cage. The bars ran from ceiling to floor in a triangle pattern, creating a prison room no bigger than a small bedroom. Once in the cage, the nits became nervous and moved to get out. Before either of them made it, Azure waved his kilve and knocked the heavy gate closed.

"How quaint," Azure said, wincing, his ear so painful he had to bend over.

"You can leave us here, but the Want will find me," Geth said confidently.

"That's where you're wrong," Azure said. "In fact, I can promise you that the Want has no interest in you anymore. He sent me to finish you."

"That can't be," Geth whispered.

"The Want has changed," Azure hissed. "I suppose now there's no harm in you knowing that."

"Changed?"

"He no longer cares for Foo."

"I don't believe it," Geth said tightly.

"Whose idea do you think your death was?" Azure asked, his ear so swollen it looked like he was holding a bloody orange to the side of his head. "Lith is dying. By the morning its soil will be added to the gloam. And your corpse will give it energy to reach. It's my gift to the cause."

"No," Geth said in shock.

"Lith's soil is a gift from the Want himself," Azure smiled. "The gloam will grow rapidly."

"It will be able to reach the fourth stone," Geth calculated out loud.

"And possibly the fifth as well," Azure added, his blue eyes flashing with smugness.

"Leven's still out there," Winter said. "You have no control over him."

Azure smiled. "I've not yet had the privilege of meeting Leven," he said. "But he soon will perform the one task the Want is most in need of. Poor boy, at this very moment he's walking blindly into a trap, and there's not so much as a common cog to help him."

"Please, Azure," Geth begged, his voice more desperate than Winter had ever heard before. "Leven's just a boy. You can't let the

Want harm him. You once stood for the good of Foo. That Azure can't be too far gone."

"Such pathetic words," Azure said. "Even before Sabine destroyed you, I had thoughts of silencing you. You do understand that the reason Sabine was able to put you in the seed was because of the power of the Want?"

Geth's eyes grew cloudy.

"He knew your soul and your dreams," Azure smiled. "He felt certain that you would never agree to what needed to be done. It also seemed that there would be no one better than you to get Leven back. What is it the dirty tharms say? Oh yes, 'burying two nits with one hole.'"

"Where's Leven now?" Winter asked.

"Hundreds of feet above us," Azure answered. "I would assume that at the moment he's being told what he needs to do to save Foo. Too bad he doesn't understand how difficult a time the Want has telling the truth these days."

"So the Want never planned to save Foo?" Winter questioned.

"The Want's plan doesn't run parallel with that of the Dearth," Azure said hotly. "But they will both serve each other in the end."

"But the gateway is gone," Winter argued. "Leven destroyed it."

"Do you think we would have let Leven ruin the only way out?"

Geth put his head into his bound hands.

"There's another gateway?" Winter asked Geth.

Geth didn't answer. He lifted his head and stared at Azure. A small fire burned behind his eyes as his entire body painfully absorbed the knowledge.

"But why did Sabine try to stop us from getting back?" Winter asked.

"Sabine," Azure laughed. "What a worthless nit. He became a liability years ago, so consumed with returning to Reality quickly that he sidestepped strategy and saw no need to appease the Want by having Leven enter Foo. Sabine and his shadows became far more powerful than we were able to control or influence. He wanted out too badly. Now Reality has killed him. Had he structured his passion, he would be alive and about to taste success alongside the Dearth."

"There can't be another gateway," Winter insisted. "Where is it?"

"There is, and I don't know," Azure said. "But the Want is willing to trade us the location and the means to open it—all for the measly price of destroying you two and, of course, taking care of Leven. Something I would have done for free."

Winter felt sick.

The giftless nits in the cage began to weep and complain. "Let us out," they cried. "We've done nothing."

"Your souls will feed the soil as well," Azure said. "Of course, giftless souls are hardly a meal."

Azure pulled at his swollen ear, grimacing at his own touch. "Take heart, Geth," he boasted. "Your death will give the troops great hope in the cause."

He turned and walked off, leaving Geth and Winter to die in relative privacy. The two giftless nits sobbed softly.

"Are you worried now?" Winter asked Geth.

Geth didn't smile.

CHAPTER TWENTY-EIGHT

Don't Let the Box Bugs Bite

There are few things as bothersome as being shoved into a small space for any amount of time. Claustrophobia is an ugly condition. Who in their right mind enjoys having no room to move and little or no air to breathe? Imagine being buried alive, or stuck in a heating vent while trying to overhear someone's personal conversation down below.

Horrible.

I once spent an entire afternoon in a barrel in an effort to elude some pesky assailants. The ruse worked, but I have been even less enthusiastic ever since about volunteering for anything involving barrels or limited space.

It seems as if it would be equally uncomfortable to be shrunk and placed in a tiny wooden box. True, your body would be smaller, but it would still be dark, bothersome, and concerning.

Leven was experiencing just such a fate.

The Want had made him as small as a toy action figure and placed him in a little box for easier transportation. Currently the box was tucked under the Want's left arm, and the Want was walking with jostling purpose toward the highest roundlands of Lith.

Inside the box Leven stretched his legs, trying to brace himself and keep his body from knocking around. The walls of the box were lined with a soft fabric that made it impossible to get a solid grip anywhere. The smell of something fruity that had occupied the box before Leven was strong and disgusting.

"Let me out," Leven yelled, knowing that nobody could hear him, but feeling he should at least yell something. "Let me out!"

The box shook even more.

Leven slid swiftly on his back to the opposite edge of the box and hit his head up against the side. His chest hurt from thoughts of Phoebe being locked up and left alone. He reached to rub his head and the box turned completely over, throwing Leven down against the inside of the lid, which still had big globs of fruit stuck to it.

Leven's right hand pushed into one of the globs. The box flipped again, and Leven dangled from the lid, his wrist caught in the fruit.

The predicament gave him an idea.

Leven reached up with his other hand and scraped off a rotted chunk of fruit. He lifted his right leg and smeared a bit on the bottom of his shoe. He then shook his wrist loose and fell back onto the floor of the box. Leven jammed his left hand into the

corner and his right hand into the crack where the sides of the box met up. He stuck his left foot against the other side, wedging himself in and giving him some stability.

"Perfect," he said.

The idea worked for a few minutes. But the Want was moving too fast, and as the box bounced up and down, Leven was having a hard time staying put in the inside corner of it. His foot slipped first, then his hand, and when the box was flipped upside down again, Leven's stomach pushed into the mushy fruit on the inside of the lid, smearing bits of it all over.

He hung suspended for a few moments and then began to rock gently back and forth. The fruit snapped and Leven fell to the floor of the box, frantically trying to grab ahold of something to stop him from tumbling about. He rolled from end to end, lightly spreading the rotten fruit with his body.

He was flipped back up into the lid, pushing even more rank fruit out and down. The slick, soft walls made it easy for the decaying food to bleed out.

Leven made the mistake of touching his face.

The box dropped a few inches, and Leven plopped down face first against the bottom of it. His arms and legs were spread-eagled, each of them glued to the sticky fabric. The entire front of him was now adhesive as well, his chest and face pressing into the fabric.

Leven was stuck.

He tried to yell for help, but each time he opened his mouth the taste of putrid fruit filled it. The only good news, if you could

call it that, was that he was no longer knocking about the box.

The Want walked faster.

The box spun in the Want's robe pocket like a pinwheel. Leven could tell from the movement that the Want was moving up some stairs. Leven half wished he was out to climb them himself.

Leven's face was pinned to the floor, but he could see small dots of white light flashing inside the box. The light increased until Leven felt like he was in center field in an arena where every spectator was taking flash photos. If his arms hadn't been stuck to the floor, he would have covered his eyes.

As the flashing continued, Leven could see that the pinpoints of light were coming from the open mouths of very tiny bugs. They seemed to ooze out of the walls, opening their mouths to expose their miniscule flashing teeth as they consumed small bits of fruit.

It would have been interesting if Leven had been looking at them under a microscope, but watching them ravenously attack the fruit droppings as they circled closer was a tad unsettling.

Leven felt the first one on his ankle. It bit down with a solid crunch.

Leven screamed, letting the taste of bad fruit fill his mouth. The bugs moved back, startled. A few seconds later they were flashing Leven again.

One reached his arm, and Leven's ensuing scream temporarily scared them back for a few more seconds.

"Clover!"

A bug bit Leven on his backside, prompting Leven to scream the loudest yet. The box went completely dark.

"Want!" Leven yelled, not knowing what else to call him.

The box was still dark.

"Anybody!"

The box slowly began to flash to life with the advance of more bugs.

Leven closed his eyes.

His gift had not worked ever since he had set foot on Lith, and he didn't expect it to be any different now. He had closed his eyes simply to avoid seeing his painful immediate future. Even in his state he couldn't help thinking that everything would be fine if he could just see Phoebe again.

CHAPTER TWENTY-NINE

SPLINTERS

The Rove Valley was filled to capacity, creatures and beings spilling up over the rolling hills and mountain slopes that created it. For many months now, Lore Coils and lobs had been drifting across the whole of Foo, subtly inviting any who longed for Reality to take up arms and gather in the Rove Valley.

It looked to Janet as if the message had gotten out.

There were pockets of nits and cogs and palehi and echoes. There were also legions of black skeletons that had come from the mountains behind Morfit. And, of course, there were rows and rows of rants.

Janet had stayed with the echoes and spent most of her time standing near Osck. He was tall and still liked her reflection on his limbs.

The entire valley was buzzing over recent events. The rants were taking on fewer shapes than ever before. It seemed as if the

dreams of people in Reality were condensing themselves. Almost every rant now was either half telt, avaland, sarus, hazen, or building. Those rants who were cursed with a left side of brick and mortar were fairly useless and had planted themselves in one large group over by the far end of the valley waiting for someone in Reality to dream of something less heavy.

There was also some movement in the valley. A large group of rants had been sent out weeks ago to gather on the shore below the Sentinel Fields where the gloam jutted out. Since their departure, steady waves of reinforcements had left daily to follow in their tracks and meet up with them.

Those still in the valley were beside themselves with the possibility of something finally happening to reconnect them to Reality.

Osck sat down by Janet on a dead fantrum tree. He looked at her large reflection in the side of his arm. In the past day he had grown even more attached to her, talking often of the two of them being more than just friends. Janet had wanted to point out how impossible that was, but it seemed as if impossible things were always happening in Foo anyway, and she rather enjoyed the attention.

"We will leave tomorrow," Osck said.

"Why?" Janet asked.

"All the echoes are ready."

"I'll go with you?" Janet asked carefully.

"Of course. I would stay if you didn't."

Janet smiled sadly.

"You're so odd," Osck said. "There's no one here like you."

"It's different in Reality," Janet replied, her whole being so much softer than it had once been. "In Reality there are many like me."

"Glorious," Osck exclaimed. "And in Reality we will be free. We will be able to bounce off every surface and texture."

Janet was quiet.

"Your face is longer than usual," Osck said with concern.

"It won't work," Janet admitted. "I can't understand how I can see that you will fail when nobody else does."

"You doubt because you don't know anything of Foo."

"I know that if we do make it back, you will drift off into the sunlight and disappear. And I will most likely return to being who I have always been."

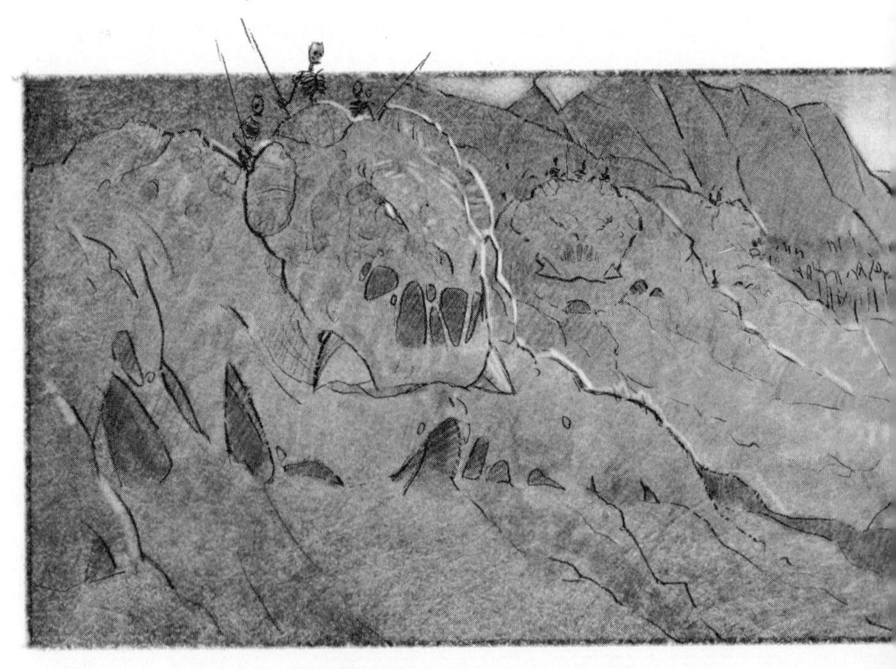

Osck tried to touch Janet consolingly under her chins. "You'll live there," he said. "And I'll sit next to you there like I do here."

"I don't want to sit anymore," Janet said sadly. "I don't even want to see myself again."

Janet had been through so much in the past little while. She had seen things of unbelievable complication and beauty. She had also witnessed acts of great selfishness and foolishness. And, even though Osck's presence was a comfort to her, it was the words of the boulder that had moved her most.

Janet wanted to reach.

She had not even extended her arms in Reality. Now, she was unable to touch or reach in any fashion. She desperately wanted to hold Osck, or feel the ground, or even comb her hair.

Janet wanted to reach.

She could see Winter in her mind, and she began to cry.

"I'm not sure it's wise to be near you when you are dripping," Osck said, afraid the tears might affect his fiery skin.

"They might hurt you if they were real," Janet said, foolishly wiping at the non-tears on her cheeks.

"Why are you doing that?" Osck asked kindly.

"I ruined my chance in Reality," Janet said with embarrassment. "I lost my own daughter."

"Well, then, the war will give you another go," Osck said seriously. "The Sochemists have promised an end to our pain."

Janet smiled at Osck. Never in a billion years would she have thought that she would end up sitting next to someone like him. And never in a trillion years would she have thought that she would allow herself to care for something like him.

"You'll get a second chance," Osck reaffirmed.

Janet smiled sincerely, and from that moment on she was a changed whisp. She was fully and wholeheartedly committed to the war. True, she had no real idea whom she would be fighting, or what it would take to win, but she knew she would give up everything for the chance to reach one more time.

ii

The day was spectacular. Warm weather had settled into the valley, and tourists by the hundreds had descended upon Berchtesgaden to eat fish and listen to the echo of the trum-

pets. Boats moved across the water constantly, taking people to St. Bartholomew's Cathedral to look at the lake from a different angle and wait for a ride back. The smell of fried fish and sound of polka music filled the light blue sky.

It had been a full twelve hours since anything odd had been reported in the world, and people felt a bit of hope creeping back into their lives.

The green water lay flat, like an emerald mirror, and swans hovered around the docks hoping that the generosity of men would move tourists to toss bread crumbs and fill their gullets.

It would have taken someone with binoculars and nothing interesting to look at to notice a small, bubbling circle near the far edge of the lake.

From out of the bubbles rose a very wet and browbeaten Dennis.

"You call that swimming?" Ezra spat, shaking water from his tassel. "If I had a newborn baby sister wearing a tutu and a tiara, she would have swum less girllike."

"I'm not a good swimmer," Dennis apologized.

"You can thank me for pointing that out," Ezra said angrily.

"It doesn't work," Dennis said. "You saw me. I stood there on the bottom of it. The gateway doesn't work."

Dennis was back to his old self. Every bit of Sabine had been blown from him and destroyed. He still had faint lines covering his body, but they didn't move and were no longer black.

The experience of being controlled by Sabine had also left Dennis with a bit of a backbone. It was as if a part of him remembered being aggressive and now wasn't about to let go of the feeling. He still wore his white shirt and wrinkle-proof pants. The water had washed his sticker off.

"Leave it to you to build something faulty," Ezra barked. "I wish I had listened to myself."

"It wasn't just me that built it," Dennis pointed out. "Where's that other guy?"

"Who?"

"The guy with the baseball cap."

"It's not ringing a bell," Ezra said, bothered.

"The one you stabbed and made fall on me?"

"Tony?"

"Maybe," Dennis faltered.

"I think he's dead."

Dennis looked down at the ground.

Ezra shook. He looked at Dennis and blinked his single eye.

Ezra couldn't remember his birth. He knew he had come from the tree that had stood as Geth. He also knew that Geth had tossed him aside, leaving Ezra to deal with all the hatred and anger Geth had once possessed. Ezra could also remember bits and pieces of Foo. He had thought meeting up with Sabine was fateful, but now he could see that the fate involved was much more subtle. Ezra hated to admit it, but he seemed to have learned something.

Ezra's tiny body burned.

He had been getting stronger every hour. His enamel body made him almost unbreakable. Now, if he could just suffocate his

hate long enough to interpret his feelings, he would be able to understand the impressions of Foo that were coming on stronger and stronger every minute.

"I think I know something," Ezra seethed.

"Like what?" Dennis asked, unstrapping his oxygen tank.

"Your mouth is moving," Ezra mocked, ignoring Dennis's question. "There's something I know."

"I've had that feeling before," Dennis admitted.

"I find that hard to believe," Ezra sneered. "Now, if you'll please push up your lower jaw and stare into another direction."

Dennis closed his mouth and turned around as Ezra struggled with his own mind. There was something Geth now knew that very few others did.

"Geth," Ezra growled. "What a pile of flesh."

"Do you remember what you know yet?" Dennis asked, still facing the other direction.

"Quiet," Ezra yelled.

"I could swim to the gateway again," Dennis said, trying to appease Ezra.

"Why don't you do that," Ezra said angrily. "But this time don't take any air, and chain yourself to the bottom of it until it works."

"But then . . . oh," Dennis replied, getting the implication of Ezra's words.

The sound of trumpets echoing off the mountains filled the air. It was so calming that Ezra forgot Dennis's less-than-snappy

comeback. Squirrels ran down a nearby tree, and a car horn sounded in the far distance.

Ezra's thoughts cleared. There had been a few times in his life when he had felt a connection to Geth. He knew he had come from him, but for the most part Ezra felt only hatred and spite for the person who had left him to be the angry toothpick he now was. But in this one clear moment, Ezra could feel that somewhere Geth had just learned something so huge that the knowledge was affecting even Ezra.

"There's a second gateway," Ezra said suddenly, the statement popping out of his mouth like a well-cooked piece of toast.

"What?" Dennis asked excitedly.

"There's a second gateway," Ezra said deliciously, rubbing his tiny hands together. "Of course there is. Thank you, Geth, and your weak, surprised emotions."

"Is this gateway near?"

Ezra looked Dennis up and down. "Why? Scared of a little effort?" he snipped.

"No, I was—"

"*Was* is such a stupid word," Ezra said. "I don't know where the gateway is exactly, but I know what direction we should head. We are going to go . . ."

Ezra pointed.

"West?" Dennis asked.

"I don't know," Ezra said defensively. "Is that west?"

Dennis turned and looked around, as did Ezra.

"I thought west was that direction?" Ezra said. "Over those trees."

"No, that's east," Dennis said, pointing. "North, east, south, and west—'never eat soggy waffles.'"

Ezra stared at Dennis with rage in his single eye. "What holds the top of your head up?"

Dennis looked down.

"We are going west," Ezra said.

Dennis shrugged and picked Ezra up. "What about Tony?" Dennis asked.

"He had his chance to be evil," Ezra spat. "Good riddance."

"I don't know that I actually want to be evil either," Dennis admitted.

"Oh, right," Ezra corrected. "How about *I'm* evil and *you* get to experience something besides cleaning out sinks and emptying trash cans?"

"Sounds fair," Dennis said.

Never had Ezra wished more for his own ability to walk better. Unfortunately for him, Dennis was necessary. There were some large limitations to being a toothpick. Ezra simply had to play nice until he got to where he needed to be and who he needed to become. Then, and only then, would Ezra finally be able to be himself.

CHAPTER THIRTY

A Reversal of Proportion

Clover had stayed invisible but close to the Want. He had followed the Want through three tunnels, an endless wing of his house, and an outdoor garden that stretched upward for miles.

It was cold outside, and the temperature was dropping. The landscape on the edge of the gardens rolled like grassy waves. They were nearing the highest point of Lith, heading into the roundlands. The purple sky became gray with thin bands of gold weaving in and out of it. A set of brick stairs wound around and through the wide, humpbacked terrain. In the darkening sky, large numbers of rovens flew in all directions.

The Want was climbing the stairs with purpose, talking to himself. "Dreams are beginning," he said. "Take this and go."

There had been more than a hundred times when Clover had wished he could materialize and tell the Want to keep quiet. But

Clover had seen enough of the Want's endearing personality to realize that bossing him around was probably a foolish idea.

The Want had placed the box with Leven in his robe and not brought it out since. Clover thought about trying to steal it away, but he felt certain he would not succeed. He was pretty sure that even though the Want had said nothing to acknowledge it, he knew that Clover was there. Leven was Clover's burn, and there was no way Clover would leave him at a time like this.

The wind picked up, and frosty black hazen drifted in circles around the roundlands. Clover looked back. The only bit of the Want's home he could now see was the tower room that they had been in earlier.

"Taste what you wish," the Want screamed to nobody in particular. "The pain will be in the digestion."

The brick stairs crested the top of Lith, giving Clover a great view of the island's highest ground. The roundlands were beautifully barren. Long grass swirled in flat circles under the fading sky while small cats sprinted like cheetahs in straight lines of four. A line of them crossed directly in front of the stairs. The Want waved his kilve and the creatures scattered in a flash.

Clover felt good about his decision to stay invisible.

In the distance the top of a large castle appeared, its skyline looking like square teeth in an expansive mouth of sky. The castle had large white flags flying from its three turrets. Emblazoned on each flag was the black silhouette of a roven skull.

The massive castle seemed to rise from the depths of Lith as

they got closer. It stood as a dark, structured mountain. Backlit by the gold in the sky, the castle looked formidable and lonely.

"Feed yourself," the Want waved at the wind. "Reach in my pockets and lose your life."

Clover felt good about his decision not to try to steal the box.

Two giant rovens flew low through the sky and landed on the top of the castle, screeching.

"Wicked, wicked dreams," the Want moaned. "How dare the human mind dream such things?"

The brick stairs led to the front of the castle, where a thin stream of robed nits were climbing off of rovens and making their way in.

The nits walked slowly, as if being drawn in by some unseen energy. The Want waved his hand, and they scattered in a flash of white light.

The castle door opened up and the Want walked through. All those in his way moved to the sides and corners to avoid his presence. The sound of chanting echoed off the walls.

The Want stepped off into a big room. A large, roaring fire was growling in the corner, and two furry chairs and a small table sat in the center of the room. The Want walked to the table and took the box from his robe. He set it down carelessly. He then waved, as if shooing away half a dozen flies, and walked out of the room.

Clover waited a good thirty seconds before he materialized near the box. He fumbled with the latch and opened it quickly.

There was a small doll stretched out facedown in the box. It took Clover a couple of seconds to register that the doll was actually Leven.

Leven moaned.

Clover reached in carefully and gripped Leven around the waist. He pulled gently at first, but when that didn't work Clover tugged as hard as he could, ripping Leven from the box.

Leven screamed, still groggy from all the pain he had recently experienced.

Clover held him up and looked him over. Leven was covered in splotches of his own blood and smelled like the trash piles near Morfit. His clothes were wet with blood and his pants were ripped. The front of his hair looked ragged and torn.

Clover looked back in the box and realized that he had ripped some of Leven's hair off when he yanked him out.

"Sorry," Clover said.

Leven only mumbled.

"Are you okay?" Clover asked.

"Perfect," Leven slurred, still trying to regain his composure.

"What was in that box?" Clover questioned, looking down into it.

"Bugs," Leven managed to say. "And fruit."

"That explains the smell," Clover sniffed.

Leven glared at Clover with tiny glowing gold eyes.

"What?" Clover said self-consciously.

"I'm four inches tall."

Clover smiled. "Here," he said excitedly. "Try sitting on my shoulder."

"What?"

"Like you're my sycophant."

"That's okay," Leven said. "Will this wear off?"

"I have no idea," Clover shrugged, looking hurt. "The power of the Want is different from any other force in Foo. He can enter the shores of Sycophant Run anytime he pleases. Our claws have no effect on him."

"Claws?" Leven asked.

Clover blushed. "Most sycophants get temporary claws while serving as posted pegs on Sycophant Run. Every sycophant, male and female, spends five years protecting our land. Here, just let me try to balance you on my head?"

"No," Leven insisted. "Where are we?"

"The roundlands on top of Lith."

"Are we far from where Phoebe is trapped?"

"She's far beneath us," Clover answered.

The door opened and Clover disappeared. The Want strode across the room as if his backside were on fire, the door closing soundly behind him. His eyes were still covered. In his right hand he held a folded robe. He stopped and looked at the open box. Leven stood there on the table trying not to look as weak and pathetic as he actually was.

"Where are we?" Leven asked.

"Quiet!" the Want said nervously.

"Where are Geth and Winter?"

"You have no need to ask such questions," the Want commanded. "There's an evil greater than you or I sneaking up on us even as we speak. You must be ready."

"I can't be ready like this," Leven pointed out.

The Want's body bubbled in and out, dimples and bumps the size of melons collapsing and billowing all over his body. He pulled his hood down and blew out.

Leven's arms began to swell. His legs stretched and his chest and shoulders inflated like a folded balloon. He could feel a strong wind moving into his head and fingers. It felt like if he were to clip his nails, he would slowly leak air.

In a matter of moments Leven was as tall as, if not taller than, he had ever been. He looked down and noticed that his right foot was still tiny.

Leven cleared his throat and pointed to his foot.

The Want sighed and Leven's foot expanded to normal. Leven fell back into one of the chairs.

"Give me grief again and you will go back in the box," the Want moaned, wind puckering through the depressions in his body. "We've no time for your slow stride or delay. The darkness rises from the soil even as we stand."

Leven was tempted to point out that he was sitting.

The Want handed Leven the folded robe. "Put this on," he said. "We'll not want anyone recognizing you."

Leven put the robe on.

The doors blew open and amber light flooded the room and spilled up against the stone walls. The light crept up the walls like a rising watermark.

"The rage begins," the Want said.

"The rage?"

"Thousands have gathered to feast on the chaos of dreams," the Want said. "This castle is a conduit for dreams, and those who are addicted to the lives of others gather nightly to taste the wants of those in Reality."

"Will I see a dream?" Leven asked, still never having experienced that for himself.

"You have not seen any?" the Want asked suspiciously.

Leven shook his head.

"Brilliant," the Want smiled. "Fate's a sneaky ride. You may very well see one tonight. Now, do you remember what I have told you?"

"About dreams?" Leven asked.

The Want howled and beat his own arms. "No!" he insisted. "About your purpose."

"Tonight?" Leven asked, bile rising in his throat.

"Yes," the Want said. "Even now, the evil rises above the soil like a weed. You must choke it out."

"I don't know what to do—"

"Stop," the Want ordered. "You stand here for no other reason than to accomplish the task at hand. You destroyed the gateway, killed Sabine, and finished Jamoon so that you could

stand where you now do and put to rest the real evil—the very voices that whisper from beneath the dust. Understand?"

Leven didn't say anything.

"You must trust me."

Leven nodded.

"You will be surrounded by darkness," the Want whispered. "You will hear my voice in the dark, and as it sounds, an object will be placed before your feet. Use it."

"I need to know what I'm doing," Leven said nervously. "It's one thing to face evil and attack it, but it is another to have to trust the words of someone I barely know."

"Perhaps it would help you to know that what you will do will save the lives of Geth and Winter," the Want said.

"It won't harm them?"

"It'll be your one chance to see them again."

The Want trembled like he was full of hot gas and about to explode. His body rumbled in sections, shifting so as to lower his left arm while his right side raised. He twisted and stretched out his uneven arms—they then came together and pointed at Leven.

"Don't ignore your fate, or the whole of Foo, as well as every dream in Reality, will be gone. You must pick up the burden, and you may well save the world. Nobody can take this from you but you."

"I'm doing the right thing?" Leven said, sweating.

The Want shook.

"What about Phoebe?" Leven asked longingly.

"I showed her to you for a purpose," the Want said. "That purpose will become clear in time. Now, you have other things to think about. The rage is beginning."

He extended his right hand to Leven. Leven took it, surprised at how warm it was. The Want's fingers were long and seemed to hold onto Leven's hand with shocking tenderness.

The feeling was almost comforting.

"You will save the world," the Want said, "or you and I will die tonight. And by the color of the moons in view, I don't think fate is done showing off. The world must go on."

Leven wanted never to let go of the Want's hand. The feeling became stronger and stronger. He could see new things in his head—things he had never imagined or actually seen. He could feel a heightened sense of perception, and warmth spread over his entire body. Every fiber of his being seemed to wake up simultaneously. The tips of his long hair opened as if taking a breath.

"Will you be there?" Leven asked foggily.

"I cannot be," the Want said. "But you will hear my voice."

"I would be wrong not to try to save the world," Leven said, more to himself than to anyone else.

"The future would be a dark place."

The Want pulled Leven from the room and into the large hall. Hundreds of dark robed beings were still flowing into the castle like black blood cells. The ceilings were brushed with broad, fuzzy strokes of deep red and black jagged cracks.

The Want stopped and removed his right shoe with his left

foot. He then extracted his left with his right. His bare feet were white and old. They looked like withered fish in need of some serious water.

The Want dug his toes into the soil of the bare floor. His robe contracted until it was the width of a street pole. He nodded almost imperceptibly, and his robe filled with movement and substance again.

"The time is finally here," the Want cried, bright bands of white light twisting around him. "It is here."

The Want fell to his knees and burrowed his hands into the soil. He dug into the dirt like a dog, soil flying up and around.

"He's in there," the Want whispered fiercely. "I can feel him."

Leven couldn't see anything but dirt.

Once the Want's hands were a couple of inches deep in the soil, he stopped. He smiled from beneath his hood, his red beard curling in multiple spots. The Want's body glowed, and the dirt around his hands hissed.

The ground beneath Leven's feet started to rumble.

"What's happening?" Leven asked.

The Want smiled and then whimpered as Leven shook.

The entire island of Lith was starting to sink into the Veil Sea, and Lith's final dream rage was about to begin.

Leven wanted desperately to see the future.

CHAPTER THIRTY-ONE

What You Can't See Can Scratch You

The waves from the Veil Sea rolled in like thin taffy, stretching up onto the shore and then snapping back into the body of water from whence they had come. The beaches were barren and darkness had won the battle with light, leaving night in full force over all of Sycophant Run.

There was no laughter in the air—only the sound of waves and the occasional shout-out from a wayward whittle bird. Two naked moons hung in the air, while two more had the modesty to have dropped their bottom halves down below the horizon.

A tight whistle could be heard.

A few moments later, another sounded.

The waves came in and out.

Rast moved from his spot to climb up a pointed stone that

sat like an angry finger on the shore's edge. He fumbled in his pocket and pulled out a pair of glasses. The frames were made of wormwood and the glass was actually rock, polished so thin you could see through it. The glasses gave anyone wearing them the power to see any sycophant, whether invisible or not. There were only five pairs in existence. Rast put the glasses on and looked out over the shore.

The sight gave him goose bumps.

As far as the eye could see were posted sycophants. They stood like stone gargoyles, rigid and ready. There were millions of them. Some had their claws out, as if anticipating trouble. Many were crouched as if preparing to pounce, whereas others were already on their toes, halfway into an extraordinary jump. They were positioned to have effect in waves. If someone were to attack, they would be covered by wave after wave of vicious, dedicated sycophants. The entire beach and cliff walls were blanketed in them. There were also thousands spreading out into the shallow water.

Rast had always loved this sight.

Sycophant Run was one of the most marvelous and comforting places in existence, but the glasses showed another side. Sycophant Run was also ready for anything. It was a comfort to see his home so protected.

Rast turned a couple of inches to his left and was surprised to see he was surrounded by four other sycophants on the very rock he stood on. He had climbed up right over them without knowing. He knew better than to talk to them. They were poised and ready. Only the order from their commander to eat

or sleep or attack could get them to change position or move.

"Remarkable," Rast whispered. "Mule?"

Mule moved up the rock and stood next to Rast.

"Take a look," Rast insisted. "I see no weakness."

Mule put on the glasses and whistled. "Sometimes I wish others could see our forces," he said. "It frightens even me to look at the sheer numbers. Think what it would do to our enemies."

"I hope no one comes close enough to care," Rast said, taking the glasses back. "It has been so many years since anyone has even attempted to come ashore."

"Sabine?" Mule asked.

"I believe he was the last to try."

"There is word in the air that large groups are settling beneath the Sentinel Fields—rants and nits and all manner of beings. And I've a feeling they're not gathering for good."

"I've heard," Rast said. "I'm afraid the Lore Coil my emotions created has given them even more optimism."

"And have you heard that the gloam grows?" Mule asked.

"So many dark things to fit into a sycophant's head," Rast said sadly. "Mankind is never willing to just move forward in happiness."

"Progress feels thin without the rumble of battle," Mule said softly.

"Fools," Rast said, shimmying down the rock. "Are the commanders ready?"

"They know everything they need to know," Mule answered. "The heart of every posted peg burns with anticipation."

"I always hated that feeling," Rast said. "It's been many years since I was a peg, but I can still recollect the discomfort I felt at the possibility of battle."

"Odd. That's a feeling usually reserved for the old," Mule said. "Me, I hungered for a fight—as do our pegs now."

"Any word from Brindle?" Rast asked.

"None," Mule answered. "I doubt we'll hear anything until he returns with Lilly."

"You seem confident that he will succeed."

"I am always hopeful."

Rast put his hand on Mule's shoulder. "Thank the sand and stars that there are creatures like you."

"Like us," Mule said.

"Sometimes, when I think of the things placed on our small shoulders, I wonder what kind of sick sense of humor fate must have."

"There's no gain in that thinking," Mule pointed out.

"I suppose not."

"Can I see the glasses one more time?"

Rast handed Mule the glasses. He put them on and looked out at the millions of tiny sycophants waiting to protect Foo's greatest secret.

"We can't fail," Mule said.

"We mustn't fail," Rast added.

Another tight whistle sounded.

"The command's making the rounds," Mule said. "Tonight we can sleep soundly."

Rast was about to agree, but his comments were halted by the slight tremor he felt beneath his feet. "Do you feel that?" he asked Mule.

"Feel what?"

"The ground. Is it moving?"

Mule jumped up and down. He dropped to his belly and put his ear to the sand. He stood back up and dusted off his small hands. "I don't hear anything."

Rast stood still. Something big was happening in Foo, and there was nothing he could do to stop it.

"Sleep," he said to Mule. "Tomorrow the world could be a different place."

Mule walked off.

Rast put his glasses back on and looked out over the crowd. The posted pegs were in position and ready, just as they had been every day since the creation of Foo.

"If not tomorrow, someday soon."

The waves jiggled awkwardly as they slapped down against the shore. Foo seemed off balance, and Rast knew it wasn't the work of the shifting siids.

"Tomorrow the world will be a different place," he said with a sad certainty.

Rast's heart ached already for those who would certainly become lost in the dust of battle.

CHAPTER THIRTY-TWO

GOING DOWN

I have met those who challenge the existence of Foo. It concerns me, but it concerns Clover even more. Imagine someone saying you didn't even exist—worse yet, that you were made up by a person such as I.

My heart goes out to anyone in a similar circumstance.

Foo exists.

The words you are reading are there simply so that you can recall something that has been taken from your memory. You saw buildings move and planes get tipped over. A boy by the name of Cade Williams rode an avaland for two states and now doesn't even recall it. There's a reason for your memory lapse. I'd go into it, but the moment's not right. Just take comfort in knowing that by the time the tale is fully told you will understand how and why. And you might even recall the uneasy, wobbly-kneed feeling you

had the moment Lith began to sink and Foo became unbalanced.

It was a feeling Geth and Winter could relate to all too well.

The prison they were locked in was as solid as the stone walls around it.

"Can you feel that?" Geth asked calmly.

"What?" Winter asked, looking around.

The two nits they were caged with, Andrus and Sait, sat huddled in the corner talking between themselves.

"Lith's moving," Geth said.

"How's that possible?" Winter said.

"I'm not sure," Geth answered. "But I have a feeling Azure is at the heart of it."

Geth turned to the nits, crouching down in front of them. "What do you know about all of this?" he asked.

"We know nothing," Sait, the fat nit, said.

"What happened to your gifts?"

Both of them looked down in shame.

"Did Sabine steal them?" Winter questioned.

"They stole mine," Andrus said. "Sait gave his away."

Sait tried to burn holes in Andrus with his gaze.

"They promised we'd be left alone," Sait said. "That we would be left to live out our lives and manipulate dreams in peace. They just wanted my gift. Mine was to see through soil. I hardly used it anyway."

"You probably could have used it to avoid capture or to read that maze we were just put through," Winter argued.

"I could freeze things," Andrus said sadly. "I was summoned

to Morfit to meet with Jamoon, and as I sat there listening to them, my gift was stolen from me."

"Were you in Morfit when you gave up your gift?" Geth asked Sait.

"No," he answered. "I was near Cusp. They stopped me on the road and promised peace and prosperity for me and my family if I simply gave up my ability to see through soil. I stepped into a large black tent, and a machine made of metal stole my gift. The moment it was gone, they bound my hands and threw me into a weld with others they had captured in the Red Grove and below Fté."

"Who was in charge of all this?" Geth asked with disgust.

"Sabine was mentioned," Sait said. "As were Jamoon and Azure and, at times, the soil."

"Soil?" Winter asked.

"At first the soil was clean here," Geth answered. "But the Sochemists claim that, as dark and dirty people were snatched into Foo and eventually died, their buried souls corrupted the dirt and gave strength to the Dearth. Now the soil whispers and hisses for power, using weak souls like Sabine and Jamoon to help it rise up above the ground and take on a life above."

"And there's some reaching for Lith?"

"For years the Dearth has pushed the gloam slowly closer and closer to the Thirteen Stones, reaching to have control of all the gifts and to use them," Geth replied. "I'm afraid now that Lith is being sacrificed for that very reason and for the same evil. We have to get to the Want."

Andrus and Sait shivered.

"What is it?" Geth asked.

They both looked in different directions.

"The Want?" Geth questioned.

"Don't say it," Sait begged. "I might cry."

"I'll throw up," Andrus said with bile in his voice. "Even though I haven't eaten for days."

"The Want's to blame for so much of this misery," Sait blurted out.

"What do you mean?" Geth demanded.

"The Want has stood still for too long," Andrus said. "His mind is not his own."

"That can't be," Geth said, pushing his hands over his face. "His mind might be heavy with dreams, but he has not listened to the Dearth."

"I'm sorry, but he has," Sait insisted.

The ground rumbled, and the thin stream of water nearby widened and began to spill gently into the cage.

"Tell me all you know," Geth begged.

"I don't know much," Andrus said. "But I know the Want has dark plans. Like I said, he has stood still for too long. Azure has mentioned that the Want simply waits for the one person who will seal the fate of Foo."

"Who is that?" Geth asked, already knowing the answer.

"Leven Thumps, of course," Sait answered.

Winter began to tug at the bars in vain as water pooled around her ankles.

"You're sure of this?" Geth asked.

"Positive," Sait replied.

"I've been played. We've got to get to Leven," Geth said, as if they had stayed there simply because they had been waiting for a reason to leave.

"Okay," Winter agreed. "Any ideas?"

The ground shook and lowered a bit. Lith was going down.

"This cage was built years ago," Geth said.

"Excellent," Winter said, her voice raising. "I was curious about the construction date of the jail that's going to kill me!"

"That's just it," Geth said. "Fate has long been an enemy of killing. When you take a life, you directly interfere with what fate had in mind for that person. The rules for murder and killing here in Foo have always been muddled. Judging by the bones on the floor, this cage has probably killed a few people."

"Again," Winter said, shaking water off her ankles, "that's obvious."

"Yes, but to ensure that their prisoners would die, whoever built this would have had to leave some way for captives to get out. That way their fate would not be sealed, and if they died, it would be in a sense their own fault for not finding an escape. We may be mortal, but Azure would not have thought that Andrus and Sait could die unless he knew there was an escape."

"I see no way out," Sait said.

"Of course not," Geth said. "They would never make it obvious, or even easy. But there might be a pattern or a code we can't see that could open it up for us."

Winter moved along the bars, feeling each one. "They're all solid," she reported.

Andrus and Sait began to tug on bars as well. The ground moaned, and water began to pour from the side in a thick, steady current.

"Keep looking," Geth said.

"There's nothing here," Winter yelled. "Unless you're talking about our impending death!"

Geth turned to her and smiled.

Winter shook her head, her blonde hair twisting. She flashed her green eyes at Geth and frowned just enough to let him know she wasn't smiling.

"They wouldn't make this without a way out," Geth comforted.

"I think that's what the gate is for," Winter pointed.

"An alternate way out," Geth clarified. "Are any of the bars thinner than others?"

Water was swirling around them.

"This one is," Andrus said, his right hand on a bar.

"Does it twist?"

Andrus gripped the bar and twisted as hard as he could. The bar turned clockwise in his hand.

"It's turning, but it's not doing anything," Andrus said.

The water was above Winter's knees and rising fast. Thin yellow snakes began to flow into the cage. Winter screamed like she might win a prize for doing so.

"They can't hurt you," Geth said. "They won't bother you unless you step on them."

The water was at Winter's waist.

"It's not doing anything," Andrus said again. "It's just turning."

Geth pushed through the water, pulling on the other bars.

"Here!" he exclaimed.

A bar on the opposite side of the cage had lowered half an inch, disconnecting it from the top.

"It won't twist any farther," Andrus announced.

"That's fine," Geth said.

"There's no way I'll fit through that," Winter hollered, staring at the half-inch gap between the top of the bar and the top of the cage.

"Of course not," Geth said. "Find another thin bar."

Sait found one and began to turn. The bar next to the lowered bar dropped a half inch. Winter tried to pull on the unconnected bars, but they were still as tight and unmovable as when they were connected.

"Find another thin one!" Geth ordered.

Winter found it and twisted as hard as she could, lowering the third bar. The water was now up to her shoulders.

"We've got to hurry," Geth said. "Lith's sinking fast."

"We're in a hurry?" Winter questioned sarcastically. "Thanks for pointing that out."

Winter twisted faster. The walls of the prison shivered, and great amounts of water moved from open caverns into new spaces, creating a huge sucking sound.

"Here's another one," Andrus yelled, water entering his mouth as he spoke.

"And another," Sait hollered.

"Twist them," Winter yelled.

Two more bars lowered.

"We've twisted all the bars," Sait wailed.

"I guess that will do it," Geth said, having to swim to keep his mouth above the rising water.

"Do what?" Winter asked in a panic.

Sait pulled himself up to breathe in the small pocket of air still left in the top three inches of the prison. He reached out to pull on the bars they had lowered, but Geth stuck his hand out and stopped him.

"No," Geth insisted. "If you pull back the wrong one, it will raise the bars back up and we won't have time to lower them again. We need to pull the right one."

"Which one is that?" Winter yelled, her mouth pushed up above the water gasping for breath.

"I have no idea," Geth answered honestly. "If we had time to think, we could probably figure out a code. I wish I had shrunk enough to slip through."

Water filled the cage completely. Winter wished for a Baadyn to help her breathe, but knew none would come to her rescue. She looked at the five bars as the entire island of Lith sank. She felt out of balance and confused. She knew that Foo was a place of limitless possibility, but that at its soul it was also a place of balance and organization. It was the off-balance disregard for what was supposed to be that was tearing Foo apart.

Winter looked at the five bars.

Her lungs felt like someone had shoved a small roasted sun into them. She could feel her insides choking and bits of flesh curling up like old flecks of paint. The five bars suddenly looked balanced to her, the middle one standing out like a solid center. She reached out and pulled the third bar. As she pulled it forward, the two on each side lowered until they were all far enough down that the captives could swim through.

The nits didn't wait for an invitation, pushing past Winter and out of the cage. Geth shoved Winter through the opening and followed her up.

The water looked to have no ceiling, but in a few seconds their heads broke through and the cooling balm of oxygen filled their flaming lungs. Winter spat and screamed. Geth spat but didn't scream. His hair was wet and hung in his face in long, dark, twisted strands. His green eyes looked amazed.

"Number three, huh?" he said. "How'd you know?"

"It seemed like the only bar with balance," Winter answered. "Right in the middle."

"I'm glad you got to it before me," Geth smiled. "I was thinking of pulling number five because it rhymed with *alive.*"

"Oh, so when you said *code,* you were thinking of a dumb code?"

Geth smiled.

He swam ahead of Winter and crawled out of the water onto a long, dry ledge. He leaned down and pulled Winter up out of the water.

"Are you okay?" he asked, helping her get her balance.

There are moments in life too big to be clocked on a watch or an odometer—times when the very act of living is so real and intense that you forget there are other people in the world. In such moments, all poverty is ended, violence is a disease long ago cured, and wars occur only in fables with happy endings. Those moments are few and far between. I've known people who have never experienced them, and in turn have never really lived. Because until you hold a moment like that in your hand and blow it away like a dandelion in the wind, you have never really breathed. You may have bookcases filled with trophies and mile-high walls covered with plaques that prove you're much smarter than you look, but unless you have stopped time for a moment in the act of truly living, then you really haven't experienced that much.

For Winter, one of those rare moments had snuck up on her and caught her completely off guard. The ground she was standing on was falling apart, but for a second everything made sense.

"Are you okay?" Geth asked again.

Winter put her arms around Geth and held onto him. For the first time in as long as she could remember, she had people in her life who cared about her. The feeling was so comforting that Winter felt temporarily invincible. Her emotion was so intense that a Lore Coil filled with nothing but comfort shot off from around her, and within a reasonable amount of time most beings in Foo would pause to momentarily feel good about themselves as the Lore Coil passed over.

Winter might have hugged Geth for a bit longer if it had not been for the "awwwws" of Andrus and Sait.

Winter pulled back and smiled again.

"Are you okay?" Geth asked softly.

"Yes," Winter said.

Sait cleared his throat.

"Leven," Geth whispered. "We've got to get to him."

Geth took Winter by the hand, and they began working their way through the crumbling insides of Lith.

CHAPTER THIRTY-THREE

FALLING JUST RIGHT

Tim was beside himself. He had no papers, no money, and nowhere to go. For some reason nobody was answering the phone back home, and he still had not found Winter.

On the plus side, most of his memory had come back to him. He was still struggling to recall anything about the last couple of days, but he had a feeling that in time that might clear up as well.

Tim did remember they had been building a gateway. He had even returned to the abandoned barn they had done the construction in. It was void of any gateway or of Dennis and Ezra, but there were bits of used wood and metal and tools still lying around.

"They did it," Tim said to himself, thinking that Ezra and Dennis had made it back to Foo. "I can't believe it worked."

Tim hiked back to the lake. He stayed off the main roads,

feeling like he didn't fit in with all the other tourists who were there to hear the trumpet and take pictures.

By midmorning he had reached the far edge of the lake where Dennis had talked about placing the gateway. Tim wanted nothing more than to return to his home and make sure his family was okay, but he also couldn't help but be curious to see if the gateway had been completed. He stepped into the cold water at the edge and breathed in deeply. He could feel the blood from his shivering feet moving up into other parts of his body and turning his veins to ice.

Without further thought, Tim dove into the water and kicked his legs as hard as he could. It was murky, dark, and filled with fish that kept thumping into him. His eyes scanned the underwater world for any sign of the gateway. Just as his lungs began debating with him over the importance of obtaining air soon, Tim spotted the faint outline of a big box. He kicked his feet and rose to the surface as fast as possible.

Tim sucked in air like a vacuum with a clean filter. He caught his breath and then dove back down under. This time he went right to the gateway. He recognized what he had helped build—the square box with the mismatched piece of street attached to the floor by a metal arm. The cement base holding the arm had been built by Hector Thumps and had survived the blast to now hold a second gateway—although it looked a bit more cracked and flimsy than Tim would have preferred.

Tim's lungs began to argue again.

He shot back up and filled his lungs with air. The cold

wasn't as painful anymore. And as Tim's head bobbed above the surface of the water, he noticed a boat motoring to the center of the lake. Tim took a deep breath and went back under.

He swam up and into the gateway. He stepped on the bottom of it, but nothing happened. He felt the walls and the ceiling of it.

Again with the lungs.

Tim pushed his feet up against the inside of the gateway to dart to the surface—but he had misjudged the gateway's front opening, and his head rammed into the inside wall. The gateway shook, and Tim grasped for the opening edge to pull himself out of the box. His frantic grasp rocked the gateway from side to side.

The concrete footing screamed and then snapped.

The ceiling of the gateway crashed down against Tim's head as the metal arm supporting the gateway broke free from its cement hold.

Tim's lungs were not just angry, they were spitting mad. He kept his mouth closed, struggling in the box as it fell deeper into the lake. Tim's body spun and his feet knocked up against all the surfaces inside the gateway.

A normal person might have perished right then and there from lack of air, but Tim's job as a garbage collector had given him superhuman strength in the lung department. There had been many times when he had been forced to hold his breath to prevent the putrid smell of other people's trash from assaulting his nose.

Now that skill was paying off.

The gateway spun as it dropped, sending Tim to the ceiling of it, which was actually the floor.

Had he been up on dry land watching the whole thing unfold as a movie, he might have noticed how his shoulder was pressed up against the uneven crack. He might also have heard the very faint sound of a trumpet pleasing the earth around it as a short German man with a large mustache played up above. He might even have wondered if, when the gateway was falling, it was passing through any water with a temperature divisible by seven.

But, of course, Tim wasn't up on dry land, he was trapped in a box, running out of air. Fortunately for him, there was a brief moment right before he ran out of breath for fate to align things properly.

The empty gateway hit the bottom of the lake and broke into more pieces than it had started out with.

ii

The night felt old. The wind was like a memorable song written long ago, and the stars were dim from years of trying to be noticed. Brindle thought even the Fté Mountains looked aged. Their outline made obvious by the light of the moons, they sat there slumped and out of energy.

"Hello," Brindle whistled into the trees. He was invisible and not yet sure that showing himself would be a good idea.

The fantrum trees shifted, their bark scuffing like coarse stones rattling against one another. Brindle didn't particularly

care for this region of Foo. True, it held some of the most magnificent scenery, but it seemed to be a breeding ground for unstable and newly birthed creatures of dreams. Brindle didn't mind a variety of fellow beings, but he liked to know how they felt about sycophants before he had to deal with them. He bounded up into a shifting tree and called out again.

"Hello?"

"It's late," a voice called back.

"I know," Brindle said. "It's important."

"I doubt that."

"I was told you might know how to get to the Invisible Village."

Two completely white eyes fluttered open and stared at Brindle from the dark.

"Why would anyone wish to visit the village?" a mouth beneath the eyes asked.

"I have reason," Brindle said.

"Sycophant?" the eyes queried.

"Yes."

The eyes came closer, moving out of the dark of the trees and into a spot where moonlight could rest on the shoulders of their owner. The being was tall, with a dark face and hands. He had a long, brown beard and solid white eyes with dark circles around them. His clothes didn't match and his shoes were on the wrong feet. His hair was combed into a style that didn't have much to do with style at all. There were smudges on his right cheek and left arm.

"I was told to look for Tosia," Brindle said.

"That's me. The village is not a place that any sycophant should visit," he said. "Your nature is one of happiness. The Invisible Village will bring you nothing but depression."

"I wouldn't visit if it weren't necessary," Brindle said. "My contact didn't know what you were. You are a . . . ?"

"One of the omitted," Tosia answered.

Brindle jumped down from the tree and materialized. "I've not heard of your kind," he admitted. "I apologize."

"No apology necessary," Tosia waved. "We've only one unique characteristic. Others can view us, but we cannot see ourselves."

"Truly?"

"Sadly," Tosia said. "I have no idea what I look like."

"What about mirrors, or glass?"

"We've no reflection."

"But I can see you."

"How do I look?" Tosia asked hungrily.

"Very nice."

"How generous of you. When I place an article of clothing on my body, it disappears to my eyes."

"Amazing," Brindle said with awe. "Why have I not heard of your type?"

"We've been here for some time," Tosia said. "But because of our condition, we're not the sort of pupil who seeks the desk at the front of the classroom. We prefer to be in the back."

"There's wisdom in watching the crowd."

"How nice of you," Tosia said. "Most would say we're cowards."

"Every breed has its noble and just."

"What a delightful little creature you are," Tosia said with joy in his voice. "You're not at all like the white one."

"White one?" Brindle asked.

"The white sycophant," Tosia answered. "She came to the village a long while ago."

"So Lilly is there?"

"She was last I had heard," Tosia said. "Her soul is sicker than many of the others. She would take up metal and destroy the whole of Foo with the hate she holds in her heart. It's a good thing she's so small and unimportant."

Brindle was quiet as he thought.

"I'm sorry if that was mean," Tosia said. "Small things can be important."

"Don't worry about what you've said," Brindle insisted. "I prefer people speak honestly with me."

"Really?" Tosia asked.

Brindle nodded.

"How's my hair?"

"Excuse me?" Brindle asked.

"I can't get anyone to tell me how I really look," Tosia lamented. "The omitted are all so insecure that we have a difficult time telling each other how we look. No one trusts anyone's opinion. How's my hair?"

"Too long," Brindle said.

Tosia looked crestfallen, and then his face lit up. "I knew

it," he said. "Everyone says it looks just fine, but I think they just want me to look worse than they do."

"What a strange breed," Brindle said kindly.

"We have a hard time trusting each other," Tosia said. "We're always scared that our neighbor is making us look bad."

"So, you can take me to Lilly?" Brindle asked, returning to the subject of his journey.

"I can take you to the mountains above the village," Tosia said, tugging at his own hair. "But I won't step in."

"Take me to the edge of the village and you will be paid well."

"I don't understand money," he said. "When I hold it, it does nothing. But others look at me differently."

Brindle smiled. "I don't understand it either."

Tosia tried to comb his hair with his hand.

"I hate to pressure you," Brindle said. "But there is some urgency in what I seek."

"Of course," Tosia waved. "Is my outfit okay?"

"Perfect," Brindle said before disappearing.

Tosia turned and began moving back into the trees. His stride was wide and almost mechanical. He walked with some unevenness due to the fact that he couldn't see his own feet.

"Where are you?" he asked the air.

"On your right shoulder."

"Should I shave?" Tosia asked.

"No," Brindle answered. "A beard looks good on you. Besides, shaving for you must be a bit precarious."

"It's never without blood."

"Keep the beard."

"Honest?"

"Of course."

Tosia increased his speed, running through the moonlit forest with purpose.

iii

Ezra peeked out from behind Dennis's right ear and growled. The front of the airport was crowded with patrons and police. Both Dennis and Ezra were sitting in the backseat of a cab in front of the Munich International Airport realizing that they were at an impasse.

"Look at all those stiff cops," Ezra whispered. "Can't a person just get on a plane and fly? Where's the trust?"

"It was lost years ago," Dennis said. "I hate to say it, but we still need Sabine. He did something to them last time to get me through."

"Your life is one big pause," Ezra seethed. "There has to be a way."

"I could stick you on someone else," Dennis offered.

"Don't think I haven't thought about it," Ezra said. "But I doubt I could find someone as dense and pliable as you to do my bidding."

Dennis felt needed.

"Are you going to get out?" the cab driver leaned back and asked. "Or were you planning to just keep talking to yourself?"

"Hold on," Dennis said. "I'm on the phone."

"Whatever," the driver said. "I'll have to drive around again. They won't let me just sit here. This is an airport."

"Then drive around!" Ezra yelled from behind Dennis's ear.

The driver, thinking it was Dennis yelling, put the cab into drive and drove out of the airport.

"We could try a boat," Dennis whispered to Ezra.

"Is there water between here and there?"

"It depends on how far west we have to go," Dennis answered.

"I don't know," Ezra snapped. "I just know that it's that way."

"So we'll take a boat?"

"I guess," Ezra said, bothered that his rage never garnered more respect.

"How far can you drive us?" Dennis asked the driver.

"Us?" he questioned.

"Me."

"As far as you have money."

"Take us to where there's water," Dennis said.

"To the shore?" the driver asked. "That's hours away."

"We have money."

"I'll need to see some of that now."

Dennis pulled out some money and promised the driver plenty if he would take them to the water.

"Will you be talking to yourself the whole time?" the driver asked.

"I was on the phone," Dennis insisted.

The cab driver rolled his eyes and signaled to get onto the autobahn.

"To be honest with you, I haven't been to the watery edge of Germany in some time," the cab driver announced. "It might be nice to see the shore. How about Cuxhaven?"

Ezra and Dennis didn't answer.

"I have an uncle there, and I think it's one of Germany's most beautiful vacation destinations," the cab driver explained.

Ezra sighed with disgust. "Don't people know that we don't care what they think?" he whispered into Dennis's ear.

Dennis sat back and said nothing, his bald head wondering what he was doing.

"Stop thinking," Ezra insisted. "Your eyes make that funny motion whenever you attempt to think."

"Sorry," Dennis said.

"There you go, stating the obvious again." Ezra looked around. "Are we still going west?" he whispered.

"No," Dennis said. "We'll have to go north to get to the sea."

"You know, you could talk to me," the cab driver butted in. "I hear you whispering to yourself and you remind me of my brother Ronald. I enjoy having conversation."

Ezra tucked himself back behind Dennis's ear, his purple fringe showing over the top.

"I guess I could talk to you," Dennis said awkwardly.

"*Sir gut,*" the cab driver said. "Let's start with what you are doing in Germany."

Dennis looked around at the world as it sped by. He could

see a river in the distance and row after row of gray buildings. He glanced down at the cab's dirty seats and dull windows. He looked at his own arms and traced the faint gray lines on his right arm with his left hand. His pants still were not wrinkled.

"What are you doing here in Germany?" the cab driver asked again.

"I have no idea."

The cab driver cleared his throat. "Just like Ronald. Maybe I begin. I have been driving a cab . . ."

Ezra jabbed his hands into his ear holes and cursed. In the history of angry toothpicks, none had ever had to endure such lazy and boring opposition. Where was the sword, the gun? Where was a true nemesis or at least a task wicked enough to cackle about?

There was nothing to cackle about!

He was in a taxi with Mr. Blandness traveling at one mile above the speed limit to a vacation spot.

Ezra jumped down from Dennis's shoulder and shoved himself into the crack at the back of the seat. He positioned himself just so that if Dennis shifted he would most likely prick his backside.

It was the most sinister thing Ezra could find to participate in at the moment.

CHAPTER THIRTY-FOUR

SHARING IS NOT ALWAYS A GOOD THING

I have seen bad things happen. It's no fun. Most humans try to avoid pain and sadness, but eventually the puddle of misery is too large to hop over or sidestep, and everyone's feet end up wet.

Leven knew the feeling of bad things happening.

When he was eleven, he had been picked as co-student of the week at Pinchworthy Elementary. On the surface, this sounds like a happy occasion, but in truth it was one of Leven's worst days.

He was in a small class, and everyone else had already been picked and had had their pictures on the wall. To make matters worse, Sally Dimp had been student of the week twice. But during one of the last weeks of school Leven's teacher was so busy grading tests that she didn't have time to review who had been

student of the week before and who hadn't. So she made everyone write down his or her name and put it in an empty box she had lying around labeled "Future Tests." She then drew a name.

"Sally Dimp."

A number of the students complained that Sally had already been student of the week twice. So Leven's teacher drew again.

"Leven Thumps."

"Who's that?" the boy who had sat next to Leven all year asked.

"He must have moved away," the overworked teacher said, putting her hand back into the box.

Leven then tried to point out that *he* was Leven, and that if he had moved, he would not have been able to write his name down and put it in the box.

His classmates just stared at him.

"Well, I can't waste time arguing this," the teacher said, frazzled from all the tests she was constantly having to grade. "Let's draw a second name, and that way if you *have* moved we will still have a student of the week."

"I haven't moved," Leven had said again.

"Still, better safe than sorry."

Leven had never felt sorrier. As he looked around at everyone he had gone to school with for so many years, he felt his soul give up. He could think of no reason to argue his existence any longer. He had known the second his name was picked that it would end up badly. Things always did for him. The misery he had felt every day of his life was so raw and painful that he decided to switch it

off and hope that when he was grown up and on his own he would be happy and appreciated.

Well, Leven was growing up. He was at least two inches taller now than when he had stepped into Foo. His clothes were tighter and his hair was in need of cutting. He pushed back that long hair from his eyes and stared at the Want.

Lith was shaking and dropping slowly.

The Want was standing in front of Leven turning in a circle and talking in multiple tongues. They were in the foyer off of the grand hall in the castle—the Want shifting in place on bare feet. An upside-down fire was burning on the ceiling above, the fire-light making the room dance with shadows.

The Want had been saying something about Leven's burden when, as before, he had become overwhelmed with incoming dreams. All Leven could do was watch as white strands of light vibrated in and out from the Want's body, his robe moving in and puffing out in small circular waves. Leven had seen the Want like this many times by now and figured it was best to let him be. It felt as if he were warming up to give the world's final sermon.

"Do you think he can hear us when he's like that?" an invisible Clover asked.

"I'm not sure," Leven said. "If he wants to, he probably can."

"I think we should get out of here."

"Not yet," Leven said, feeling oddly comfortable.

"You don't have to stay."

"I need to see what is required of me," Leven spoke.

"Still, something doesn't feel right."

Leven wanted to argue that point. Whereas the moment his name had been picked to be student of the week he had known something bad was coming, the opposite had happened here. The moment he was returned to his full size, he felt as if something good were approaching. His desire had been to get away, but now his head was filled with warm thoughts toward the Want, and strong images of Phoebe being freed. A terrific surge of possibility filled his being. He could see Winter and Geth, and he felt hopeful. The feeling was so unusual and surprising that Leven had to stop himself from smiling.

He let one slip.

"Are you smiling?" Clover asked in confusion.

Leven stood there smiling, unaware that he was gaining strength from the wake of emotions Winter's Lore Coil had created.

"I can't help it," Leven said. "There's something about this place."

"Like the fact that it's sinking? Or that your gift doesn't seem to work on this island?"

"This is the Want's home," Leven said. "He sets the rules."

"What about what he wants you to do?"

"I don't like to think about it," Leven admitted, the warm feeling fading just a bit. "But at the moment I can feel nothing but happiness."

"I'm worried about you," Clover whispered.

The Want stopped rambling and turned to face Leven. He whimpered just a bit and then stood tall.

"Are you okay?" Leven finally asked him.

"Fine," the Want replied kindly. "Are you ready?"

Leven nodded.

"Such a large weight to place on your shoulders," the Want grieved, stepping out across the room.

The happiness Leven felt dropped like a falling roller coaster. The Want scared him, but Leven also cared for him. He wanted desperately to make him proud and to restore Foo. He wanted to feel all the time the sense of peace and happiness he had recently been experiencing. He wanted to live in a place where beauty and dreams were powerful and vast.

Leven thought of Winter. She had been on his mind so strongly ever since he had seen the longing locked in a cage underground.

"You're warm," Clover whispered from on top of his head.

"Sorry," Leven said.

"It's kind of nice."

"This robe's so itchy," Leven complained, tugging at his sleeve.

"But it makes you look like you're a lithen or something," Clover said. "I wish I had a mirror."

"No, thanks," Leven said. "I don't want my reflection giving me grief again."

"Your reflection?" Clover asked.

"Last time I looked in a mirror, the way my reflection acted made me nervous."

"Your reflection acted?" Clover said, confused.

"Yeah," Leven said. "You know, how it speaks to you."

Clover laughed. "Reflections don't speak."

"Mirrors don't talk?"

"I think someone was messing with you."

The Want stepped back in, halting their conversation. His robe was billowing as wide as possible.

"The crowds have gathered," the Want said. "It is time for your sycophant to go. You must tell him to leave."

"Why?" Leven asked.

"This is not a place for alternate voices," the Want said. "You must listen only to the ones fate places in your head."

"Clover can be quiet."

"I know that," the Want said. "But we can't take the risk. Tell him to go."

"Go, Clover," Leven said firmly into the air.

"He's probably still there, isn't he?" the Want said.

"Probably," Leven agreed.

The Want sighed. "I can't stand the breed."

The Want clapped his hands and the entire room lit up like an undeveloped negative, revealing the outline of Clover clinging to the back of Leven's right leg. The Want's hands swooped like frantic ravens to wrap around Clover's neck and pull him off of Leven. It all happened so fast that Leven could barely register what had taken place.

Clover materialized, dangling from the Want's grip.

"It's a little tight," Clover complained. "I was just leaving."

"Let go of him," Leven insisted.

"I'm only assisting him in his exit," the Want said. "Now, leave us."

Clover looked at Leven sadly. The Want opened his grip, and Clover dropped to the bare dirt floor. He dusted off his palms as if disgusted and walked back toward the direction they had just come from. "I'll be right outside if you need me," Clover said bravely.

The Want clapped again.

"Okay, I'm leaving."

Clover reluctantly walked out.

"He wouldn't have ruined anything," Leven said.

"Your eyes are too young to see the hurt I am saving you from."

Leven looked back to where Clover had gone. The ground rumbled beneath his feet, moving enough to make Leven reach out to steady himself. "Will Clover be okay?" he asked.

"Sycophants always are," the Want said gently.

The Want faced Leven. There was still no visible sign of his eyes, but Leven had grown to be able to read his nods and gestures.

"They're waiting," the Want said kindly, an odd tinge of hope in his voice.

"I'm not sure I'm ready," Leven admitted, the gold in his eyes pulsating.

"Perhaps fate will spare you."

"Is that possible?" Leven said with hope.

"I suppose, if fate's design is for Foo to fall."

The Want faced the door and it opened. The grand hall was filled with thousands of dark robed beings. Everywhere there were hooded nits chanting and turning in circles. Groups of them were spinning together, creating swirling sections of moving blackness with white smoke ascending from them as they spun.

The ground rumbled.

The grand hall was oval shaped, with a tall, elaborately carved stage at the front end. A balcony ringed the entire oval except over the stage. Around the ceiling, the upper walls were lined with roven skulls, giving the place an uneasy crown molding. Firelight flickered behind every skull, causing those who looked up to feel as if they were being watched. Long, blood-red curtains ran from beneath the balconies to the floor, covering all the windows and blocking out any light the night might hold.

Both balcony and floor were filled to capacity, robed nits crowding the aisles and walkways. Their chanting was infectious, filling Leven's troubled mind with images of power and aggression.

"I feel weird," Leven said.

"Don't ignore it," the Want said back.

He opened his arms and the sea of nits parted, allowing him room to walk through. The crowd quieted like a scream covered by a thick pillow. Some touched the Want as he passed. Leven followed closely, letting the muted chanting fill his senses.

The Want stepped to the stage and stood behind a tall, well-polished tree stump. The front of the stage was carved to be a

map of Foo with images that moved as the eye followed. Behind the Want, ten nits sat playing instruments that Leven had never seen before. The music the instruments produced was intoxicating. Leven couldn't tell if he should listen or leave.

The room grunted as the ground shifted even more.

The Want stood behind the polished trunk. He reached down and grabbed the hem of his robe, then bolted upright, pulling his robe up over his head and completely off. Leven felt compelled to look away, but the Want was wearing a sheer orange robe underneath. He looked thin and frail, his eyes still covered.

The Want mumbled something.

Leven looked around at the empty faces of those gazing at the Want. They looked like pictures a child had drawn, round mouths and white eyes. A feeling of invincibility and completeness ran through Leven's veins like warm butter.

The floor began to glow as a mass of dreams pushed slowly up into the hall. Leven couldn't see the actual dreams, but he could feel the light. The floor bubbled like simmering white cheese. All around Leven, nits began to fall to the ground and roll in the light as brighter beams blasted up into the balconies.

The chanting increased and the music became louder.

Nits scattered nonsensical words around like bird feed. The Want shook and then without warning lifted his hood.

Light shot from his eyes, filling the grand hall with blazing whiteness and billions of tiny images. He trembled and bowed. As he moved, the light crystallized and settled like snow over the heads and shoulders of all those in the building.

Leven felt an intoxicating sensation settle over him.

Millions of dreams pushed in through the ground. Nits were lifted and flew about as they grasped to manipulate and participate in as many dreams as they could. Leven watched a group of nits float to the ceiling and hover in the substance of a hundred dreams.

The sound of uncontrolled appetites gasping for more filled the air.

Leven couldn't see the dreams, but he could see telts and avalands and sarus floating around the room. He could see people's homes and their aspirations. He wasn't in the dreams, but he was being buffeted from side to side by their presence.

He wished his gift would kick in. He wanted to be lifted to the ceiling and to feel the strength of manipulating a dream himself, as the others did. He reached out, hoping to hold onto a dream.

The ground shook.

No one paid it any mind, feasting on the dreams as quickly as they could. Two nits began to fight over a particularly dark dream coming in. The taller of the two held the dream and shook.

Leven could feel images and creatures moving through the air. He watched the Want standing there with his eyes glowing. The Want was counting on his fingers as if he were working some math out in his head.

The ground snarled and the music played on.

The balcony on the up side of the castle tilted, the front of it

bending down. Nits spilled like black beans down onto those below. Their peril didn't slow the dream gorging at all. Voices grew louder and Leven fell to the floor. His palms burned against the soil.

Something was under there. Leven pulled his hands back and looked at them as if they belonged to someone else.

A big nit dropped from a dream and landed across Leven's back. Leven rolled over and stood up. He reached down to help the nit who had fallen on him.

The nit just rocked back and forth, moaning and talking to himself, wanting no help. Everywhere Leven looked there was chaos and darkness.

The land rocked back and forth and dropped two feet rapidly. A second balcony fell as the wall behind it crumbled. Darkness from the outside plugged up the holes in the wall.

Two laughing nits flew into Leven. Leven fell flat against the floor again. There was definitely something in the dirt. The floor felt comfortable and soothing.

"Get up," a deep voice sounded in Leven's head.

Leven pushed himself to his feet and looked around. There were plenty of people speaking, but none of them were talking to him. He tried to spot the Want, who was no longer up behind the polished stump.

The ceiling began to break apart. Not a single nit seemed to care, however. Leven covered his head and ran past a large brick pillar that was collapsing on a swirling group of nits. Since the destruction was accidental, the nits found their lives expiring as quickly as the castle crumbled.

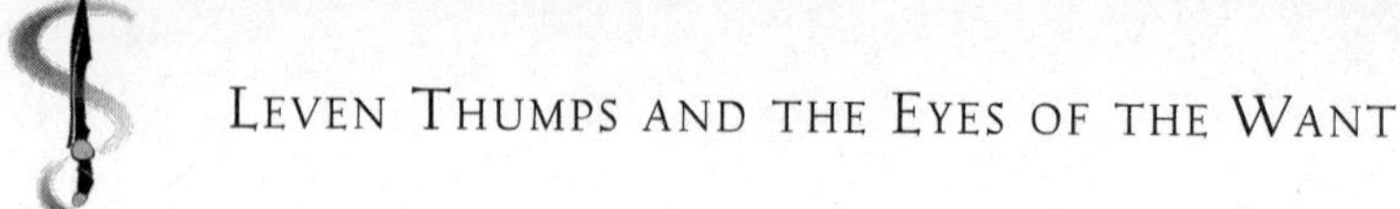

"Move," the voice sounded again.

Leven looked around, expecting to see the Want. He was not there. Leven moved through the crowd, dodging bits and pieces of the disintegrating castle. Fire broke from the fire pits, climbing the walls and boasting as to its swiftness, flame leaping from any raised point.

Another section of balcony moaned and then slid from the wall, crashing down like a waterfall of brick and mortar, drowning any in it or below it with dirt and stone.

Leven ran down the center of the room, dodging and weaving between nits too hopped-up on others' dreams to realize the severity of what was happening to them.

The ground wobbled like Jell-O. Leven flew against a wall and into a mess of dream-drugged nits. The remainder of the ceiling started to cave in, pulling the outside walls down with it. Leven worked himself up and moved into a hallway covered with arches. Large masses of dust billowed like storm clouds across the ground.

Leven ran down the arched hallway with the castle imploding behind him. A huge stone blew into the side of his left foot, spinning him around and into a tall pillar.

The castle was done for.

Leven slid against the floor, his head smashing into a stone column that had not yet fallen apart. His eyes crossed and his mind introduced him to a whole new level of darkness.

He was out, but his eyes burned gold beneath the closed lids.

CHAPTER THIRTY-FIVE

AWKWARD MOMENTS

Winter was scared. It was a feeling she was not entirely comfortable with. The very caverns they were racing through were simultaneously falling apart and filling with water. The two nits traveling with them, Andrus and Sait, were behind her and Geth was in front, feeling through the darkness for any possible passage or way of escape.

As Lith collapsed, it seemed to be going underwater faster and faster, its expiration date growing closer with each movement of soil.

"It's a dead end," Geth shouted back, digging at the wall for any loose rock. "Nothing but stone."

"I can't see anything," Winter said.

"Neither can I," Sait whined.

Lith shook.

"We'll have to go back a bit," Geth said. "Find another way."

"No," Andrus complained. "There's too much water."

"Well, there's no way out here," Geth added. "We have to go back."

A giant slurping sound echoed in the space behind them.

"Every pocket of air is being filled with water," Winter said.

Sait started to whimper.

"We could have used your gift now," Winter added, still disgusted that he had willingly given it away.

"Where's *your* gift?" he snapped back.

"Stolen."

Geth stopped.

He could feel something burning inside of himself. He thought back to being a toothpick and being pinned in the leafy weeds on the banks of the Washita River in Oklahoma. He remembered the feeling of turning his life over to fate—something he had done thousands of times. Since he had stepped back into Foo, however, he had let his feelings focus too much on what he should be doing. He had been upset by Azure's betrayal, sickened by the Want's abandonment. Now all his family and those who knew the true ways of Foo were either buried or dead.

Geth couldn't let that happen to him.

He was a lithen, and because of that he traveled by fate. Here he was showing his lack of faith by digging at a wall for a way out. Geth had stepped off of cliffs and walked through fire in his lifetime, knowing that fate would sort out the effect. He couldn't stop believing now. His heart felt as if all of Foo rested on his next action.

Geth folded his arms. Winter bumped into him as she moved forward. "What's happening?" she asked.

"Nothing," Geth said honestly.

"Then move."

Andrus and Sait bumped into Winter.

"Are we stuck?" Sait whined.

"No," Geth said his green eyes dark. "We're waiting for fate."

"Did he say death?" Andrus asked, not having heard correctly.

"Perhaps," Geth answered. "If that's what fate has in mind."

"This is ridiculous," Winter said. She motioned to Andrus and Sait, but it was too dark for them to see her.

The ground shook so violently that even the air was knocked around. Andrus moved closer to the group. Dirt and stone began to tumble all around them. The sound of water splashing and stone tearing was almost deafening.

"We have to get out of here!" Winter screamed. "We've got to get to Leven."

"I know," Geth hollered back.

"I'm going," Winter announced. "It's not fate that we die here standing around."

Geth grabbed Winter's arm to stop her, and for a second time seemed to stand still, waiting for her to make up her mind. In that instant she knew. The moment called for trusting in fate.

"I'll stay," she yelled.

"I knew you would," Geth yelled back.

"You'd better not be smiling."

"I'm not," Sait said, thinking she was talking to him.

"Nor am I," Andrus added. "The world is falling apart and we're just standing here."

"Hold on," Geth hollered.

Giant slabs of stone ripped from the cavern walls and pummeled the water. Waves washed over the four of them, trying to knock them down. Lith was breaking up.

"No offense," Andrus screamed, "but standing here seems like a really stupid strategy."

"No offense taken," Geth yelled back. "Hold onto each other."

All four of them huddled together as Lith pushed downward into the depths of the Veil Sea. The cavern cracked open and the stone that surrounded them relaxed its futile hold and dropped down. Geth leaned protectively over the other three as dirt and water beat against them like an angry rain.

The ground beneath Winter began to slide. "Geth!" she hollered.

Geth pulled her closer to him, moving into Andrus and Sait's personal space and onto what seemed like the last stable piece of soil. Winter stood on top of Geth's feet and Sait stood on Andrus's. Everything was dropping down and away from them.

"Don't let go of me," Sait begged.

"We won't," Winter yelled.

The rest of Lith's innards continued to shift and rumble. In what seemed like hundreds of minutes later, the roar of falling objects began to subside. In another five minutes there was

nothing but the sound of water far below and silence in the air.

"Look," Andrus exclaimed, motioning upward with his head. "Light."

Hundreds of feet above them there was a small crack in the surface of Lith. Small drops of moonlight dripped through and down onto their heads. With each bit that oozed in, the scene around them became clearer.

It wasn't good.

All four of them were standing on a piece of ground no larger than four square feet. The piece of ground was at the top of a column of thin stone that stretched at least two hundred feet high. They were four people occupying four feet of rock on a precarious pillar in the belly of Lith.

Andrus shifted and the rock column swayed just a bit.

"Don't do that," Winter said.

"Sorry," Andrus said. "My feet are asleep."

"Are you smiling now?" Winter hissed at Geth.

"We're alive, aren't we?" he pointed out.

"I hate to be a problem," Sait said. "But I don't know how much longer I can stand still. My legs are throbbing."

The moonlight continued to pour in. The crack up above was about five inches wide and a foot long. It was comforting to see the light, but it was an uneasy feeling to realize that it was most likely illuminating their end.

"Could we climb down?" Winter asked.

"I don't think so," Geth said. "The second any one of us shifts too much, this whole pillar will collapse."

"So it was fate's idea to save us just so it could finish us off in a clever fashion?" Winter asked.

"Maybe we could just jump down," Andrus said. "It might be nothing but water below."

"Go ahead," Winter said.

"I'm just suggesting."

They had their arms around each other, Winter still on Geth's toes and Sait on Andrus's. Dust in the air made Sait sneeze.

The column rocked.

"Don't do that," Winter whispered fiercely.

"I can't help it," Sait said apologetically.

The moonlight dripped off their heads and spiraled down the column. Geth looked down. There was no sign of a bottom.

"Seriously, Geth," Winter said. "We have to do something."

"I know," he said. "I just can't think what that something is."

"Aaachoo!"

The column swayed again, and everyone held on tightly to each other, anticipating that the thin stone support was going to snap at any moment.

"Achoo, achoo!"

Winter was about to plead with Sait to stop breathing in dust when she heard a faint "Gesundheit."

"Did you hear that?" Winter asked.

"Hear what?" Geth said.

Sait sneezed again.

"Gesundheit."

"Someone's up there. Up above us," Andrus said unnecessarily.

"Hello," Geth hollered out.

There was a long pause and then the sound of a very familiar voice.

"Toothpick?" Clover yelled down.

"Clover?" Winter yelled up.

"Help us," Sait yelled out.

"What are you doing down there?" Clover called, his voice echoing off the hollow walls of Lith.

"Never mind that," Geth said. "Is Leven with you?"

"No," Clover said. "He's with the Want. I had to leave."

"Well, can you find a rope or something?"

"Just give me a minute," Clover said.

"All right," Winter answered. "But we probably don't have much more time than that."

Andrus's right foot slipped and he started to fall. Geth held him up with his arms, but Andrus couldn't support his own weight with just his left foot. It slipped off the lip of the stone pillar, and his body slid down. Geth kept ahold of Andrus's right arm while Andrus clung to Winter's ankle with his left hand.

"Don't let me fall," Andrus yelled, scraping his feet against the stone column in an attempt to find footing.

"Hurry!" Winter screamed, knowing she couldn't hold Andrus for much longer.

Sait, who had been standing on Andrus's toes, fell to his knees. His right knee slipped off the column, but he was able to put his arms around Geth's and Winter's legs to keep from falling.

"Really hurry," Winter yelled.

Geth felt something tickle his nose. He thought at first that it might be a bug, but as it brushed against his arm he could see it was a white strand of thread.

"What's this?" Geth yelled.

"It's all I could find," Clover hollered down. "I took it from those awful people Leven used to live with. They never used it—besides, there's nothing else long enough to reach you from up here."

"There's no way this will support us," Geth said.

"Just tie it around your waists," Clover yelled, his voice sounding huge in the echo of the cavern. "I have an idea."

Geth pulled the thin string down. It was slick and smelled minty.

"That's going to save us?" Winter said. "It's dental floss."

"It's all we've got," Geth said. "Circle it around your waist and Sait's a couple of times. Then have Andrus tie the end to himself."

"We don't exactly have free hands," Andrus pointed out.

"We'll help."

They worked the dental floss around them twice, using their fingertips and mouths. Eventually they got the end tied to Andrus.

"I don't want to be a downer," Andrus said. "But if this is the best we've got, we're going to die."

Moonlight dripped down through the hole up above and rolled along the length of the dental floss. It circled around them, coating every bit of the floss.

"Interesting," Geth said.

"Moonlit floss?" Winter said sarcastically, her green eyes huge. "I guess I can stop worrying."

"Hold on," Geth said. "If heated, the moonlight here can become quite rigid and strong."

The next wave of moonlight flowed down the floss, coating the first layer and making the floss even thicker.

"How coated does it have to be to support all of us?" Winter yelled.

The ground began to rumble again.

"I hope not too thick," Geth answered.

More moonlight raced down the floss, making the rope about a quarter-inch thick.

The ground rumbled even more. Stone from the ground above them broke off and fell down. The thin column their lives were depending on wobbled like a rubbery carrot as the moonlight continued to flow, dripping slowly along the line as it wound around the four of them.

"I can't hold on much longer," Andrus said, barely clinging to Winter's heel.

Geth shifted his hold and tried the strength of the line. "It's getting there. Hang on."

"My knee is slipping," Sait cried. "And I can't feel my legs."

"Just hold on," Geth encouraged.

"This is crazy," Winter yelled. "We're waiting for the moonlight to make a strand of dental floss strong enough to hold us? I bet Clover doesn't even have the other end tied off."

"That would be a problem," Geth said calmly.

"That would be a horrible problem," Andrus wailed.

"I'm going to jump," Sait said. "There's got to be water down there. I can hear things splashing into it."

"If you jump, you take all of us," Winter said frantically. "And for every splash I hear down there, I also hear a crash."

"But my knee."

"And my legs."

Moonlight spiraled down the floss for another coating, making the string about the width of a heavy plastic cable. The ground shook and the column moved enough to cause Winter to lose her balance. She fell backwards a few inches before Geth was able to steady her. His grabbing ahold of her caused the pillar to sway more.

"I'm going to throw up," Andrus said.

"I'm going to jump," Sait threatened again.

The cavern shook, and a spectacular crack rang out as the column snapped in two and dropped to the ground like a gigantic broken arrow.

Winter screamed. Andrus wailed. And Sait passed out as the stone dropped out from beneath them. There was a rush of wind and then a jarring stop as the moonlit floss miraculously held strong. The looping around the four of them wasn't as perfect as it should have been, but it was holding. Andrus was hanging from his knees, Sait was cinched up to Winter's left side, and Geth and Winter were tied side by side at the waist. They all four swung like an abstract pendulum.

"Amazing," Geth chimed in.

The ground above and below continued to rock and rumble.

Clover stuck his head down in the hole and smiled at the sight. "It worked," he clapped.

"Perfectly," Geth said.

"Now get us up," Winter pleaded.

"Up?" Clover asked. "I guess I hadn't thought that far. You want to know how I warmed it up?"

"What?" Winter asked, not caring about anything besides getting up and getting untied.

"How I heated up the floss?" Clover clarified.

Only his echo responded.

"I tied the other end to a fantrum tree and then told the tree a bunch of stories about cute girls. I've never seen a fantrum tree go so red so fast. It not only heated up the string, it melted a bunch of bark off its crown. I've got some great stories."

"Fantastic," Winter yelled. "Now get us up."

"I'm going to need to get some help for that."

"Well, get it fast," Andrus whined.

"Right," Clover said, dashing off, all humor gone from his voice.

Geth and Winter and Andrus and Sait were left to swing under the dripping moonlight.

"You must think fate's pretty clever," Winter said, her arms going limp from the loss of circulation.

"I'm never disappointed," Geth said. "Fate *is* pretty clever."

"Clever? I'd write that down if I had a pen," Andrus said

sincerely. "Or a piece of paper. Or actual feeling in my hands."

"Don't worry," Sait said. "He'll probably say something like it again before the night's through."

Winter smiled. The four of them swung gently in the night as the destruction of Lith proceeded.

CHAPTER THIRTY-SIX

SWIG OF FOO

Surprise parties are fun. Unless, of course, the ones waiting to surprise you are a group of murderous thugs who think you took something of value from their possession and now want it back. If that is the case, I suggest you give it to them and run.

Fast.

But the kind of surprise parties with cake and streamers and piñatas that you had no idea were coming can be very satisfying. Who doesn't like walking into a room where they thought there was nothing but leftovers to discover a ring of friends and a cake? If you meet people who say they wouldn't like that, do not trust them in any aspect of life. In fact, I suggest you run.

Fast.

Tim was surprised.

It was as if the forces of the universe had gotten together and said, "You know that brilliant garbage man with the pretty wife

and two children? Let's throw him a surprise party that will not only catch him off guard, but will change every thought he ever has from now on."

Tim was very surprised.

One minute he was in a lake drowning, and the next he was standing on a dirt road facing a row of spectacular mountains and being swarmed by small furry creatures who insisted he was brilliant and would be best suited by picking them.

Tim screamed for only the third time in his life.

He batted and swatted and kicked. He danced and punched and rolled over and over against the ground. Still the sycophants covered him. A brown-haired one took his hand and begged him to consider choosing it. Tim flung the poor thing off to the side of the road. A red-haired one latched onto Tim's right arm and kept telling Tim how good it was and how safe he would be if only he would choose it. Tim pulled the sycophant off his arm and tossed it to the ground. Another planted itself on Tim's foot and looked up at him with wide eyes, pleading to be the one. Tim kicked his leg and sent the sycophant flinging a good half mile into some trees.

"Stop it," Tim yelled. "Get away from me."

"You'll do fine," one said.

"I think you'd be very smart to pick me."

"You're a wise human, and I am here to serve."

The sycophants fought with one another, kicking and punching until only a handful of the most dominant ones were still fighting over Tim. Two knocked each other out, leaving only a fat gray one and a wiry blond one. Tim swatted at both of them, but

they kept disappearing and then reappearing to tell him something positive about himself.

The fat one kicked at the blond one, but as it kicked, the blond sycophant pulled the fat one's leg up, spinning its confused adversary into the trees.

The blond sycophant materialized on Tim's right arm.

"And then there was me," it said.

Tim screamed for the fourth time in his life. His foot

slipped on the dirt path and he fell to the ground face first.

"You're okay," the sycophant said, disappearing quickly. "You're in a place called Foo."

Tim pushed himself up and stared in the direction of the sycophant's voice.

"This is Foo?" Tim asked with excitement.

"Yes, this is Foo."

Tim smiled a weary smile.

"You know about it?" the sycophant asked, surprised. "How can that be?"

"I've been trying to get here," Tim said, standing slowly. "I can't believe it exists. What are you?"

"I'm a sycophant. My name is Swig. But, as is customary, you can rename me if you wish."

"A sycophant?" Tim asked.

"We are aware that the term has been perverted in Reality," Swig said. "But it was our word here first. Somehow it leaked through dreams into your vocabulary long ago."

"And where exactly is here?"

"Foo."

"I know that," Tim said. "But where is Foo?"

A horselike creature with six legs flew across the sky, landed gracefully, and galloped into the trees. Tim stared at it with awe.

"Foo exists in the folds of your mind," Swig said.

"Impossible."

"Really?" Swig said sincerely. "And yet here you are."

Tim looked at himself. He looked down at his arms and

legs. He shuffled his feet against the dirt and ran his hand through his hair.

"I'm here," Tim said. "I can't believe it's real."

"Believe it," Swig said. "And I'm here to help you in any way I can."

"It would help if I could see you," Tim said.

Swig materialized instantly. He was about eleven inches tall, with blond fur all over his body. He was wearing a dark brown robe that hung open at the front, showing his furry stomach and chest. Swig had soft purple eyes and ears that looked like flat maple leaves that had been pressed in a book for years. His feet were bare, as were his knobby, long fingers. He smiled in a submissive, unassuming way.

"I'm looking for someone," Tim said.

"Really?" Swig said, having never heard of a nit who had come to Foo looking for something, much less one who already knew of Foo.

"A girl," Tim said. "She goes by the name of Winter."

"Nice," Swig replied seriously. "I've got a sister named Spring."

Tim looked deflated. "I guess it would have been too much to hope that you knew her," he said.

"Foo's a giant place," Swig said. "But if you must find her, fate will put her in your path. It brought you here."

"Fate?" Tim asked, looking around. "Are there people around I could ask?"

"The city of Cusp is just a couple of miles down," Swig said.

"All new nits are welcomed there. Perhaps someone there has heard of this Winter."

"Which way?"

Swig pointed.

A light rain began to fall. Lightning flashed far away in the valley of Morfit as a small storm passed through. Tim could hear faint whispering in the wind.

It was insulting.

"Ignore the thunder," Swig said, noticing Tim wince. "It can be quite rude. Now, I've had one burn before you. He preferred that I walk behind him. Do you have a preference?"

"No."

"Would it be too forward if I asked to ride on your shoulders?"

Tim reached down and pulled Swig up onto his left shoulder as the distant thunder called him weak-chinned.

"It's like it knows me," Tim said, referring to the thunder.

"Foo is a stranger to no man," Swig said. "A surprise, maybe, but no stranger."

Tim moved quickly in the direction Swig had previously pointed. He was bewildered and confused, but a larger part of him was relieved to have finally found Foo.

CHAPTER THIRTY-SEVEN

DANGLING

Geth, Winter, Andrus, and Sait swung in small circles at the end of the moonlit floss. The rope holding them was now as big around as a quarter. The rumbling had increased to the point where they had to yell to one another to be heard.

"We can't hang here forever," Andrus cried.

"I've got no circulation in the bottom half of my body," Sait said. "Can't someone just loosen the rope a bit?"

"No," Geth insisted.

"You lithens are infuriating," Andrus said.

"Loosen the rope and we all fall," Winter pointed out.

Clover slid down the moonlit cord and landed softly on Geth's head.

"Everyone doing okay?" he asked.

"I've been better," Winter admitted.

Clover looked at Geth closely. "Are you losing weight?" he asked. "Because you look great. I didn't think diets made you shorter."

"He's shrinking," Winter said.

"Oh, Leven had that problem," Clover said. "Anyhow, it seems that Lith is falling apart. From up top, I could see the Want's house crumbling in the distance. It's gone now."

"Our heart goes out to him," Winter said, frustrated. "I hope we live to see the wreckage."

"Lith's not exactly falling apart," Geth said, ignoring Winter's frustration. "The soil is slithering beneath the water to join with the soil of the gloam. By morning Lith will be completely gone. Just a spot on the water."

"I wish I had one of those cameras from Reality," Clover said. "I know I'll always have the memory of this, but the details—I forget some . . ."

The cavern bellowed and hissed. The cord they were hanging from bounced up and down.

"The moonlight's spongy tonight," Clover said.

Winter had a clever response to that, but it was drowned out by the loud scraping of sheets of rock breaking free and crashing to the ground. At the same moment, the five of them were pulled upward about six feet in a long, dragging motion.

"We moved!" Sait exclaimed.

"And it was up," Andrus added.

"I'll see what's happening," Clover said.

He scampered up the rope, hand over hand, and disappeared out of the hole and into the great above.

The rope dragged upward another four feet. This time, after the initial pull, the rope kept moving up slowly.

"Have you thought about what might happen if we actually make it?" Winter asked, her neck hanging back from the position she was tied in.

"The circulation will return to our bodies," Andrus said.

"It's not that," Winter said. "I'm pretty sure the hole isn't big enough to pull us through."

Everyone looked up.

"It's not big enough to pull even one of us through," Sait wailed.

"Any suggestions?" Winter asked Geth.

"Fate's gotten us this far," he replied.

"Remind me never to be in peril with you again," Winter said passionately. "This isn't a test to see if you believe, it's the last moments of our lives, last moments we should be using to save Leven."

Clover scrambled back down headfirst. When he had almost reached them he lost his grip on the slick, moonlit rope and fell, crashing into Geth's head.

"Sorry. It's the trees," Clover said breathlessly. "And the bushes and even stones. They're all uprooting and moving to higher ground. The tree you're tied to is trying to get up to the roundlands. All the stones are rolling to the sea."

"They know Lith is sinking," Geth said quietly.

"That's not such a hard thing to figure out," Clover said. "I bet the island is halfway underwater. I can hear the water rising beneath you even now."

"That tree better hurry," Sait said.

The small stream of moonlight lit the cavern enough that they could fully witness its falling apart.

"What about the opening?" Geth asked Clover as they continued to jerk upward. "Can it be widened?"

Clover ran back up the shaky rope.

"Seeeeee," Geth said to Winter, his voice shaking from the movement. "It'll work ouuuuut."

Twelve seconds later Clover was back down.

"There's nothing I can do," Clover said. "The ground is too hard to break apart."

"Well, we're not going to fit through that," Sait complained as the rope dragged them closer.

"Then we're going to die," Andrus said softly, as if he had just now realized the true severity of the situation.

"Careful," Geth said. "We escaped from the cage, had a pillar to stand on, and are now being suspended by moonlight. I'd say fate has something besides death in store for us."

"I guess we'll find out momentarily if you're right," Winter said.

The tree on the other end must have been getting desperate, because they were now moving up in a series of rapid jerks.

"Wow, that tree must be jumping," Geth said.

"How sad," Clover observed. "It probably abandoned its

roots. It won't live even if it does find dry, solid soil."

They were twenty feet from the opening.

"This is bad," Sait bawled.

Ten feet.

"My pathetic life is flashing before my eyes," Andrus said. "And I'm embarrassed by how pointless it is."

Three feet.

"Hold on," Geth said unnecessarily, reaching up to touch the ceiling.

He grabbed at the edge of the opening and tried as hard as he could to pull at the ground. It was solid stone, and his strength was not enough to do anything with it.

The tree pulled them up farther, shooting Geth's arm through the hole and cramming his and Winter's heads against the cavern's ceiling.

The moonlight holding them creaked as the scared tree frantically tried to climb higher. The rope twisted and pinned Andrus and Sait right up under Geth and Winter. Clover hopped around all of them looking for anything he could loosen or some way he could help. The cavern rumbled and choked as the sound of rushing water filling in holes increased below.

"I can't breathe," Andrus gasped. "The rope."

"My lungs are being smashed," Sait added.

Geth's and Winter's faces were pushed tight against the ceiling, preventing them from speaking as freely as those with bound lungs.

Up above, the frightened tree pulled as hard as it could. Just

as the rope was about to cut everyone in half, the moonlight broke and Geth, Winter, Clover, Andrus, and Sait fell hundreds of feet into an entirely different mess.

The freed tree, meanwhile, hopped its way to a higher ground that would soon be nothing but water.

CHAPTER THIRTY-EIGHT

INTO THE DARK

The air above the castle was filled with hundreds of confused rovens. Their panicked screaming competed with the sound of Lith being dragged under. Over half of Lith was underwater, and every tree and bush that had ever grown on the island was tearing up roots to get to where the castle once stood.

The roundlands on the top of Lith were filling in like an old forest. Other trees, unable to make it that far, plummeted off cliffs and mountain walls down into the Veil Sea, their limbs waving desperately as they fell to their wet deaths.

The great castle that once had been was now several smaller structures covered in debris and fire. Nits by the hundred were fleeing from the scene, only to be trampled by trees or brought up short by the increasing lack of land.

Lith was disappearing.

Leven heard the sound of feet running and tried to open his

eyes. His head felt like someone had filled it with lead and was now jumping on it. He could smell smoke and feel heat on the right side of his face.

He willed his eyes to open, but they wouldn't.

His thoughts were abstract and confusing. He kept seeing his mother and Antsel, only to have their faces replaced by those of Addy and Terry. He could see the first time he had met Winter, and the dark center of the earth where he had first been introduced to Geth. He could see Clover under his bed and Geth as a man. He could see his mother and her smiling at him. He could see the Want's eyes, shriveled and dangling.

"Help me," Leven whispered as he lay there between the mounds of rumbling debris.

There was no one to hear him. Even if there had been any nits nearby, they never would have stopped, too concerned for their own lives.

Leven could hear the cries of the rovens and the screams of people running about. All the noise was punctuated by the ripping apart and disintegration of Lith.

"Move," the Want's voice sounded.

Leven's body shook with chills. The voice seemed to push through his skin and scrape up against his bones.

"Move." The Want's speech was like the sound of water being poured over hot coals.

Leven opened his eyes. There was fire to the right of him and smoke everywhere. But there was no Want. Leven's right hand was bloody from a gash he had suffered while being blown off his feet.

"Arise."

Leven stood slowly, his black robe moving in the odd wind. He was surprised by all the trees everywhere. One tree in the distance caught fire, and he watched it jump off the edge and down into the water. Leven could see some nits still with their faces to the ground sucking on the last bits of dreams and refusing to run for their lives.

"Come," the voice whispered directly to Leven's soul.

"Where are you?" Leven asked the air, not expecting an answer. The Want's voice seemed to originate more from inside of him than from some other place.

Leven turned.

There was a large portion of the castle still standing. The far side of it smoldered, and all around it lay stones and rock that had crumbled from its face. Hundreds of trees huddled together near it, as if it offered safety.

"Quickly," the voice hissed.

Leven stepped through the wreckage and around a rectangular fire. The trees circling the castle were not about to let him through. Almost instinctually, Leven raised his hand, and the trees reluctantly parted.

"Come," the Want's voice whispered.

Leven's heart was torn. His soul was so confused. Ever since he had seen the longing, his feelings for Foo had intensified. He wanted nothing but to set her free and let the whole of Foo feel as he did. He knew fate had a path it needed him to walk, but Leven wished the Want would just take care of whatever fate wanted so that he could release Phoebe.

"Come," the Want's voice said sternly.

Leven kicked at a large wooden plank that had most likely been a door at some time. He reached down and pulled it out of the way and stepped into an archway that was covered with stone and as dark as decay.

"Come."

Leven's heart beat like the slamming of doors—each thump more painful and perceived than the last. He moved down into the dark and found a large room still intact. Light from a fire lit it just enough for him to see his way.

"Forward," the voice sounded.

The word seemed to give Leven a bit of hope, as if he were moving in the right direction. The ground beneath him shook like a beaten carpet. He could still hear the faint screams of rovens and nits outside. At the end of the room was a dark hallway almost entirely hidden by long, gray drapes. Leven parted the fabric and stepped behind it. The drapes settled back into place and silenced all noise from outside.

Leven looked into the dark. He moved forward, reaching out into the blackness. His hand trembled and his heart pounded loudly enough for him to hear it.

A thick, screeching form sprang from the darkness and pounded Leven in the chest. He fell backward onto the ground, grasping at his assailant, tearing away handfuls of stringy blackness. Leven rolled over, pulling the being with him. He shifted and wrapped his arms around the form, squeezing the breath out of it. Three thin lines of moonlight scratched across the attacker's face.

"You," Leven whispered in disbelief.

"I need the key," the Want's shadow demanded, shoving his dark fist into Leven's face.

Leven saw stars and felt the earth move.

"Give me the key!"

Leven tore at the shadow's face, ripping bits of black from its chin and neck. As quickly as Leven tore the pieces away, the shadow regained its shape. The shadow screamed and bit Leven on the cheek.

"The key!" it shrieked.

"No," Leven yelled, turning to hold the shadow around its neck.

The shadow disappeared and reappeared, holding Leven in the same position.

"You can't defeat me," the shadow hissed.

Leven tried clapping his hands, remembering how he had gotten rid of Sabine's shadows. The trick didn't work. Leven was not surprised, as the Want's single shadow was so much more substantive and humanlike.

"I need the key!" The shadow tore at Leven's robe, grasping for the key that hung around his neck.

Leven pulled himself up onto his knees and swung, plowing a hole right through the shadow. The dark form screamed as the hole filled back in.

It was so dark that at times Leven couldn't even see what he was fighting. But he could feel the shadow grasping at the key and trying to pull it off of his neck.

Leven pushed forward, shoving the shadow up two stairs and into a wall. The wall, already weakened from the rumbling ground of Lith, pushed out. Leven and the shadow rolled into a half-collapsed room with no roof.

Leven wriggled from the shadow and kicked it in the jaw as he stood up. The shadow flew back, disappeared in a puff of black, and reappeared two inches in front of Leven, sending a swift kick to Leven's gut. As Leven bent to breathe, the shadow ripped the leather cord from around his neck. Leven reached out, grabbing the key as it was being pulled away. He yanked the key so hard that the leather strap broke, leaving him with the key and the shadow with the cord.

Leven clutched the key as tightly as he could.

The Want's shadow stood there staring at Leven's closed fist.

"It's mine," the shadow hissed.

"I don't think so," Leven panted.

"I held it and I want it back," the shadow screeched. "He who casts me is a fool to have let it go."

The shadow lunged, tearing at Leven's clenched fingers. Leven pulled back and the shadow stilled itself.

"I want it."

Leven relaxed his grip just a bit. Moonlight pushed in between his fingers and sparkled off the key.

The shadow moaned. It sprang toward Leven just as the surface of Lith made a giant rocking motion. Leven's left foot slipped, and as he reached out to steady himself, his fist slashed against the Want's shadow. The bit of key sticking out sliced off

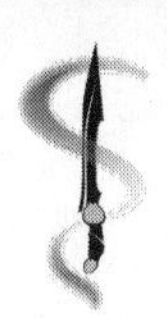

a portion of the shadow's right cheek. The chunk of black fell to the ground wriggling and hissing. Unlike before, the missing piece did not re-form on the shadow.

Leven looked at the key. "The metal," he whispered.

The shadow lunged again, and this time Leven swung his arm in a broad arc, slicing off the shadow's right arm. The arm fell to the ground and crawled out of the room hissing.

The shadow disappeared and reappeared behind Leven. It kicked Leven in the back of the knees. But as he fell, he turned and sliced off the shadow's two legs. The shadow fell to the ground. It screamed and hollered, its eyes focused on the key the whole time.

Its severed legs made such a huge hissing sound that rovens up above took notice and began to circle.

"I want the key," the shadow wailed. "I want to hold it again."

"I won't make that mistake twice," Leven said.

He stepped forward and sliced the shadow's neck. The shadow's head fell to the ground and screamed.

"Never," Leven whispered.

A huge roven picked up one of the shadow's legs and flew off. Another roven took the screaming head, and a couple of others moved in and began to fight over the body.

Leven looked around him. Lith was falling apart even further. The sound of fire and water and crumbling stone filled his head.

"Was that what I was supposed to do?" Leven yelled to the sky.

A strong wind blew down and brought behind it a momentary silence. It was as if the sound had been muted. Leven turned

to look back toward the direction he had come from.

A soft voice whispered, "It is time."

At first Leven had seemed to hear the voice in his heart. Now he was clearly hearing it in his mind.

"Fate is ready," the voice said.

Leven stepped back into the dark hall and down the steps. The hallway opened into a stone-walled chamber. His soul was unsteady and disappointed that there was still more for him to do.

A low wind blew and a ray of moonlight slipped through a thin crack, exposing a sword resting by itself on the ground. It lay there like an infant nobody wanted.

It had not been there before.

Its hilt was egg shaped, and the center of it glowed a soft yellow. The blade was sharp on one side and covered with jagged teeth on the other. It wasn't as long as a typical sword, but it wasn't as short as a knife either.

Leven looked at it lying there and felt a great sense of danger swell within his body. It was as if the very air was planning to kill him. He reached down and picked the sword up with one swift movement. He held it in his left hand, not wanting to get blood from his cut hand on it. He marveled at the metal that had been used to create it.

"They can see you," the Want's voice said.

Leven looked around anxiously, wielding the sword. The moonlight shifted and disappeared, leaving the stone room pitch-

black. A feeling of suffocating dread filled the air. Leven heard someone stepping closer.

"Who's there?" Leven shouted.

Heavy footsteps pressed against the stone floor.

"Who is it?" Leven demanded, still energized from the fight he had just survived.

"Thrust the sword into the dark," the Want's voice said.

"I can't," Leven said strongly.

"Thrust the sword into the dark."

Leven's body burned. He longed to make Foo right, but his heart was too confused to obey. He hefted the sword in his hand.

"Thrust the sword into the dark."

Leven's body took over. He pulled back and thrust the sword. His hand seemed to glide effortlessly through the air, coming to a stop against something solid and cold. Whatever he had hit crumbled to the floor with a soft thud. Large patches of clouds shifted in the dark sky above, and moonlight burst through a thousand openings, illuminating the room in sparkling shafts.

There on the ground in front of Leven lay the Want.

CHAPTER THIRTY-NINE

Too Late

Geth, Winter, Clover, Andrus, and Sait hit the water like a gangly stone, arms and legs flailing like a fight scene in the Sunday comics. The rope around them tangled, making it almost impossible for them to swim up for air.

Winter pushed at the rope. She could feel Sait pulling her under as he tried to get up above the water. The rushing water was trying desperately to find a way out of the cavern. The group of tethered beings spun as they were pushed up against and around giant stalagmites and walls. If it weren't for the rope binding them, they would have been separated at every turn.

Sait screamed.

Clover bounced around from Andrus's knee to Geth's head to Winter's shoulder. All five of them dropped six feet as the water fell suddenly to a lower level.

"Hang on," Clover said.

It was dark, and every precipice and wall came as a complete surprise. They hit another stalagmite and the water pulled them around the side of it.

The roar of water up ahead was almost deafening. A moment later they dropped twenty feet, dipping down into the water and then bobbing back up like a barrel. A rock fell from above and hit Andrus on the left shoulder.

He screamed but could barely be heard.

"We'll get through this," Geth said. "Lith is a series of caves and caverns, but there are many openings as well."

"What if the water has already risen above the openings?" Winter screamed.

"I hadn't thought of that," Geth said almost cheerfully. "It'll be interesting to find out."

Sait passed out, obviously lacking interest. His body became dead weight that beat up against the rest of them.

"If Lith is halfway under, then—" Water filled Geth's mouth, causing him to cough and sputter.

"If Lith is halfway under," he tried again, "then there should still be a few openings."

"Light," Andrus shouted.

It was faint, but the others could see it as well. There was an opening, and the night sky wasn't quite as dark as the cavern walls. The opening was wide enough for them to get through, but showed no signs of what was on the other side of it.

"We're moving too fast," Winter yelled. "What if there's a drop?"

"We had to have been at the very top of the island," Andrus said.

"I didn't think we were that—" Geth never got a chance to say "high." The thick sleeve of water they were caught in reached the hole and spat them out with force. All five of them blew out of the cliff's wall. Unfortunately, they were hundreds of feet above the Veil Sea.

Winter screamed, her voice trailing like a falling star.

Andrus used the moment to imitate Sait and pass out. Clover grabbed onto Winter's head, covering her eyes with his hands, and Geth spread his arms and, like a true lithen, enjoyed the ride down.

ii

Leven fell to his knees.

The sword he had thrust was piercing the side of the Want's left shoulder. It would have been a superficial wound to anyone else, but fate had guided Leven's hand and found the weak spot.

There is only one way to kill a Want. It is not an easy thing to do. I would have never even thought it possible if I had not been reading a dusty old book I stumbled upon in an abandoned candle shop in Ohio. In it was a story that spoke of the Want's possessing a weak spot—a small, red circle that travels across his skin, constantly shifting and moving. There are, of course, many spots that drift across the Want's skin, but only one is the weak spot. If someone who is picked by fate hits the Want on the right mark, then it is meant to be, and the Want will die.

"No," Leven said angrily. "Why would you?"

He picked the Want up in his arms. He felt so small and light. The Want's eyes were still covered, but Leven could see him smiling.

"I'm so sorry," the Want said, laughing lightly.

"Why?"

"Purely selfish," the Want choked. "I have lived too long. I'm so tired of all the dreams and the desires. This will be your problem now."

"I don't understand," Leven said carefully.

"How could you ever understand?" the Want coughed. "There are so many who need you. I used you to free me. I have given up my integrity to fulfill my fate. Now the fate of Foo is yours. I will worry myself no more."

"How could you?"

"It was my design all along. I betrayed you and Antsel and Geth. I'm afraid I also did some things that will make your fight even harder. But my fears are calmed by the fact that I'm free."

The Want's chin was pale and relaxed. As if on impulse, Leven reached out and lifted the hood he was wearing to look into his eyes.

Leven gasped. The Want's raisin eyes hung in their slimy wet sockets. Leven could see miniscule objects twisting around the withered eyes. A light glowed from behind them, but even now the light was dimming.

"I've seen too many dreams," the Want said with glee. "My eyes are yours now."

"No," Leven insisted, reaching up to feel his own eyes.

"The transition will take time," he laughed. "But you're the Want now. And your moods and your thoughts and your actions will curse or bless all of humankind."

"What if I refuse?" Leven argued.

"It won't change a thing," he coughed. "You will still be the Want and I suppose Foo will crumble and you'll be left alone. The Dearth will simply take over sooner rather than later."

"What?" Leven questioned.

The Want smiled lightly.

"I don't have to worry about any of it," he said happily. "Even my shadow is destroyed. Sorry about that; he wasn't supposed to interfere."

"Why me?" Leven asked, upset. "I don't understand."

"It's your blood."

"What does my . . ."

Leven stopped to look at who he held. His hands and mind trembled.

"You can see it, can't you?" the old man asked, his withered eyes looking directly at Leven. "You can see the truth?"

"I don't know what I see," Leven whispered. "If what I think is true, you're supposed to be dead. Now here you are alive."

"Only momentarily," Hector Thumps said.

Leven was dumbfounded. He looked closely at the face of his grandfather, searching for some bit of recognition.

"I don't believe it," Leven whispered.

"Yes you do."

"Did Amelia know?" Leven asked softly.

"No," Hector gasped. "She thought me dead. I would have been, if fate had not put me in line for the life I have since lived."

"Does Geth know?"

"He suspected," Hector said. "That was one of the reasons I sent him to take care of you. I knew that only my blood could take the reins. Up until now you were too young. Now you have come and pierced my shoulder, but fate has found it fitting to let me pass on."

"How could my own grandfather do this to me?" Leven reasoned. "You brought me here for this?"

"It was time. I have lived too long. I'm done," Hector coughed. "I've seen too many things. My mind has not been my own for years. I want out of the pain of knowing everything. It's now your turn."

Leven was so confused. He wanted more than anything to hold his grandfather and cry. Every bit of family he had encountered in his life had disappeared as quickly as they had come into the picture. He couldn't comprehend the madness his grandfather must have been suffering to sell out not only the whole of Foo but his own grandson as well.

"Someday you will understand," Hector choked.

"I'll never understand," Leven said, hurt, his eyes burning a new shade of gold. "I'll never understand what kind of grandfather could do this."

Hector Thumps laughed. "Sorry," he choked. "But it just feels so good to think of other things. Besides, the events set in

motion cannot be completely fulfilled while the sycophants still live. You hold the key that I promised to Azure. It was my single move to prevent him from grabbing all he was reaching for and satisfiying the Dearth.

"The Dearth?" Leven asked.

"Fate cannot hold him below forever," Hector rasped. "There must be opposition in all things, and he will prevail unless you are strong enough. Show your key to no one. If they know what it looks like, they can try to re-create it. There's still a chance that Foo can be saved. You need only . . . no, no. I won't even think about what you should do. The tone of all mankind's dreams now rests with you, and I am free. And, sadly, I'm afraid you have not known peril yet."

"But I haven't even seen a single dream," Leven argued.

"That's not my concern."

"It should be," Leven said boldly.

"Then release Phoebe."

"What?" Leven asked.

Hector Thumps pulled out a thin strand of leather from around his own neck. There was another key hanging from the leather.

"Take this," Hector choked. "Phoebe's release will change the whole of Foo."

Hector smiled one final time as his withered eyes turned cold and dimmed.

"I've lived such a long time," he coughed.

Leven held his grandfather and cried with anger and sorrow.

CHAPTER FORTY

SWABS

Dennis climbed onto the boat with Ezra tucked under his collar. The day was gray and the skies looked full of moisture and mischief. The Russian ship would be leaving the German dock soon, on its way to Newfoundland. Dennis and Ezra figured it was a good start toward getting where they needed to go.

"We'll see where I'm drawn to once we get there," Ezra had said.

The crew chief of the Russian ship had raised his eyebrows when Dennis had informed him that he had only an American driver's license and no passport. But the crew chief had said yes in the end because they were shorthanded, and it took a lot of hands to get a boat as big as they were sailing safely across the Atlantic Ocean.

"No weapons?" the crew chief had asked.

"None," Dennis had replied, wondering if he needed to declare the toothpick he was packing.

Dennis found his bunk and was handed a broom by a tall man with bad skin and big teeth. The man pointed to the floor as if Dennis might not be accustomed to the act of sweeping.

Dennis was all too familiar. As he moved the broom in a nice pattern, he thought of how strangely his life was turning out. He looked at the faded marking on his skin and wondered if he would ever be completely back to normal.

"Look at you, broom boy," Ezra said, surfacing from his pocket. "Can't get away from who you really are."

Dennis didn't even acknowledge Ezra.

"What's the matter?" Ezra mocked. "Manhood got your tongue?"

Dennis pushed the broom into the corner and pulled out a long trail of dust.

"You need me," Dennis said calmly.

"Excuse me," Ezra raged, his one eye blinking madly. "I'm letting you tag along."

"I found you," Dennis said bravely. "I carved you. And I kept you when Sabine wanted to toss you aside."

Ezra stared at Dennis with his mouth open. Dennis looked away and kept sweeping.

"My little janitor has grown a backbone," Ezra finally said. "It's about time. You're going to need it where we're going. How fast did you say this boat can go?"

Dennis took an educated guess.

"That's it?" Ezra spat.

"Maybe a little faster once we're out to sea," Dennis added.

"It's going to have to do better than that," Ezra said.

Ezra slipped back under Dennis's collar while Dennis gave the deck a second sweep. The calm sea was in stark contrast to Dennis's state of mind.

He finished sweeping and stood at the bow of the boat as it worked up speed. Wind ran over his aerodynamic head and blew his wrinkle-proof pants. Dennis put his arms to his waist. He felt as if he were heading to war and he was the only person who knew the plans.

"Are you thinking again?" Ezra asked with disgust.

Dennis nodded, realizing that he rather enjoyed the feeling.

ii

Addy came home from work in one of her moods. She had two of them—moods, that is—mean, and stinking mean. She slammed her car door getting out. She slammed the mailbox after checking for mail. She slammed the screen door and then the door behind it. She stomped across the floor like a spoiled mountain. She reached into a kitchen cabinet and pulled out a glass. She then slammed the cabinet. She retrieved a piece of stale cake from the fridge and slammed that door too. She slammed her fingers in the drawer after finding a fork.

She then moved from mean to stinking mean.

She could see Terry from the corner of her eye. He was

watching TV with the volume up too loud as usual. She was also still upset over the fight they had had that morning over him stealing her dental floss.

"Sit here all day?" she asked cruelly, not expecting to get an answer. "The world's falling apart, and you wouldn't know it. I watched the Washington Monument get up and walk on CNN today. Sitting there folding napkins and watching the world fall apart. And here you are doing nothing."

Terry's recliner-rocker swiveled around. Terry was sitting there wearing the robe he had found—which, unbeknownst to him, had belonged to Antsel—and looking as smug as a toad who had just successfully swallowed a whole eagle.

Cake fell from Addy's mouth.

"Where'd you get that?" she said, spraying small crumbs into the air.

"Found it," Terry said, brushing the right arm. "Looks like my metal detector is paying off."

"That ain't metal," Addy pointed out.

"Still," Terry said, standing. "I wouldn't have found this without it."

Addy set down her plate and walked slowly around Terry. The robe he had on was threadbare in a few spots, but still remarkably regal looking. It didn't appear to be something purchased from a discount store. It looked black, with a pattern of rectangles running along the hems, but as Addy circled around a second time she could see that the robe was actually a very dark purple.

Addy couldn't believe how handsome it made Terry. His

unshaven face looked rugged, while his dirty hands testified of a man who knew how to work. The roguish way he slurred his words almost made her smothered heart flutter. And if Addy wasn't mistaken, it appeared that Terry was hovering a couple of inches above the floor.

"I bet this cost over fifty bucks when it was new," Terry bragged.

"Fifty?" Addy said. "I've seen dresses like that for almost three hundred."

Terry lowered himself and then sat back down as if light-headed.

"That metal detector paid for itself and then some," he whispered reverently. "I'll tell you something else. I think this thing can do things."

"Do things?" Addy said with a smirk.

"I put it on and the dirt around me began to bubble."

"There's something about this Oklahoma soil," Addy said in awe. "Frozen houses, bubbling dirt."

Terry's show came back on—he swiveled around toward the TV and away from Addy.

"Is that the last piece of cake?" he asked over his shoulder.

"Yes," Addy replied, still thinking about how Terry looked. She stepped over and handed him the portion she hadn't eaten yet, brushing the bite that had fallen from her mouth off of the plate and onto the floor.

Terry looked at her leaning into him and flinched as if he were being handed a bomb.

"Here," Addy said. "Take it."

Terry was in awe. His red eyes burned, and he scratched his nose.

"Paid for itself and then some," he said, shoving a bite into his mouth. "Paid for itself and then some."

Addy couldn't have agreed more.

iii

Janet was so disappointed. She felt as if she had changed greatly in the short time she had been in Foo. But when she looked at her reflection in the moonlit water, she appeared every bit as sour and stubborn as she had once been.

"I don't feel like I look," Janet said to Osck.

Osck stared at her, even more taken with the way she reflected off his fiery being. He had become obsessed with her—so much so that he looked for every chance he could to stand by her.

"You look beautiful," Osck said. "I've never seen a sunset that looks anything like you."

"Thank goodness," Janet said.

"I don't understand," Osck said honestly.

Osck's hair was high and orange. It moved like a slow flame as a light wind blew through. His neck reflected the others around him while his body and legs reflected the image of Janet. His hornlike ears flinched and twitched as he talked.

Osck stood and walked into the trees.

Janet stayed sitting. She and the rest of her group of echoes were gathered around a small fire on the up shore of the Green Pond. There were stars in the sky outlining the moons and reflecting in the water. In the distance Janet could see lightning over Morfit as it was being picked on by a small storm. She had no idea the thunder was calling her names, thinking instead that it was just her conscience finally speaking up.

"Selfish."

"I know," she thought.

"Ugly."

Janet began to cry.

"Nasty and unfashionable."

Her conscience was getting specific.

"Coward."

"Not anymore," Janet said aloud.

The sound of churning dirt and rattling bones pulled Janet from her thoughts. She looked up to see a black skeleton sitting high upon an avaland. The giant beast stopped at the edge of the firelight. The skeleton on top was silhouetted by the second moon. One of the echoes near the fire questioned him.

"Where are you coming from?"

"The Sentinel Fields," the skeleton said, its sinewy joints shining under the moon's reflection. "There's word that the gloam grows rapidly. It has stolen the soil of Lith. The Sochemists have sent locusts, and the very act has created Lore Coils that confirm it. I am to gather the rest of our kind."

"What of the Want?" another echo asked.

"It is unknown," the skeleton said. "But a lithen will lead us into battle."

"A lithen?" the echo said. "Lead us where?"

"We are to attack Sycophant Run," the skeleton said. "Our escape is there. The gloam will have reached the stones, and the soil will begin to possess the gifts it needs to control Reality."

The echoes all cheered.

"It's happening," a short echo with thick legs said happily.

"March quickly," the skeleton said, "or you may well miss the whole thing."

All the echoes began to chatter and reflect off of one another as the skeleton motioned the avaland to continue moving. The excitement was so palpable that the small fire began to sing songs of battle and triumph. Osck stepped back out of the trees holding a fistful of plum blossoms. Even in the poorly lit conditions Janet could see they were for her. He stared at the exiting avaland and then back at Janet.

"Thanks," she said, unable to actually take them from him.

"Ingrate," the distant thunder whispered.

Once again Janet mistook it for her conscience.

"You're very kind," Janet strained to say to Osck. "But I can't actually hold them."

She was surprised how much she liked the way the words sounded as they left her mouth. She was even more surprised to see both Osck's cheeks burst into flame as he executed a smile of sparks.

CHAPTER FORTY-ONE

TREE DIVE

The fall was spectacular—it made the drop they had taken inside the cavern feel like the jolt one receives stepping off a single last step. The distance down had actually been long enough for Winter to scream, catch her breath, and then scream a second time.

They hit the water sideways, rolling down under twenty feet before the momentum was limp enough to allow them to frantically paddle back up to the surface.

Geth gasped for air, feeling born again. He had left their situation to fate and they had succeeded in spectacular fashion. He looked around and dragged a sputtering Winter up over the surface. The drop had loosened the loop around her. He pulled it over her head as rocks and dirt splashed down like hail.

"Thanks," Winter coughed.

She bent backwards and slid the rest of the rope down.

Andrus popped to the top, floating belly up. Sait had come to during the fall and was happy to discover that he was still alive.

"We made it?" he asked incredulously.

A huge, creaking tree smacked down twenty feet from them. Its branches writhed and thrashed until it was still.

"Where's Clover?" Geth asked.

"Clover!" Sait yelled.

"He said he was going for Leven," Winter said.

"Good," Geth replied.

The moons were all lit to full capacity, every one of them curious to see what was going on down below. The Veil Sea was filled with dead trees and bushes that had taken the plunge in an effort to live. Currents of water pulled in odd and awkward strands as Lith continued to go under. One of the smaller moons was bold enough to dip down level with Lith, backlighting the island perfectly.

Geth watched in awe as the island lowered, its massive body dropping like a sand castle. The fall had pushed them out quite a distance from the land mass, and the sound of its demise was almost deafening.

Trees and bushes and grass showered the water.

"We've got to swim away," Geth said. "Lith will drag us all under if we stay this close."

A huge stone dropped right next to them.

"Or we'll be smashed," Sait said.

"Drag Andrus as far as you can toward the other stones," Geth shouted.

"What about you?" Winter yelled.

"I'm going for Leven," Geth said. "It may not be too late."

Winter looked up. The top of Lith was still a long way up, but it was lowering rapidly.

"You'll be killed," Winter said. "I'm going with you."

"No," Geth insisted. "Get them to the other stones. I'll make it, I promise."

"I can't imagine how," Winter yelled, looking up at the still-towering Lith.

"Well, Foo will fix that."

"I don't think I can swim much longer," Winter reasoned, hoping Geth would stay.

"Find a tree," Geth said.

Winter was already reaching out to the large one that had fallen nearby. She wanted Geth to stay, but she knew he needed to go for Leven's sake.

"Go," she said. "We'll be fine."

"Of course you will."

Geth turned and swam toward the sinking island as Winter and Sait dragged Andrus in the opposite direction.

CHAPTER FORTY-TWO

The Realization

Leven felt his heart sink like the very ground around him was doing. He had carried his grandfather out into the open and laid him down on a bed of dirt and wind. He had then draped his grandfather's arms over his chest and pulled the hood down over his empty eyes.

Leven gathered rocks like a sad child looking for Easter eggs. He piled the rocks up over his grandfather, creating a stony grave.

Leven stood tall and gazed around in wonder. His eyes were gold and, unlike before, the light from them shot into the far distance. Leven felt like a lighthouse sweeping the ruins of his stormy life for any sign of hope. He blinked and watched patches of light flash out from his eyes and float off.

Leven pulled the hood of his robe up over his head and slipped the sword into the leather band across his back.

Lith was falling fast, and each minute brought a different

view of the stars above. The trees had long ago fled, realizing that there was no safety anywhere on Lith. Every blade of grass and weed that had ever grown on the soil was also long gone. All of it had rolled or hopped or dragged itself into the sea to face a watery death.

Likewise, every nit that had been there gorging on dreams had left. Some had flown off on the backs of rovens; others had rushed to the sea, hoping the ships they had come in were still intact.

Lith had sunk so low that only the high, wide roundlands still protruded above the water. In a matter of minutes, however, even those would be sunk.

Nothing was left on the roundlands but the remains of the castle and some burning fires. A few rovens had stayed around to feed on anything the toppling castle had killed. They ate nervously as the soil crumbled. One by one they realized the danger and flew off.

Leven had never felt so alone.

He looked up at the sky and wondered why he of all the people in the universe was standing there. He missed Winter and Geth. He hoped that wherever they were, they were safe. He missed Amelia, and wished he could have known his grandfather under circumstances that didn't involve betrayal and selfishness. Leven missed the mother he had never known, and he missed Clover. He felt a restlessness in his limbs that made him shake out his arms.

The ground dropped twenty feet rapidly. Leven swayed and balanced himself.

"I was about to comment on your sea legs," Clover said. "But then I remembered we were on land."

Leven smiled, and his eyes burned even brighter and farther.

"Wow," Clover said. "Someone's lit up."

"I don't know what I would do without you," Leven said as Clover materialized, hanging on his left arm.

"Why are you staring at a pile of rocks?" Clover asked.

"It's a grave," Leven said. "My grandfather's."

"That's where Hector Thumps was buried?" Clover said in amazement. "It's held up well. I'm surprised nobody's knocked it over, or the rocks haven't walked off years ago."

"I just buried him," Leven said. "He was the Want."

"Your . . . he . . . ?" Clover questioned in amazement. "That was your grandfather?"

Leven nodded, his robe billowing in the wind.

"So, the Want's dead."

"No," Leven answered honestly.

"But you just said—"

"It's a long story."

Lith dropped twenty more feet. Every last roven flew off as a new small fire leapt to life in the distance.

"I wish I knew where Geth and Winter were," Leven sighed.

"Don't worry about them," Clover said. "They're fine."

"You've seen them?"

"I just left them. I think they were swimming," Clover waved, as if they were off vacationing at some resort. "I'll be honest, Winter looked tired, but they seemed okay."

Leven stared at the rocks as Lith began to spin in a downward motion. Leven watched the stars slowly turn.

"The Want betrayed us all," Leven said somberly.

"People are hard to peg," Clover said, thinking of other things. "What do you suppose we'll do when there's no longer any land to stand on here? I mean, I'm a good swimmer, but if I remember correctly, you sort of struggled with water in Reality."

Lith dropped and spun faster.

"Don't worry about it," Leven said. "I have my Waves."

"*Your* Waves," Clover said in awe. "You mean . . . ?"

Leven looked at him and let the light of his eyes explain everything.

"Of course," Clover whispered. "My offing, the Want. Does this mean you'll be going mad and your eyes will go all googly?"

"I hope not," Leven said. "It means that, no matter how I feel, the battle to save Foo is unavoidable for me."

"It's always been that way," Geth said, stepping up from the side and causing both Leven and Clover to jump.

Leven settled down and turned to face his friend. Geth offered Leven his hand.

"You're okay?" Leven said with happiness.

"Of course," Geth replied.

"Where's Winter?"

"Floating toward the stones on the back of some dead trees," Geth said. "She was moving in the direction of the fourth stone with a couple of nits. The grave?"

Leven looked at the rocks. "The Want's dead," he said.

"That's impossible," Geth replied, his green eyes showing shock under the moonlight.

Both Leven and Clover gasped.

"Impossible?" Leven questioned.

"There's no way for the . . . well, there's only . . . he would have to have been . . ."

"My grandfather?"

Geth looked silently at Leven and then back to the grave.

"I'm the Want," Leven answered almost sheepishly.

"Fantastic," Geth whispered quietly.

"He thought you might have already known," Leven said.

"I've suspected but never known," Geth answered. "How fortunate for Foo that you are here."

"Fortunate?" Leven replied. "He freely sold me out."

Geth remained silent as Lith spun and dropped ten more feet.

Leven's eyes burned, sending bright rays of light out over the landscape. There was little of Lith still standing above the water. "I suppose we should find Winter and begin this war," Leven said.

"There's still much amazement to save," Geth added with respect. "Azure will be counting on the Want's death and the soil's new gifts that Lith is providing. But, with luck, you will cultivate the power to stop him."

Leven nodded, "I hope so."

"We can be only what we give ourselves the power to be," Geth said, sounding like a wise toothpick.

The ground twisted and dropped. Large pieces of Lith broke

from the edges and crumbled into the vacuumlike sea. A tremendous snap rang out across the entire sky. The noise was coming from across the Veil Sea. Leven and Clover put their hands to their ears as Geth crouched, looking into the distance.

"What was that?" Leven asked, lowering his palms from his ears.

A violent, hissing sound rose into the dark night, filling the air and sounding as if Foo had sprung a leak.

"Leven," the air hissed. "Leven."

Clover shook.

Geth stood as tall as he could at the moment. "The Dearth."

Clover shook harder.

The hissing slowed and faded until all that they could hear was the sound of Lith being sucked under.

"The Want spoke of a Dearth," Leven said anxiously.

"It appears that the movement of Lith has started the wheels in motion for setting the Dearth free," Geth said solemnly. "It seems likely that the very soul who controlled Sabine and who moves Azure will finally rise above the soil. The master is alive."

Geth almost looked scared as he shrank a bit more. "We are near the end," he said. "Or a great new beginning."

"He whispered my name," Leven pointed out uneasily.

"He knows the one person who can stop him," Geth answered. "The first Want enslaved him. Only you can hold him back."

Clover stopped shaking to look proud of Leven.

Lith sank even lower.

"Do you think maybe we should get going?" Clover said.

Leven stepped back away from the grave and extended his right arm, instructing Geth to lead. Leven followed Geth down a small path that led to the edge of Lith. Even from where he was, Leven could hear the water down below. The sounds it made swallowing the last bits of Lith were repulsive but hypnotic.

Leven stopped.

A small spot of light bubbled up out of the dirt in front of him. It blocked his passage, rising from the soil in swirling, feathery patterns. The circle grew to the size of a bathtub and pushed up in a well-lit spire. The light arched and moved in Leven's direction.

"Can you see that?" Geth whispered.

"What is it?" Leven asked.

"A dream. A very rich dream," Geth smiled. "Your first, I believe."

Leven reached his palms out as if acting like a slow mime in a glass box. The warmth of the dream rippled across his hands. His fingers vibrated and clattered like loose silverware.

Leven wanted more.

He stepped into the light and let it circle around him. The feeling was unlike anything he had ever experienced. The dream squeezed in through the soles of his feet and the underside of his chin. It seemed to draw out the confusion in Leven and fill him with hope. It felt holy and personal, so personal that Leven closed his eyes to let those things happening around him happen in privacy. His closed eyes could not keep out the images. Leven could see the outlines of a dream, their pictures flashing through his

mind like a spot of bright sun on a black day. There was a faded child in the dream, and a man. The man was tall, wearing a red shirt and blue jeans. He had dark hair and brown eyes that looked as unsettled as the sea they were sinking into. The man wore glasses and seemed to be looking frantically for something.

The man stopped.

He turned to stare at Leven with a frightened gaze.

Leven collapsed and fell to his knees. Color drained from his face as the dream slid back down into the dirt.

The last bit of Lith turned and tipped sideways.

Geth lost his footing and had to push himself back up. He put his hand on Leven's shoulder. "You'll be weak for a while," Geth said. "The first dream can be quite taxing."

Leven looked up at Geth. "Do the dead dream?" he asked, the sound of water so loud he almost couldn't hear his own voice.

"Not in the ways we can see," Geth answered. "Why?"

"That dream belonged to my father," Leven said with emotion.

Clover didn't know whether to clap or nod reverently. So he sort of shuffled his feet and clicked his fingers.

"Your father's alive?" Geth said.

"If the dead don't dream."

"Fate is pulling out all the stops," Geth smiled, shrinking just a bit more.

Leven could no longer fight the overwhelming feeling in his heart to run. He was more than he had ever thought possible. He could clearly see the moment he had decided to step into Foo. He

knew now that it had been under false pretenses, that he and Geth and Winter had been tricked. But he also knew that what had happened had to be, and that he was a large part of what was to come.

He could still hear the whisper of the Dearth bouncing around in his mind. There was evil greater than he yet understood.

Leven stood up and pulled his hood down. The white streak in his long, dark hair glowed. He reached down and pulled Clover up onto his shoulder.

"Ready for all this?" he asked his sycophant.

"Of course," Clover replied.

Leven took off running as fast as he could, a faint trace of gold energy buzzing around him. Geth followed closely behind. They reached the edge of Lith and leapt forward into the dark air.

Geth shouted as if he had just received a great inheritance, while Leven breathed in deeply, never doubting for a moment that the Waves would catch them and take them to Winter.

Clover, on the other hand, closed his eyes and held tightly to the neck of the Want.

GLOSSARY

Who's Who in Foo

Leven Thumps

Leven is fourteen years old and is the grandson of Hector Thumps, the builder of the gateway. Leven originally knew nothing of Foo or of his heritage. He eventually discovered his true identity: He is an offing who can see and manipulate the future. Leven's brown eyes burn gold whenever his gift kicks in.

Winter Frore

Winter is thirteen, with white-blonde hair and deep evergreen eyes. Her pale skin and willowy clothes give her the appearance of a shy spirit. Like Sabine, she is a nit and has the ability to freeze whatever she wishes. She was born in Foo, but her thoughts and memories of her previous life are gone. Winter struggles just to figure out what her purpose is.

GETH

Geth has existed for hundreds of years. In Foo he was one of the strongest and most respected beings, a powerful lithen. Geth is the head token of the Council of Wonder and the heir to the throne of Foo. Eternally optimistic, Geth is also the most outspoken against the wishes of Sabine. To silence Geth, Sabine trapped Geth's soul in the seed of a fantrum tree and left him for the birds. Fate rescued Geth, and in the dying hands of his loyal friend Antsel he was taken through the gateway, out of Foo, and planted in Reality. He was brought back to Foo by Leven and Winter.

SABINE (SUH-BINE)

Sabine is the darkest and most selfish being in Foo. Snatched from Reality at the age of nine, he is now a nit with the ability to freeze whatever he wishes. Sabine thirsts to rebuild the gateway because he believes if he can move freely between Foo and Reality he can rule them both. So evil and selfish are his desires that the very shadows he casts seek to flee him, giving him the ability to send his dark castoffs down through the dreams of men so he can view and mess with Reality.

ANTSEL

Antsel was a member of the Council of Wonder. He was aged and fiercely devoted to the philosophy of Foo and to preserving the dreams of men. He was Geth's greatest supporter and a nit. Snatched from Reality many years ago, he was deeply loyal to the council and had the ability to see perfectly underground. He was a true Foo-fighter who perished for the cause.

CLOVER ERNEST

Clover is a sycophant from Foo assigned to look after Leven. He is about twelve inches tall and furry all over except for his face, knees, and elbows. He wears a shimmering robe that renders him completely invisible if the hood is up. He is incredibly curious and mischievous to a fault. His previous burn was Antsel.

JAMOON

Jamoon is Sabine's right-hand man as well as a rant. Because he is a rant, half of his body is unstable, transformed continually into the form of the dreams being entertained by humans. He is totally obedient to Sabine's wishes. Jamoon believes Sabine's promise that if he and his kind can get into reality, the rants' unusual condition will be healed.

HECTOR THUMPS

Hector Thumps is Leven's grandfather and the creator of the gateway. When fate snatched him into Foo, he fought to find a way back to the girl he loved in Reality. His quest nearly drove him mad.

AMELIA THUMPS

Amelia is old. She is the woman Hector Thumps married after he returned to Foo a second time. She is Leven's grandmother and

lives between Morfit and the Fundrals of Foo. She was the protector of the gateway to Foo.

TIM TUTTLE

Tim is a garbage man and a kindly neighbor of Winter. In Reality, Tim and his wife, Wendy, looked after Winter after being instructed to do so by Amelia. When Winter goes missing, Tim sets out to find her.

DENNIS WOOD

Dennis is a janitor whom fate has picked to carry out a great task. He leads a lonely life and has never dreamed.

JANET FRORE

Janet is a woman who believes she is Winter's mother but has no concern that Winter is missing. She has spent her life caring only for herself.

TERRY AND ADDY GRAPHS

Terry and Addy were Leven's horrible caregivers in Reality.

OSCK

Osck is the unofficial leader of a small band of echoes. He is deeply committed to the meshing of Foo with Reality. He has also taken a very strong liking to Janet Frore.

THE ORDER OF THINGS

BAADYN

The Baadyn are fickle creatures who live on the islands or shores of Foo. They seek mischief to a point, but when they begin to feel guilty or dirty, they can unhinge themselves at the waist and let their souls slide out and into the ocean to swim until clean. The clean souls of the Baadyn have been known to do numerous good deeds.

BLACK SKELETONS

These great warriors rose from the Cinder Depression many years ago. They occupy the land nearest Fté, and are known for their ability to tame and ride avalands.

CHILDREN OF THE SEWN

The Children of the Sewn live beneath and amongst the roots of the Red Grove. They are patched together from dreams and imaginations. They are the only framers in Foo. Their task is to frame the strong dreams so that they can be focused on and achieved, and to frame the darkest dreams so that they are contained and stopped.

COGS

Cogs are the ungifted offspring of nits. They possess no great single talent, yet they can manipulate and enhance dreams.

THE DEARTH

It is said that there is none more evil than the Dearth. His only desire is for the soil to have the last say as all mankind is annihilated. He has long been trapped beneath the soil of Foo, but has used his influence to poison Sabine and Azure and any who would stand still long enough to be fooled. In his present state, the Dearth works with the dark souls who have been buried to move the gloam and gain greater power on his quest to mesh Foo with Reality.

ECHOES

Echoes are gloriously bright beings that are born as the suns reflect light through the mist in the Fissure Gorge. They love to stand and reflect the feelings and thoughts of others. They are useful in war because they can often reflect what the opponent is really thinking.

EGGMEN

The Eggmen live beneath the Devil's Spiral and are master candy makers. They are egg-shaped and fragile, but dedicated believers in Foo.

FISSURE GORGE

Fissure Gorge is a terrific gorge that runs from the top of Foo to the Veil Sea. At its base is a burning, iridescent glow that creates a great mist when it meets with the sea. The heat also shifts and changes the hard, mazelike air that fills the gorge.

GIFTS

There are twelve gifts in Foo. Every nit can take on a single gift to help him or her enhance dreams. The gifts are:

See through soil
Run like the wind
Freeze things
Breathe fire
Levitate objects
Burrow
See through stone
Shrink
Throw lightning
Fade in and out
Push and bind dreams
Fly

GLOAM

The gloam is the long arm of dirt stretching from below the Sentinel Fields out into the Veil Sea. It is said that the Dearth uses the black souls of selfish beings buried in Foo to push the

gloam closer to the Thirteen Stones in an effort to gain control of the gifts.

GUNT

The gunt are sticky creatures that seal up and guard any hole too deep, thus preserving the landscape of Foo and preventing disaffected beings from digging their way out. Once gunt hardens in the holes, it can be harvested to eat.

LITH

Lith is the largest island of the Thirteen Stones. It has long been the home of the Want and a breeding ground for high concentrations of incoming dreams. Lith was originally attached to the main body of Foo but shifted to the Veil Sea along with the other stones many years ago.

LITHENS

Lithens were the original dwellers of Foo. Placed in the realm by fate, they have always been there. They are committed to the sacred task of preserving the true Foo. Lithens live and travel by fate, and they fear almost nothing. They are honest and are believed to be incorruptible. Geth is a lithen.

LONGINGS

A near-extinct and beautiful breed, longings were placed in Foo to give the inhabitants a longing for good and a desire to ful-

fill dreams. They have the ability to make a person forget everything but them.

LORE COIL

Lore Coils are created when something of great passion or energy happens in Foo. The energy drifts out in a growing circle across Foo, giving information or showing static-like images to those it passes over. When the Lore Coil reaches the borders of Foo, it bounces back to where it came from. It can bounce back and forth for many years. Most do not hear it after the first pass.

NIHILS

Nihils are black scavenger birds that pick at the leaves and bark of trees, searching for and eating small bits of leftover dreams that have settled in the trees. They are aggressive and a nuisance.

NITS

Niteons—or nits, as they are referred to—are humans who were once on earth and were brought to Foo by fate. Nits are the working class of Foo. They are the most stable and the best dream enhancers. Each is given a powerful gift soon after he or she arrives in Foo. A number of nits can control fire or water or ice. Some can see in the pitch dark or walk through walls and rock. Some can levitate and change shape. Nits are usually loyal and honest. Both Winter Frore and Sabine are nits.

OFFINGS

Offings are rare and powerful. Unlike others who might be given only one gift, offings can see and manipulate the future as well as learn other gifts. Offings are the most trusted confidants of the Want. Leven Thumps is an offing.

ONICKS

Raised near the Lime Sea, these winged beasts travel mostly by foot. An onick is loyal only to the rider on its back, and only as long as that rider is aboard.

PALEHI

The palehi are a group of beings who refuse to take sides. They run people through the Swollen Forest. They are pale from all the frightening things they have seen. Their arms are marked with rings that keep count of how many trips through the forest they have made.

RANTS

Rants are nit offspring that are born with too little character to successfully manipulate dreams. They are constantly in a state of instability and chaos. As dreams catch them, half of their bodies become the image of what someone in Reality is dreaming at the moment. Rants are usually dressed in long robes to hide their odd, unstable forms. Jamoon is a rant.

RINGS OF PLAGUE

The Rings of Plague were created by Sabine. There were originally two, but Geth defeated one of them. The remaining Ring consists of twelve nits plus Sabine, each possessing one of the different gifts of Foo. Collectively having all the gifts, they are a threat to most.

ROVENS

Rovens are large, colorful, winged creatures that are raised in large farms in the dark caves beneath Morfit. They are used for transportation and sought after because of their unbreakable talons. Unlike most in Foo, rovens can be killed. They are fierce diggers and can create rips in the very soil of Foo. When they shed their hair, it can live for a short while. They often shed their hair and let it do their dirty work.

SARUS

The sarus are thick, fuzzy bugs who can fly. They swarm their victims and carry them off by biting down and lifting as a group. They can communicate only through the vibration of water. They are in control of the gaze and in charge of creating gigantic trees.

SIIDS

There were originally seven siids—humongous, mountain-sized beasts whose weight helped balance the landscape of Foo. Siids have the gift of killing and in turn can be killed. Years ago

some were hunted and killed off, and now many in Foo feel that the unbalance and darkening of Foo are somehow connected to their absence.

SOCHEMISTS

The Sochemists of Morfit are a group of twenty-four aged beings who listen for Lore Coils and explain what they hear. They are constantly fighting over what they believe they have heard. They communicate what they know to the rest of Foo by using locusts.

SYCOPHANTS (SICK-O-FUNTS)

Sycophants are assigned to serve those who are snatched into Foo. Their job is to help those new residents of Foo understand and adjust to a whole different existence. They spent their entire lives serving the people to whom they are assigned, called their "burns." There is only one way for sycophants to die, but nobody aside from the sycophants knows what that is.

THARMS

Tharms are short, smelly creatures who populate the Swollen Forest. They have a third arm where a tail would be. They are mysterious and love to capture and bury things in the forest. They also like to ransom those they have caught for favors.

THIRTEEN STONES

The Thirteen Stones were once the homes of the members of the Council of Wonder, with the thirteenth and largest, Lith, occupied by the Want. Each of the smaller stones represented a different one of the twelve gifts. With Foo in disarray, many of the stones are empty or are being used by others for selfish reasons.

TURRETS

The turrets of Foo are a large circle of stone turrets that surround a mile-high pillar of restoring flame. The turrets sit on a large area of Niteon and are surrounded by a high fence. The main way to the flame is through the gatehouse that sits miles away.

THE WANT

The Want is the virtually unseen but constantly felt sage of Foo. He lives on the island of Lith and can see every dream that comes in. He is prophetic and a bit mad from all the visions he has had.

WAVES OF THE LIME SEA

The Waves of the Lime Sea are a mysterious and misunderstood group of beings who guard the island of Alder. Their loyalty is to the oldest tree that grows on the island.

WHISPS

Whisps are the sad images of beings who were only partially snatched from Reality into Foo. They have no physical bodies, but they can think and reason. They are sought after for their ideas, but miserable because they can't feel and touch anything.

Here's a sneak preview of

Leven Thumps and the Wrath of Ezra,

available in hardcover from Shadow Mountain.

The Trappings of Comfort

There's some great real estate in Foo—beautiful spots that bring new meaning to the word *gorgeous*. I love the property above the Sun River and just below the Pillars of Rant. I also wouldn't mind buying a lot near the mountains at the edge of Morfit. But without a doubt the long span of land on the back side of the Devil's Spiral reaching over to the start of the Fté mountains is some of the most beautiful land in all of Foo. There isn't a bad blade of grass to be found growing anywhere on it. For this reason most of the elite and pompous have filled the land with castles and mansions. They have also built many walls in an effort to keep the un-elite from getting too close to them.

It was down from one of those walls that Leven dropped, hitting the ground with a soft thud. The night was dark, but the large house in the distance was well lit. It sat there like a proud mother showing off all her rooms. The land was miles back from the Devil's Spiral but the sound of rushing water could still be heard faintly in the distance.

Leven waved and Winter dropped down behind him.

"Looks cozy," she whispered.

Leven pulled his kilve from behind his back and swung it forward. The long wooden staff glowed slightly at its top.

"Geth should be in place by now," he said quietly. "Clover, you here?"

Leven felt something shiver on his right shoulder.

"Good, let's go."

Leven stepped quietly along the wall and down through the brick courtyard. Large stone statues, shaped like roven in various attack positions, lined the path.

"Makes you feel so warm and welcome," Winter said.

Leven looked at Winter and thought of Phoebe. The longing his grandfather had shown him before Lith was destroyed weighed constantly on his mind. He tried to shake off the feeling, but it was so powerful it kept creeping back into his soul. Looking at Winter only reminded him that Phoebe was still trapped.

"I smell mice," Clover whispered, bringing Leven's thoughts back to the situation at hand.

Winter pulled out her kilve.

"I wish I could just freeze them," she said.

"Mice?" Leven asked.

Leven and Winter moved behind two statues and listened carefully. Leven could see a pack of large creatures running towards them. They were three feet high with long legs and square noses that twitched as they ran. Their round ears and long, rubbery tails gave them a rodentlike silhouette. There were at least a dozen of them.

"Those are the mice?" Leven complained.

Winter didn't answer; she was too busy knocking the wind out of the closest one. The poor beast slid across the stone and up against a far statue.

Leven looked at the creatures. Their faces were expressive and he could see and feel what their small brains were thinking. Leven's heart pumped with confusion and then clarity. Without understanding his own actions he stepped forward and held out his hands. The mice stopped and looked up at him. Their heads twitched and their feet tapped as if being forced to stay in place.

"What are you doing?" Winter whispered.

"I don't have any idea," Leven replied.

The mice folded their legs inward and fell to the ground.

"Wow," Clover said. "That's helpful."

Leven and Winter stepped carefully though the large, resting creatures.

"Seriously," Winter said, hushed. "How did . . ."

"Leeeven," the sky said softly.

"What?" Leven asked, looking around.

"Leeeven," the sky whispered.

"Someone's calling my name," Leven said quietly.

"Well, it's not me," Winter whispered. "I didn't hear anything."

"Me neither," Clover said. "Sometimes the wind can sound like a person humming."

"I don't think it's the wind."

Leven shook his head. They moved closer to the house. Through the large side window they could see someone sitting inside near a huge fire.

"That's him," Winter said. "Knoll."

Knoll was a traitor—a lithen who had turned his back on Geth and Foo. His place was to occupy the sixth stone, but he had given up his responsibility for the opportunity to live lavishly on the mainland of Foo.

Knoll was sitting by the fire, his long braids hanging over the back of a soft chair. The ends of his dark mustache were woven into his braids and he was wearing a long white nightshirt. His cheeks were red from the warmth of the fire and his eyes were halfway closed. All around him large pieces of furniture sat draped in the hides of roven. In his right hand he held a fat wooden cup.

"Are you ready?" Leven asked.

"Of course," Winter said.

"Me too," Clover added. "In case you were wondering."

Leven tilted his head, nudging Clover.

"Good to know."

Leven walked up and gently took hold of the large wooden doorknob that was sticking out of a twelve-foot-high door. The knob was carved into the shape of an eye.

It didn't budge.

Leven motioned for Winter to move back. He lifted his kilve and slammed it down directly onto the knob. The eye cracked in half and Leven kicked the door directly below the knob. The door flew open as Knoll leapt up from his spot.

"Stay where you are," Leven demanded.

Despite the warmth of the room Knoll froze and then coolly relaxed his shoulders.

"How dare you come into my house and tell me what to do?" Knoll said casually. "My mice should have stopped you, but since they didn't I suggest you leave while the opportunity is still available."

Winter moved in behind Leven.

Knoll saw her and shook his head. "How hard is it to kill one simple girl?"

"I'm not that simple," Winter replied.

Where is he?" Leven said, ignoring Knoll's obnoxious statement.

"Get out," Knoll insisted.

"Where's Azure?"

"Again," Knoll said, stepping forward. "This is my house and your questions are not welcome."

Knoll sprang forward, grabbing his kilve as it lay resting against the edge of his chair. He whipped it up over his head and threw his arms forward.

His hands were empty.

Knoll looked back in confusion. Geth was holding the kilve and smiling as if he had just been invited to test out every ride at a new amusement park. Knoll tried to shelve his shock, but it was obvious from his twitching that he was unhappy to see his one-time friend Geth.

"How's my timing?" Geth asked.

"Perfect." Winter smiled.

"Where's Azure?" Leven asked again.

"We should sit," Knoll said, shaking. "I see no reason why this—like all problems—can't be talked through."

"You're welcome to sit," Leven said, continuing to stand. "Where's Azure?"

"You bother me to find out about another? It's too late." Knoll smiled faintly. "Azure's on to other things. I want nothing to do with him."

"What of the Dearth?" Geth asked.

"That fable?" Knoll laughed. "I know nothing of the Dearth," he insisted. "You must believe me, my part is finished. I am out of the tempest and alone in the lull."

"You're a horrible actor," Geth said, looking around. "You must know what Azure has planned for the Dearth. You seemed awfully close to him last time we saw you. You know, that time when we were bound up and you did nothing."

"My hands were tied," Knoll apologized. "It pained me to leave you."

"I'm sure it did," Winter said.

"Where's Azure?" Leven asked, bringing the conversation back around.

"I don't know," Knoll said. "My part is done. Let me rest."

"Don't tell me you bartered your integrity and sold out all of Foo for this?" Geth motioned to the lavish surroundings.

"I live very comfortably now," Knoll said. "I served Foo for many years with no reward but the health of mankind's dreams. Now I have something to show for myself—a warm place to drink and sleep."

"I don't believe what I'm hearing." Geth was disgusted.

"You always were stubborn," Knoll said.

"Where is he?" Leven insisted.

"Azure fights for more complicated things," Knoll answered.

"The meshing of Foo is no concern of mine. So it happens, so it doesn't, I'll sip my ale in front of a warm fire regardless."

Geth looked stricken.

"The Dearth exists," Leven spoke up. "I've heard him."

Knoll looked at Leven. He brushed his mustache and tugged on his braids as if he were milking a cow. His body shook. The warmth of the room was so great everyone began to perspire. Knoll rubbed his forehead and spoke.

"So you're Leven Thumps," Knoll said nervously. "It was quite masterful how the Want played you. Give someone a task and tell him it's important and most anyone will follow. What brings me the most joy is how you, Geth, were strung along."

Geth pushed the sharp end of his kilve up against Knoll's chest. Knoll stepped back up against the wall. He held his drink in his hand and tried not to look as concerned as he really was.

"You can't kill me," Knoll said.

"We could apply some of the dirty tricks you have been

using," Geth said seriously. "Apparently you've become quite good at causing accidents."

"Why fight against us?" Knoll said. "You could have all this. You've done your part and fought hard. Reality must have been a task. So enjoy what you deserve."

Geth still held the kilve up to Knoll but said nothing.

"You could have it all," Knoll said. "Just say the word."

Geth stared at him. "No." He pushed the kilve hard against Knoll's chest.

"Fine." Knoll sighed. "Azure's not here, but I have no reason to keep what I know from you. If it means I can get back to my drink, I'll speak. I am not the calendar by which Azure sets his movements, but it is public knowledge that in three days' time he will be meeting with the Twit of Cusp, cementing Cusp's part in what's to come. Have at him. Of course, you're fools if you think you can deter Azure—fools of the highest caliber. Will you leave me now?"

"I don't think so," Geth said kindly.

"We had a deal," Knoll scolded.

"That was your deal, not ours," Geth replied.

"Azure will kill you," Knoll raged. "You need me to save your lives."

Geth nodded at Winter. "Go ahead."

Knoll looked confused right up until the moment Winter hit him with her kilve on the back of his head. Knoll slouched forward onto his knees and fell face first onto the carpet, his drink spilling into the fire. The flames sizzled and snapped.

"Feel better?" Leven asked.

"It's a start," Winter replied, pushing her blond hair out of her face. "That's for the way he talked to Geth and me when we were tied up in the council room."

Leven bound Knoll's hands with rope while Clover rummaged through Knoll's things.

"Do you think he wants this?" Clover asked, holding up a small starfish wrapped around a tube of wood.

"Don't take his things," Winter said. "We're not here to steal."

"But this looks like something he's not going to use."

"Leave it." Leven smiled.

Clover sighed and let go of the object.

Geth bent down and hefted Knoll over his right shoulder. He carried him outside with Leven and Winter following.

"The onicks are up beyond the road," Geth said. "I didn't want to bring them in and give our presence away."

Leven stood still and clapped like he knew what he was doing. His gold eyes blinked with surprise.

The sound of the onicks' hooves clomping closer could be heard. The three onicks marched up the road and stopped directly in front of Geth. The largest one exhaled, his breath like thin, spiraling spiderwebs.

"Not bad," Geth said with excitement. "Controlling an onick from afar. Nice trick."

"He messed with some mice earlier," Clover said. "Made them lie right down."

"It'll be interesting to see how you end up," Geth said happily.

"Interesting or frightening?" Winter asked.

Geth threw his prisoner onto the back of an onick. Knoll was still unconscious and slumped over the rear of the beast. He looked out of place in his white nightshirt and long braids.

"Leeeven," a voice whispered, rising from the dust.

"Somebody had to have heard that," Leven insisted.

"What?" Geth asked.

"Lev keeps hearing people call him," Winter said. "I think he's getting a little full of himself."

"A little?" Clover laughed. "He can't pass a mirror without stopping."

"That's you," Leven pointed out. "So nobody heard that?"

"The Dearth knows you," Geth said seriously. "Don't stand still for too long. Now, do you want to lead?"

"Of course," Leven replied excitedly.

They all climbed onto their onicks and rode out of the gates toward the direction of Cusp. The wind blew softly.

"Leeeven."

Leven tried to think of other things, like longings, or wishing for a clear head—anything but the fact that the Dearth seemed to know him personally.